IMPOSSIBLE

I moved closer and tried to peer around Didi to see the reconstruction of the skull's face. There wasn't enough room. "Why the screen?"

"It's been hell," she said without turning. "Goddamned hell. Press. Indians. Smithsonian boobies. The woman's getting no peace."

"So it's a woman. I'd like to see."

"Just one sec." Her hands flew over the face molded with clay and resin and intuition, and she moved them lightly, tweaking here and massaging there.

Her shoulders slumped. "Almost there. Try like hell, I can't make an Indian out of this skull. You look."

Didi backed off, and the light beamed down onto a strikingly beautiful face.

I suddenly felt dizzy. I knew that face. "Omigod."

I walked closer to Didi's clay reconstruction. It seemed to pulse beneath Didi's single spotlight. I raised my hand, but didn't touch. The hair was pulled back, tight, and she wore bangs. Her cheekbones were high, the whole face angular, right down to her jutting chin. Her lips were thin and sculpted and wore an almost-kiss. Her large eyes tilted up at the corners, just a bit. She was exquisite in every way, and I knew her....

The Bone Man

Vicki Stiefel

LEISURE BOOKS NEW YORK CITY

To Peter and Kathleen.
Family is more than blood. Love you.

A LEISURE BOOK®

September 2007

Published by

Dorchester Publishing Co., Inc.
200 Madison Avenue
New York, NY 10016

ISBN-10: 0-8439-5937-1
ISBN-13: 978-0-8439-5937-6

The name "Leisure Books" and the stylized "L" with design are trademarks of Dorchester Publishing Co., Inc.

Printed in the United States of America.

Visit us on the web at www.dorchesterpub.com.

ACKNOWLEDGMENTS

Without the following people, I could never have written this book. Blame me for any errors, not them.

To my darling husband, Bill Tapply, for his invaluable critiques and even more invaluable love; To my beloved family—I could never, ever write these books without you: Blake and Ben and Sarah and Mike and Melissa; Mum T; Peter, Kathleen, and Summer.

To my dear friend, Donna Cautilli, whose spirit and homicide counseling experience continues to inspire me; Dr. Rick Cautilli, for sharing his exceptional medical expertise; Mass. State Police Detective Lieutenant Richard D. Lauria, for his invaluable insight and assistance.

To Lynette Esalio of Zuni, who answered so many questions. To Bob McCuen, owner of Zuni Mountain Lodge, Thoreau, NM; Pam Lujan of the *Cibola County Beacon* in Grants, NM, who helped with all sorts of nitpicks that I needed to get right; and thanks to Sheila Grant.

Hats off to Dispatcher Alvita Sarracino of the Cibola County Sheriffs Department; to Martha's Vineyard realtor Cathy Goudy; to Phil and Shirley Craig, who introduced me to their wonderful island; to Sarah Tapply, whose help and patience with Salem locales was fantastic.

To Mandy Harmon, National Park Ranger at Chaco Canyon. Mandy helped me with everything from pots and petroglyphs to the roads and the apartments at Chaco.

To the members of Mass. State Police Canine Corps, human and canine, who enable Penny to continue her work; the MEs, Crime Scene Services teams and support staff of the Office of the Mass. Chief Medical Examiner. To Dave Badger of the Badger Funeral Home; Wanda Henry-Jenkins and Paul T. Clements, whose work with

Philadelphia's GAP is legend; Dr. Barbara Schildkrout, for her psychiatric expertise; Andrea Urban for traveling so many miles.

To John and Kim Brady, for their continuing support; to Danielle and Henry Pedreira for my wild Carmen. To Kate Mattes of Kate's Mystery Books, Willard Williams of the Toadstool Bookshops, and all the book stores and libraries that support the work of writers everywhere.

To Lisa Souza, Susan Gray and so many other dear friends. Without their encouragement and patience, I couldn't write these novels; to the fabulous Hancockites who create a writing environment beyond compare; to Carolyn Boiarsky, Saundra Pool, Barbara Fitzgerald, and the Wannabes (D, Linda, CJ, Pat & Suzanne), all of whom support my writing in myriad ways.

To Barbara Shapiro, Bunny Frey, Tamar Hosansky, Pat Sparling, Jan Brogan, friends and critiquers; my amazing editor, Don D'Auria; and Dorchester's terrific Brianna Yamashita; editor Leah Hultenschmidt, and to Diane Stacy, Carol Ann and the gang—you're the best.

To my agent, Peter Rubie, for his continuing work and faith in my writing.

To the many incredible Zuni fetish carvers and traders of Zuni art including carvers Fred Bowannie, Thelma and Lorandina Sheche, Aaron Chapella, Lena Boone, Alonzo Esalio, Gibbs Othole, Jeff Tsalabutie, Dee Edaakie, and many more; and traders Harry Theobald of Zuni Mountain Trading, Kent and Laurie McMannis of Greydog Trading, Corilee Sanders and Melissa Casagrande, Janet and Diane of Zuniart.com, and Darlene and Dave of Zuni Spirits, Greg Hofmann, and so many more...I wish I could name them all.

Finally, to my beloved Maggie Roe, Cindy Johnson, Dorothea Ham, Joni Hullinghorst, and Phil, dear Phil. We'll meet again.

I thank each and every one of you for helping to make this book a reality.

AUTHOR'S NOTE

No Massachusetts Grief Assistance Program exists within Boston's Office of the Chief Medical Examiner, whereas Philadelphia's Grief Assistance Program continues to work out of the Philadelphia Medical Examiner's Office. There are many grief assistance programs throughout the U.S., and they continue to do amazing work with the families of victims of violent death. I applaud them all. Please remember that Tally and her gang at MGAP live in a world of fiction.

*No trumpets sound when the important
decisions of our life are made.
Destiny is made known silently.*
—Agnes de Mille

Cherokee Legend

An old Cherokee is teaching his grandson about life.

*"A fight is going on inside me," he says to the boy.
"It is a terrible fight and it is between two wolves.
One is evil—he is anger, envy, sorrow, regret, greed,
arrogance, self-pity, guilt, resentment, inferiority,
lies, false pride, superiority, and ego."*

*The boy nodded, and the old man continued, "The
other is good—he is joy, peace, love, hope, serenity,
humility, kindness, benevolence, empathy, gener-
osity, truth, compassion, and faith. The same fight is
going on inside you—and inside every other person,
too."*

"Which wolf will win?" the grandson asks.

The old Cherokee replied, "The one you feed."

CHAPTER ONE

More than 365 days had passed since Veda died. One whole year had flown by since my foster mother, the only mother I'd ever known, left this earth. I still didn't understand her death. Not at all.

How could such a vibrant person die?

A friend said that energy never disappears. It just takes another form. I liked believing that. On good days, I did.

In the past year, I'd left MGAP, the Massachusetts Grief Assistance Program I'd founded. I'd ignored the invitation to create a grief assistance program in New Mexico. I'd also tabled a similar position from the state of Maine.

Instead, I'd hung out.

Ah, you're thinking that I was so sunk in grief that depression held me prisoner.

Wrong!

In fact, with the substantial sum of money and property left to me by Veda, I'd traveled to Greece, visited New Zealand, and driven across country with my faithful former Canine Corps dog, Penny, at my side.

I'd scuba dived and sky dived and parasailed and sailed. I'd ballroom danced and fly fished and skeet shot.

At the moment, I'd gotten off my merry merry-go-round and begun to look for a place to buy, an expensive one, in Boston. For now, I still lived in my rented first-floor brownstone apartment in the South End. My apartment was nice. Very nice, in fact. But what the hell? Why not, right? Go for the gusto. Spend the filthy lucre. Live it up.

I had no homicides to deal with. No weeping families. No revenge-choked husbands. No newspapers chomping for a "blood and guts" story. No watching victims sliced and diced during autopsies. No helping families ID the bodies of their loved ones. No cops, no killers, no lawyers, no rapists, no rampaging crazies. No nasty Acting Chief Medical Examiner Fogarty nipping at my heels. None of it.

How would I not love this life? Except I didn't. Everything felt hollow as hell after the dozen years I'd counseled the families of homicide victims. Boring, too. Tough to trump that one. True, normal people wouldn't have a problem with this stuff. Me? I found it bizarre living what others might call a traditional life.

I should love it. My problem was that I missed my former life. All of it.

Which was really messed up.

I had to face reality, a reality I found deeply disturbing: I was *not* a carefree-type person.

I couldn't decide between Maine or New Mexico. Certainly Penny was no help at all. I wasn't much in the mood to ask anyone else.

Which was why I now stood in Harrisville, New Hampshire, near the site of my last case—face-to-face with Charley Paradise and beside his wife, Laura—while a fiddler fiddled and a caller hollered out near incomprehensible steps of a contra dance.

I liked it. When I was sweaty, I didn't have to think

about much at all. And, believe me, I was good and sweaty. It oiled my forehead, dampened my armpits, and sheened my forearms. The hall was roasting even here in New Hampshire in late September. Indian Summer was in full bloom, and I felt like a barbecued chicken.

Charley, with his black curly beard, flannel shirt, and red suspenders, grinned across from me as the steps quickened. He wanted me to pick up the pace, and I did. Oh, yeah. The music grew louder, the dance faster and faster, and I was breathing hard, watching Charley's feet and arms flail away. When I glanced at Laura, in her cool cotton shirt and whirly skirt, she winked.

I tilted my head back and laughed. Damn, this was fun.

And suddenly, just as Charley took my hands and twirled me around and around and around, I sensed that something was coming, something important. I was certain my stress-free life was about to end.

For no good reason, it scared the hell out of me.

We stood around the punch bowl—fifty-cents for a cup, a donation for the town's latest fund-raiser—and sipped tart lemonade made with fresh lemons. Divine.

"Penny needs a pal," Charley said.

"No," I said. "She doesn't. I'm her pal."

"You should see these pups," Laura said.

"You gotta see 'em," Charley added.

I wasn't stupid. They were trying to lure me in. I was not going to be lured. "I won't see those puppies. I do not want to hear about those puppies. Those puppies do not exist for me."

"What a chicken." Charley ladled us each a punch refill, then offered a shot of vodka from his sterling flask.

"Not for me," I said. "But thanks. And, yeah. I'm a chicken." I gulped down my punch. "Basset puppies are easily the cutest creatures in the entire world. If I see one, I'm done."

They both laughed, and as I headed to the ladies room, their laughter followed behind me.

I took one look in the mirror and scared the hell out of myself. My Medusa hair had reached new heights. Coils? Dreds? I didn't know what to call the halo of blond curls that wove toward the ceiling. I splashed some water on my face, and just as I was drying my hands, my cell phone chimed.

I flipped open the phone. "Gert?"

"Hoi, Tal! How *you* doin'?"

Gert's Brooklyn-ese combined with her Joey Tribbiani imitation made her near incomprehensible.

"You've got to get over Joey," I said. "So what's up?"

"Ya don't sound so good. You okay?"

"I'm great. I've been dancing." Sounds of the fiddle danced into the bathroom. My feet started moving. "I don't have much time, kiddo."

"You there with a fella?" she said in a way-too-hopeful voice.

"No, Gert. Get to the point. I've been contra dancing. You don't even need a partner."

She snorted. "Perfect for you."

"What's that supposed to mean?"

"Nevah mind. We got some late breakin' news here. They've just appointed the new chief."

My heart sped up. I knew what was coming, and I hated it. "Thanks for calling, hon. But I knew it'd be Fogarty. What can I say? It sucks. I've gotta run."

"Holdit! Holdit! It's not Fartin' Fogarty."

Shocker. Tom Fogarty and I had a long history of aggravation, grudges, and spats. I was sure he'd segue from acting chief to chief. Except for all our friction, I admitted that he was a fine ME. "Now I'm feeling guilty that Fogarty didn't get it."

"Well, don't," Gert said. "He's still onboard to drive you crazy. Thing is, the new chief says she knows ya."

I leaned against the beadboard wall. "She?"

"It's some chick named Adeline Morgridge. She knew Veda, right?"

Addy Morgridge. An old buddy of Veda's and a fabulously talented medical examiner. Veda. I couldn't get away from it, could I? I missed her every day.

"Addy Morgridge is great. Simply great." So why wasn't I overcome with the urge to cheer?

My voice sounded tentative, my breath short. "Yes, Addy's an old friend of Veda's. Right."

"She needs to see ya in the morning," Gert said. "Pronto like. And on the QT. She's got a problem and needs you, Tal. You."

Swell. So this was why I'd been feeling that sense of dread. I wasn't eager to find out what it all meant.

The following morning, I sat on my tiny back deck, which overlooked my teensy backyard and even teensier garden. Small it might be, but I loved such greenery in the heart of Boston. Penny sat beside me, her large German shepherd ears pointed forward, on alert. She knew something was up.

I sipped my coffee, relished the warm breeze as summer said its final farewell. All too soon it would turn to fall's damp chill.

I was stalling. I didn't know if I would go into The Grief Shop or not. Addy had summoned me. She might now be the Chief Medical Examiner for Massachusetts, but that didn't mean I would do her bidding. I was obligated to no one and nothing.

Geesh, that sounded hollow.

For so long . . . forever . . . I'd been the founder and director of the Massachusetts Grief Assistance Program. Although MGAP rented space at OCME, we were a private, nonprofit organization. Our job was to aid the bereaved when their loved one was the victim of a homicide. We walked with them during the aftermath of their devastating loss, we counseled them—often for many, many years—and we also helped them deal with more practical stuff, such as legal matters, the courts, the press, and the cops.

We made a difference, and that compensated for the sorrow we lived with each day.

Fewer than sixty professional homicide counselors existed in the United States. I'd always been proud to be one of them. At least, I used to be.

Dr. Veda Barrow, my foster mother, had pulled me into the profession after the murder of my father. She'd been Chief Medical Examiner for Massachusetts longer than I'd run MGAP. Her death rocked my world.

If I went into The Grief Shop today, I'd see Kranak and Fogarty and Didi and all the others I'd worked with for countless years. I'd brush into old feelings, both good and bad. But that wasn't it. Not at all. I would come face-to-face with the absence of Veda. The emptiness. Her *lack* of presence, that was the worst.

Veda had called Adeline Morgridge "Addy M." She'd liked her an awful lot. If I thought about it, Addy was a lot like Veda. Even tougher, in fact. No nonsense Addy. Right.

And I just couldn't take it.

I flipped open the phone to tell Gert I wasn't coming. Except just then the front door buzzed over and over and over. Even on three legs, Penny easily beat me to the door.

When I looked through the peephole, I saw . . . *Damn.* "I'm not home!" I shouted through the door.

"Yeah, you are," Gert hollered back. "C'mon. This taxi's meter is workin' ovahtime. Hurry up." She crossed her arms and blew an immense purple Bazooka bubble. She popped it. She didn't smile.

I swung open the door. "Dammit, Gert!"

She wagged a finger made more powerful by the fake nail manicured with the stars and strips in honor of 9/11. "You comin', all right. Yes, you are."

"This isn't defeat," I shouted as I scrambled for my

purse. "Just a minor setback." I slipped on my sandals and hooked up Penny to her leash. "Let's go."

Gert popped another bubble. And smiled.

I sat across the desk from Addy Morgridge in the office once occupied by Veda. I'd met Veda here a thousand times. Except for the art Addy had hung on the walls, everything was pretty much the same—carpet, desk, drapes. Yet I was okay with it. Veda didn't live here, anymore than she lived at the house in Lincoln.

But she was with me, all right. Every second of every day.

Addy handed me a mug of coffee. "Smells divine," I said.

She smiled, and the warmth reached her soft brown eyes. She had the look of that marvelous actress Alfre Woodard, wise and knowing and rich with history.

"The coffee is divine," she said, "because I brew it up myself. No Starbucks for this woman."

I chuckled. "Same ol' Addy. How does it feel?"

She leaned forward, her tented hands tapping her lips. "Good. It feels damned good. It's been a long route, Tally."

"I know it has, Addy."

"Becoming chief means the world to me."

I nodded. "I know that, too. Fogarty's your chief assistant, yes?"

"He was with Veda. He is with me." She straightened some papers on her desk, tapped the folders twice. "And that's why I need you. Here."

"Pardon?" I shook my head. "I can't. Don't want to."

Her lips tightened. "We need balance, Tally. We need your firm, intuitive hand."

I laughed as I shook my head. "My dear—"

The jangling of the phone interrupted us. Addy snatched the phone off its cradle. "Hold my calls, I said." She listened, nodding, then held up a finger to me. "Put him through." And to me she mouthed, *One sec.*

Her expression hardened to one of fierce annoyance. "I

am so sorry, Governor Bowannie, but it is not our fault here at OCME if the *Boston Globe* calls the skull Anasazi. I know you don't care for that name. I understand, and I am sorry, but we have no control over what they print. We really do not. Dr. Cravitz will be a few more days at least."

More nodding from Addy. Then, "Until then."

She placed the phone on the receiver with such feigned gentleness I thought it might explode.

"That damned skull," she said.

Boy, was I interested. I was dying to see what was left of the ancient pot from Chaco Canyon. "I read about it. The one found in the smashed Anasazi pot, yes? The Southwest is a passion of mine, but I've never heard of a skull being inside an ancient pot. It's highly unusual."

"Don't I know it, dammit." She opened a desk drawer and slid out a cigarette and lighter and small plastic ashtray. "You?"

I shook my head. "I wish."

She lit up and inhaled deep and long, then exhaled out her nose. "The whole thing has given us a raft of problems we don't need. First off, it's not PC to call them Anasazi, since that name was given to the Old Ones by their enemies, the Navajo. Or so they say. Who knows? I haven't told the Zuni governor that I'm half Navajo. That would really rip him up."

"If he's a Zuni governor," I said, "I'm sure he can handle it, Addy. I take it Didi's working on the reconstruction. Is it done yet? I'd love to see it and the pot."

"Let me check with Didi." Addy shook her head and flicked her ash into the tray. "Everybody's having a festival with this ancient skull thing. Who owns it? The Smithsonian's salivating. So are a bunch of other institutions, not to mention the Zuni. The Hopi have gotten into the act, too. And National Geographic. It's slowing Didi down."

I smiled. "Right up your alley, kiddo. Listen, I've got to run."

She took a drag. "I want a commitment from you, and I want it today."

Cripes! She looked like some indignant Afro-Indian princess. OCME didn't know what it was in for. "Sorry, Addy. It's a no-go."

"Without you, the program dies."

"Without me," I said, "it'll be just fine. Gert's amazing."

"She is, but she's lost heart. They all have. They miss you terribly."

I tried to shut out the violins. "I've had offers from Maine and from New Mexico. Lots of money. Carte blanche. All the bells and whistles. I've put them off, too." I stood to leave. I walked around the desk to give her a hug.

"I'll call down," she said. "See if Didi can see you."

"Great."

She blew out a stream of smoke and stubbed out the cigarette. "I've got some news on your boyfriend. He is your boyfriend, right?"

That stopped me short. "You mean Hank?"

She winked. "Don't count The Grief Shop out, yet. That's all I'm asking."

"What about Hank? C'mon, Addy."

"So what do you say?"

"Okay, fine," I said. "I won't close the door on Boston."

She stood and hugged me. "Good thing."

"You smell like smoke."

"Perfume works wonders."

"You're a terrible blackmailer," I said. "What about Hank?"

She smiled, and there it was again, that Alfre Woodard look. Whew. I couldn't help smiling back.

"Word is," she said, "might be just a rumor, but they say that your Sheriff Cunningham has taken a position with the AG's office. State police homicide investigator."

"Holy shit."

I wanted out, and I wanted out fast. Addy's buzzer

sounded. Perfect timing. I waved "bye" and turned to go.

"Hold on!" she said. "Hold on, Tally!"

I sighed. "Sure."

While Addy talked into the intercom, I tried to picture what the hell Hank Cunningham was up to. He was the sheriff for Hancock County in Maine, so why rumor said he was taking a job as a state homicide investigator made no sense to me.

Cripes, Hank and I talked almost every day. What Addy said was crazy.

She hung up, and I said, "I've really gotta race." As much as I wanted to see the Ancient Ones' pot, I wanted to find out about Hank more.

"Of course you do," Addy said. "But that was Didi. She'd love for you to stop down and see the reconstruction."

I shook my head. "I know I said . . . but . . . well. I'd better get home."

She began walking me to the door. "She's been working like a dog on this thing. She's like a proud parent. She's dying to show it to you. C'mon, girl. No matter what your sweetie's up to, a few minutes won't make a difference."

Of course, she was right.

CHAPTER TWO

I trotted down the stairs, headed for OCME's "back stage," which is where Massachusetts's medical examiners and pathologists do their work. OCME is a state facility. It houses the administrative offices and operations for the Massachusetts medical examiner system. OCME, aka The Grief Shop, was a pretty intense place. I'd been called intense too, which I guess was why I fit in so well.

The Grief Shop was on Albany Street in a bland, three-story brick building dwarfed by the campuses of Boston City Hospital; Boston University Medical Center; and Boston University Schools of Medicine, Dentistry, and Public Health. OCME was also smack at the crossroads of Boston's South End and Roxbury neighborhoods.

Medical pathologists, administrative staff, an elite State Police Crime Scene Services unit, and MGAP inhabited The Grief Shop. The building contained a state-of-the-art forensic pathology center, one immense autopsy theater, two cold storage facilities, a trace evidence room, and specialized rooms for family counseling and identifying human remains.

In addition, OCME had one of the top forensic anthropologists in the country—Dr. Dorothy Cravitz. Addy was right. Of course I had to see Didi's hard work. She was old and crotchety, and I adored her. The eminent doctor had no kids of her own. Her reconstructions were her children. She was at her happiest when a skull began looking human again.

And now she had one from A.D. 1100 to work on. Of course she was proud. Honestly, I couldn't wait to see the reconstruction of an ancient Puebloan ancestor. A couple of my Zuni fetishes were replicas from that era, not to mention that the Old Ones were said to be the ancestors of the Zuni.

And their pottery? *Spectacular* was an inadequate word for the beauty they'd imbued in such serviceable vessels. I just wished I hadn't heard that rumor about Hank's "adventure" until after I'd seen Didi's work. Boy, I needed to process Hank's latest move.

I walked down OCME's halls at a fast pace. If I didn't know better, I'd swear that Addy Morgridge was a reincarnation of Veda. Sure Veda had been old, and Addy was only in her fifties. Veda had been Jewish, and Addy sure as hell wasn't. But I'd never consciously realized how alike they were. Shook me up. That and the "little" tidbit she'd dropped about Hank.

I sighed. I thought Hank and I had gotten over the hump I'd caused by my ill-conceived romantic foray with CSS sergeant, Rob Kranak. I'd explained to Hank where my feelings had come from—Kranak was my good buddy, and he was there when my need for safety and security in a world falling apart blotted out all else. Hank was in Maine, and Rob was here. Wrong headed, but honest.

I thought Hank understood. For heavens sake, he was a county sheriff in rural Maine. Okay, so he'd once been an NYPD homicide detective, but that was . . .

"Hey, Ms. Whyte!"

I stopped short. A young man in his twenties, fresh-faced and eager with piercing blue eyes, looked across the lobby at me. I had no idea who he was. "Um, hello."

His smile was self-effacing. So why didn't I believe it?

"I'm Adrian," he said. "We met at a party. I'm the Harvard grad who's working in MGAP now. You know, for my doctorate."

"Ah, of course." I held out my hand, and we shook. "Nice to see you. How's it going?"

He frowned. "Okay. You're missed."

I smiled. For some reason, the kid was annoying me. "If I know Gert, she's doing twice the job I ever did."

He shoved his hands in his pockets. "Yeah, sure."

"Sorry, I've got to run."

He petted Penny behind the ears and followed me to the reception desk.

"Hey, Sarge," I said. "Would you punch me inside?" I'd always known the code. Not anymore.

"Can I come?"

I turned. Adrian was still there.

"Sorry, Adrian," I said. "No can do. Sarge?"

The buzzer sounded, and I pulled open the heavy door that led to the autopsy suites.

I looked back. Adrian stood there, hands on hips, with a petulant frown marring his face.

Gert had to have her hands full with that one onboard.

The first thing I noted was the impeccable cleanliness and order where there had been chaos a year earlier when Veda was taken ill. The linoleum floor glistened, and not a single corpse on a steel gurney lay in the hall awaiting autopsy. I looked through the window into the large refrigeration room. The dead were carefully lined up in a rectangle around the four walls, the way Veda had preferred they be arranged.

All the order was bugging me, too. I sighed. I guess I wasn't in the mood for exploring, or even for reflection.

Emotionally, things were finally easing for me. At last I was settling into a good rhythm. No point in bringing up memories of dead children and murdered loved ones.

I hooked a sharp left and walked toward Didi Cravitz's office-lab. The room I remembered was small. Forensic anthro was a late-comer to OCME. Just outside her office door sat a table with one of her earliest reconstructions—a handsome young man whose skeletal remains had been a mystery at OCME for nearly a decade, until Didi came on the scene.

I knocked, peered inside the darkened office. Didi had no window, and I could only see the clutter in silhouette from the light pouring through the office door.

"Didi?"

"In here."

"Can I flip on the light?"

"No!"

I walked inside the small office. No Didi. "Where the hell are you?"

"Behind the screen," came the disembodied voice. "Hang on for a minute, all right?"

"Sure!" Didi always loved the mysterious. I walked over to her worktable. There were the pot shards, or potsherds, as I'd been taught to call them. Beautiful things, even broken. These were a deep reddish brown with designs in black of mazes and cross-hatchings and spirals. Next to the potsherds, Didi had sketched a diagram of the pot, before it had been broken. Her notes read twelve inches at the base, eighteen inches where it bowed out, and around six inches at the neck. Sort of like a blowup beach ball, round and full.

The ancient pot had to have been built around the skull. I wondered about its purpose. In all my reading about the Anasazi, I'd never heard of that.

I slipped on some latex gloves from Didi's dispenser and touched each of the potsherds. I'd never been to Chaco

Canyon, the most revered of the Ancient Ones' sites, nor had I ever held any Chaco potsherds. So this was a real treat.

"I'm amazed at how vivid the markings are on the potsherds," I hollered to Didi.

"I know," she said back. "New Mexico's dry air has really preserved an incredible number of pots and petroglyphs and pictographs. But I'm over the moon about this skull, my dear. She's precious. Wait until you see this woman!"

"I can't wait," I said. "Hurry up!"

"Just a few more minutes," Didi said. "I've got to tweak her nose a bit. My calculations tell me it's off."

I lifted the largest potsherd, which was about the size of a deck of cards. From all the pieces on the tray, I saw where Didi got her sketch for the pot. "It's a shame that the pot's broken."

"But without that, we'd never have found the skull."

"True." The most sacred site of the Anasazi, Chaco was abandoned around A.D. 1200. I'd often wondered why. A legion of others did, too, yet the mystery was yet to be solved. Nowadays, it was believed that the Hopi and Zuni and other modern tribes were their descendents.

I'd been to the fabulous cliff dwellings of Mesa Verde and others near Sedona, Arizona, but I knew someday I'd see Chaco's sandstone cliffs and ancient city. I wished Hank had more of an interest. Ah, well.

I lifted another potsherd. A rust hunk of rock sat beneath it. To my eyes, it resembled a primitive fetish carving. Maybe a wolf, maybe a mountain lion. The stone was warm in my hand, like the sun on the desert rock. I turned it over. It was maybe three inches long, an inch high. I didn't think it was from the Chaco era at all, but much later.

"Where's the rock from, Didi?" I said.

"What rock?"

"The one that was with the potsherds?" It felt heavy in

my hand, too heavy for sandstone. "What's it made of, do you know?"

She leaned around the edge of the screen, gray hair askew, clay streaking her face. "What's with you this morning, twenty questions?"

I made a goofy face. "Sorry. I've been collecting Zuni fetishes for a long time, but this past year, I've really gotten into it. This looks like a fetish to me, one that started life as a concretion."

"What's that?"

"Y'know, a found rock shaped like an animal that the carver enhances. I just wonder where it came from." I held up the rock.

"No idea." She disappeared behind the screen. "It came in with the pot and skull. Come on in."

My blood quickened. This was going to be very cool.

The gray folding screen blended perfectly with the office's cinderblock walls. I walked around the screen. Didi was in her lab coat, her back to me. Her arms moved in a smooth rhythm, like a symphonic conductor, and her gray hair shot out in all directions, as if following the music of her arms. A narrow beam of light shined on what I guessed was her reconstruction of the ancient skull found in the Anasazi pot.

"Glad you came!" she barked over her shoulder.

"So this is the famous American Indian skull that you're reconstructing."

She nodded. "Wish it wasn't so damned famous."

I moved closer and tried to peer around Didi to see the reconstruction. There wasn't enough room. "Why the screen?"

"It's been hell," she said without turning. "Goddamned hell. Press. Indians. Smithsonian boobies. The woman's getting no peace."

"So it's a woman. I'd like to see."

"Just one sec." Her hands flew over the face molded

with clay and resin and intuition, and she moved them lightly, tweaking here and massaging there.

"God, I'm tired." She swiped the back of her hand across her hair, leaving a streak of clay. The color blended perfectly. "I'm too old for this crap."

"No way. But what about that 3-D computer stuff? I hear it's pretty good at reconstructing."

"I need my fingers," she said. "I need to feel it, Tally. To see the individual come alive beneath my hands. I need to sense it, to find the face. I can't do any of that with a computer. Not a bit."

"I understand, Didi. I do."

Her shoulders slumped. "Almost there. Try like hell, I can't make an Indian out of this skull. You look."

Didi backed off, and the light beamed down onto a strikingly beautiful face.

I squeezed the rock in my hand so tightly it hurt. I suddenly felt dizzy. I knew that face. "Ohmigod."

I walked closer to Didi's clay reconstruction. It seemed to pulse beneath Didi's single spotlight. I raised my hand, but didn't touch. The hair was pulled back, tight, and she wore bangs. Her cheekbones were high, her whole face angular, right down to her jutting chin. Her lips were thin and sculpted and wore an almost-kiss. Her large eyes tilted up at the corners, just a bit. She was exquisite in every way, and I knew her.

The lights blazed. Addy Morgridge and Didi Cravitz sat across from me. I sat on a tall lab stool as I sipped bourbon from a coffee mug and tried to steady my heart rate. It wasn't working.

"I know her, Addy," I said. "I know her well."

She sighed. "You can't possibly know a thousand-year-old woman."

I rolled my eyes. "I understand that. Believe me. That's why what I'm seeing makes no sense. This woman, my friend, is our contemporary. She's obviously not from A.D. 1100."

Didi turned to Addy. "I told you she didn't look like an Indian!"

Addy snorted. "Not *your* image of one. Of course she's an American Indian, and she's been dead for almost a thousand years."

"We don't know that for certain," Didi said. "There was a huge protest when we tried to carbon date the skull. The governor found the idea disrespectful. So we had to let it drop."

Addy brushed a hand across her clipped Afro. "I need some of that bourbon." She sighed. "We'd better test it, no matter what the governor says. That this woman—"

"We can't test the skull," Didi said. "It's absolutely forbidden by the federal government."

I poured Addy two fingers of Wild Turkey, splashed it with water from Didi's sink, and handed her the glass.

"Remember," Addy said. "The pot was broken during a Peabody installation. Salem's Peabody has one of the best American Indian collections in the U.S. The pot is old. No doubt about it."

"Aren't either of you listening to me?" I said. "This poor woman's skull was somehow put into an ancient pot. I don't know how or why. I recognize her, for heaven's sake. I doubt she put her skull in there of her own free will."

Addy knocked back her bourbon. "No matter who she is, you're right about that one, Tally."

Didi draped some moist cheesecloth over the reconstruction, then washed her hands. "I *knew* it. She was too good to be true. From the very first. She never felt right."

"Oh, come off it, Didi," Addy said. "You can't buy into Tally's fiction. I'm telling you, this is the real deal. She just *looks* like someone Tally knows."

Addy made some sense. "It's possible, I guess," I said. "I

remember an ancient skull they found out in Washington State."

"You mean the guy," Addy said, "who looked like Star Trek's . . . What's his name?"

"Patrick Stewart," I said. "The reconstruction really did look like him. I remember."

Addy wrapped her hand around my arm. "The museum found her *inside* that damned pot."

Didi lifted a bony hand to the covered face. "Morgridge has a point, for once."

Addy snorted.

"I see your point," I said. "But what's unnerving is that I know the woman. I recognized her. She's a friend."

"There easily could be a resemblance between the two women, that's all," Addy said. "You're mistaken, Tally. The pot's almost a thousand years old. Think about it."

I slid my glass onto the counter and stood. "You're right. Of course you're right. Seeing it . . . her . . . just spooked me. Sure. I'll call her. She owns a shop on the Vineyard. We'll chat, and I'll feel about a million times better."

Shouts from outside in the hall. "What the hell . . ."

Gert appeared at the door. "Hey! National Geographic's here. And they're makin' a big brouhaha."

"Shit!" Addy said. "I forgot the Geographic people were coming today to look at her. They planned to do some filming."

"The governor said that was a bad idea," Didi said.

"His problem." Addy waved at the cheeseclothed head. "Now they can't anyway. They absolutely must not see her until we're sure she an old Indian. I mean, I know she is, but I'll feel better once Tally has talked to her friend. The magazine's doing a piece on the skull, The Peabody Essex Museum in Salem, Didi, me, the Ancient Ones. Cripes."

"I won't talk to those people," Didi barked.

I slid off the stool. "I'll go call my friend right now."

"Hurry up," Addy shouted.

I varoomed to my old office. Gert followed, and we closed the door. I began to shake.

"Tal?" Gert rested her hand on my shoulder.

"Nothing. It's just settling in. A friend's *head* is on Didi's table. God, that head could be her twin. I swear." I dialed The Native Arts on Martha's Vineyard. A woman answered on the third ring, and I asked for Delphine.

The voice was young yet authoritative. "I'm afraid Ms. Delphine isn't here."

"This is Tally Whyte," I said. "Are you Delphine's daughter, Amélie, by any chance?"

"No. Sorry. But I'm sure I can help you."

I looked at Gert and shook my head. "I've bought some pieces from your shop, and I'm a big fan of Delphine's. She knows just what I love. Not that you're not wonderful, but I really need to speak with Delphine."

"She's on a buying trip out West. She left before Indian Market in August, and we don't expect her back until November first."

"How about her cell?"

"I'm sorry. We're not allowed to give out private information."

November—a month and a half away. I remembered Delphine went on big buying trips in the fall. I wanted to scream. "November's too late, I'm afraid. Um. How about *you* call her, tell her who called, and have her give me a ring?"

A pause. Then, "I can do that. Sure."

I gave her my numbers—my cell, my home, and even Gert's office. "This really is urgent," I said.

"I'll do my best."

"I'm sure you will . . . ?"

"Zoe."

"Thanks, Zoe. So when should I expect to hear?"

"Later this afternoon or tomorrow morning at the latest."

"No sooner, huh?"

"I'm sorry," she said. "But no. Like I said, I'll try. But the coverage out there stinks. Sometimes Mrs. LeClerc is out of range until late at night. You know, the time difference."

I knew. The waiting would drive me batso.

Time. Time. Time. It's a river that flows north to south, yet parallel, too. At different speeds, no less. We were all sort of bobbing heads in the river. Dear God.

Was that skull Delphine's? Or was I crazy? It was only Didi's construct, after all. Tweak it and the woman would be transformed.

"Tal? *Tally!*"

I looked up to see Gert frowning at me.

"Sorry," I said.

She handed me a Diet Coke. "This should help."

"The only thing that'll help is a phone call." Shouting screeched through my former office door. "What the hell?"

We flew down the hall to find Addy in the lobby getting screamed at by a man with wild hair, a blue hoodie, and an unfashionable mustache. Addy's arms were crossed, and she remained patiently silent while Mr. Mustache gesticulated wildly with his arms.

"Excuse me busting in?" I said.

Mustache-man's head swiveled, snakelike, and I bit my lip so I wouldn't laugh.

"The dead live here, mister," I said. "Have some respect."

"Oy," Gert hissed.

A sandy-haired guy in a pressed denim shirt stepped forward. He could have been an outdoor model. Or maybe a news anchor. Or maybe Thor, what with those lightning bolts embroidered on the tips of his collar. "Ma'am."

Ick. I smelled bullshit ten feet away. "Yes?"

"We have an appointment with Dr. Cravitz. Our time is valuable." He hitched his thumbs over his belt. "We are, after all, with National Geographic."

I smiled my most obsequious smile. "And I, after all, am representing all the dead folks here. Got it?" I girded myself for a diatribe when Sergeant Rob Kranak stormed out of the CSS offices, his face a mask of fury.

"One more word, motherfucker," Kranak said, "and I haul your ass behind bars."

The string bean with the wild hair rolled his eyes. "Do you know who I am?"

On that note, Kranak hollered for backup, whipped out his cuffs, slammed them on Mr. Mustache.

All hell ensued, and by the time Dr. Addy Morgridge sorted it all out, the National Geographic people were grateful to postpone for a week their story on the finding of an ancient skull inside an Anasazi pot.

CHAPTER THREE

Hours later, I dropped my water bottle into the sink in my kitchen and splashed my face with tap water. I leaned on the edge of the sink, gasping. One glance at Penny, and I felt even worse. She wasn't even breathing hard. I freshened her water dish, and she drank deeply.

In the living room, I looked at my collection of Zuni fetishes. Most had been carved in the past ten years. I had wolves and mountain lions and bears and moles and eagles and badgers. A few of my carvings were old, from the sixties and seventies. I picked up the Edna Leki I loved. The coyote was a beautiful piece from the seventies that was more than three inches long and made of travertine marble, with an Edna face—rounded and distinctive—and a coyote's jutting tail. Though simple in line, it was far more descriptive than the red rock I'd held that morning.

Yet both made me shiver.

Or maybe I was just chilled. I laughed, put the Edna back in its place, and plucked a towel from the rack. I pulled a Southwestern pottery book from my collection, grabbed the phone from its cradle, and walked out onto the deck. I sat on my tattered wing chair, slung the towel around my neck, crossed my ankles on the deck railing, and sighed.

Our run had been good, but I was still out of shape. Penny appeared, and I scratched her behind her ears. My three-legged dog would always beat me on a run. She just humored me by keeping pace.

"Good girl." I opened the book, hoping to find examples of that afternoon's pot markings in the catalog.

And there they were. Huh. No word from Zoe. It was still afternoon in New Mexico, and if Delphine were on some buying excursion, she'd most likely still be out of range.

Except I could only picture her as dead.

Ridiculous. I understood the physical impossibility of a contemporary skull being found inside a thousand-year-old pot. But, cripes, I couldn't get the image of a dead Delphine out of my head.

I jumped three feet when the phone bleeped. I scooped it up from the deck floor and pressed it on.

"Yes?"

"You're breathless tonight."

"Hank!" I said. "I, um, I was expecting an urgent call." I shivered. Dusk had fallen, and my damp shirt gave me goose bumps. I walked inside and shut the French doors behind me while Hank filled me in on a case he'd been working in Winsworth.

"So you see," he said, "it was that damned Percy after all."

"I'm not surprised. He's one sad case with real mother issues."

Hank snorted.

I wanted to ask him about the job with Massachusetts State PD, but I hesitated. He should tell me. I shouldn't have to ask. So I switched gears. "Something strange happened today."

He chuckled. "Tal, with you, I expect strange."

"Very funny. Now listen." I told him about the smashed pot and the skull and my thinking it was shop owner Delphine. "At first, I was sure. Now? Not so much."

He grew quiet on the other end. I heard his breathing, then a hiss. "You know, Tal, I usually tell you to go with your gut."

"I know. I agree. But it makes no sense."

"No, it doesn't. It sounds highly unlikely, in fact. So why don't we go to the Peabody this weekend, if I'm still invited for the overnight. We'll find out just where those pots came from."

"Of course you're invited." Just the thought of Hank here, in my bed, made me lust. "But we won't need to go to the Peabody. I'll be talking to Delphine, at the latest, tomorrow."

"Plan on a field trip, hon."

"But, Hank, I . . ."

"I know you," he said. "I doubt talking to the woman on the phone will satisfy you."

My gut tightened, and I gnawed a nail. "I hope you're wrong."

"Gotta run," he said. "See you Friday, sweet cheeks."

"Um, Hank?"

"Right here."

I sat on the couch and dragged the afghan onto my bare goose-bumped legs. "Sure. Of course. I, um, I heard a rumor today. Pretty interesting one."

"Ayuh," he said, sliding into the Maine-ese he used to muddy a situation.

"Aren't you curious what it was?" Here he went again.

"Nope-suh. You know how I feel about rumahs."

"God, you're a frustrating man," I said.

He chuckled. "Yup-suh."

"Cut the Maine crap, Hank. It was about you."

"Like I said, gotta run, Tal."

"Don't you dare—"

Click.

The bastard had rung off.

That night I watched a BBC mystery. I clutched a pillow to my gut, was lazily scratching Penny, and failed to find distraction in a most compelling *Waking the Dead.*

Every so often, I stared at the phone, willing it to ring, urging it to have Delphine's voice on the other end.

No such luck.

Before I tucked myself in for the night, I checked my cell phone and made sure it was charging. I dropped a pair of special glasses and a wig I'd used on a years-ago dance with death into a L.L. Bean bag, so I'd be all set for the morning. I gave the night sky one last look, then slid into bed.

That night I dreamt of Delphine and saw her face melt from her skull. I snapped awake, smelling of sweat and fear, and decided that a dreamless five-thirty was better than a sleeping alternative.

"Didi, just give it a try." I stood in Didi's office beside the uncovered bust of the mystery woman. In less than thirty minutes, retired Zuni tribal governor Ben Bowannie was to arrive and give the real skull, along with Didi's construct, a cleansing ceremony. I needed to be done before then.

Didi ruffled her hands through her wild gray hair, making it even wilder than usual. "I cannot put that old ratty wig on this head. Nope. Can't do it. Can't slip on those ridiculous glasses, either."

I held the glasses up to the reconstruction's face. "C'-mon. Delphine wears reading glasses similar to these!"

"I don't care if she wears Fig Newtons on her eyes," Didi said. "I promised the governor the head would be untainted with Anglo anything. It must be pure, according to him. I'm trying to accommodate. Get it?"

"I respect that," I said. "I do. But I told you, she looks so much like this woman I know. The wig will help. It's how she sometimes wears her hair. And the glasses will—"

"No." She pursed her lips as she sat at her desk. "No. I *am* sorry, Tally. Perhaps after the governor leaves. Yes, that might work. Believe me, this guy's sharp. He'd know if we put something like that on her. Whether the skull is American Indian or not, I feel it's appropriate to go along with this guy for now. Have to, Tally. They say he's high in the Bow priesthood, the most secret and sacred of Zuni clans, or whatever they call them. I believe that. He's got power, and he knows it. So just don't keep pushing me."

I understood I had to respect Didi on this, I just didn't want to. I knew about the Zuni Bow priesthood from my Zuni fetish collecting. She was right. It was a powerful entity. I pulled out my cell phone and started taking photographs.

She plucked the phone from my hands. "That's not allowed, either!"

"Christmas, Didi!" I snatched back the phone. "What's wrong with you? You're always more than willing to share—"

"Not today. Not her. I will not be accused of profaning a holy American Indian person."

"Fine." I slapped the phone shut.

"Delete them." Didi's pale eyes, aged and tired with overwork, burned. She wasn't kidding.

I'd known Didi for years. A curmudgeon, yes. But this was different. And strange.

"Did you hear me?" she repeated. "Delete them."

"Sure." I flicked some buttons and moved my fingers across the phone.

Two knocks, then, "Delete what, ladies?"

Fogarty. "Don't sneak up on people like that," I said. "It's creepy."

He frowned. "You. I truly believed we were well rid of you."

"Gee, Tom," I said. "You're always such a welcoming fellow. And here I was going to congratulate you on your appointment as assistant chief medical examiner. Shucks. So are you butting in on this, too?"

He crossed his arms, crinkling his starched lab coat. "I never barge where I don't belong."

I winked. "Of course not . . . unless publicity is a factor."

He puffed up. "Why you—"

My attention was distracted by a shadow that blurred the doorway. I looked closer, yet for some reason, it was difficult to see. Lousy lighting at OCME.

The shadow said, "Hello," and coalesced. How had he done that? He'd been watching us, I was sure. His sun-browned face wore a quizzical smile. He was short and heavy set, with a barrel chest and large bones and a bladed nose that implied authority. His vibes were curious—jolly yet powerful. His chocolate eyes were laughing, apparently at us. Yet I was sure there was more to it than that. He'd heard everything we'd said and found it amusing. He'd tied a bolo around the neck of his turquoise snap shirt, and his black jeans were pressed to a knife edge. His cowboy boots were well used yet gleamed with polish. He carried a small rawhide bag that I guessed he would use for the ceremony.

I was staring, and though I knew it was rude, I couldn't seem to help myself. His presence was compelling. Then again, I never trusted that first, charismatic reaction. Charisma often had a short shelf life.

Didi thrust the black wig back into my hands, walked over, and embraced the man I assumed was the Zuni governor.

"Let me introduce you," she said. "This is Governor Ben Bowannie."

I nodded, smiled. "Hello, Governor Bowannie. I'm so pleased to meet you. You live in a place of beauty."

"Suck up," Fogarty hissed. "Governor!" He shook hands with the governor, who was obviously uncomfortable with Fogarty's faux friendliness.

"Come, Governor," Didi said. She turned to Fogarty and me. "If you would excuse us, this is a private ceremony."

"I insist on staying!" Fogarty said.

Didi waved a hand. "Go, Tom. Shoo, shoo. This is private. Come back later."

"I refuse—"

"Shall I call Dr. Morgridge?" she said. Her exasperation was palpable. "She assured me the governor and I would have privacy."

Fogarty flushed. He pushed the bridge of his glasses higher onto his nose. "As you wish." He stalked out, lab coat flying behind him.

The governor bent down to pet Penny, who accepted his affection as a queen would a courtier. He'd certainly passed that test.

"Fogarty is such a drama queen," Didi muttered.

"I know." I hadn't missed him one bit. I turned to the governor, who had begun unloading his bag onto Didi's desk. I spotted a sage stick, but the other items I didn't recognize.

His smile was gentle, his eyes suddenly sad. "We'll talk later."

I didn't know what to say. "I . . ."

The governor turned toward the clay head. Didi began to close the door.

"Didi, can't we just tell the governor that—"

She shook her head. "Please, later." She closed the door, and I heard the snick of the lock.

I hesitated, then walked to my former office, the one Gert had proudly decorated in pink and green and yellow—

the colors of spring, as if that could banish Massachusetts's dour winters.

She answered my knock with, "Come in." I found her awash in a sea of paperwork.

"Horrible, isn't it?" I followed Penny to the sofa. "All that paperwork."

She blew a pink Bazooka bubble. "I kinda like it."

"*What?*"

"Yeah. It's contained, y'know. Ya finish a stack and you feel you've done something. Ya can see it."

I got it, but . . . "You're such a people person, Gert."

She nodded. "Don't tell, but I get sad."

I knew just what she meant. "Mind if I make a call?"

She pointed to the phone. "You know the routine."

I did, and soon I had an outside line. I dialed Delphine's gallery on the Vineyard. No one picked up, not even the machine. Disturbing. The woman was a sharp businessperson. Someone *always* answered her phone during business hours.

"Back in a sec." I crossed the hall to MGAP's central office, waved at Donna, a longtime employee, and sat behind one of the workstations. As soon as I logged on, I found Delphine's Vineyard gallery and the hours it was open.

The elegant Web site told me I could call now and get knowledgeable help. Well, dammit, where was that help? Where was Zoe? The phone rang and rang and rang.

I rubbed the pendant I'd purchased from Delphine the last time I'd visited her shop. The carved frog was set in silver on a long silver chain. The frog was nutria jasper with azurite by a Zuni master carver named Ricky Laahty. He'd mined the stone himself. It was smooth and warm beneath my fingers as I rubbed and rubbed.

I didn't care if it sounded crazy or made no sense, Delphine was dead. Her skull, here. I felt it in my bones.

* * *

I felt compelled to wait until the cleansing ceremony was complete, so I called up to Addy to see if she was free for lunch. She wasn't, and so I wandered down the hall and across the lobby to CSS to find Kranak. He'd been his usual ballsy self with the Geographic guys. Made me chuckle.

I peeked around the corner. "Rob?"

He hadn't heard me because he and that new lab tech—what was her name?—were eating subs. Looked like the subs were from my favorite place in the North End. Bite for bite, the tech matched Kranak's gusto. They were laughing at something. I wondered what.

I backed away, right into the officer on duty at the desk.

"Ma'am?" he said.

I smiled, but felt a wistful sadness creep up from my belly. The officer didn't know me, nor I him.

There was a time when I had known *everyone* at The Grief Shop.

"Ma'am?" he repeated.

"Sorry," I said. "The fellow I was looking for isn't here."

I guessed I wouldn't wait after all.

That night I ate with my old pal Shaye at Antico Forno on Salem Street in the North End. It was far away from touristy Hanover Street on a narrow street reminiscent of Europe, which is why I liked the setting so much. The food was pretty fabulous, too.

Shaye was a shepherd to homeless women, and I respected her greatly. But we argued, as usual.

"The tribe should get their skull back," she said.

I zipped my trap as the waiter delivered my steaming plate of *frutti di mare*, then I stabbed a piece of calamari onto my fork. "You can't say that."

"Sure I can." She swished her bread around the herbed oil and chomped down. "It's easy."

"We don't even know if the skull is an American Indian ancestor."

Shaye smirked. "Right. It's a fucking white guy from Spain or something."

"Cripes, Shaye, quiet. This is a family place."

She scooped a hunk of vegetarian lasagna into her mouth, dabbed her lips, and hissed, "Pussy."

"Geesh, you're foul."

A beatific smile crossed her face. "I know. It's one of my many charms."

"Seriously, Shaye, it's a matter of knowing the skull's history. I can see why the Smithsonian would want to study it."

"Shit."

"C'mon, Shaye, look—"

She shook her head. "Not that. The door. Don't turn your head."

The inevitable furred my spine with chills. I glanced sideways and there, walking into the restaurant, was Harry Pisarro himself.

"Does that creep follow you everywhere, or what?" she said.

My back was to the door. I kept it that way. I lifted fork-fuls of lobster and mussels to my mouth, sipped a delicious cabernet and poked at my spring greens salad. I tasted nothing but ash.

Pisarro and his two goons were here because of me. I knew it, and I hated it. Somehow I was unable to completely extract the leech of a mobster from my life.

I laid some bills on the table, tossed my napkin down, and left the restaurant.

"Why, my dear Tally . . ." Pisarro began.

I brushed past him without a look, and the sound of his familiar baritone laughter followed me down the street.

* * *

When I arrived home, I showered, something I always did after an encounter with sleazeball mobster Pisarro. Having counseled him after his daughter's homicide and dealt with him on several other cases, some of which he caused, he now felt I was his personal property, a view I sure didn't share. One thing good about leaving MGAP was I didn't see Pisarro so often. A real blessing.

Hank would be here in another day. I couldn't wait. I turbaned my hair, let Penny in, and responded to the blinking light on my phone.

I scoonched on the couch and pulled the afghan across my legs. I flipped channels on the muted TV while I listened to my voicemail—my broker's suggestions, all of which sounded silly; a request to donate money to my alma mater, Cornell; and Gert's invite to Hank and me for dinner on the weekend to meet her newest flame, a guy named Incredulous, or Cred for short. A rapper. With dreds. Gert loved dreds.

"Good heavens, Gertie," I muttered.

Penny's ears pricked.

I didn't recognize the final voice. "Zoe here," she said, "at Delphine's. I wanted to call you, Ms. Whyte. I spoke with Delphine. She's good. She's pretty intense about her buying trip, and so she's not being really good about answering her phone. She's staying with friends, but she asked me to give you her cell number. I hope that's okay."

Relief flowed to my fingertips as I jotted the number on a Post-it.

"If you have any questions," Zoe added, "just give me a shout. Bye."

I took a breath. Progress. But I wouldn't feel truly great until I spoke with Delphine. I dialed her cell, got her voicemail, and left a message.

I unmuted the volume so I could watch a repeat of *Life on Mars*, one of my favorite Brit mysteries. I pulled out a scarf

I was knitting, and off I went. As the gorgeous alpaca silk flowed through my hands and onto my needles, I relaxed.

Addy sure made a compelling case for my return to MGAP. So did Gert. I missed her. Missed the gang. Missed the *belonging*.

I dozed, and dreamed of Indians and skulls and . . .

A sound on the TV jerked me awake. It was late. Time for bed, the real one. Delphine still troubled me. The reconstructed skull had looked so like her, right down to her Romanesque nose. At least, I thought the reconstruction's nose matched Delphine's.

Damn. I'd go back, talk to Didi again, and photograph the reconstruction. I didn't care how much Didi objected. I simply couldn't believe the resemblance to Delphine was a coincidence. Not for one minute.

CHAPTER FOUR

I awakened later than planned. I called, checked Didi's schedule. She'd be at The Grief Shop all day, and so I felt comfortable taking a run with Penny down Appleton to Peters Park, our favorite dog park, before I went to see her. I checked my watch. I had to make sure Addy didn't spot me, or I'd be grilled again about returning to MGAP. I wasn't really ready to think about that. Choices and more choices.

Now that she and the governor had that cleansing ceremony, maybe I could talk Didi into carbon dating the skull.

Penny and I got a good workout at the park, where we met some friends—canine and human—chased balls and Frisbees, and generally had a swell time. So I didn't much mind leaving Penny home when I went to The Grief Shop, since I planned to scoot in and out.

Lucky me, I didn't meet much traffic on the way over, and as I pulled open the side door to OCME, I swore the thing got heavier each year. The lobby was empty. Sarge was probably on one of his frequent breaks. But I found it odd that one of the CSS crew wasn't standing in for him.

As I crossed the hall, I saw that CSS was curtained. A meeting or they were performing some of their forensic mumbo jumbo they made look so easy, but was actually intensely complex. I'd hoped for a glimpse of Kranak.

I punched the keypad, hoping they hadn't changed the combination from the previous day. The buzzer sounded louder than ever.

"Damn."

I glanced around. Still no one. I let out a small sigh. I eased the door shut and headed down the hall, then to the left. I waved at a tech I recognized who was trotting toward the large autopsy suite. That's where everyone was, of course, busily carving and sawing away in search of the truth.

I rounded the corner. A red ballcap lay on the bench. Someone must be in with Didi. I slid it over and sat. I unhitched my purse, weighted down with my digital SLR camera. My shoulder ached, and I rotated it a couple of times.

I opened the book I'd bought on the Old Ones and read. Interesting stuff, particularly their rock art, which was gorgeous.

Several chapters later, I checked my watch. I'd been sitting there for twenty minutes. Enough was enough. Whoever was in with Didi was taking forever.

I knocked, breezed on in, and screamed!

My voice ricocheted around Didi's small lab, then quieted. Blood pooled around Didi's sprawled form. She looked like a red snow angel. Blood had sprayed her face, dripped down to her ears and stained her pewter gray hair.

He'd slit her throat. And stabbed her.

I pressed my back against the door. "Didi!" I shouted. "Didi!"

I blinked faster and faster as I gasped breaths. I desperately tried to hold back the bile surging from my belly.

Her eyes were open, staring blankly into nowhere. Her head lay at an awkward angle, almost detached from her neck, which . . .

What was that on the floor? I looked around, saw no one. He couldn't still be there, could he?

I inched to the left. Didi's right arm was slung over her body, her bony index finger, its tip reddish brown, pointing the way, like in some '30s horror movie. Writing on the linoleum floor. *Bloodfet*

I turned my head and vomited. When I was empty, I wiped my mouth with the sleeve of my jacket.

Why had I reacted so powerfully to the words she'd written in blood? I didn't know. Didn't really even know what they meant. *Bloodfet? Oh, Didi, I don't get it.*

Where the hell was everyone?

Somehow, I couldn't move, except to push my back harder against the door. With one hand, I rooted around in my purse and dragged out my phone. I flipped the phone open, hit a button and mumbled "Gert."

Nothing happened.

I closed my eyes, yet as soon as I reopened them, they fastened on the wreck of Didi. My eyes burned with unshed tears. Didi didn't deserve this. She didn't.

I wanted to kneel in front of her, hold her, stroke her face. I didn't dare. That would damage the scene. "Oh, Didi, I'm so sorry." I raised the phone again to my lips. "Gert!"

The phone dialed itself, beeping as it did so. I couldn't stop shaking. I was crying now, and my tears fell to the floor where her blood was congealing.

What if Didi's killer hid behind her desk when I'd entered the room?

"MGAP," said the voice. "How can I help you?"

"Gert," was all I could say.

"She's not here," the voice said. "Can I help you?"

I panted, two, three times.

"Hello?" the voice said again.

"This is Tally Whyte. Go to the CSS offices. Get some officers over to Dr. Didi's office."

"Tal, this is Donna. We've got a bunch of—"

"Go. Now. Do it."

I flipped the phone closed and slid down the door to the floor. A finger of Didi's blood pooled around my foot, and I wept harder.

"Tal?" Kranak said.

I blinked a couple times. The hall was abuzz with forensics, an ME I didn't recognize, and someone sobbing. I couldn't see who. Someone, probably Kranak, had plastered crime scene tape across the door to Didi's office. I looked away and into Kranak's soft bloodshot eyes the color of charcoal.

Funny. I felt a burst of happiness at seeing him.

"Yes," I said. "Yes. I'm okay. I've seen worse. But this is . . . Geesh, poor Didi. Damn!"

"Yeah," he said. "I gotta go back in. Gertie's on her way."

I grabbed his sleeve. "Wait. The skull, the reconstruction. Where is it?"

Even before he shook his head, I knew. I sighed, leaned back against the cinderblock wall, and sucked on the piece of ice Kranak had given me.

Of course whoever done this had stolen the skull, the potsherds, and Didi's reconstruction.

I paced Kranak's small cubicle, which wasn't an easy thing to do. I waited and waited, and finally he lumbered in. He slipped off his wrinkled suit jacket and rolled up his sleeves.

"Better," he said. He sat on the leather-padded bench that rested against the cubicle wall. He shifted his bulk so the cubicle's corner embraced him.

I poured him a cup of tea from his stash and popped my Diet Coke.

"Anything?" I asked as I handed him the steaming porcelain cup.

He sipped, nodded, then scraped a hand through his bristly crew cut. "Little. Some trace. Shit. She was a friend."

I sat beside him and leaned against his shoulder. "I know." Her bloody image flashed before my eyes. How long would it take to get rid of that damn picture?

"Anything at all on the skull? The restoration?"

His lips thinned. "We think that's why . . ."

"Me, too," I said. "Even so, there was a huge amount of anger in her killing. A lot of passion."

He snorted. "Knew you'd say that."

"Well, sure. Obvious, isn't it?"

"Maybe," he said. "Yeah. I guess. Or the killer's trying to make us think that. For all the hell we know, the guy was out for bucks. Big market in those things, ya know."

"Reconstructions? No way that . . ."

"The old skull, Tal."

"I can't believe that. But I guess . . . well, I'd believe anything right about now." I scraped my fingers through my hair. "So, what do you think '*bloodfet*' means?"

He took a sip of tea. "Huh?"

"What do you mean, 'huh'? The words Didi scrawled in her own blood."

"I don't know what you're talkin' about, Tal."

I stood. I didn't get why he was shining me on. "This isn't funny, Rob."

He slid his teacup onto his desk before he shrugged on his jacket. "Ya got that right, at least."

Was I losing my mind? "C'mon." I dragged him back to Didi's bloodstained office. Fewer people. The spatter guys, one of whom was perched on a ladder, were still taking measurements, but Didi's body was gone. I'd soon be talking to her family. Except . . .

I shook my head. I couldn't quite see where she'd been resting. I moved forward, slipped under the tape to get a better look.

"So?" Kranak said.

I stared to the right and to the left of markers that indicated where her body had rested. I saw pools of blood congealing on the linoleum, but no words. None.

"This is creepy, Rob. Didi wrote the word '*bloodfet*.'" I pointed to where she'd inscribed the word. "Right there. I saw it."

"Hey, Bruce," Kranak said to the guy on the ladder. "You find any words? Anything like that?"

Bruce shook his head. "Nope, Sarge.

"What about under that pool of blood," I said. "Maybe it oozed over the word or something."

The blood spatter specialist peered down at us, shaking his head. "When we get there, I'll look again. But I doubt it."

"Well, don't doubt it. Just find it." I turned and left.

Kranak said something I couldn't hear, then followed me. "Bruce's the best blood guy I know, Tally."

I stood in the hall, my body flushed with anger and a touch of fear. "Whatever. What about the crime scene photos?"

"They show nothing like you describe."

"I know what I saw."

"Bruce'll check. Promise."

"Sure. He sounded awfully certain he'd find nothing." I walked through the keyed door and into the lobby, headed for MGAP. Kranak stopped me with a hand on my arm.

"Hold up, Tally," he said.

I faced him. "Something hinkey's going on. I know what I saw. I don't much enjoy being treated like a three-year-old. Or doubted. Or questioned."

He snorted. "You're not. But the word may be gone, Tally. You, of all people, know how the mind imagines stuff."

"I didn't imagine this." I got a pen and a pad at the front desk and wrote out the word I'd seen scrawled in Didi's blood. "Here. She wrote it. I don't know why it's gone, but it matters. Understand."

"Sure do. But you know as well as I that I can't do anything without evidence."

"Just keep an eye out, okay?"

"Promise." He looked at the paper. "Promise."

I kissed his cheek, nodded, and looked down. The toe that peeked from my open-toed pumps was stained with Didi's blood. "Oh, hell."

It was hard handing off Didi's sister and brother-in-law to Gert and her team. But I didn't work there anymore.

Still, I ached for them, for Didi, for her friends and family at OCME. She was this wild-haired wonder, and she didn't deserve to die that way. Not at all.

Right after the viewing and ID, I slipped back inside the far reaches of OCME to say my farewells. They mattered, at least to me they did, those good-byes. Funerals and such were different. The remains were embalmed to waxy perfection and often dressed and dolled up in clothes and makeup they'd never have worn in life. I remembered seeing a good friend's nails painted bright red in her casket, her newly manicured hand clutching the Bible, King James Version. She never would have used red on her nails. Nor would she have allowed a Bible in the casket with her.

The remains we all saw at funeral homes were really about the bereaved, not the deceased. Or so I believed.

So I made it a point with my cases and with my friends to say my good-byes privately.

I stood in the large refrigeration room, a place I knew intimately. Didi lay on a steel gurney, just like all the others. She was encased in a white plastic bag, and, I guessed out of respect, someone had covered her with a sheet. She hadn't been autopsied yet. I didn't envy the ME that one. Cutting one of your own was hard.

I sighed and rested my hand on her forehead. I stroked her wiry gray hair that was still matted with blood. "You were crazy, Dee. Just nuts." I ran my hand up and down her arm, as if that soothing motion might help her. One truth—it helped me to deal.

She was frozen in time, just like one of her reconstructions. I slipped two fingers over the bruise that had bloomed on her cheek. "Who hit you? Why? Who did this to you?"

The mole she'd always talked about removing remained beside her left eye. It was sexy, but Didi was not.

Had the Zuni governor come back? Or maybe the Geographic people? Someone else—who?—wanted to possess that which he shouldn't. I saw Didi fighting him and . . .

I smoothed my hand across her thin forearm. "Oh, yes, Dee. We'll find out. That we will. Never fear. We'll make him pay."

"What do you mean there are no photos of Didi's reconstruction and the skull?" I stood, arms folded, and stared at Addy Morgridge until I was sure she'd relent and tell me she was mistaken.

"Sorry, Tal. No." She waved a hand. "Please sit! You're obviously distraught and dealing with that terrible sight of Didi's corpse."

"No, I'm not!" I said.

"Sit."

The leather squeaked as my tush landed hard. "I am not distraught. Much. Not too much." Suddenly I was fighting tears. "Why no photos?"

"The governor. His request, our acquiescence. We had to respect his wishes, Tally."

"Ah, jeez."

Addy lit a cigarette. Boy, didn't I wish . . . "She was something, that one," Addy said.

I nodded, chuckled. "A character. One of a kind."

"All that talent, gone." She inhaled deeply and allowed the smoke to dribble out her nose. "And here. How dare they."

"Have you called the governor? Told him about—"

Addy nodded.

"Mind if I talk to him?"

She stubbed out the cigarette. "Yes."

"Why?"

She lit another one. "Sergeant Kranak said you'd be trouble."

A prick of pain. I was sure Kranak hadn't said it like that, but . . . funny how those words hurt. I guessed he'd moved on, just like me.

"Sergeant Kranak's right," I said. "But I don't work here anymore, which sure looks like a good thing." I contemplated telling her about the two snaps I had of the reconstruction, the ones I'd taken with my phone and only pretended to erase. Later. I'd tell her later, after I'd talked to the Zuni governor.

Outside Addy's office, I made sure I e-mailed the photos home. If they were the only pictures of Didi's reconstruction, they were priceless.

Once I got home, I brought up my e-mail. There were the two images, one a full face and one in profile. I wished I'd ignored Didi and taken more. Didi. I'd caught her on camera, too. Just her back, bent over some hunk of unformed clay, her bony hands and slightly hunched shoulders a portrait in intensity.

She was so damned good at what she did. So devoted to her work, to the past she wished to bring back to life.

The photo said it all. Life, there now, then—poof.

Gone. In a blink. I looked at her image again. She was alive there, intensely so. And now . . .

I could not see the value in stealing a skull, a bunch of potsherds and a clay bust. I couldn't see the value at all.

I failed to find the Zuni governor that night, at least in the flesh, so I Googled him instead. He appeared to be a complex man who aimed to blend old and new Zuni ways into one, much to the frustration of certain young Zuni firebrands.

He carved Katsinas for a living and also for the tribe. I flipped through pages of pictured Katsinas, once called Kachinas. According to Barton Wright, who wrote extensively about American Indian art, Katsinas represented the spirit essence of everything in the real world. White noted that the idea of the Katsina Cult is that all things in the world have two forms, the visible object and its spirit counterpart, a dualism that balances mass and energy. Katsina dolls are never toys—I'd known that—not even when given to Hopi or Zuni children. These spirit "dolls" can assist with prayers. They're carved from cottonwood root, which had become increasingly scarce, and painted to represent the real Katsinas or spirit beings.

I'd seen Katsinas many times on my visits out West. Governor Bowannie was obviously a master carver. His pieces were sought after by many high-end collectors. They were worth thousands, and I knew the traders and retailers profited mightily. I had no idea what the governor himself received.

I continued searching, in part out of fascination, but found no way to communicate with the governor or learn where he was staying in Boston. Someone at OCME had to know. After all, he was now part of Didi's homicide investigation.

Since she was killed at OCME, she would fall under state, rather than Boston, jurisdiction. I knew a couple of detectives I could call. I'd rather leave Kranak out of it, if possible. I'd wait a couple of days, let things settle, then get the governor's location.

I tapped a few keys and looked up the Steamship Authority's ferry schedule on my computer. Plenty of ferries were running to the Vineyard. No more phone calls. I'd hop a ferry tomorrow and visit Delphine's shop myself.

Chapter Five

Indian Summer—there was nothing like it. The drive to Woods Hole was spectacular, and Penny and I made the 10:45 A.M. ferry to Vineyard Haven with ease. On this late-September Wednesday, with the sky a glossy blue and the air crisp with promise, I could hardly imagine murder staining someone's life.

I stood on the top open-air deck and wrapped my hands around the rail. Gulls wheeled and cawed and dived for tidbits tossed by passengers. It was loud—the crossing always was—with the sea and surf and wind in my ears. I tightened my sweater from the sea-chill.

How I loved the ocean! The sea brought memories of my dad and Veda and the possibility of the infinite.

I laughed and ruffled Penny's fur. Hank always said he loved when I "waxed poetic," as he called it. I usually found my yammerings, in retrospect, pretty silly.

We debarked at Vineyard Haven, and I immediately relaxed. I was crazy about the Vineyard, especially when the summer people had fled. Then you could feel her bones. She was old and no matter how much they flossed her up, her earthiness reappeared each winter. She was a working island, where life was hard and could be cheap. In the old days, folks struggled to survive. I admired their determination and grit.

As I stepped on the dock, I spotted a tall, hearty-looking man with a wispy beard and a seaman's grin. Dan Black and his wife Belle were dear old friends. She'd grown up on the Vineyard, but of the two, he looked like the stereotypical Old Salt. In truth, he was a cowboy from Durango, Colorado, who'd come east to college on a fencing scholarship.

"Dan!" I waved and was suddenly engulfed in the kind of wonderful bear hug where you can hardly breathe. I laughed and returned it. Penny barked.

"Where's your lovely bride?" I asked upon my release.

"Putting together some bluefish pate for lunch before you head off on your big adventure. Delish!" He caught my eyes and the smiling glint faded to sadness. "I'm sorry about Doc Cravitz. She was a good one."

"Yes," I said. "She was."

He smoothed a hand over my tangly hair. "Are you all right?"

Was I? "I guess. It was tough, finding Didi that way. I've sort of been possessed by this whole thing, y'know?"

"I hope not too much. Sounds like this was a real nasty one."

"Yes."

"I'll take my murders fictional, as you know." He hefted my backpack and led us through the crowd.

"I want to drive by Delphine's shop, okay?" I said as I slid into the passenger seat of Dan's red Jeep Cherokee. The truck backfired, seemingly in protest, and his hands tightened on the steering wheel.

He snapped me a nod, then took a right, and then another onto Main Street. I wished we had time to stop in at Bunch of Grapes books and the Sioux Eagle jewelry store, two of my favorite shops in all the world.

"Next time we'll stop and shop," said mind-reader Dan.

"Oh, you know me too well."

He grinned and tipped his cap. "Which is pretty nice, isn't it?"

"To have friends like that?" I said. "Yes, it is."

We continued down Main, through the shopping area where I'd once seen President Clinton and Chelsea leave their motorcade and shop for books. At the time, I'd talked to Buddy, the president's chocolate Lab. He was a handful for the Secret Service agent who held his leash—a wild and sweet dog, and I was saddened when I heard about his untimely death.

Dan turned left, then made a right onto North William Street.

"Pretty," I said. "I love this drive. One of these days I'll make it out to West Chop."

He chuckled. I never seemed to get beyond Delphine's shop and her American Indian artifacts. We were only minutes from her shop and home, and I felt the usual anticipation.

"Belle and I are thrilled to have you here, so don't take this wrong, but you shouldn't . . . I'm not good with you going to that shop."

"Why? We've always had a kick going there before. You're the one who introduced me to Delphine."

He nodded. "To plenty of people. She's a good woman. I wanted her to thrive, but . . ." His fingers danced on the steering wheel.

"You don't have to tell me, Dan."

He nodded. "I know. Delphine had an affair with my brother-in-law. More than twenty years ago."

"But he was married to—"

"Belle's sister? Yes." He lowered his window, and the air slapped our faces. Penny scooched closer so her nose poked out the window.

"Why are you telling me this now?"

He nodded. "It matters. What with the doc's death and all. Belle's sister killed herself over it."

I hadn't known. Sad stuff, and all too typical of human relationships and frailties. I was glad I hadn't told him about the reconstruction, just that I wanted to visit Delphine's shop.

"You're up to something," Dan said. "Oh, you haven't told me what, but I feel it, my dear. Of course I do. You plan to ferret stuff out." He almost smiled. "You're the best ferreter I know."

"Gee, thanks. I would never—"

"I can't have Belle, well, upset," he said. "You know? Can't have it."

He made the left onto Old Lighthouse Road, and we were soon bumping and thumping down the potholed dirt surface.

About half a mile up the road, I spotted Delphine's large nineteenth-century Greek Revival home that also served as her shop. "Park under this tree, please?" I said. "Right here. I'll walk the rest of the way."

He looked at me, straight on, and my jocular friend had vanished beneath a fierce and disturbing exterior, one that held a silent threat.

Penny growled.

"Dan?"

His barrel chest bellowed, then sank. He rested his chin on his chest. "I never should have told. Jerry was a fool. Delphine would never breathe a word of it. But you, Tal . . . that's why I told you. That's all. Delphine has that death on her head."

I didn't like the sound of that one bit.

*   *   *

Penny stayed by my side as we set off down the road, hugging the tree line. I didn't mind the walk. It felt good to be outside, and I would call Dan when I was ready to go back to his place. The side of the road was sandy, another thing I loved about the ocean, and sand slipped inside my sandals. A soft breeze lifted my tentacled curls, brushing one across my face. I pushed it away. A car rounded the curve, and I stepped into the shadow of an overhanging oak.

Once the car passed, I walked on and soon came to the end of a white picket fence flooded with long-past rosa rugosas. I peeked out from a large flame bush beginning to turn.

A woman stood in the stoop of the front door shop entrance. She wore a T-shirt beneath her billowing lavender jumper, granola-style. I couldn't see her face, but she bore the stance of someone young and bristling with life. Long, tiny braids flowed from her bandana-bound hair. The braids were white-blond and dangled to the small of her back, while wispy curls danced around her face. They swayed as she talked on her cell phone, and I felt her smile even this far away. Her left hand waved and dipped, and her braids bobbed like bouncing puppets when she nodded.

I'd bet that was Zoe. The shop was obviously open, but not busy. A perfect time to chat, take a look around and get a sense of what was going on.

I took a step forward. In that moment, a pink Cadillac convertible rounded the corner and beeped. The thing was a boat, circa 1960, complete with fins. My, my. Damn, someone was primed for shopping and . . .

"Tally!" hollered the woman in the driver's seat.

The woman wore a pink scarf wrapped tight around her head and neck, a la Kim Novak in *Vertigo*. Except, this woman I knew and . . .

Penny began barking like crazy, full of excitement and joy. Who the hell? "*Carmen?* What are you doing here?"

The Cadillac halted in a screech and billows of dust.

"Geesh, Carm," I said. "I'm trying to be secretive here!"

My best friend's face fell. "Crap. Sorry. Belle told me you were on the Island, going to Delphine's shop, so I came looking for you."

I looked back at the shop. The girl on the phone had disappeared, presumably inside. Ah, well. So much for stealth.

"This is obviously *not* a coincidence, dear friend," I said. "What are you up to?"

"Me? Nothing. Coincidences *can* happen. I was vacationing here. Down from Maine."

"Where's the family?" I snagged Carmen's arm as she moved forward. "And what's with the pink car and scarf?"

She gave me one of her goofy looks, a la Lucy. "The restaurant's been doing, um, not so hot. We needed something else. Bob, well, he's, let's just say it's up to me. I'm not entirely here to vacation. Nope, I'm also here as Ms. Organic Mary Kay."

"*Pardon?*"

"It's a new company called Organic Pink. Same getup as Mary Kay, but organic. I even brought the car over on the ferry. Pretty neat. Get it now, duh?"

It sounded like a recipe for a lawsuit to me, and Bob . . . I was disturbed to hear there was a problem. And as for coincidences . . .

But that was for later. "You look great, hon." Carmen, at six-foot-plus, would be astonishing in a MK pink outfit, yet the scarf and car, oddly enough, worked. I hugged her. "You're fabulous, Carm. Always."

She laughed. "Yup suh. Sure am, and don't I know it."

"C'mon," I said to Carmen. Penny leapt into the Caddy's backseat, and I hopped in front. "Why don't you come with me to visit the shop?"

"Love to." She put the boat of a car in gear. "Afterward, I'll give you a lift back to Dan and Belle's. Lots to tell."

"Knowing you, Carm, I can only imagine." I gave the humongous pink convertible Cadillac another look. "I've really never seen a car like this in the flesh."

She winked. Cripes.

The bell jingled as we entered the shop. I poked my head in. "Zoe?"

No answer.

Persian rugs, old wide-board pine floors, exposed beams—Delphine's shop was a feast for the eyes. Penny's nails went *clack-clack* on the wood floor as we turned left, into a modern room filled with American Indian art from contemporary artists. It drove me crazy not to look at all Delphine's new pieces, but I needed to find Zoe. The shop took up the entire first floor of the classic Greek Revival home, and one room led into another to form a perfect square. We walked through the front, contemporary room, through an arch and into the second room, one at the back of the house. It was filled with Delphine's collection of American Indian and Southwestern sculpture. I wondered what Didi would have thought of the place. I smiled. Unless there were bones, I doubted she would have found it very interesting.

"This stuff is gorgeous," Carmen said.

"Yeah, it sure is." This shop was where I first had seen the wonderful sculptures by Roxanne Swentzell and Allan Houser and Nila Wendall.

Carmen walked to a bronze of a full-figured woman, reclining, her hand raised, a sweet smile on her face. Carmen smiled back, and she caressed the sculpture's hand with her own large, capable one.

"Don't touch that sculpture!" barked a voice.

We both turned. Penny let out a low growl.

The girl in the violet jumper and long white-blond braids stood in the doorway, her eyes frightened, cell phone in hand.

"*Sedni*," I said to Penny in Czech, her native language and one I often used for commands. "Sit. Good girl. Zoe?"

She snapped the phone shut. "Yes. Please get that dog out of here. She'll ruin things."

"She really won't," I said. "She'll be fine. Promise."

I introduced myself and Carmen. "I don't think that Carmen will hurt the bronze, either."

"No. I guess not." She moved toward us with a tentative smile. One of her front teeth was slightly crooked, which made her looks even more endearing. "No. No of course she can't."

Zoe stared at the sculpture with a look of longing, and, I mouthed Go to Carmen. *Take Penny.*

"Ayuh," Carmen said in her thickest Down East accent. "Pretty stuff. I'm gonna browse the shop, yup suh. Take the dog. Okay by you?"

"Of course," Zoe said. "Yes. It's fine. But I've got an errand I have to run in fifteen minutes. I hope that's all right. I'll have to lock the shop."

Her expression was sweet and kind, a look that would melt a man. But her skin was mottled, her eyes puffy. Crying about what, I wondered. And her nervous fingers played with the cell phone in her hand.

As soon as Carmen and Penny left the room, I said, "Are you okay?"

She bit her lower lip. "I'm fine. Thanks."

"You sure? Is it . . . is it Delphine?"

Her blue eyes widened and tears pooled on her lids. "How did you know?"

"I, well . . ." I drew in a deep breath. "You know I want to talk to her."

She sniffled.

I dug a tissue from my purse and handed it to her. "Want to talk about it?"

"I shouldn't." Her voice was a whisper.

"It might help. Let's go sit someplace and—"

"No." She rested a hand on my arm. "I'm being silly. I should be used to it by now."

"Used to it?"

She walked over to the Swentzell sculpture and wrapped her hand around the sculpture's much smaller one. "I yelled at your friend because, um, well, she's my friend. At least I think of her that way. I'm sorry."

She straightened, brushed her hands down her linen jumper. "There. Better. I shouldn't let her get to me. That's so dumb."

"Delphine?"

She nodded. "I love her. She's really good to me. But when she's on these trips, she can be such a witch. She gets crazy with work, and she was just yelling at me when you came in. I . . . I lost it, I guess."

I walked closer to Zoe, so I could see her eyes. "Delphine. It was Delphine on the phone."

"Yeah. I told her you wanted to talk to her. But, no. She didn't have the time. She never has the time. I wish she didn't lay all this stuff on me."

"I understand." But I wasn't paying total attention. Delphine really was alive. Alive. Yet . . . why couldn't I just let it go?

"You want to call her back?" Zoe thrust the cell phone in my direction.

"I thought she said no."

Zoe shrugged. "So? She can't always have it her way."

I took the phone, flipped it open and pressed the button for calls received. Delphine's cell number popped up. I pressed send and held the phone to my ear.

But what I saw was a woman in panic. Zoe looked terrified. She turned away. Delphine's phone rang once, twice . . .

"What do you want now, Zoe?" growled the voice.

Delphine's voice. Angry. I flipped the phone closed.

* * *

Carmen varoomed the Cadillac around island curves, while I held on to Penny with one hand and dug my heels into the floor.

"Cripes, Carm. Drive slower around these . . . dammit! You're crazy!"

I looked across at the lapping water. Not that far, really, but enough to kill us if we flipped over. And I thought *I* was a wild driver.

Penny whined.

"Oh, come on, you two," Carmen said. "It's fun."

"Fun? It's crazy. You're being crazy and scaring Penny!"

"Well, in that case . . ." Her foot eased off the pedal, and the car slowed to a nearly normal speed for the serpentine roads.

I checked my watch. "Are Dan and Belle expecting us at any time?"

"Not really. I don't think so. Belle said they'd have cocktails waiting whenever we arrive."

"Okay. So how come we're taking this scenic journey?"

"I need to let off some steam," Carmen said. "I'm pissed."

"Because Zoe yelled at you?"

"Are you kidding?" She snorted. "That story about how the Delphine woman yelled at her. What a bitch. I hate people like that."

I puffed out some air. "Yeah. But I never saw that side of Delphine. I really didn't. Which is why I found the whole thing sort of strange. I wonder . . . Let's go back."

"Huh? Where?"

"To the shop."

"Why?" she said.

"It's complicated, Carm. Go."

"I am not your chauffeur," she said. "What's going on?"

"You're right. I'm being unfair. Just gimme a sec, okay? I've got to think this thing through. While I'm doing all my thinking, will you *please* turn around?"

Her U-turn sent the tires screeching and Penny howling and my heart just about leaping from my chest. I was thrilled, *thrilled* that no cars had been headed our way.

"Carm, how the frick many years do you think that took off my life, huh? How many? And Penny's? That's it. I am never letting you drive again. Never."

A grin of satisfaction split her lips. "I know exactly what I'm doing. Speaking of . . ." She careened to a stop at the side of the incredibly narrow cliff road, pressed a button on the dash, and the canvas roof began to canopy over us. "We can go faster this way."

"Oh, joy," I muttered to myself.

She straightened her head-scarf, cleaned her sunglasses. "You can always walk, you know."

"Shut up, Carm."

"Why are we going back?"

The top flopped to a stop, and Carmen pressed levers that secured the top to the windshield.

"Something's off," I said. "I'll explain as we go. I should have talked to Delphine. Not hung up like that. I thought it was her voice, but . . . well, maybe it wasn't, y'know?"

Of course, when we arrived back at the shop, we were greeted with a sign that said BE BACK SOON and a clock dial pointed to three P.M. Bummer.

CHAPTER SIX

We drove down a neatly paved road lined with trees and
very little retail and a few houses, yet we were on the main
road from Vineyard Haven to Edgartown. We were headed
for the Blacks' home. They lived on Third Street or
Fourth Street or maybe it was Seventh Street—I could
never seem to remember—which was a side road off the
main one to Edgartown.

"You know where you're going?" I asked Carmen.

"Sure."

I sat back and relaxed. Carmen was incredibly compe-
tent, which impressed me from the day we became buddies
in kindergarten in Maine. She turned left, and we bumped
down an unpaved road. We soon saw the pond, a lovely
body of water connected to Nantucket Sound. I could
never pronounce its Indian name. Minutes later, I spotted
my friends' driveway.

"There," I said.

"I know," she answered, and turned left into their dirt
driveway. The bursts of flowers that rimmed Belle and
Dan's fence and outlined their post-Modern home had

started to yellow. Some had already turned brown and died, and a few of the trees sported their bright autumn party colors.

New England's fall always came later and stayed longer on the Vineyard, which held great appeal to me. But I could never stand her summer tourist crowds for very long.

We parked in front of their garage and walked down the path to their screened-in porch. Belle stood on the steps, beaming. I rushed forward, and she gave me a big hug.

"Hey, hon," I said. "Thanks for having us on such short notice."

Her Egyptian brown eyes gave me the once-over. "It's been tough, yes?"

I compressed my lips, nodded. "Veda. Yes. And Didi, too. I'm okay, though."

"Of course you are." She smothered me in another Belle hug. "You two come on in. Cocktails await."

We sat around their harvest table spooning chowder and sipping wine. All except for me, with my Diet Coke, of which Belle and Carmen heartily disapproved.

"How do you guys know each other?" I looked from Carmen to Belle to Dan.

Dan's deep laugh bubbled up, and, as always, I saw him as the perfect Santa. A very cool one.

"We met years ago," Belle said. "Long story. But when Hank called, we—"

"Pardon?" I said. "When *Hank* called?"

Belle's chagrined smile told the tale.

"You weren't supposed to tell," Carmen said to her.

"Of course I wasn't," Belle said. "Ouch."

Carmen looked at me. "Well, Hank, he suggested I come down to the Vineyard and keep an eye on you. He said you were upset about your friend's murder, and he was worried."

Anger squeezed my gut. I tightened my jaw, forced myself not to explode when all I wanted to do was scream. I leaned forward, and the trio mirrored my movements as they recoiled in their chairs.

"Just like last time." My voice was a whisper. A hiss. "Hank is doing his paternal thing again. Just. Like. Last. Time. And you, Carmen, are his minion!"

A collective sucking-in of breath.

"I do not need a father," I said.

Carmen threw her balled up napkin, and it bonked me on the nose. I glared at her. "I'm in no mood, Car—"

"Get over it!" she said. "Just get over it. Hank means well. I wanted to come. I needed the break. So what? End of story."

I turned away in a sulk. I was really sick of Hank and his control-freak attitude. "So your being on the island wasn't a coincidence."

"Duh," Carmen said. "Of course not. But I have made some really good sales here."

"You mean all the Pink Organic stuff is true?"

"Ya got that right," Carmen said. A giggle.

"This isn't funny, Carm."

"Yo-uh chowda's gettin' cold," Carmen said in her best Down East dialect. "Ayuh. Colda than a witch's tit."

Belle giggled.

I did, too. Ticked or not at Hank, I couldn't stay mad at them for long.

Carmen, Dan, and I were washing dishes. Belle had gone to lie down. She was in the midst of a Lyme's disease relapse, and I worried about her.

"Something's not right," I said.

"So you say." Carmen handed me a freshly rinsed dish to dry.

"Sounds like," Dan said. He took the dish I'd dried and put it away. "Mebbe."

"Something's off. You know what I mean, Dan. I've got

this really weird feeling, like the whole scene with Zoe was a performance. I'd like to go back up there now."

"When didja say that girl was getting back?" Dan said.

"Three." I folded the damp dishtowel and laid it on the counter. "I'm not going to wait. Mind if I take your car?"

"I'll come with," he said.

"You're nuts," Carmen said. "The both of you. I'm sure not going."

Boy, it'd be nice to have Dan come along. But his son was a cop, which meant bad news for father and son and Belle if a misadventure occurred. I stretched on tiptoe and kissed his cheek, while I reached for the car keys on the table. "Thanks, but no. I'm just going to walk around, check a couple things out. Keep an eye on Penny, eh? And *no* surveillance, Carm. Got it?"

"Scout's honor," she said.

"Good." I looked at my watch. "One-thirty. Back in a flash."

I parked down the street and walked to the back of the shop. I'd brought my Leatherman and crowbar, just in case some tool might come in handy. Behind the house, a huge screen of trees, planted millennia ago, blocked prying eyes. What I was about to do was wrong. But then I imagined Didi lying in her own blood, throat slashed, gasping for breath, and I couldn't seem to help myself. A large rock off to my left invited sitting. I put the Leatherman in my pocket and sat.

What I planned was plain stupid. I heard Hank's voice. And Kranak's. And Veda's.

But Veda also always told me to listen to my gut. That same gut was telling me something was very wrong with Delphine. Okay, so I'd heard her voice on the phone. Maybe. Be easy enough to fake.

Except it, the voice, whatever was off. Only as Carmen

and I had driven around the island did I realize how wrong. The words, the tone almost sounded canned.

No, I had to learn more. Had to.

I picked up my Leatherman and worked at jimmying one of the back windows open. Vintage windows looked great, but were lousy at keeping out drafts and people. A dog yipped, and I jumped.

I looked around, saw nothing. I was cool. Of course the place was alarmed. I wanted the cops to come, just not too soon. If I bumbled much more, they'd be here before I'd made it inside.

"Damn!" I sucked my bloodied finger. I wasn't so hot at this. Plus, my jimmying efforts weren't working. All I'd achieved, besides stabbing my finger, was wrecking the poorly painted white window trim which, sadly, was the thing keeping the window from opening. The paint was like glue. I reached for the crowbar.

"Idiot!" hissed a voice.

I dropped the crowbar on my toe. "Shit!"

"Stop with the noise and the cursing," Carmen said as she crouched toward me across the back lawn.

"I'd like to bop you with the damned crowbar. What happened to Scout's honor?"

She grinned. "Who said I was ever a Scout?"

I stood and stared. She'd doffed her Mary Kay kerchief for her iconic red bandana and overalls. Carmen in full granola mode was Valkyrie-esque and a welcome sight.

"Babe," I said.

"Don't 'babe' me, Tal. You couldn't break into a laundry basket. You really suck at this." She walked up to the shop's back door, looked around once, and pulled out her picks. "I just hope you haven't triggered the alarm yet."

Insulting. "Of course I haven't." Talk about memories. We'd done this before, with teeter-totter results. "I thought there was no way."

"*Way!* I just didn't want Dan to know I was an expert lock picker."

"So what's taking you so long?" I was thrilled to see her, but the last thing I wanted to do was admit it. "You've gotten slow in your dotage."

"My ass." I watched with fascination as she tugged on a pair of latex gloves and went at the doorknob with the care and gentleness of a lover. She inserted one pick, moved it around, withdrew it, then glided another pick into the lock. She appeared to have all the time in the world.

"There," she said as she twisted the knob. "We're in."

I heard the silent alarm in my head shrieking *Break in.*

She closed the door behind us, and we walked down a short passage lined with treasure-stuffed shelves. The pieces were contemporary, and none warranted a second look. We spilled out into a room we hadn't seen earlier that day. It was filled with cases and shelves that held vintage and new baskets and Inuit carvings.

Carmen walked toward the right, where we'd been earlier that morning. I went straight ahead in search of the artifact room. A board creaked, and I jumped. We had minutes. That was it.

I passed beneath an arch that once must have divided front and back parlors and entered the room. In that instant, I knew what I feared, and there it was—a large photograph of Delphine holding an Old Ones pot.

It was she. Didi's reconstruction. Delphine's face had been on that bust. And it felt as if I were face-to-face with her.

I'd been trying all week to believe Delphine was alive, but all it took was one look at that photograph. My doubt vanished.

Delphine was dead, her skull somehow impossibly planted in an old Anasazi pot.

And right in front of me, beneath the photograph, a similar pot sat on a plinth. Naked. Not under glass. Nothing but air protecting it.

* * *

"*Shouldn't they be under glass?*" *I had asked Delphine nearly a year ago.*

"*These ancient artifacts need to breathe, Tally,*" *she answered.* "*Some are beneath glass, but some need to be free. You know?*"

"*I'd hate to see one broken, Del.*"

She shrugged in her Gallic way. "*C'est la vie. Meant to be.*"

I sighed. "Oh, Delphine."

"Don't be sad, sugar."

I flew around and stared into the grinning face of a Gene Hackman look-alike, a guy with a day-old beard and green Izod-style shirt. He stared back me. His sweet smile matched his thick Southern drawl. Too bad all that contrasted with the chill pulsing from his eyes. This man was a predator. All else was a costume donned for show.

"I . . . I . . . oh, um. I'm not sad. Not really." I shoved my hand into my pockets. The cops would be here any minute. I could stall him. I'd be fine. "How can I help you?"

His brilliant smile widened, revealing a gold canine engraved with a Z. "I'm here to meet Miss Zoe, of course."

Here to meet Zoe . . . what was he doing . . . what did he want . . . cripes. "Of course!" I repeated. I smiled, breathed deeply, tried to slow my racing heart. I had to ignore the evil I felt from this man, or he would hurt me. Somehow I knew that. "Here I am. So how can I help you?"

"Whelp me? What are you talking about?"

"Help. I said help, not whelp."

He pressed a finger to his left ear and turned. He chuckled, shook his head. "Damn hearing aids. Way too much rock n' roll as a kid. Better." He lifted my shaking hand and kissed the palm.

I forced myself not to pull it away. Not yet. I hoped it didn't shake too much. "Me, too. Now—"

"M'dear, you know just how to help me."

He tried that charmer smile on me again, but his eyes remained flat and dead. Killer eyes. I batted my eyelashes, gave a sly smile. "Sir, perhaps I've forgotten." I straightened my spine, threw back my shoulders so he'd notice my boobs, and tossed my blond curls.

The police. Any minute. Carmen? Where was Carmen?

A knife flashed. He grabbed my arm, flipped me around. A movement, swift, then pressure, then pain and . . .

I shrieked.

He pushed me away.

I pressed my hand to my face and felt a warm wetness, lowered my hand and saw . . . my palm smeared with blood that glistened and dripped. My blood. I bit my inner cheek, fighting the pain. Couldn't let him see it or my terrible fear. I spit at him. "Creep."

"Now you listen, little Miss Zoe," he said. "I don't mess around, m'dear. You should know better than to play coy with me. Now, do tell, where is the fetish? The one they used. I'm sent to get it."

He held on to my forearm while he bent and wiped his knife on my jeans. He didn't lower his head, and his lizard eyes held mine. I had to control the fear. The fury, too. Bastard. I wouldn't let him get the upper hand, not completely, or he'd kill me. He'd enjoy it, too.

He ran a finger down my cheek, where he'd cut it. His touching it burned. My eyes watered in pain, but I didn't cry. He raised the finger to his lips and licked off my blood.

His grin was lipstick-pretty from the blood on his lips. Christmas. I forced a wink. "So cool you don't mind HIV."

His wide smile faltered, just a touch. I wasn't dead yet. But the fetish? I had no clue. And I had to control the situation. Somehow. Had to. Calm. He wanted something from me. I'd try to give it to him. "Follow me." My voice rasped with pain.

I led him to the back room, where I'd seen the Zuni fetishes. No sign of Carmen. The smell of my own blood dripping down my neck sickened me. I shook my head. I'd keep it together, dammit. I had to. I tugged my shirttail out and dabbed at my face. He didn't say a word, just followed behind me.

Delphine had lined the terra cotta room with her modern American Indian treasures. I glanced at a pot, a huge one. It sat on the nearest glass counter. Good. Okay.

Now to find the fetishes. I skirted a display of Katsinas and one of small seed pots. Finally . . . "Here." I pointed toward the case that held dozens and dozens of Zuni fetishes. Wolves and mountain lions and bears and moles and corn maidens and many, many more.

He stood behind me, close, tight, his breath fetid and warm on my neck. His hands wrapped around me and pressed my breasts. He squeezed, gently massaged them, just like a lover.

I grew dizzy with hate.

I lowered my head. His hands were long and slim. Pianist's hands. I opened my mouth to bite one.

He squeezed tighter and tighter and the pain, blinding. I struggled, tried to bite, elbowed him, clawed at those torturous hands. But he was too close, pressed too tight against me.

My legs trembled from pain, and I reached up behind me, found his face with my fingers and ripped.

He pushed me away, and I smashed into the case, and it toppled backward.

"Bitch!" he said.

I gasped for air, bent almost in half, arms crossed over my breasts, which pulsed with pain.

"I want that blood fetish, and I want it *now*. Y'all hear? If I don't get it, sweet peaches, I'm gonna cut you into little slivers and feed you to my carp."

"It's in the case," I said.

"In the caves? Where? Which cave, goddammit?" Face bright red, scored with my nails, eyes boiling fury turning icy and calm. Very calm. Happy, almost. He pulled a gun from its sheath above his ankle. "First, the left kneecap. A crippling bite. Here . . ."

A cacophony of windows breaking and wood shattering and screams. A woman. Carmen.

I twirled. In the doorway, there she was. "No!"

The boom of a gun, and I ran to Carmen, expecting to see blood bloom on her shirt. But her eyes stared past me, and I grabbed her and shoved her to the floor.

Silence. The pounding of my heart.

I was afraid to look, knew he was standing over us, the stubby barrel of his gun pointed at us.

"Ma'am?" Footsteps. "Ma'am?"

I tuned my head. Boots. I followed up the leg and found the face of a police officer. Dan's son, Riley.

"I . . . hello," I said.

"Tally, get off."

Carmen was talking. *Get off?* Oh. Right. I rolled onto my back, stared at the beautifully painted ceiling done in . . . What was I thinking?

"Tally?"

An arm around my shoulders, helping me sit up.

"Carm?" Tears fell down her face. "I'm okay. Are you?"

She sniffled. "Ayuh. Just peachy."

"Stop stealing my lines." I hugged her tight.

We helped each other up. Across the room, the man who'd attacked me lay on his back, blood seeping into the wood floor from the hole in his chest.

"Thank you, Sergeant Riley," I said.

Lips compressed, he nodded. "Timely."

"Yes. The alarm?"

He shook his head. "This lady here."

"Oh, Carm."

"Ma'am—"

"Call me Tally, please."

"Ma'am." His eyes soft and sad. "I'm sorry, but you have the right to remain silent. Anything you do or say . . ."

CHAPTER SEVEN

Carmen and I sat on the same bunk in the cell in the Edgartown jail. The thin mattress smelled, and the air was thick with old sweat and cheap antiseptic. Through the bars and glass, we could see black thunderclouds scudding across the gray sky.

Technically, we'd been told, we were in the Dukes County Jail, which was *in* Edgartown. Somehow, the finer points of the jail locale failed to move me. Yet the thing was, I felt safe. From my years of practicing psychology, I knew I was experiencing a sort of post-traumatic stress disorder. It felt good to be in an enclosed space where no one could get at me. Or so my psyche imagined.

I lay down and dozed. Again I saw Didi's body in that pool of blood and her writing on the floor that . . .

I sat up abruptly, scratched my scalp. I'd found it.

"Blood fetish," I said.

"You've been dreaming, Tal," Carmen said.

I nodded. "Yeah, in a way. That's what Didi had been writing with her own blood on the floor. She wrote *bloodfet*. See? She'd been starting to write *blood fetish*." I swallowed a sob. "She didn't get to finish the words. And that's what the thug demanded I find—the blood fetish."

She rested a hand on my shoulder. "So what does it mean?"

I walked across the cell trying to piece together something, anything. "I have absolutely no idea. I've collected fetish carvings for years, but I've never heard of it. Never. You heard the guy ask for it, yeah?"

She pursed her lips. "Actually, no, Tal. So what?"

I heard his voice—clear and ugly—in my mind. "I guess it shouldn't matter, but . . ." I sat beside her, took her hands in mine. "See, no one but me saw Didi's bloody words. They were gone by the time forensics got to her office. Somebody wiped them away. I have no idea who. I'm the only one who saw the words and now I'm the only one who heard that thug ask for the blood fetish."

"So?"

"I don't know. It feels . . . odd, is all. I can't explain it."

Carmen laughed. "To much woo woo, if you ask me. Or maybe not enough."

"What the hell's woo woo?"

She waved her hands. "The supernatural. Creepiness. You know, woo woo." She lifted a finger to my cheek, but didn't touch. Concern lined her face. "It's looks okay, Tal. The EMTs did a great job. And I watched the doc at the hospital sew it. You're all set. Yup suh. All set."

I gave her a quick hug. "Don't worry, Carm. It'll be quite fetching." I began to pace the cell, counting the steps. "A faint scar and all. I refuse to snivel."

Carmen stood and wrapped her hands around my shoulders, effectively stopping my pacing.

"Oh, go on," she said. "Snivel."

I had trouble meeting her eyes. I shook my head. "He was about to blow out my kneecap with his nine millimeter. Thanks, Carm. Thanks for the rescue."

"You'da done the same for me, Tal." She bit her lip, stifled a sob.

"It's okay." I hugged her again, tight. "Really. I'm fine."

"It's not okay. I shouldn't have left to get the cops. I . . ."

"You didn't have a cell. The shop phone was off. What were you supposed to do, yodel?"

She laughed, looked at my face. She was smiling. "Tally, you're a piece of work. When I think about it. Shit. Without the cops, we'd be dead."

"That you would," came a male voice.

We turned. Dan stood outside our cell, a crooked smile on his face. The guard smiled. "You ladies are out of here. Good thing I have some pull on this island." He laughed. "They didn't charge you. At least, well, not yet they haven't. So I thought I'd take you home for some chowdah."

The guard swung open the door.

I stepped forward, then hesitated. What if Izod got out? What if he came after me and . . .

I looked from the guard to Dan to Carmen. I shook my head. "I'm being silly, but . . ."

"He's dead, Tally," Dan said. His face grew tight and grim. "You saw him. Drowned in his own blood."

"Oh. Okay." So how come I still didn't feel safe?

Carmen took my hand and tugged and out we went.

Dan wrapped an arm around our waists. "Belle's made a huge meal. Ha! It's gonna be delish. And a friend of yours is here, Tally. Rob Kranak."

Oh, hell.

The following night, a gorgeous sunset dressed the Vineyard in party colors that turned the sea almost painfully beautiful. I was glad I'd brought my camera. We sat on State Beach, just the two of us, Kranak and I. A sweet wind blew from the east, ruffling the frizzed corkscrews of my hair that I hadn't captured beneath my ball cap. My feet were bare except for their red paint, and I squished my toes in the chilly sand.

When I closed my eyes, I heard the whisper of the sea. That was all. I rested my good cheek on my knees. The wind brushed my damaged cheek like a lover's caress. I could sit like that for hours.

Kranak held my hand in his beefy one. He'd doffed his shoes, but still wore the thin brown socks I knew he'd purchased at Brooks Brothers. I knew a lot about Kranak. Why he wore suits instead of more casual wear. Why he no longer hid his diabetes. Why he thought he was in love with me, but wasn't really. And why he was so furious with me, he shook with it.

"You never told me who called you," I said.

"Riley and Dan. We're old pals from Dan's law enforcement days. He wanted me to check out the scene. And you."

He'd brought his CSS kit, and earlier he had gone over Delphine's shop and home with a Kranak-like precision. And now we sat on the beach, holding hands, saying nothing, until . . .

"Does Cunningham know?" he said in an almost-reasonable growl.

"About me being cut? No. Not unless Carmen told him, which is possible."

He snorted. "You tellin' me that you're afraid he'll think less of you because of that . . . ? Jesus, Tally, the guy cut you. I'd like to fucking rip his—"

I squeezed his hand, then wrapped both of mine around my knees. My eyes clung to the sunset. "He's dead, Rob. So it's over. And I didn't call Hank because he'd hotfoot it down here, just like you. Then he'd yell at me really, really quietly, which is far worse than anything you can dish out."

"Oh, *yeah?*"

He wore sunglasses, like Nicholson, which meant he probably couldn't see a damned thing. They made him feel less vulnerable, and I understood that. "Christmas, Rob. Everything isn't a contest with Hank!"

"Yeah, yeah, yeah."

Music came from down the beach. I saw a couple holding hands, him carrying a picnic basket and an old-fashioned boom box; her, a blanket. In their own world. He lifted her hand to his lips and kissed it. I ached to taste Hank's lips on mine.

Why hadn't he told me about moving to Boston? "Let's, just for a few minutes, talk about the case. Okay?"

He cradled my jaw and turned my head. He searched my eyes, seeing things I didn't want seen. He slid his sunglasses from his face, to make sure that I saw the pain in his. Hard as it was, I held his charcoal eyes, although I desperately wanted to look away.

"I am sorry," I said. "I know I've upset you with this. I've upset me, too. We just wanted to—"

"Don't." His eyes narrowed.

Now would be when we kissed. Except we wouldn't. We'd learned from past mistakes.

"I know what you were doing, Tally," he said. "I get it. Every fucking time you get in trouble like this, it takes years off my life."

I nodded. A friend was killed. Murdered. Didi. She'd been his friend, too. "I can't change. Not this."

"I'm glad we're not lovers, Tal." He dropped my hand.

"Me, too. It's better." Funny how much it hurt.

He turned toward the sunset. "I'm getting cold. Let's wrap this up."

"Sure," I said. His brusque tone was painful, but I had to live with it. My choice. But it was still hard. "What did you find at Delphine's antique shop?"

"Some blood on the floor in that room you call the artifact room."

"Human? Old? New? What?"

"Human. New, not old."

A catboat scudded across the waves, sail billowing, jib flying. I pointed. "Pretty catboat, eh?"

He tsk-tsked. "See the jib? It requires that bowsprit, that pole extending forward from the vessel's prow. So, even though it looks like a catboat, it's really rigged like a sloop. Traditionally catboats were gaff rigged. Now they use the more modern Bermuda rig."

"You do love your sailboats, don't you?"

"I live on one don't I?"

"Because it takes you away from everything." I lifted my camera and snapped off a dozen shots. My dad would have loved to sail here. I pictured him at the tiller of our small Blue Jay. I'd swear he acted as if he were captaining a schooner. I shook my head. I loved those glimpses into the past, but they never helped with the now.

"How much blood did you find?" I asked.

"Not a lot."

"I don't see her being killed there," I said.

"Her? That Delphine woman you keep talking about?"

"Yes."

He raked a hand through his crew cut. "Who knows? Plastic on the floor, like a drop cloth, some escaped. We don't know she's dead, Tal."

I removed my glasses, rubbed my eyes. "I know. But I believe . . . What does Zoe say?"

Kranak jiggled his foot.

"What?" I said. "I told you, the guy thought I was Zoe. Obviously he hadn't met her. Is she okay?"

"She's vamoosed."

The following day, Friday, with Riley, Dan's son, as police escort, Carmen and Kranak and I again went over every inch of Delphine's shop. I'd brought Penny along, and let her sniff her happy heart out. She was certain to react to anything unusual. At the same time, Carmen and I re-

moved every single Zuni fetish from the damaged case.
Amazing, but most had survived the crash intact.

We found a safe haven for them in a long case in front.
We began to replace the carvings one by one, using the
care each deserved.

The Zuni or Shiwi, as they're also called, are *the* preem-
inent fetish carvers, just as the Hopi were famed for carving Katsinas and Navajo for their fabulous weaving of rugs.

The Zuni call fetishes *wemawe*, and most are carved for
collectors, although some are part of the complicated Zuni
religion. Those religious fetish carvings represent the animal they depict, with the animal's spirit residing in the
stone. Of course, they say it's all about the relationship between the carving, the carver, the stone, and its owner.

I always marveled at the carvings and their beautiful di-
versity. I held a mountain lion and walked him to his new
case. Mountain lion was the hunter god of the North. The
one I held was carved from angelite, a bluish-violet stone.
The figure had a smiling face and highly animated body,
left paw raised, haunches tight as if to leap. His eyes were
coral, his bundle a lapis arrowhead, with some turquoise
and abalone tied to the sinew that bound the arrowhead to
mountain lion's back. Jeff Tsalabutie had carved him, and
he was highly collectable. As we handled them, I recognized many of the stones—serpentine and travertine,
pipestone and turquoise, jasper and azurite, as well as carving media such as mother-of-pearl and amber and jet. I
held bears and mountain lions and badgers and moles and
eagles and wolves, the classic six directionals of the North,
South, East, West, Above and Below.

But the Zuni carved much more, and I saw skunks and
dinosaurs and horses and dolphins. Not so classic. I knew
almost all of the carvers, too, as each fetish in the case was
modern and carved for purchase, and not a Shiwi ceremony. I carried another carving, this one done by Aaron
Sheche. The carving was contemporary, but old—Aaron

was deceased—and this, too, was a mountain lion. As with many of the Sheche family carvings, it resembled fetishes from the late 1800s found in a classic book by Frank Hamilton Cushing. Carved from yellow jasper, it was a highly subjective piece, intended to resemble old-style fetishes.

"Look, Carm." I held up the Aaron fetish and the Jeff T. one. "Aren't these mountain lions cool?"

She tilted her head. "Yeah. I see one looks like a mountain lion, but that other one?" She pointed to Aaron's carving. "What makes you say it's a mountain lion?"

I ran my finger across the back of the fetish. "See how the tail goes up and over the back, almost to the shoulders? That represents a mountain lion's tail. All the classical carvings of mountain lions indicate the tail going up and over the back."

"Huh." She took Aaron's fetish from my hand. "Really primitive looking. I like it."

"It's based on old fetishes, ones used in Zuni religious ceremonies, not for trade."

She nodded, but kept staring at the carving. "It's mesmerizing."

I smiled. "Yes. Many carvers believe it's the owner who brings life to the fetish. So a fetish carved for sale, for art, can still be transformed into something more . . . magical."

She looked at the price tag on the bottom of the carving, reached into her purse, and drew out her wallet.

"What are you doing?"

She cradled the carving in one hand. "I'm buying him." She left a hundred-dollar bill and a scrawled a note to Delphine. I understood. Completely.

"Get him some cornmeal," I said. "They like to be fed."

We finished removing the carvings from the broken case. Regarding the fetishes carved by Zunis unknown to me, I took photos. I would e-mail these unknowns to Harry Theobald of Zuni Mountain Trading, Kent Mc-

Mannis of Grey Dog Trading, and Corilee Sanders and Melissa Casagrande. At least one of them would know with a certainty who had carved each piece.

Next, we examined the seven older carvings in the artifact room. These were under lock and key. Again, I recognized four as being carved by midtwentieth-century carvers. A tiny Leekya Deyuse wolf, a Leo Poblano bear, a Theodore Kucate bobcat, and a Teddy Weahkee frog.

"Are any of those the carving you're looking for?" Carmen asked.

"No." Each was worth thousands, but none was a ritual fetish. All had been carved for trade. The three I didn't recognize, I again photographed and would send to the traders. I also would ask them to take the photos of carvings they didn't know to Zuni. Someone would know the answers. All we could do was wait.

"I've read a lot about Zuni fetishes, you know," I said to Carmen. "But there's something strange going on. I've never heard of a blood fetish. It could be ritual. Still . . ."

We looked in nooks and crannies and on shelves and in closets, but nowhere did I find any kind of ritual fetish. I wasn't surprised, as I didn't believe Delphine would sell one. Ritual fetishes were carved for an individual's use or for the tribe, and not meant to be sold. She respected the Zuni too much and wouldn't break that taboo.

Yet that was what Izod man had been looking for. It had to be. I ran my fingers along the slash in my face, now stitched by the Vineyard hospital and covered with a bandage. Had he really wanted something else? We'd found nothing suspicious in Delphine's shop.

I climbed the center-hall stairs. Zoe had left. Why? Probably out of fear. Had she known Izod man was coming? Maybe. But if not, then why did she run? Could someone else have gotten to her? Sure. There could have been more than one man. That was always a possibility.

Earlier, Kranak had said there was no progress in finding

Didi's killer. A ton of people not normally seen at OCME had visited Didi since the skull had arrived. A million prints and no suspect. Except I didn't quite believe his story about no progress.

I wished I could stop seeing Didi in the sea of blood, her blood. My steps slowed. She hadn't been a young woman. She should have lived out her life happily putting old bones together, not dying on a linoleum floor.

The old maple banister beneath my hand felt warm and smooth, cared for, loved. I was about to enter the bedroom of a woman I believed to be dead.

My foot hit the landing's wide pine boards, and I moved forward, down the hall.

CHAPTER EIGHT

Up here, out of customers' sight, Delphine had decorated in modern and clean Southwestern style. Tony Abeyta and R.C. Gorman and Greg Lomayesva paintings hung on the terra cotta–painted walls. A Navajo runner lay beneath my feet. It led me to Delphine's large and airy bedroom filled with Southwestern-style furniture, old Spanish icons, and a gorgeous clay mask by Roxanne Swentzell.

I peeked in and was surrounded by the soft scent of chamomile. I stepped into the room. Nothing looked odd or out of place. Photos of Delphine's daughter, Amélie, lined the walls and sat on her dresser. I smiled. Most of them pictured a happy kid, then a serious student. I guessed she was in college now. I walked over to one that showed mother and daughter hugging. The little girl was around three.

With my sleeve, I brushed the dust off the glass and frame. I thought of old cases and long-gone girls; of having my own child and wondering if she'd resemble me, the way Delphine's daughter looked just like her mom. I returned the photo to its home on the dresser.

A pair of gloves sat on the dresser—hand knit, they felt like silk. I slipped them into my pocket. If I needed Penny to hunt for Delphine's remains, they would come in handy.

On the window seat in her bedroom, she'd placed three gorgeous pots, one of which was much like the one broken at the Peabody. The terra cotta color remained deep and rich, even after nearly a millennium. It was decorated with triangles and spirals and some white squares.

Silly, but I fetched a yardstick from downstairs and carefully poked it inside the pot's narrow mouth. Empty.

How could a contemporary skull have gotten inside an ancient pot? Impossible. Yet I imagined it, even though it made no sense.

I lifted all the pots. Checked inside each one. All fine, all empty. Nonetheless, I photographed them, as I'd photographed everything downstairs in the shop. If in good condition, they'd be worth thousands, but I suspected Delphine had them up here because each was blemished in some way, which diminished their attractiveness to collectors. I had no idea about their imperfections, but I'd show the photos to the expert at the Peabody, and I knew I'd get answers.

I heard Penny's nails clack on the wood floor. I was about to hold her off, when I realized it would be good to have her check up here, too.

She put her moist, clever nose into niches and beneath the bed and in front of closed drawers. I opened a low door and found a long, narrow, and empty closet. I pulled on the light, just a bulb, and Penny and I walked to the end. There sat a cardboard box stamped Jimmy Choo. I crouched down and saw it was posted from Albuquerque. I didn't like it. Not one bit.

No way would the stylish Delphine put a box of Jimmy Choo shoes, at $600 a pair, at the back of an empty closet. So what was it? Should I move it? Open it? What the hell to do? I could holler for Kranak, but what if it was just some old Christmas wrap? He'd think it was pretty funny.

I knew it wasn't Christmas wrap.

Damn.

"Pens?" I said.

Nope, she didn't answer. But she did poke her nose at the box.

Whatever was inside wasn't human. Penny would have reacted more strongly. It wasn't food or drugs, either. I waggled it. It was heavy. And it made a strange noise.

Crap.

I put the box down, flipped off the top, and screamed.

"It's dead," I said. "I know, I know, I know. But it scared the living hell out of me."

The box, with the dead and taxidermied rattlesnake in it sat on Delphine's kitchen table. Kranak, Carmen, and I sat around that same table, staring at the covered box.

Carmen reached for it.

"Do *not* open the frikken' box," I said.

"It's *dead*, Tally," Carmen said.

"I don't give a fagarwie. It's way too alive for my taste. Cripes, the thing is all coiled up, with its mouth open, ready to strike. I'd swear it was six feet or more. Horrible. I bet Delphine found it horrible, too."

Kranak scratched his chin, which bristled with hours-old growth.

"This Delphine woman," Kranak said. "She was as scared as you are, Tal?"

I ran my gloved fingers across the box top littered with black fingerprint powder. "Maybe. Possibly."

He notched his head. "A message. That's what this little baby was."

"I guess," I said. "Yes. But messages often insist we do things, or they're a promise of things that will be done to us. What was the message here? One of terror, for sure. But something else, too."

"Like what?" Carmen asked. She laid the pizza she'd gone to fetch, along with Diet Cokes and juice for herself in front of us.

"Yuck," I said. "Don't put them by the snake."

Kranak closed the box with the stuffed rattler and set it on the counter beside his CSS kit.

I snagged a slice of pizza and chomped. "Zoe was either afraid of Izod man or maybe she was involved with him. Either way, she's disappeared. Vanished." I ran scenarios around my head.

"I don't like that look, Tal," Kranak said.

Carmen grinned. "I do. So what's up?"

I took a swig of Diet Coke. "I'm not sure."

"Ayuh," she said. "You are. Better tell us."

"No, really," I said. "Something Izod man said reminded me of . . . well, that's the problem. I don't know. He triggered a memory, except now it's gone. I hate when that happens."

Kranak began to pack up his kit. "We're done here."

I stood. "How can you say that, Rob? Delphine's missing. So is Zoe. Izod man broke in and would have killed us."

"I got what I needed." He snapped his kit closed. "Izod man? Speaking of the bastard who cut you, so far we got nothing on him. He's a mystery man."

"Swell," I said. "I was hoping he'd come up in one of your databases."

"He didn't."

I filled a glass of water at the sink and sipped it slowly. When I was finished, I said, "They're connected."

"Who?" Carmen asked.

"Didi and Izod man." I rinsed the empty glass and put it in the drainer.

Kranak shook his head. "How? And, yeah, even more important, how come?"

"The pot, the skull, the break-in, Didi's murder." Outside, clouds rumbled in, threatening rain. "They have to be. You know I'm not much for random."

Carmen nodded. "I agree."

Kranak poked a finger at her. "You, missy, are not a professional."

She bellowed a laugh. "You'd be surprised."

"I'm going," he said.

"I'm coming with," I said. "I need to hammer you some more."

Saturday morning, we said our farewells to the Vineyard. Good-byes were hard with Carmen, they always were, but she was staying on the island for a few more days. I hated saying farewell to Belle and Dan, too, but I'd see them again soon. Kranak and I took the Steamship Authority ferry from Vineyard Haven. This, the height of leaf-peeper season farther north in New England, and still the Vineyard was crowded with travelers embarking and disembarking from America, as the Vineyardites liked to call the mainland.

"Maybe I should get a boat," I said to Kranak. No matter how gloomy I felt, I stepped on a boat and instantly relaxed.

We climbed the metal steps to the top deck, even though Kranak was lugging his heavy CSS kit and I my rollie pack. Penny's nails *clack-clack*ed on the steps, their uneven cadence somehow a comfort. We walked to the rail. Blue canopied our heads where only hours earlier, the sky had threatened rain. The ever-hungry gulls wheeled and careened, and passengers tossed tidbits of whatever was handy to see them perform their stunts.

A touch of melancholy drifted across the deck, most likely from folks regretting their leave-takings and the thought of going back to the real world once they left the ferry.

Now that I was off-island, I was eager to get home. It

was all about Hank, of course. No matter how he frustrated me, I couldn't wait to feel his arms around me, to smell his scent and see his grin beneath the retro-mustache he refused to shave. We had issues, sure, but he'd be driving down from Maine right now. I felt excited as a teenager.

"Tell me again about Didi," I said. "You're keeping something from me, and I wish you'd tell me what it is."

"We've got nada. That place had a revolving door, especially after that stupid TV report. A helluva lot of people visited her office to see that damned head. A million prints worth of people. They saw that Zuni governor leaving. I think he's prime for it."

"I don't see it, Rob," I said. "Him killing her."

"He wanted that damned skull and pot really bad. Really bad."

"Yes, of course. He believed they belonged to his people. That the skull was one of his ancestors. But I don't—"

"You don't buy that spiritual native voodoo crap, do you?" Kranak's bushy eyebrows beetled.

"Maybe . . . in a way, I do. The governor is a hard man, but a good one. I felt that strongly in him. As desperate as he was for the return of what he saw as one of his people, he wouldn't have stolen it, and he sure wouldn't have killed for it. Talk about bad joss."

Kranak shook his head. "Sometimes you lose reason, Tal. He's one tough dude. I could see him killing Doc Cravitz in a flash. See, I got him going back home a hero. Him going back to his tribe with the skull and the broken pot, and becoming a BMOC. Power. That's a huge motivator."

I shook my head. "I know it can be. But just not with that man, not with the governor. So what is it you're not telling me?"

He held out his hands, palm up. "I got nothing, except we found two of the pot shards under a counter. That's somethin', huh?"

I smiled. He'd closed up for the day, but I knew he had something more than two potsherds. So how come he wouldn't tell me? That worried me.

We grew quiet, and I lost myself in the elegant gray waves that cradled the huge steel ferry. A breeze chilled my face.

I brushed a finger across the gauze that covered my left cheek. The island surgeon who'd stitched me together had said I'd need plastic surgery to erase the scar. Hank would not react well to this injury. Not one bit.

The gauze felt funny. Kranak had a long scar on his face that I loved. But, honestly, he was a guy. I stroked the line where I'd been cut. It would uglify me. I could handle that, except it would also define me. *That* I didn't like.

"I love it, ya know," Kranak said.

Startled, I turned. For a moment, I'd forgotten about Kranak. "The sea, you mean? I know you do, Rob. Me too."

He clasped his hands. "Yeah, ya do. But not like me. With me, she's an ache, day in, day out. I need her to breathe. I need her close by, or I suffocate."

I smoothed my hand across his clenched ones. "Why not join the Coast Guard?"

He smirked. "And leave my cushy berth? Yeah, right."

He was full of it. His "berth" was anything but cushy. "You can retire soon, right?"

"Ten years isn't soon."

"I didn't realize."

"If you and me, well . . ."

Crap. "Rob, I . . ."

"No worries." He turned from me and stared far beyond what I could see. "We wouldn't've worked. I know that. But it felt nice for a while."

His beefy profile and mean scar spelled love to me. Always had. But with Hank, it was different. A quickening. More. "I know."

I dug around my purse and found a plastic pack of crackers, ripped it open, and sent them sailing. The gulls dived for the treats.

Kranak wrapped his arm around my waist, and I leaned my head on his shoulder as we approached the dock.

"Tally! Hey, Tally!"

The call came from far away. I peered over the rail. I didn't recognize the tall, beefy man with a trim beard at first. He was waving. I looked and suddenly . . . "Hank!"

I disengaged from Kranak, but it wasn't fast enough.

I'd seen Hank as mad, but only once before. Minutes later he clutched my hand as he tugged me from the ferry landing toward the bus that would take us to the parking lot miles away. He'd been cordial to Kranak, who'd left as soon as he'd unloaded his police car from the ferry, but now . . .

"That hurts, dammit," I said. "Cut it out."

His grip loosened, but his scowl deepened. Hank in a beard. He looked great. Different, but great, even if the beard did hide his dimple. I wished he hadn't seen my affection with Kranak.

"You've got to believe that Kranak and I aren't a number," I said. "I guess it's too much to ask."

"Too much."

"Carmen called, didn't she? She told you what ferry I was taking?"

"Ayuh."

Ah, we were in terse Maine-speak. It was colder here in America. I zipped my fuzzy and slipped my pink Boston Red Sox hat on my head. "You should trust me, Hank."

He was silent on the crowded bus ride back to the parking lot. I refused to be drawn into his snit, and so I chatted with a neighboring passenger who admired Penny.

As we disembarked from the bus, Hank didn't even spare me a glance, but plucked the keys from my hand and beeped open my 4Runner. I tried to open the back, but it was still locked. "Beep it again, dammit."

"Thing's a pain."

"So, you could have brought your own car."

"I got a ride. Thought we'd drive back together." He beeped the keylock.

"It's still locked, Hank. You've got to beep it twice in a row."

He stabbed with the remote, as if it were a person he was killing. I heard the click and lifted the back. I flung my rollie into the cargo area, slammed the trunk shut with way too much force, and stomped around to the driver's side. "I'll drive."

He didn't move. "Get in."

I snorted, walked around, opened the back door and waited while Penny gathered herself and leapt. I slid into the passenger side and grabbed the handle.

"Where's Peanut?" I asked, missing Hank's giant Irish Wolfhound.

"Not here," he said, pronouncing "here" like "heah." I laughed.

As expected, Hank crept out of the parking lot at the speed of sludge. He paid, and we were on our way back to Boston, which, given his driving style, would take years, if not decades.

CHAPTER NINE

Amazing that Hank could move even slower going across the Sagamore Bridge. He knew it drove me batso when he crawled along in the car. The more irritated he was with me, the slower we went. Revenge. That was what this was all about.

"Nothing happened, Hank."

"Yup suh."

"You know," I said, "I'm so frickin' glad to see you, and all you can do is scowl. Dammit. I was with Kranak because he was investigating a crime scene. Nothing more."

He didn't move.

"I can't even see your eyes behind those stupid cop sunglasses."

The glasses remained on his face.

"You drive me crazy." And he did. But the whole story about why I was on the Vineyard and Izod man and my cut face avalanched out. "Satisfied?"

He slipped on a Bluetooth earpiece, which I somehow found shocking in my retro fella. He pressed and mumbled something into the earpiece I couldn't hear, nodded. Then he pushed the off button.

I waited a good ten minutes while the tarmac of Route 3 plodded by. "C'mon, Hank," I finally said.

"It's your face, Tal."

Not a trace of Maine-ese. "I know. It's a mess."

"He cut you."

"I had it stitched on the Vineyard. It'll be fine. I . . ." *He hates it. He thinks I'll look ugly with a scar snaking down my cheek. He . . .* Well, I guess I hadn't thought he'd react that way.

I peered out the window, saw nothing, felt that hollow place inside.

A warm hand, more like a bear paw, covered mine. "I don't give a fuck about your scar, Tal. I'm pissed the fella's dead, 'cause I want to kill him myself. I'm trying to get a handle on that fury. Y'know?"

I tried to cry, let out a string of epithets. I leaned closer to Hank—wished the 4Runner had bench seats—kissed his cheek and lay my arm across his belly for the rest of the ride home.

Nothing was better than making love with Hank Cunningham. He touched my left breast, pinched my nipple lightly. Geesh, I wanted more. "Christmas, Hank."

His rumbled chuckle drove me higher, and I rubbed his groin with my pelvis. His hardness made me feel full and wet and electric. I pushed my toes against his, opened, and when he slid inside me, I arched like a quivering bow.

"Oh, Hank, what you do to me, love." The scent of him drove me crazier.

"Let's ride," he gasped.

Lips on mine, pace tormentingly slow, hands pressed to my back, my arms wrapped around his shoulders. We found nirvana again.

* * *

Monday morning, I heard Hank open and close the front door.

"Did you get the paper?" I said.

He winked and tossed it on the bed.

"What are you up for today?" I checked the headlines, then lounged on the bed, scratching Penny's ears, while he dressed.

He shot me a long, sexy look and wiggled his eyebrows.

"Yeah, yeah, big boy. Don't do that if you can't play."

He laughed. "You're a ball-buster, Tal."

I flipped onto my belly, grinned. "Now you're hurting my feelings."

"Not gonna sell that one," he said in his best Maine-ese.

He pulled out the one tie he kept in my closet and knotted it around his neck. What the hell?

"No, seriously." I sat up, dragged on the silk Japanese robe he'd given me. "I don't get this. What's up?"

"Just gonna meet with some friends."

He walked out of the bedroom, and I trailed after him into the bathroom. He trolled for his razor, couldn't find it, and poached my pink Venus.

"That's for girls," I said.

That sideways grin. God, I could melt. "That's why I like it," he said. He scraped away everything but his out-of-fashion mustache that I so loved. "The new beard gone?"

"Ayuh." He then tugged his short-bristled brush through his hair.

"Tell me, please," I said. "I don't like this."

He cupped my chin. "Can't tell you anything I don't know. When I do . . ." He moved me away from the door and left.

Hank was the most open guy I'd ever known. The kindest. The most straightforward. So who was the guy who'd just left my apartment?

I recalled what Addy had said—the rumor about Hank

joining the AG's office as a homicide detective. He was being awfully secretive.

I tossed on a pair of jeans and a shirt, leashed up Penny, and followed.

I shouldn't follow him. I knew that as I drove down Tremont. Honestly, I felt illicit and guilty. I did it anyway. He was headed for Route 90, and I felt a small burst of satisfaction when he merged onto the Mass Pike. That morning, the Pike wasn't bad going west, but I didn't envy those headed east. Traffic was brutal.

Maybe twenty minutes later, he turned onto Route 9. I knew now where he was going—Massachusetts State Police Headquarters in Framingham.

I had to see it, though. I couldn't believe he was having some interview or assignment or something and hadn't told me.

I really did wish I still smoked. I hadn't even eaten that morning. My stomach rumbled. Penny gave me the "look," which meant I was an irresponsible mom for not feeding her.

Oh, screw it.

I took the right and then the U-turn and ended up back on Route 9 going east. Just as I suspected, Hank ended up at Mass. State Police Headquarters. Addy had been right. Although it made no sense. None at all. He had a great job as Hancock County's sheriff. After all he'd been a detective in New York for years, yet he'd moved back home to Maine to get away from the bile of the city.

I switched lanes. No point in hanging around. I guessed he tell me at some point. Or not.

I stroked my bandage. He could have been lying about my sliced cheek, too, and how he felt looking at me. It was pretty creepy looking. Sort of.

I suddenly felt empty inside.

* * *

Back home, I fed Penny, then took her for a run at the doggie park. She bounded around like the puppy she no longer was. At least I could still thrill someone. She wouldn't mind my scar. Not one bit.

I ran home beside Penny, relishing the cool late September air and the blush on the turning leaves. As I rounded the corner to Appleton, I slowed, then stopped.

A man stood beside my front door facing the street. His hands were clasped behind him, his posture tight and tall, although I wouldn't call him a tall man, inches-wise. His eyes were closed, his face slack. He stance implied patience and calm, and he seemed out of place in the hustle and bustle of Boston.

I walked slowly toward my front steps. I thought about what I would say to him, how I would approach him. He could be a friend, an enemy, or something in between.

A neighbor yelled, "Hi!" and, "That guy's been there for an hour. I'd call the cops."

I thanked him and walked on. When I reached the bottom step, I recognized the stranger. I'd met him days earlier.

Penny and I eagerly trotted up the cement steps. "Hello, Governor Bowannie," I said. "How can I help you?"

Inside, while I made us some coffee, the governor admired the collection of Zuni fetish carvings that sat on my mantel.

He pointed to a favorite amber bear of mine by a carver name Dee Edaakie.

"She's pretty, isn't she?" I said from the kitchen.

He laughed. "How do you know she's a girl!"

"Just look at her," I said.

"You've got some fine young carvers here. Dee Edaakie. Alonzo Esalio, Jeff Tsalabutie." His smile widened. "Even Fred Bowannie, an exceptional carver. Despite the name, we're no relation."

I walked into the living room and handed the governor his mug. I picked up Fred Bowannie's jasper bear. "He's wonderful. Look at that sweet face. They all are wonderful. They mean a lot to me." I slipped Dee's amber bear into my shirt pocket, just above my heart.

"Dr. Cravitz told me you were a collector."

I shook my head. "A very modest one. It's partly because I love animals so much. And stones of all kinds. Fetish carving combines both."

He nodded toward my desk, where four of my favorite carvings lived.

"They help you work?" he said.

"You betcha."

"You like the old ones, too." He held my marble Edna Leki to the light." "She was amazing, Edna. What a carver. You could really see the spirit in the stone. She learned from the best, her father, Teddy."

"I hope to have one of his, someday."

He nodded. "It's good to see something of my home here."

"I understand. The feeling of home is important."

"Yes. Home." He ran his hand across his upper chest.

"Is everything all right?"

"As much as it can be."

"Shall we sit here?" I gestured to the couch.

He pointed to the partially open French doors. "How about in the sunshine?"

We sat out back on my tiny deck, Penny lounging between us. The breeze was sweet with the promise of fall, and, as always, I tasted a hint of the sea in the air.

The metal tray between us held more coffee and cream and sugar.

"Is it too chilly for you out here?" I said.

He patted the arm of my tattered wing chair that lived on my deck. "This is good. I've been inside too much."

I touched his leathered hand with my index finger. "You said you were here for help. What can I do?"

He again massaged the spot on his chest above his

heart. He frowned. "Dr. Cravitz is dead. Executed. I am suspected in doing the deed."

I should be afraid. But I wasn't, not with Penny beside me and the belief that this man wouldn't kill for a skull, even a sacred one. "From what I've heard, yes, you are a suspect in Didi's homicide."

"You don't fear me?" he said.

"Should I?"

He unsnapped his shirt pocket and drew out a pack of generic cigarettes. From his jeans pocket, he pulled out a worn Zippo and flipped it open. His hand shook when he lit the cigarette. "Can't give them up."

"I'm jealous," I said. "I gave up a pack-a-day habit, and I miss them. Ha! Silliness. As I said, what do you want from me?"

He inhaled long and deep, then pursed his lips to exhale. The wind stole the smoke, while the familiar smell flip-flopped my stomach. I waited.

"I am not afraid of being locked up," he said. "I did not kill the good doctor, and there is no evidence. But I feel bad that she's dead. She was a dedicated woman who meant well. I do fear that I will never recover the skull."

I stroked Penny's soft fur. "For your people, you mean. For the Zuni."

"No, I do not mean that. I believe that the skull is no more Zuni than you are, found in the Old Ones' pot or not."

A leveler. "I agree with you, actually," I said. "But why? What makes you think that? I'm sorry. I thought you were so sure."

"I was." He flicked his ash over the rail. "Until Dr. Cravitz created that woman from the skull. The doctor was too skilled to make a serious misstep in her reconstruction. That woman was no Zuni. Nor Hopi. Nor even Navajo. I don't think she's Indian at all. So *who* is she? Somebody's playing some bad game, and because of that, Dr. Cravitz is dead. So, yeah, I want that skull. I want the people who took it, too."

I rubbed my hands up and down my thighs. "Well, I have a theory. I think that Didi's re-creation was of a friend of mine. A modern woman. I don't know how her skull ended up in an Old Ones' pot. But that's what I believe."

"Yes," the governor said. "Well, it's a crazier theory than mine, even."

"Which is?"

"That her head was witched in there."

"Switched in there? How?"

He chuckled softly. "Not switched, Tally Whyte. *Witched.*"

Not what I'd been expecting. "Ah. You're a shaman. Am I right?"

He laughed harder, put his cigarette out on the bottom of his boot, and slipped the butt into his shirt pocket. "I'm not sure what you Anglos call it, what I am."

I almost told him about events on the Vineyard, but held my tongue. I trusted him, but I'd done that before with disastrous results. His chocolate eyes said "truth," and his body language conveyed relaxation, not guilt. Yet for once I resisted my innards and didn't spew forth all that I knew.

"And you want me to . . . ?" I said.

He waved his hand. "In a minute. You want something from me, yes?"

"How did you . . . Whatever." I leaned forward. "Yes, I do. I'd like you to tell me about the blood fetish."

His head snapped around, and his eyes blazed. "That's deep, my dear. Deep. I can't help you. I can't talk about it. Or even name it."

"Can't or won't?"

"They're much the same. You should talk to my son."

"And how would I do that?"

His eyes warmed and his leathery face folded into a smile of such quiet joy I wished to reach out and hold him and feel that warmth, that love of life. I reached into my shirt pocket and pulled out my amber bear. "Please take her."

He looked from the bear to me, and his long brown fingers slipped Dee's bear from my palm. He pulled out a pouch from beneath his shirt—his medicine pouch—widened the mouth and placed Dee's bear inside.

"That is a great gift." He slid the pouch back beneath his shirt.

"She's a sweet bear."

"Yes. I've seen you and, now, your home. You are in tune with the Indian as much as any white can be. You have authority, presence."

His flattery made me uncomfortable. I respected his slow pace, but he wasn't being completely forthright with me.

"You won't tell me, will you?" I said. "About the fetish."

"It's not part of my story. Aric, on the other hand . . ." He inhaled smoke from his cigarette, and his lungs expanded. "Good. It's good."

"It will kill you."

His ironic smile gave me pause. I wondered . . . "So . . . what can I do for you?"

"I want you to come with me to recover the skull."

I laughed, all nerves. "Come with you where?"

He nodded. "To Zuniland."

Zuniland. I'd been there once, years earlier, and I'd loved it. I always felt at home out west. Yet . . . "I can't, Governor. I have things here. Obligations. This should be left to the authorities."

He stood and leaned on the balcony's railing. His eyes narrowed, and everything about him said he desperately missed his home, his mountain—Corn Mountain—and the sun above the mesa. His place.

"Governor?" I said finally.

He straightened his spine. "The authorities, as you call them, are your authorities. Not mine. They know less than nothing. They have not seen the face of the woman. She is pleading for help."

"The reconstruction?" *Pleading for help.* Maybe that's what I'd been feeling for days, Delphine's plea.

"Not that, ma'am," he said. "Dr. Cravitz. Her face. I shall never forget. She is not resting yet. Not yet."

He stood and drew a card and a pouch, much like his medicine pouch, from his jeans pocket. "Here is where I'm staying. I wrote my cell phone number on back. I leave tomorrow. Please call me."

His card read *Professor Ben Bowannie*, with numerous initials after his name, and followed by *Archeology Department, University of New Mexico*.

"You are full of surprises, Professor," I said.

He grinned. "I try to keep the young ones hopping."

"I'll call either way. But please don't count on me."

"One more thing." He held up the pouch. "This, too. It's for you."

"Really?" I took the pouch from the governor. It was soft and warm, perhaps made of deerskin. I looked at him with questions. "Governor?"

"Just open it."

I widened the neck and spilled what was in the pouch into my palm. I gasped, smiled. "The red rock from the Old Ones' pot! I just assumed the thieves had taken that, too."

He nodded. "The doctor told me how much you admired it." His lips curled into a grin. "I thought you would like it."

"I love it." I couldn't believe I held the red rock in my hand. The rock from Chaco. It was warm and the essence of the mystery and beauty of the Southwest. "It reminded me of a fetish. It just feels . . . *good* in my hand. You know?"

His two large hands encompassed mine and the red rock. "I do know. A small piece of Chaco. It's mine to give." He chuckled. "As long as those Navajo don't find out!"

I hugged him. Inappropriate or not, I couldn't help myself. He laughed and hugged me back. "A great hug like that for a little red rock. Marvelous."

The governor stood to leave.

"I wish you didn't have to leave so soon," I said.

"Time."

I walked him to the door.

"One more thing," he said. "Someone is tracking you. He slouches, like a bum, and blends in well. If, for some reason, I fail . . . it matters that you find the skull. You, Tally. I don't mean to burden you, but truth is truth." He walked slowly down the steps as if he'd aged ten years.

Following me. What made me so interesting? I peeked out my bedroom window. My bucolic street looked lovely, the leaves on the trees turning vermillion and orange and yellow. A few had already drifted to the ground. They and danced on the breeze.

A couple held hands, swinging them like a pendulum, smiles on their flushed faces.

I pictured them living simple and beautiful lives—work, movies, books, making love, cooking, vacations at the shore. I should picture myself doing those things. Yet I couldn't imagine it for me. My life had never been simple, pleasant, or comfortable.

Life could be that way now. I had the money. The time. No encumbrance. Except I was itchy. Waiting for that other shoe to drop.

Outside, no one else appeared on the street. So who was following me and why? Or maybe the governor was imagining things, like witches. God, these dramas got tedious.

I let the curtain fall back across the window.

I sat on the bed and leaned forward to scratch Penny's belly. "Belly rub, Pens!" She sprawled onto her back, per usual. "You are shameless."

Kaboom! Shards of pain stabbed my back and head.

CHAPTER TEN

"What the *hell!*" Hank said as he squeezed his large frame into my emergency room cubicle at Brigham and Women's Hospital.

I yawned, tightened the nasty johnny they'd wrapped me in after cleaning the glass shards from my back. "I got some Demerol," I said. "Not sure why. Hell, by the way, has nothing to do with it." I smiled. Hank looked so darned cute when he was angry.

He wrapped his paws around my upper arms.

"Ow! You're mean."

He instantly freed me. "Dammit, Tally. What happened? The nurse outside won't say shit."

He had the cutest, bushiest mustache. It was auburn, and it tickled when he kissed me. I licked my lips and leaned forward. I puckered up.

"Tally, dammit! First your face, now this!" His hand brushed the bandage on my cheek, and I giggled.

Hank was scowling again.

"Gee," I said. "What's a girl gotta do to get a kiss around here?"

"You sound like a Playboy bunny, fa Christ sake!"

A white-coat poked her head in. "Sir. You'll have to keep it down."

He flipped open his billfold and held it up to her face.

"Rude," I said. "Rude, rude, rude."

The doctor squinted. "You're a police lieutenant? Are Ms. Whyte's injuries a police matter, Lieutenant Cunningham?"

"Ayuh," he said. "Dammed well straight."

"Hank," I said. "You sound so . . . *Maine*. My window just broke."

Fury ripped across his face. "Someone shot the fucking window out, Tally."

Shot. Oh. "Maybe." I leaned against him and closed my eyes. Lieutenant Cunningham. I liked that. Sounded good. A good name. But he was Sheriff Cunningham. My sheriff. My lieutenant. Lieutenant?

"You're not a lieutenant." I giggled and swung my legs. "Oops. Shouldn't fib."

"Lie down, Ms. Whyte," the doctor said. She lifted my legs onto the gurney and pulled a blanket to my chin. "I'm a nurse, dear. Why don't you try to rest?"

I was so tired. But . . . "Hank Cunningham! Tell her the truth. You are a *sheriff!*"

"Dear," the nurse said.

"Don't call me 'dear.' I'm not your dear." I sat up. "And he's a sheriff, *dear.*"

A feminine hand shoved a badge into my face. "No, *dear*, he's a Massachusetts State Police lieutenant."

"Tally, I . . ."

The world got all fuzzy and bright yellow, and white noise hissed in my head. Hank? A Mass. State Police officer? And he'd been lying to me the whole time. Lying to me. He'd been . . .

I turned on my side and slept.

* * *

Gert fetched me from the hospital. I had no idea what day it was. Demerol does that to me. My ferocious headache had quelled, and now all I wanted to do was get out of there. I was really okay. Just achy. Very, very achy.

And pissed. Very pissed at Hank Cunningham. I had asked him not to come back, and he hadn't. Did he think I meant it?

"How long was I in the hospital?" I asked.

"Twenty-four hours," she said.

"That's more than enough for me." A moment of panic. "Who's got Penny?"

"Your hunky landlord. Yum, yum."

"He is adorable, isn't he? But definitely off limits, Gertie. He likes a smorgasbord, not one dish."

"I know." She frowned. "What a shame."

On the drive to my apartment, Gert remained disturbingly quiet but for the popping of her Bazooka bubbles. They filled the air. Purple bubbles. Smelly ones.

"I'm fine, Gert. Really. So no worries. Okay?"

"Don't," she said. "You're a mess."

I didn't have the energy to fight. Not then.

I used Gert's arm and the railing to climb the small flight of stairs, thrilled that my apartment was on the first floor. Someone had nailed a plywood board across the yawning bow window in my bedroom. I guessed it was my landlord, Jake.

Inside, Penny greeted me with her usual bouncy exuberance. I was prepared for the place to be a shambles. Except for some residue fingerprint dust, it was neat by even my Aunt Bertha's standards.

"Wow," I said. "I thought it would be a wreck. Who cl—"

"Mr. Maine," Gert said.

"Hank? Wow again."

Gert slid my purse off my shoulder and laid it on the kitchen counter.

"Thanks, Gertie."

"Sure, Tal," she said. "How about I make you some soup or something?"

"Not now. Maybe I'll just take a snoozle." I opened the door to my bedroom. Another shock.

"Impressive!" Gert said.

New sheets, new duvet cover, new everything. A few down feather escapees from the vacuum floated on the air. Other than that and the plywood, I never would have known anything had happened.

"Boy," Gert said. "I'd marry that guy really fast."

"Great plan. Not." I sat down hard on the edge of the bed. "He'd have gotten me good if I hadn't leaned over to pet Penny. There are worse things than flying glass." I ruffled Penny's fur. "I'm glad she wasn't hurt."

Gert's blue eyes widened. I recognized the fear in them. I took her hand. "Don't worry, hon. All is well. Really."

She slumped down beside me. "How can you say that? You've just had your window blown out by a shotgun, and you're not talkin' to the guy who did this great cleanup, and I'm afraid you won't come back to MGAP and—"

"Sshhhh." I wrapped an arm around her shoulder. I walked to a bowl on the bedside table. Someone had placed a small pile of shot in it. I picked up one of the small pellets. I looked from the bed to the boarded-up window. "Huh. Bird shot. I think it was supposed to be a warning, not meant to hurt me at all. Certainly this wasn't meant to kill. Bird shot's too small."

"Yeah? That's just *special*, Tal. C'mon! That's almost as awful."

I tugged on one of her blond locks. "But not quite, right? How about that soup."

I sat up on the couch. I'd slept for a few minutes, that was all. Except my clock said I'd been out of it for ten hours.

"Cripes." I ran a hand through my hair. Greasy and gross. Yuck. I needed a shower. Bad. I looked for Gert, but didn't see her. The place was dark, too. Not enough lights on.

"Gert?"

Nada. Maybe she'd gone out for food. Was I hungry? I didn't even know.

I unfolded myself from the couch. I ached in so many places I wasn't sure which to groan about first. I let Penny out back, walked into the bathroom and . . . Some guy was . . . "Shit!"

I slammed the bathroom door and shoved the club chair in front of it. That wouldn't keep him in.

I twirled. The redwood table! Weighed a ton. I began to pull. The thing was massive, but I could do it.

"Tally!"

I turned. Somehow he'd wedged the door slightly open, and a hairy arm flailed from the crack. I leapt at the door.

"*Fuck!*" he bellowed.

I pushed and pushed, but I wasn't making any headway.

"It's Rob, goddammit."

Rob. Kranak? Oh, crap. I stopped pushing, and the arm slid back inside. I tugged the chair out of the way. "Rob, I—"

"Don't utter a frickin' word," he said from behind the door.

"I'm so sorry, I thought you were an intruder."

"Brilliant."

"You can come on out now. I'll get you some tea." Kranak loved tea.

Behind me, a large and looming presence coalesced as I filled the kettle with water and put it on the burner. "Rose hips, cinnamon, orange p—"

"Bourbon flavored."

I looked over my shoulder. "I am *so* sorry."

He was shirtless, and a nasty red mark blotched his forearm. His right hand held my bottle of Rebel Yell.

"I really am, Rob." I poured his tea, and he dumped in a solid dose of comfort from the bourbon.

"You'll be sorrier when you hear what I have to say."

I leaned back on the couch, reminded how much my body ached from all those nasty little cuts. Penny sprawled beside me, her large head in my lap. Kranak had put on his shirt, and as he buttoned it, I saw that the bottom button was missing.

"I can sew that on for you," I said.

"You with a needle? That's the last thing I want." He finished buttoning, then rolled up his sleeves. "Some bad shit's come down, Tal, and I think you should know about it."

"The guy on the Vineyard?"

He shook his head.

"Your sweetie pie." His lips curled in distaste.

"C'mon, Rob, don't do that."

He notched his chin. "Whatever. He's with us now."

"The state police. Yes, I know."

He snorted. "You coulda told me."

"I only just found out, Rob."

He tipped the bottle of Rebel Yell one more time. "Sure you did."

"I did! Dammit, Rob." My head jabbed with pain.

"So loverboy figures that the governor did Doc Cravitz. He's been working on it. Circling like a vulture."

I leaned forward. A chill skated up my spine. "Why does he think that? I can't believe this. What about other suspects?"

Kranak slammed his mug on the table. "None that he wants to see. And he's a *De-tec-tive.*"

"C'mon, Rob, don't. You refuse to be anything but CSS, and you know it. Listen, I had no idea. None. Not until I was in the hospital. I *would* have told you."

He shrugged. "Yeah, well, he's got his own ideas of who

to tell. I'm sure as hell not in his loop." He checked his watch.

"What?" I didn't like the way this conversation was playing out. Or Rob's whole self-satisfied aura. Not one bit. "Why are you being so smug?"

The clock on my mantel chimed. I looked from it to him. He smiled, and it wasn't pretty. I stood. "What the hell is going on?"

"Smug? Well, maybe. See right about now, loverboy's arresting Mr. Governor Pooh-Bah. It's a fucked-up get, but he's doing it anyway."

"Dammit." I raced to the bedroom and slammed the door. I shucked my nightie, pulled on some clean jeans, and grabbed a turtleneck and socks. I might smell, but at least my clothes were decent. I snapped my jeans and began to fasten my bra, thought better of it through the haze of pain in my back, and slipped on a camisole instead. Turtleneck, check. Socks, check. Shoes, wallet.

I raced the front door, lifted the leash off it hook. "Come, Penny. *Ke mne!*"

"Hold the fuck on, Tal," Kranak yelled.

I ignored him as I flew outside and down the steps.

I ran, Penny beside me, until we hit Tremont, where we hopped a cab. Quicker that way than driving myself. I gasped out Seaport Hotel—one of Boston's biggies—and the guy knew just where to go.

"You in a rush, ma'am?" he asked in a thickly accented voice.

"I am."

He varoomed.

It still took us fifteen minutes, what with Boston's crazy roads and nasty traffic. We were near Boston's World Trade Center and the fish pier, and I knew I'd have to run again. I leashed Penny, got the money out, and was off the minute traffic clogged on Northern Avenue.

Good thing. Up ahead about a block, I spotted a yellow sawhorse and a uniformed cop standing duty. I slowed, regulated my breathing, gave Penny a treat for being such a good girl. Then I walked quietly, unhurriedly. If I sped up, the cop would suspect something.

"Hi," I said. Penny stood beside me, on alert, and I believed the police officer sensed her tension. The kid looked about twelve years old.

"What can I do for you, ma'am?" he asked. His eyes continued to roam the scene.

"I'm with OCME." I flipped open my wallet with my out-of-date credentials. I suddenly felt an utter loss of identity.

He looked over his shoulder, as if searching for someone. "And you're here because . . . ?"

"Oh, sorry. I . . . yes." I waved toward the plaza and the hotel where the governor was staying. "Him. We got a call."

"We." He looked nervously at Penny, then quickly looked away.

"I know, three legs. She's Canine Corps. She does the work of most four-legged dogs. We were called."

"By . . . ?"

"Detective Lieutenant Cunningham."

He lifted his walkie-talkie.

"Huh," I said. "So the situation isn't so dire, eh?"

He pale cheeks flushed. Confusion muddied his eyes. "Pardon?"

"You wouldn't be calling if things were really bad." I smiled. Gave it all I was worth. "I'm relieved." I made sure to sound chirpy.

"Well, um."

I pushed a hand into my jeans pocket. "See, we're only usually called when things go south. Penny here is a great tracker. They've called for other dogs, but Penny was closest."

"Um, well I . . . sure. Just a sec." He slid the crime scene sawhorse out of the way. "I'll walk with you."

"Great." Half a loaf was better than none. "Your name is . . . ?"

"Officer Enoch Gillano."

"Nice to meet—"

"*Down!*" he screamed. "Get down!"

Someone knocked into me, and I flew off my feet and slammed into the concrete, palms first. I shouted "*Lehni*, Penny! Down!" as bullet booms and bings exploded around me.

Screams and more shouts and what sounded like a hailstorm of fire burst around me.

I rolled over to Penny. She seemed fine, and we cowered together, one hand covering my head, the other wrapped around my dog. It felt like I was living in molasses time as I breathed in and out and shivered. My palms burned from the gravel jammed into them when I fell.

Hank. Dear God, Hank.

I peered around. From my pancake position all I saw were the undercarriages of cars. The noise was deafening, with bullhorns and bullets and shouts. Then it got quiet, and I wanted to move. I thought maybe I'd crawl to my knees and see if I could spot Hank. But just as I was about to push to my knees, I realized that if the bad guys didn't shoot me, Hank would if he caught me doing something that stupid.

My cheek throbbed where Izod man had cut me. I checked Penny again. She was fine, hadn't been hit. If this was all about the governor, this was the stupidest . . .

The gunfire slowed again, and I turned my head toward Officer Gillano. His flushed face was now pale, and fear furrowed his brow, but when he saw me looking, he gave a thumbs up and a wink.

I gave it back to him, and the pounding started all over again. I scooched Penny closer to the sedan parked by the curb. Maybe smart, maybe stupid. I just didn't know.

Still, then noise, then still again. The back-and-forth seemed like forever. But then things quieted, not all at once, but the way the rain gradually slows, then stops all together.

I heard shouts, recognized Hank's voice. Thank God.

I yelled, "Hank!"

Someone hollered, "All clear!"

I pushed to my knees. "Ouch!" My palms were raw from the fall. "Come on, Pens. Let's go find Hank." I scratched her behind her ears. Her tail wagged, and she licked my good cheek. She was fine. "Hey, officer, I could sure use a hand up." I turned toward Gillano.

He stared at me, unblinking, eyes glazed.

"Officer?" I scooched over to where he lay prone on the ground. And then I saw one hand unnaturally twisted and a sluggish drool of deep red dripping from his mouth to the pavement.

"Enoch?" I whispered.

In the distance, muffled chatter. But here, silence. Penny whined.

"Enoch?" I pressed to fingers to his neck, praying for the *tha-thump* that said "life."

I found death in the flesh that had lost its resilience. When I looked for his wound, I saw the back of his head had been blown away.

I took Enoch's hand, the one that lay by his side, and held it in both of mine. "Oh, Enoch, I am so sorry. So sorry. I pray you walk in beauty now, and in places far sweeter than these."

I stood off to the side, arms crossed, trying to keep warm on a perfectly warm day. Penny leaned against me, for comfort, I knew, and I waited while Hank spoke with the ME assigned to the "incident."

I didn't have the heart.

Hank finally walked over, hands shoved in his pockets. I

expected an arm around my waist that would lead me to safety. Instead, he notched his chin, as if to say "over there, lady."

Tears jammed my eyes, and I blinked a lot. Couldn't let them fall. Wouldn't. I slid on my sunglasses. They were cracked down the center, a victim of today's "fracas," as the police were terming it to the media, at least until the dust settled.

"Can we go inside?" I said. "I'm cold."

He jammed a toothpick between his teeth. "You've gotten soft."

I thought about that for a minute. "Yes, I think I have."

CHAPTER ELEVEN

The trendy Cafe bar at least had comfortable booths where I could hide. The lighting was poor, which I liked, too. Penny slid under the table, now invisible. I sure hoped she was. I needed at least one friend with me.

The waitress set down our coffees, and I fixed mine with the pink stuff and milk. We each took a long sip, eyes locked. I wasn't used to Hank's fury, at least not when it was directed at me. His anger after the Vineyard seem like a practice session compared to this.

He set down his mug with a disturbing gentleness. "You got him killed, Tally. Enoch. He was a good officer. A good kid. A boy."

"Yes." I had so much more to say, but the words choked my throat.

He swiped a bear-pawed hand across his face. "I'm sorry. I don't really believe that."

I did.

"You shouldn't have been there." He drilled me with his eyes.

"Yes, I should have. You should have left the governor alone." His bushy brows beetled, so like Kranak that I winced.

"Nope suh," he said. "There you're wrong, Tal. He killed Doc Cravitz."

"No, he didn't."

He clenched the paper napkin he'd worked into a ball. "We've got proof."

"I don't care." I took a pull on my coffee, hoping my words sank in. "Governor Ben Bowannie did not kill Didi. He's a shaman. He wouldn't kill her. He wouldn't kill anyone."

His blue eyes lasered mine. "He was with you, wasn't he?"

Where was the sweet man I'd fallen in love with? The one who believed in me, comforted me? "Hank, what's happening? I don't understand. What are you doing here? Why have you left Winsworth? Is the governor dead?"

"Is there an order to those questions, Tally? Or you just spitting out anything that comes to mind? Did he or did he not visit you, Tally?"

"Yes, he did, dammit. So what?"

A plainclothesman leaned into the doorway of the café. "Lieutenant?"

Hank held up a hand. "One sec," he said over his shoulder. "We'll talk later," he said to me.

"Just tell me if the governor's dead."

He shook his head. "He's gone. No sign of him."

"The shooting?"

"His associate. He's dead."

I closed my eyes. I didn't understand any of this. I said a prayer for the Zuni who traveled with the governor. Nothing was right. Nothing fit anymore. When I opened my eyes, I expected Hank to be gone.

"You're still here," I said.

"Ayuh."

"We've got to talk," I said.

"Do something you're good at," he said. "Take care of Enoch's family." He slid out of the booth.

"See you later?"

"Not today," he said. "Not soon."

I slipped on my counseling skin and called MGAP. I told them what was happening as I headed for the ME's office. I asked permission to take charge of Enoch Gillano's family, and Gert okayed it. I stopped off at home, showered, and cleaned up my cuts and scrapes.

Had I killed Officer Gillano? I didn't know, but I loathed the idea that I even had to ask myself the question.

I arrived at MGAP just in time to greet the young officer's mom and dad and fiancée. Hank was right. I knew how to do this and do it well.

I assisted the father as we walked into the ID room and stood before the large curtained window. We took two of the chairs and waited, I knew, for the ME on the case to clean Enoch's face so it would be presentable to his father. I was beeped that they were ready, and so I pressed a button signaling that we were, too.

The curtain parted, and Enoch lay before us on a gurney tilted to a near-standing position. He looked even younger than I remembered.

"Yes," his father whispered. "Yes, that's my boy."

He reached for my hand, and I held his tight. I nodded, and the curtain closed.

I held it together until I said farewell to the Gillanos, having assisted them with a sheaf of paperwork and the beginnings of funeral arrangements. They'd all need follow-up, especially the fiancée. It was a particularly tough case for me, having been with Enoch when he died.

Unlike the old days, I couldn't hide out in the office that was now Gert's.

I felt compelled to give Didi's office a quick look-see and found myself shivering. I swear I still saw Delphine's head atop Didi's pedestal, her hair a deep brown, her eyes calm and accepting. Except I wasn't accepting.

When I finished, which was pretty quick, I went in search of Addy Morgridge. Someone said she was in the main autopsy suite. I headed around a corner and down the hall. Then I heard a noise from behind. I turned and slammed right into Fogarty.

I rubbed my nose. "Damn, that hurt."

He shook his head. "We can't get rid of you, can we?"

"Not a chance." I wasn't in the mood. I attempted to go around him, but he blocked my path.

"Come to see the specimen?" he said.

I had no clue, but I'd be damned if I didn't play it cool. "Of course."

He shook his head. "Just like you. Well, you can't. You simply can't." He breezed on, full of his own self-importance.

Down the hall I called for Addy. I was still annoyed with Fogarty for piquing my curiosity. What the hell was the specimen? Probably some disgusting thing in a jar that fascinated him.

I turned to go, got ticked off all over again that Fogarty could get to me so easily, and went in search of the "specimen."

I found one of my old friends, a tech, and she led me to the decomp refrigerator.

"I hate this room," I said. Here was where they brought waterlogged corpses and once a bubonic plague victim. And a woman who'd been so badly mauled by a mysterious animal that fluids leaked slowly from her body. It was a small room of horrors, and when I'd worked in the building, I'd once found myself locked inside, facedown on the floor, having been knocked out by a killer.

I visited decomp as little as possible.

The small red-tiled decomp suite hummed with filters

and fans that ran not nearly well enough for my twitchy nose.

"Where's the specimen?" I asked.

She pointed to the inner room, where decomposing remains were often stored. I realized I wasn't up for it.

"Thanks, Chris," I said. "I'm, well, not today, I guess."

She waved her hands. "No, no, wait. You don't understand. He's fine. Really. The joke is Fogarty put him in here because he's superstitious."

A horrific feeling of panic overwhelmed me. I flung open the heavy steel door to the inner room. The light burst on and I saw . . .

"A fox?" I said as I turned back to Chris.

She crossed her arms and nodded. "Fogarty says it's a spirit animal. He's afraid of it."

"But it's a poor little fox," I said. "How did it even get here?"

She wagged her fingers. "No idea, but I have a feeling that it's from Mount Auburn Cemetery."

I nodded. "Sure, the one with all the bird species and wild animals. But this poor creature doesn't deserve to be in our decomp room."

"What can I say?"

A noise from outside the room. "I'd better go. Hey, have you see Dr. Morgridge?"

Chris swung open the door. "Last I saw her, she was in the fridge."

I spotted her leaving the refrigeration room, followed by another ME and a tech hauling a gurney.

"Addy!"

She turned and stepped in front of the gurney. But she hadn't been fast enough.

"Addy?" I ran down the hall and slammed to a stop in front of Addy and the body she was trying to shield. "Addy, don't."

She moved aside.

My hand flew to my mouth. Governor Ben Bowannie's bullet-riddled corpse lay naked on the cold gurney, with only his medicine pouch slung around his neck. At least they'd had enough respect to leave that.

I bit back a sob. Hank had lied to me.

I walked to the gurney, lifted the governor's hand, and held it to my cheek. The cold, so familiar. He'd been such a warm presence. His long gray hair was unbound, his eyes closed as if in sleep. He'd been shot—I counted—six times.

"Tally?" Addy said.

"One sec, huh?" He looked at peace, but I had none. That he'd died here and not in Zuniland. I wished I'd known him better.

Oh, I am so sorry that you have left us. So sorry. Dear Lord . . .

"Damn. Damn, damn, damn!"

I knocked on Gert's door.

"Cripey, Tal," she said. "You look like crap."

Had to smile. "Leave it to you, Gertie. Can I come in?" She hugged me as she closed the door behind us. I told her about the governor and Enoch.

"Oy, what a lousy day, Tal."

I nodded. I wanted to vent about Hank, but didn't see the point. Gert was such a dear, and so endearingly empathetic. But what I really needed was Carmen's earthy common sense.

"I've got to go, Gert." I walked to the door. "You've been a huge help. Thanks, hon."

"I don't like that look you've got," she said. "What are you up to?"

"Just some stuff."

"You been saying *that* for a year."

"True."

"We need you here, Tal. I need you."

I hugged her again. "That's sweet. But you really don't. You and the staff, you're doing a terrific job."

She crossed her arms. "It's not the same. Doc Morgridge needs you, too. Come back. Please?" She blew a bubble.

I smiled. "Honestly, Gertie, it feels good to hear you say these things. Better than good. But there are things I need to do."

"Like *what*?"

That I need to fix, I thought. Yes, that was it. "Gotta run, hon." I slipped into my coat. Penny yipped. She knew.

Gert walked to her desk and retrieved a pink slip of paper. "Here."

I read the note. *Virgil Soto, Gallup, NM.* "This is . . . ?"

She popped another pink Bazooka bubble, wouldn't look at me, but straightened papers on her desk. "The guy on the Vineyard. The creep who cut your face."

Was he Didi's killer? I wondered. I slid the note into my pocket, kissed Gert's cheek, and headed for New Mexico.

I drove down Storrow Drive, and folks walked their dogs beside the Charles River, and rowers pulled skulls through the water, and a few day sailors' jibs luffed in a sudden wind.

It was one of those blindingly bright days that had warmed to where I took off my jacket and still felt warm. I wished that Penny slept beside me, curled in a ball.

I sighed. I'd made the right decision, leaving her with Jake. He loved her almost as much as I did, and I trusted him totally. We'd had a sad farewell. She knew I was going somewhere without her. But if anything happened to me, my Penny was in good hands. The space beside me felt empty. She wouldn't be around to watch my back, either.

I switched lanes. I had a long way to travel, and since I didn't want whoever had taken the potshot at my bow window to come after me, I bagged Logan for the more distant airport in Manchester, New Hampshire. It was smaller, less crowded, and I could observe the comings and goings of people more easily.

I kept seeing Delphine's head. And that damned pot. And Didi and the governor and poor Enoch and the governor's aide. Ghosts. *Chindi*, the Navajo called them, an evil force left behind by the deceased that returns to avenge an offense. I wondered . . .

Yet Zuni didn't believe in *chindi*, not the way the Navajo did. Zuni did not fear their own dead. I preferred that point of view.

Gert answered on the first ring. "You okay?" she asked, worry threading her voice.

"Fine, Gertie. Yeah. I've got a thought."

"You've got lots!"

"You're a laff riot, kiddo." I checked the rear-view mirror. All clear. "A favor. See if you can get one of those potsherds carbon dated."

"You mean that antique one, that was with Doc Cravitz's corpse?"

"That's the one."

"Have you been doin' drugs?"

I chuckled. "I wish. Look, the thieves missed a couple of shards that fell under a table. Kranak told me. See if you can make it happen, Gertie. They might be able to help you over at the Museum of Science. You know, that guy you dated."

"Yeah, I know, all right. I dumped him. He was too weird."

I sighed. "Somehow. Please try?"

"Yeah, yeah, yeah. First, I gotta get 'em from evidence. That won't be easy. Hey, how come?"

"Honestly? Maybe the pot was a fake. A fabulous one. But fake. I don't know. It doesn't make sense, since it came from the Peabody Museum, but someone could be pulling a scam. Say Delphine found out. They killed her."

Gert popped a bubble. "And then why would they put her skull in a pot, huh? How's that make sense?"

"Well, yeah," I said. "It doesn't. I don't know where else to look. It can't hurt, right?"

"Whatever," she said in her strongest Brooklyn-ese. "Lotta murder for a bunch of pots, if you ask me."

"We've seen worse, Gertie."

"Yeah. By a long shot."

"Just give it a try for me, okay?"

"Yeah, yeah, yeah. Will do."

"Thanks. I owe you."

The sound of Gert's enormous Bazooka bubble popped in my ear. "You owe me about a million."

I sure did.

Sun beat through the windshield. I lowered the visor and slipped on my sunglasses.

The Chief Medical Investigator for New Mexico, the fella who'd offered me that luscious job, was waiting to interview me at the other end. I didn't think he'd mind my additional agenda. He wouldn't even have to know. And the job made a perfect cover for me being out there.

I pressed play on my iPod, which I'd plugged into the car I'd rented for the drive to New Hampshire. Ella Fitzgerald's voice filled the car, which was why, as I sped up Route 3, I didn't hear the siren over Ella's wail.

I looked in the mirror to change lanes just after crossing the New Hampshire border. Behind me, a sedan flashed a police light, one of the kind they stuck on the hood.

I checked my speed. No way was I going too fast. So . . .

Oh, crap. Hank? Unbelievable. He'd followed me. Now what?

CHAPTER TWELVE

He kissed me long and slow and held me tight, but gently, oh, so gently. I was lost again in that kiss. Thank heavens we'd found a pull-off beneath some pines where we could walk deeper into the woods.

The scent of pine and wood smoke and Hank made me delirious, and I let my brain relax. I surrendered to the joy of his touching me.

His lips began soft, but soon became hotly demanding. He pressed his body against mine, and I felt his erection and that neon urgency flushed though me. We unzipped, and he lifted me. I folded my legs around his waist, and he held me with hands that warmed me, while they somehow did magic on me. And I rode him, and he pumped me, and we slid into a rhythm that brought moans to my lips that burst from my mouth when I came.

Oh, God, I loved this man.

"I do, you know," I said as we lay on the pine needles.

His face, flushed and smiling, tilted up to a patch of sky that pierced the bushy trees.

"Know what?" he said.

"Love you." He smelled glorious, and the *tha-thump* of his heart sang a sweet song.

"Love you, too. But that's old news."

"Never."

He chuckled.

"What?" I said.

"You drive too fast, ma'am. Swear I was going to get a speeding ticket. That would not be appropriate, not now that I'm a loo-tenant." He chuckled again.

"Why did you leave Winsworth, Hank?"

"Had to."

"Why?"

His long pause comforted me. This was the Hank I knew, not that stranger who'd questioned me.

"You know, Tal."

"Do I?"

"Ayuh. Couldn't live without you."

And suddenly I didn't want to go to New Mexico, didn't want to learn about Delphine, didn't want to know why the governor was dead and Didi, too. No, I didn't care. Not much.

It was Hank. I hugged him tighter. This was real. *He* was real.

"I want to tell you something, Tal."

Uh oh. So serious. "Hank?"

"Heard you saw that Zuni governor."

I looked away. I hadn't reconciled that the man I loved caused Ben Bowannie's death. "I did."

"Well," Hank said. "I know you've already tarred me, but it wasn't us. We didn't kill the aide, either. Somebody else was the shooter. Not a cop."

I searched for the truth I knew I'd find in his eyes. I always did. A burst of joy, and I hugged him. "Oh, Hank. Then who?"

"Good question. One I don't have an answer for yet. Not yet. I will. You betcha."

Okay. Now I should tell him.

"So where're you going?" he asked.

It was as casual as pie, the way he said it. But I knew the notes of his voice too well. He was suspicious. He wanted something. He was back on the case.

Long moments with threads of ideas swimming through my head. Finally, "Shopping. Pheasant Lane Mall. A few other places." I feigned excitement. "Want to come?"

His burst of laughter sounded sweeter than Mozart to my ears. I cringed.

"You *know* I don't," he said. "I hate malls."

I smiled, a fake one, so I didn't look right at him. "I know. But, well, I thought maybe this time . . ."

"I will if you'd like. If it'll make you happy."

I kissed the tip of his nose and rubbed his slight Buddha belly. "No, hon, it wouldn't. Because you'd hate it. I'll go it alone."

I was still cursing my lies as I boarded the plane for Albuquerque.

On the flight, I tried to recall all that I'd seen and heard over the past month.

Delphine's head and Didi's homicide. The governor and his aide's death. And Enoch. I couldn't forget him. What a waste. For what? That's what I didn't get.

Virgil Izod man and his search for the blood fetish. The one they used. I wished I understood what he'd meant. The governor's son did. Or so Governor Bowannie had said. I wished that wonderful man was still alive.

And what about the stuffed rattler? Threatening Delphine? Why? What was the deal there?

And who'd blown out my window?

It was all connected, and it all had begun out West. The source, which was exactly where I was headed.

* * *

I deplaned feeling groggy. Beneath the bandage on my face, my cheek throbbed where Izod had cut me. I guessed I'd slept on it.

I walked toward baggage claim, past shops and sculptures and the buzz of humanity going somewhere, anywhere. The clack of cowboy boots surrounded me. The West was different—tall Stetsons and concha belts and rattler earrings for sale.

I loved it out here—the people and the food and the art and land and the Southwestern seas of sand. I bought some Tic Tacs and water at a news store. I was parched and itchy. Hungry, too. But for what?

What I was doing was a little bit crazy, flying cross-country for a position I didn't intend to take with New Mexico's ME's office. At least I didn't think I intended to take it. Okay, it had appeal. A new start. A new life. Newborn.

I was hungry with interest.

Except I loved Hank, and he'd just moved to Boston. I hadn't asked him to move. I felt trapped in a tangle.

Carmen hadn't liked it when I'd told her where I was going. To Hank, Gert, Kranak, and Addy, I'd said nothing. They'd be less pleased than Carm.

I handed the pretty brunette cash for my purchases, picked up a paper and added that, too. "Thanks," I said.

She smiled. "Sure. You look happy."

I tilted my head. "I . . . I guess I am."

Had to be the strange sense of freedom and joy at the prospect of learning the truth. Or maybe it was simply no counseling the families of homicide victims. No tears. No anger. No feelings of betrayal. No looks asking me to fix things that were unfixable.

I shook my head, unwilling to accept that a part of my life might have ended with a sharp slice to my face. The cut was a defining moment, I now believed. But I had to fix this thing with Delphine and Didi, had to find the skull before I could move forward.

The governor had wanted me to look for the skull. He had felt it mattered. I did, too. I just wish I understood better.

At the luggage carousel, I wedged between dozens of other travelers jockeying for their bags. After a long minute, I had my rollie bag and the carry-on, which I slung over my shoulder along with my purse and my Mac laptop.

Cripes, I felt like a camel.

"Let me help you with that," said a soft voice.

I turned to see a medium-sized woman with butternut skin and classical Pueblo features smiling at me.

"Um, thanks so much, but I really can handle it."

"I'm sure you can, Dr. Whyte, but I'm here to pick you up."

Huh? "Pick me up?" I definitely hadn't had enough rest.

"Doc Joe plans to woo you, I guess." She bowed at the waist. "So here I am, your Girl Friday. Doc Joe's waiting for you at the Office of the Medical Investigator. I work there. My name's Natalie. I'll also be your tour guide during your stay."

Good *god*. How to get out of this kindness by Dr. Philip Joe? "Gee, Natalie, thanks. How lovely. But I've rented a car. I'm doing some other vacation stuff, too."

"We can come pick your car up later," she said. "I bet you're exhausted."

I ponied up a smile. "Not so bad."

She shrugged. "Okay. I'll meet you at the office."

I followed, and with each step my load grew heavier. My bags clanked together, and I swayed. *This was stupid.* "Natalie, hold up!"

She pivoted and tried to bury her I-told-you-so face beneath a smile. She reached for my shoulder bag, which easily weighed twelve tons. "Feel better?"

Glorious relief. "Yes. Absolutely. But, y'know, I would really like to have my car with me. How about I follow you?"

She nodded and grinned. She snagged my large rollie bag. "You're a determined one, aren't you? That's what Doc Joe said. So let's get going."

Natalie's purple van was easy to follow in my white Toyota, which blared *rental!* I wished rental companies didn't do that. Buildings only half as tall as Beantown's ringed Albuquerque's fabulous blue sky. I cranked up the AC, but the soft dry heat seeped into my bones, lightening them.

I saw Spanish and Pueblo and Anglo souls mingled on streets shiny with newness. Unlike Boston, the streets were straight and the hills were far in the distance. You could see long, long away out here. One of the things I loved about it.

Natalie wove between traffic with a smooth skill and knowledge I admired. OMI wasn't far, according to my reckoning. It was located on the UNM campus, which I found odd. I never really got that, other than the Chief Medical Investigator had access to all sorts of outstanding researchers.

Like Massachusetts and Maine, New Mexico had a statewide system. A good thing.

Natalie's blinker came on, and she turned left. As I did the same, a lightbulb seemed to switch on in my brain. Something wasn't quite right about our conversation. But what?

Well, *hell.* I'd see ghosts at a petting zoo. I was being ridiculous.

An elderly woman dragging a rolling cart stepped off the curb. I jammed on my brakes and stopped just in time to avoid hitting her. She didn't even look up, but continued across the road. I plucked a tissue from my purse and wiped the sweat from my face.

So close. I spotted Natalie's van hovering just beyond the turn. I waved and began the turn. What was it that . . .

Right. Natalie had called it the Office of the Medical Investigator. Except *everyone* I knew out here called it OMI.

So why had she referred—

Glass shattered, and I was flung toward the passenger side and suddenly the pop of airbags, the screech of wheels, the sound of metal crunching and . . .

Darkness.

I tried to open my eyes, except they were leaded with pain. I sighed, and even that hurt. A moan. Mine? Then a soothing voice in a language I didn't know sang to me.

I sank back into the hazy world of shapes and songs and scents of sage.

I awakened with a start. The air felt crisp and clean on my body. When I moved, I ached, but at least I was mobile. I seemed mobile, anyway. No searing pain. A good thing, since that pain felt too familiar.

I didn't understand. The darkened room enveloped me. A slice of light from outside cut across a linoleum floor covered by scatter rugs. The room was cool, and the blanket that lay over me was soft and fuzzy and comforting.

I massaged my hands, stiff from inactivity.

Why didn't I hurt more? A memory poked inside. I saw with horror a vehicle slamming into my driver's door. I couldn't tell, car or truck. But after that . . .

Where was Natalie? Had she led me to the accident or was she a victim, too? Damn. Pleasant as it was, I needed to know who'd helped me, where I was.

I groped around the low bed. Someone had watched over me. I'd drunk, yes, I remembered that. But by the rumbling in my stomach, I hadn't eaten. Now I had to pee.

I slid my legs over the side of the low-slung bed, and a sweet stab of pain shot through my thighs. I moved my hand lightly over what I pictured as splotches of black and blue. I moved a bit, so I caught some of the light. A few bruises had already evolved to a sickly yellow. *How many days had I been here?* I rolled my ankles, cracking the stiffness out of them. They hurt, too, but not so bad.

I forced myself to remain silent.

A thump, and then a flood of light blinded me.

"Hello?" I said.

"You feel better."

The voice was low and melodic and female, with an odd cadence that I'd heard before. But where?

"I do," I said. "At least, I think I do. Um, where am I?"

"Have some water."

My eyes adjusted, and a small, square woman bent over me. She held a red Alsop's mug in her hand.

"Thank you." I emptied the mug. The warm water cleared my throat. I longed for a cold Diet Coke. "How long have I been your guest?"

"About two days. Maybe a little more." She set a pitcher on the floor.

"Is Natalie here, too?"

"I'll return."

"But I . . ."

The door curtain flipped back, and it was dark again.

Was I in a mess? A captive? Being helped? I didn't understand. Not at all. And, dammit, I still had to pee.

I stood, wobbled, and staggered through the curtained doorway, across a large, darkened living room. I opened the front door and peeked out.

"Ohmigod." Above, a vast and cloudless bluebird-blue sky canopied my head. I stood on a small rise surrounded by mud-and-stone buildings. Straight ahead was a mesa—all orange and gold—that seemed perched on the edge of the world. My memory felt foggy, teasingly elusive. *Had I been here before?* I felt a coming-homeness, yet I couldn't quite anchor myself.

The wind gusted, and fine granules of sand brushed my face and bare legs. I looked down. My feet were bare, too, and showed what was left of that silly peach polish I'd applied on my and Carmen's toenails what felt like eons ago. My hand brushed the soft, brightly colored cotton skirt that I didn't recognize. It billowed in the wind. And a T-shirt. Yes.

I plucked at it. The shirt was peach, like my toes, and complemented the skirt's flowers of turquoise and red and yellow.

My face . . . !

My hands felt rough, my fingernails cut short as I ran them across my face. It ached, in a way that said I was black and blue. The tip of my nose felt rough, and my fingers skittered across a bandage on my forehead. Cotton gauze. My cheek bandage felt different, too. Someone had replaced it.

I leaned on the door frame and shielded my eyes with my hand. I saw no one. Nothing.

A scruffy red-and-white dog with a wagging stub of a tail and a black short-haired pup gamboled on the path in front of me. They spotted me, and I sat on the wooden steps as they trotted over. I let them sniff me. The rough-haired one licked my toes, tickling me, and I laughed and felt a good kind of release. I scratched them behind their ears. Each woofled in turn. Dogs could make the world right, at least for a moment.

I had to get out of there, but I had no idea how. My brain felt like it was made of cheesecloth. Nothing seemed to be sticking. My toes dug into the warm earth. Yet there was a chill in the air, which I didn't associate with Albuquerque. I rubbed my arms, climbed the wooden stairs, and went back inside my prison with no bars.

CHAPTER THIRTEEN

I awakened with a start. Singing? Chanting? I felt better. I ached, yes, but at least I wasn't zombie-girl.

I *had* to find a bathroom. I sat up on the low bed. No one was in the room. I was alone. At least, it felt that way.

I walked through the living room and found a blue-tiled bathroom. The room was small and narrow, the light dim. I peed, washed my hands, and splashed water on the parts of my face where there were no bandages, a disturbingly small amount of real estate. I looked in the mirror. Whoa. I was a sight. My right eyelid was swollen almost closed, and the rest of my face unlandscaped by bandages was either blue or a sickly yellow.

I still felt out of sorts and dizzy, but I needed to get out of there. I'd been sleeping on a cot just off the living room in a small alcove. The dining area was behind the living room and on each side was a bedroom. The kitchen was off the dining room. There I found a back door.

The home had a strange fifties aura, decorated with linoleum and Formica and avocado appliances and plywood kitchen cabinets with curlicues over the sink window.

I tried the back door. Unlocked. I guessed I was only sort of a prisoner. I leaned against the old-fashioned hutch made of maple, the kind you'd find back home in shops selling retro antiques. Maybe I'd stepped into a time warp or something.

Back in the living room, curtains hid all the windows, and so I inched open the front door. That gave me enough light to hunt for my shoes.

After a half hour of futile searching, I was exhausted. And I sure as hell couldn't fit into the size fives I'd found in a closet in the large bedroom. Effective, I guessed, as a way to keep me inside, given I was somewhere in a village in the middle of the desert.

Exactly *what* desert remained a question.

I began a hunt for my other things—my Mac, my purse, my bags, the magazines I'd bought for the plane. Anything. I found zip. Nothing. Not one thing.

I walked back to the low bed and sat on the edge. I felt naked and alone and afraid.

That girl, Natalie. She'd led me into a trap. She'd known what was going on. Natalie, like the woman who'd given me the drink, was American Indian. Same tribe? I had no clue.

Seemed to me I had two choices. I could sneak out and run away and try to find what Anglos termed "civilization."

Or I could try to figure things out first.

I liked option number one better. Get away. Get safe. Except it struck me as stupid. I didn't think these people wanted to kill me. I suspected I was in a village or a pueblo, say, Acoma, Zuni, Hopi, Cochiti, San Ildefanso, Navajo? Except Navajo weren't Pueblo Indians. I sighed.

Even funnier, I had no idea where any of them were actually located.

Sure, the governor. He was Zuni. But this could be any Indian reservation in the Southwest. And why was I here? Who'd brought me to this place? Changed my clothes? Bandaged me and . . .

The door opened with a whine, and sunlight splashed in. A man stood before me. Bare chested, jeans, red bandana tied around his head. His broad, chiseled face was Indian, and he had a blade of a nose, high cheekbones, and tight thin lips.

I stood. "Yes?"

He turned and left.

That really wasn't so cool.

"Hey," I said. "Hey!" I followed him out. "Look, what's happening here? Have I landed on Mars? Am I time traveling?"

He turned, looked at me, crossed his arms and said nothing.

"C'mon, talk to me," I said. "There's no one around. I was in a lousy car accident, and I'm feeling really uncomfortable about all this. So what's the deal? And where's Natalie? I'd like to know where that girl is."

I cringed. I sounded crass and unappreciative, haranguing this guy who kept looking at me with unnerving passivity.

He shrugged and walked away from me.

Well, dammit, I wasn't about to return to that room like some little sheep. I followed him.

Stones bruised my feet as I walked the hard-packed dirt path after the bare-chested man. Sweat poured down his back, even though the chill in the air had deepened.

He was bronzed and well built, and if Hank weren't around, I'd be sizzling. I'd acted revoltingly. I might be scared, but Veda would have shot me for such poor manners. *Hey, Vede, you'd love this pickle I'm in.*

My eyes teared up at the thought of my dead foster mother.

A presence behind me. I whipped around, but all I saw were the two dogs trotting after me.

This is stupid.

I paused and stepped behind the adobe wall of a church. I slid my hands into the pockets of the skirt. I didn't know what I was looking for—money? Right. That made no sense.

But, wait a minute. If I were in a town, there must be stores, cafés, something for commerce. Maybe my brain was functioning again. I stopped following Mr. Silent, and turned back the way I'd come. I began to wend my way higher up the slight hill. There *had* to be something with all the homes around. I'd find it and get out of here.

The hill wound between trailers and small adobe houses and sheds made of wood and metal. When I looked behind me, a whole village was spread out in a small grid. The bell in the church tower clanged.

I could go to the church. Except it might not have a phone. I needed a phone. I sure as heck didn't have my cell anymore.

Beyond the homes lay that mesa I recognized. But from where? When? Damn.

I shook my head. No time now to think about it.

My feet hurt from the stones. What the hell, I could live with it. Everything else about me was banged up, why not make it a complete package with my feet?

Voices chattering in the distance. I widened my strides and sped up. As I crested the hill, a car zoomed by on a highway that apparently bisected the town. I stepped back. Fast. The main drag, as in many Western villages, went on forever in both directions. I saw a few stores on each side of the highway and diagonally across from me, a small, narrow adobe restaurant or cantina with a gas station attached.

I ran across the highway, up the steps and through the narrow door that slapped behind me. Two dozen Indian faces and a few Anglo ones looked up. I smiled, mouthed *sorry*, and walked to the counter. I hoped no one noticed my bare feet.

I slid onto a blue vinyl stool and forced myself not to twirl. People, humanity—I was thrilled. A woman in bangs and a white *More Cowbell* T-shirt was wiping the worn Formica.

"Hello," I said. "I need to use a phone."

The woman's eyebrows shot up, but she didn't stop scrubbing. "You got a cell?"

I shook my head. "I don't, actually. That's why I'd like to use your phone. I'll reverse the charges."

"I see. One minute." She walked through a striped curtain at the far end of the counter and disappeared.

I relaxed for the first time in I-couldn't-remember when. Ahhh, that felt great. I wiped the sole of one foot on the upper arch of the other and repeated the process in reverse. Better.

My back prickled. A dozen pairs of eyes were fastened on me, and I couldn't stop glancing at the door. Someone was coming after me. It was the "when" I didn't know.

I hadn't asked her where I was. *Idiot!* I did a three-sixty of the place. Nothing shouted back at me.

I wished the woman would hurry.

I studied the ancient red counter until she finally brushed through the curtained door. In her right hand, she held a sponge. In her left, a portable phone.

Yes.

She smiled at me as she handed me the black portable phone.

"Thanks so much," I said. "Um, where am I?"

Her face scrunched up in that you're-crazy-lady look.

I smiled. "Never mind." I slid off the stool as I punched out "O" for Operator. I gave him Hank's cell phone number. It rang and rang and . . . dammit. Who knew why he wasn't picking up.

I couldn't leave a voicemail. Not without any money.

Something bad was going to happen. I just knew. My eyes scanned the restaurant again. Everyone was eating and smoking and chatting, but they were watching me, too.

"Gee,'" I said to the woman. "Anyplace I can call that's a little more private?"

She nodded. "Out back." She wagged two fingers toward the back of the restaurant.

"Thanks." I hustled to the back, where I found a cubicle just in front of the kitchen. I called Hank again, got nowhere. Maybe I should call Gert or Jake or Kranak. Except calling Boston made no sense.

I stared at the phone, shook my head, and dialed 911.

"Yes," I said. "I need help. I'm on some reservation. Pueblo. I don't . . ."

A door slapped, and I whipped around. A couple with a little girl in a frilly blouse and pink jeans.

"Hello? Hello?" came the dispatcher's voice.

I hunched over the phone, trying to make myself small. The chatter rose and fell, an ocean of voices, nothing alarming. "Sorry. I'm in a strange place, and I . . ."

"We need some idea where you are, ma'am. We can't seem to locate you."

"I don't *know* where I am. On a pueblo. In a small restaurant. I was in an accident in Albuquerque and I woke up here." My voice rose. I tried to control it, but a sob burst out. "Damn. I need some help here."

"We will. We will, ma'am. If you can, take the phone outside and describe what you see."

I breathed in. *Calm*, I told myself. "Yes. Okay." I headed outside. As I passed the woman, who was serving eggs to a man at the counter, I held up my index finger and mouthed, *one sec*.

She nodded, and I relaxed a bit. I took a breath. Hoped I could get through this.

I stood on restaurant's wooden stoop, read the name of the restaurant to the dispatcher and described the main street.

"Okay," the dispatcher said. "We got you. Just hold on. We're on our way."

Relief became an ocean tide, and I shook. "Thank you. So much."

"On our way. Now just hang on, and we'll come get you."

"I will. Yes. Hang on."

I walked as casually as possible down the stairs and pressed against the side of the restaurant. I took deep breaths, and every few seconds I'd reconnect with the dispatcher. I checked my watch. My wrist was bare. Gone, too. So I tried to keep track—five, ten, maybe fifteen minutes passed.

A brown car with an unlit bubble light atop ambled down Main Street. I waited. I needed to make sure that this was my ride back to sanity. The car's windows were blacked out. But as it neared the restaurant, it slowed down.

I'd been standing in shadow. They couldn't see me.

"I'm here. In the shadow," I said to the dispatcher.

But the dispatcher had hung up. It had to be them. I stepped out of the shadow. The police car stopped and an officer got out. He wore a brown hat and uniform and he smiled and waved.

Relief flooded me, making me dizzy. I smiled back. "I'm glad you're here."

"Come on," he said. "We'll take you back to Albuquerque. Sort this thing out."

"Great. Super." I began to climb the stairs.

"Stuff inside?" he said. "I'll go with you."

"No need. I just want to return the phone."

He strode over, grinning. "We want you safe, little lady."

"Thanks." I reached for the door.

"Hold on!" came a shout.

The sun was in my eyes. All I saw was a clump of people running toward me. I dropped the phone and ran to the car. The officer gripped my arm as he flung open the back-seat door.

"No!" someone shouted.

A frission of fear and insight. What was I doing? "Wait," I said.

He grunted, shoved me into the back, and slammed the door.

Wrong. All wrong. I reached for the door as he slid in beside me.

He shifted the car into gear, and I shoved open the passenger door.

Now? Never?

I flung myself out the door, rolled, and sputtered to a halt sprawled on the tarmac. My head spun. What the hell had I just done?

Tires screeched, and the brown sedan spun around, so that it was facing me. I was still pancaked on the road, dizzy, uncertain. What had I done? I couldn't seem to move. Not fast enough.

The sedan barreled toward me.

Holy hell!

Someone grabbed my shoulders and hauled me out of the way as the sedan flew by and raced out of town.

Juiced with adrenaline, I peered into a woman's face. It looked frozen, as if in fury or fear.

"I . . . I'm sorry," I muttered. "I . . ."

Arms tightened around me, and I was smothered by a large-bosomed hug. "You are one lucky *chica*."

I couldn't argue with that.

I sat at a table in the café across from the bare-chested Indian, now wearing a snap shirt. Another man, much older, with drooping eyes and a face etched and jagged with age, sat beside me.

Neither man said a word.

The seat across from me was empty, yet a menu was placed in front of it by the waitress. We were waiting. The woman who'd saved me had disappeared.

"Where am I?" I said.

The younger man pressed a finger to his lips. "Sshhhh."

I shook my head. I stood to leave. "I can't do this anymore."

"Don't," the older man said. "Please, wait."

His tone was flat, but his eyes begged. How could I refuse? I gave my order to the waitress while she flirted with the younger of the two men. When I looked around again, the café was empty except for us.

I excused myself to the bathroom. The men exchanged looks, but didn't try to stop me. When I returned, a woman was sitting in the chair across from mine. She wore a white shirt and black pants. A large silver Zuni bracelet circled her right wrist, and a turquoise petit-point clip held her long white hair to the side. Her face was lined, the color of butternut, and rich with age.

When I sat across from her, her apple-green eyes sparkled. I could tell her smile came often and gladly.

"Where's the woman who saved me?" I said.

"My daughter?" the old woman said. "She had other things to do. You'll see her again."

Had I slipped down a rabbit hole? I decided to try to be normal. "Hello. I'm Tally Whyte."

She smiled again, nodded, and that's when I got it. She was related to Governor Bowannie. I wondered if she knew he was dead. I got sad all over again, just thinking about him.

"Don't be sad," she said.

The younger of the two men snorted. I almost said "wiseass," but held myself back.

"Thank you, ma'am," I said. "But I am sad." I nearly blurted out that I was sorry, but I waited for her to speak. I wanted to be considerate, to wait, to be kind. Minutes passed, long ones, then more minutes. My tether finally snapped.

I stood up. "Whatever happened here, I don't get. Thank you for saving my life. But I've got to go. I have dead friends and something important to do."

The old woman smiled. "Well, it's about time, Tally Whyte, that you found your *cojones*."

"*What?*"

She kept smiling. Her eyes sparkled with humor. I wanted to shoot her.

"*Cojones?*" I said. "Believe me, I've got *cojones* to spare! Maybe not literally, but . . ."

She laughed, slapped her thighs, and the men laughed, too.

"What is the problem here?" I said.

"You," she choked out. "You almost went with those villains. You would most likely have been killed. We've worked so hard to keep you alive. Don't you see the irony?"

I was too tired for irony, but I laughed anyway. "How did that man, the pretend cop, find me?"

"Police scanners," the old man said. "These people are good. Real skilled."

The old woman nodded, looked again at me. "Fine to see you recovering." Her hand shook as she reached into the pocket of her black pants. She slid out a folded piece of paper. Her knuckles were gnarled, her fingers scored with a thousand cuts.

I tilted my head. "You're a carver."

"Yes."

"I should have known. Of course. I'm in Zuni."

She beamed. "Yes. Your brain is working again. Thank heavens. You've been a mess."

"Thanks a bunch," I said. Not that I could take offense. She was a very cool lady.

CHAPTER FOURTEEN

The waitress brought my *huevos rancheros*, coffee, and OJ. I sipped the coffee, found my brain kicking in even more.

The old woman smelled of sage. She nodded when she got her cocoa, and she held her mug with two hands as she sipped. A wave of overwhelming sorrow jarred me. I gently lay my fork on the plate. I dabbed my lips with my napkin. The two men kept forking eggs into their mouths.

We locked eyes, the old woman and I. The same painful sorrow stole my breath.

I reached for my coffee. "What is it?"

"You'll see."

And I suddenly knew. "Where's Natalie?"

The old woman notched her chin. Tears washed down the wrinkles of her face like a many-fingered river. "Dead. For you. My niece. You had better be worth it."

I wasn't. Not in trade for a young woman. Natalie had a lot more life to live than I. I shouldn't have come out here.

"How did she die?" I said.

"She pulled you from the wreck," the younger man said. "They shot at her, but she got you out. A good thing to do." He nodded. His face was dark with anger and tight with pain. "She was a good girl, our Natalie." His lips thinned, and he caught my eyes with his. "A good girl. You were out of it, and she dragged you to her van and pulled you in. I guess that's when she got hit." He shrugged. "I don't know."

"Shot?" I said.

"Hit," he said. "Yes. She drove toward the res, them tailing her. Shooting. Her bleeding. She wanted you safe. I don't know why she didn't go to the hospital there in Albuquerque. She called and we met her around San Rafael. She was weaving all over the place, but nobody stopped her. I guess they thought she was just another drunk Indian."

"Why didn't she call the police?" I said.

The older man shook his head. "It's not something we'd do. We whooped and hollered and went after those guys, the ones chasing her. They hightailed it outta there." He rubbed his fingers back and forth across the Formic. "Boy, did they ever. You never saw anyone run so fast. Yeah, they got away. She died. We got you."

I rubbed my eyes to keep the tears at bay. Damn, but I wouldn't cry. Not now. Later. I stuttered in a breath. "I'm sorry. I really . . . I don't know what to say. I never wanted this. Natalie deserved better. A lot better."

The old Zuni man's hand slid atop mine. "Don't," he said. "It was for you, but you didn't do it to her. They did. There's a reason. It matters. It mattered to my brother, her sister, his niece, and his nephew."

His hand was dry and comforting. I squeezed it. With two fingers he held up a folded piece of paper.

I unfolded the paper. It read: *The Bone Man, Land's End Trading, Route 404.*

I walked back to the old woman's home with the younger of the two men. I had a million questions but couldn't seem to voice a one. The same two dogs greeted me, and I wished I had treats for them. I crouched down and scratched their chests. I missed Penny, but I was glad she wasn't with me. She'd be dead.

"Please tell me your name," I said.

"Aric. Aric Bowannie." He notched his head. "Ben's son. Natalie's cousin."

The governor's son. I hadn't guessed. What a loss he must be feeling. "And the old woman?"

"Katie Poblano. My auntie. Ben's sister. Enough?"

"Thank you."

The streets beneath my feet felt ancient. No longer a village of adobe, but the homes clustered together as if they were trying to accomplish what once consisted of the pueblo. We neared the church and bore left, and shadows darted like knives in the late afternoon. Above all, Corn Mountain, guardian, home, everything to Zuniland.

My feet ached from slapping the hard ground without shoes. Aric's confident steps mocked my tentative ones, his running sneakers finding easy purchase on the uneven earth.

The Bone Man. Talk about creepy. "Why the mystery?" I said. "The secrecy?"

He chewed his lip. "My father died when he was with you. We wanted to make sure you weren't from them, particularly after Natalie. She was good people. You shouldn't go back to Albuquerque. Not until you have what you came for."

"I'm not sure what I came for," I said. "At one point, your father asked me to come out here with him."

My thighs ached as I climbed the wooden steps that led to the darkened house. Someone had carried wood to the crate left of the door, and a low fire burned in the kiva fireplace. I walked across the cool linoleum floor and warmed my hands by the fire.

Aric gestured me to the couch.

"Now what?" I said.

He stood before me, looking every inch the macho man. "We go. Soon. Find the skull."

"Find my friend Didi's killer," I said. "Your father's, too, I suspect. Natalie's. An art dealer named Delphine. Too many more."

He shoved his hands into the back pockets of his jeans. "Yeah."

"It's a big job."

"Be right back." He left the room, and for a few minutes I allowed the fire to mesmerize me. I wished for the comfort of the familiar, for Hank and Penny and Carmen and Gert. For my apartment, The Grief Shop, Newbury Street.

I needed my bearings, and I wouldn't find them here.

I turned away from the fire. I felt like crap, and not just physically.

Just beyond the fireplace, a door yawned wide. I didn't remember it from earlier. I suspected I was too busy, too frantic. I slid off the couch and hobbled through the door. My feet killed.

Tools and rocks cluttered the narrow room. Dust covered every inch of every surface, including the large windows. So much dust that I couldn't see outside to the rapidly setting sun.

If I'd seen this room earlier, I would have known I was in Zuni, for here was where Katie and her family made hundreds of Zuni fetishes every year. Here they carved the rock with powerful tools, sanded it so it was smooth and gleaming, wound rawhide or gut around the carvings and attached arrowheads and coral and turquoise and heishi bundles. Chunks of serpentine and marble and pipestone lay in a basket, and a fine piece of turquoise sat on a shelf beside a pack of Marlboro Lights.

It was hard and dirty work to create such beauty.

Someone had wiped a circle on the dust-covered window. I peeked through and saw the mountain. I shouldn't be surprised.

"Ready?" came the voice.

I spun around. Aric wore jeans and a button-down shirt and loafers.

"You could be a teacher at some Boston high school," I said.

"I'm not," he said.

"No. Right. I need to change. Shower. Get some shoes. My purse."

He handed me a plastic bag. Inside were a few of my belongings clumped with a new toothbrush, toothpaste, deodorant, other toiletries, and a pair of slip-on sneakers.

I pulled the sneakers on, and he nodded. "Good."

Aric's face, so sad. "This is very hard on you," I said.

He nodded.

"Your father, Natalie. My dad . . . I've been through it."

Again, lips compressed. He nodded, said nothing.

I sighed, moved closer, studied his eyes, which met mine dead on. "I could help," I said. "I'd like to. It's what I do."

"Let's go."

I assumed we were heading out to The Bone Man and the trading post, but instead, I followed him through winding streets and alongside homes until we arrived at a larger building. Bound by a fence, the two-story adobe building looked cozy and inviting. It was trimmed with bright red and turquoise paint and carved posts that supported the porch roof.

We walked around back to a flagstone courtyard. There, a dozen people sat on folding lawn chairs while women and men in native costume milled around. We took seats in the first row, and then Katie Poblano arrived and the crowd hushed.

She sat beside Aric and the older man I'd met earlier. She nodded, and the dancers, drummers, and chanters began.

A spell draped me in mystery, one I would not repeat. Ever.

The old woman whispered in my ear, yet if I had to tell what she said, I couldn't. Seeing the dance, smelling the sage, hearing the chants, the music—I was part of it now, the hunt for the evil. I had been woven into the fabric of events I hadn't begun, but needed to end.

"Aric?" I said.

"Don't be afraid," he said. "All right?"

I wasn't. But I'd stepped on a train that I couldn't get off until the ride reached its appointed destination. Confusing.

So I watched and listened and smelled the spicy scents. I cried, but only a little.

Dust billowed around us, even as the temperatures rose into the sixties. I'd awaked refreshed, and yet I couldn't say exactly what had happened the previous evening. I guessed it was a healing ceremony for Ben Bowannie, his aide and Natalie. All I knew was that I felt well for the first time in weeks and that I'd slept comfortably and long.

Aric Bowannie and I had left Zuni that morning, headed to the trading post and the Bone Man. On the way, Aric handed me my burnt cell phone, my wallet, and my can of pepper spray. We stopped in Gallup, where I bought two pairs of jeans, a broom skirt, some tops, a jacket, a purse, a pair of gloves, and a new cell, one of those untraceable prepaid ones. I did all of that with cash given to me by Aric, as he rightly cautioned me about leaving a credit card trail. He also warned me not to use the phone unless it was an emergency.

Now a blanket of stars and full moon made the desert seem like I was in a planetarium, which Aric found ironic, as did I. Outside the truck window, the desert glowed with cacti and sage and rock and sand and night creatures foraging for supper. I thought I spotted three coyotes, but couldn't be sure if it wasn't simply a rock formation, coupled with my wishful thinking. And cows. Lots of cows. Home on the range and all that.

I opened the window, and the chilly night breeze fingered my hair. The pavement slid by as we rode farther and farther from Zuni to who-knew-where. I didn't ask. Didn't much care, as I felt the intensity of Ben Bowannie's quest that was now mine, too.

"I'd like to tell you what happened in Boston," I said.

Aric said nothing.

I explained about the re-creation that looked just like my missing friend, Delphine. I told him about Didi's homicide, my adventures on the Vineyard, and the death of his father. He wanted every detail of his father's death, and I told him all I knew.

I didn't think about why I trusted him, other than I had to. But it felt right.

"Your father wanted the skull," I said. "He didn't believe it was an Old One, though. But he felt it mattered, and that it would cause trouble."

He shrugged. "I'm not surprised he knew something else was going on. We always have problems. Drugs and booze coming in, pots and sacred stuff going out. Fake fetishes purported to be ours. And traders ripping us off, making a bundle where we only make a few pennies."

"Not all," I said.

"No. There are some good ones. But this illegal stuff. That's bad. That, more than some old skull, was what my father was investigating." More to himself than to me, he said, "I wish he'd told me more."

"About the blood fetish?" I asked.

"What?"

"The blood fetish. Didi scrawled it on the floor. And the guy on the Vineyard was looking for a blood fetish, an old one, he said. Except . . . well, it's as if I'm the only one who knows about it. It feels weird. Have you ever heard of it?"

He shook his head, flipped open a can of Beechnut

chewing tobacco, pinched a wad, and packed it into his cheek. He cracked the window. "Nope."

"C'mon," I said. "Really?"

"Really."

But there was something. Maybe a hitch in his voice? A look in his eye? Something. "I don't believe you."

"I don't care what you believe," he said. "You're hunting the guy who killed your friend. Well, someone's hunting you, lady."

I flinched, looked in the rear-view mirror. The lonely road streamed behind us like a girl's hair ribbon. I could see for miles, and no other cars were in sight. I breathed deep, calmed myself.

Maybe someone *was* hunting me. But why? What did I know? What had I seen that would make me a target. Sure, I was here looking for Delphine and Didi's killer. But how did the killer know that? And why was I such a threat?

It had to do with some kind of pot thievery or fakery or . . . But, geesh, it felt like there were a dozen threads, none of which added up to much.

It sure was tough to get rid of that itch between my shoulders when I'd almost stepped inside a fake cop car. I clenched my hands to white-knuckle tight. "So what's our agenda? And where did this paper, the Bone Man, come from?"

He hooked a sharp left, and I held on to the dangling strap inside the ancient Land Rover.

"You're angry," I continued. "Your father. His aide, who I'm guessing was your friend."

Aric remained silent. His fury came from some deep and passionate source, I was sure, even beyond the death of his father. It chilled me.

In the distance, the land flattened more, and I saw blinking neon surrounded by nothing but desert, cactus, and cows.

"*Where* did the paper come from, Aric?"

"Natalie. It was in her pocket, inside an Altoids tin. The only thing that didn't burn."

We neared the neon, which read DESERT DREAMS MOTEL. The clean blacktop and good paint job said "success." I guessed I shouldn't fear bedbugs. I couldn't help scratching my arm.

Natalie. All I could see was the girl I'd met at the airport. Open faced and smiling. Warm. "These people have a lot to answer for," I said. "A lot. When do we reach the trading post?"

He pulled into the parking lot in front of a sign that read OFFICE. A minute later, a potbellied man, unsmiling, cigarette dangling from lips, leaned against the driver's side window. He held up a key, and Aric swiped it out of his hand in what seemed to be anger.

Smoking Man smirked. "Now *you* owe *me*, ma brother."

CHAPTER FIFTEEN

I wished motel rooms smelled different. They all must use that same noxious disinfectant. They all seemed to have identical magazine subscriptions, too. I couldn't believe I had forgotten to pick up a book to read in Gallup. I snagged the *New Mexico Magazine* on the bedside table. It was from the last century, which I found really annoying. I paged through the magazine while Aric moved around the room. He flicked on the TV and flipped through the channels to ESPN. Swell.

"Look at that face," he said. "You don't like sports?"

"Not a whole lot."

"Can you live with it?"

Hadn't I forever? "Sure."

I smelled the tobacco when he stuffed it into his cheek.

"Gross," I said.

"Tough."

I found an article on Carlsbad Caverns and began to read. Good stuff. Aric finally went in to take a shower, which was when I called Gert about the potsherds. I hoped she'd been able to get them carbon dated.

"They've got 'em in evidence," she said. "And they're hangin' fast. No luck so far."

"What about Kranak?" I said. "He might go for the idea. That would have to do with evidence, the date of the pot."

"Yup," she said. "He's tried. He would have to get some kind of court order. Carbon dating wrecks the object or something."

Swell. "Thanks, Gertie. Keep me posted, okay?"

"How the hell can I when I don't know where you—"

"Tally?" Aric barked from the bathroom.

I covered the mouthpiece. "What?"

"What the hell are you doing?"

"Reading," I hollered back. I closed the phone and slipped it back into my purse, picked the magazine back up, and sat on the chair just as Aric opened the door.

"What was I hearing?"

He leaned out of the bathroom, bare chested, towel around his waist. Whoooeee, he was pretty to look at.

"You heard me singing, I guess." I smiled. "How about a sample? I can do *Oklahoma!* or *Brigadoon* or the Dixie Chicks."

He lifted a towel to his head and began to dry his hair. "You're full of shit. Go take a shower, lady, if you can pull yourself away from your concert."

I walked with great dignity into the bathroom steamy from his shower. Boy, did I miss Hank.

When I opened the door outside the next morning, the sun had not yet risen. The stars had fled, and the sky was a murky blackish gray. Aric had gotten me up *way* too early. I'd asked the manager if I could take the *New Mexico Magazine*, as I wanted to finish the article on the caverns. His "whatever" meant I'd have something to read on the road.

I chewed on a stale bagel while Aric stuffed a fresh piece of chaw into his cheek. He was decked out all Western, from his Stetson to a pair of shiny cowboy boots.

"You look like a fake cowboy," I said.

"Well, thank you, ma'am."

"That's the point, isn't it?" I said.

"Yup."

Two hours later, the sun yawned from the sky as we made yet another turn onto a desert dirt road that looked like a twin to the one we'd just left.

"How do you not lose your way out here?" I asked.

"It's where I live."

I imagined the streets of Southie and the North End and Beacon Hill and a hundred more places I knew by heart.

"How far to the trading post?" I said.

"Not long."

"You said that an hour ago."

He smiled.

"So what's our plan?"

"The old man, he'll know about the Bone Man. All we have to do is get him to tell us about him. Here," he said. "Hold out your hand."

I did, and he dropped a turquoise petit-point-style ring onto my palm.

"We're here to buy pawn," he said.

"Jewelry pawned by your people?"

"And Navajo and Hopi and others. Yes. But it's mostly all fake by now. Not fake Indian made, but fake pawn. Keep an eye out. See if he has anything that might relate to the Bone Man."

"Why would he sell something like that to strangers?"

"Because he wants to get rid of it. Evidence. Maybe." He raised his hand. "Or maybe we'll have to trick him. So put on your domestic face, Tally Whyte."

"What's that supposed to mean? I'm domestic! I do stuff at home."

He smiled. "Just stop looking like city girl."

"Easy." All I had to do was remember life in Maine. As I scraped my hair into a scrunchie, my heart squeezed.

We pulled into a parking lot in much need of refurbishing. Dust billowed around the truck as we backed up to the single red gas pump. Not another vehicle was in sight.

"This is it," Aric said. "Do a good job now."

My retort was lost in the slam of his door. Aric hauled over the nozzle and began filling up.

"Hurry up," he said. "This is a busy place. The only joint around. No shopping."

I almost laughed. What did he think I was going to do, dawdle in the aisles looking for trinkets? "Yes, sir."

He notched his head toward the shop/trading post/coffeehouse housed in the red adobe structure with an arch above the front door and turquoise slatted shutters in need of paint.

I slid out and flattened my broom skirt that billowed in the wind. I pulled on a ball cap and sunglasses.

"Don't," mouthed Aric.

He was right. Too sharp-looking for my character. I tossed them on the seat, groped in back for the straw hat I'd purchased in Gallup and headed for the front door.

I looked back once. Aric was watching me as he held the nozzle to the gas tank. The Bone Man. Okay. *Here goes*.

I reached for the screen door. The wind gusted and door flapped in the breeze. I stilled. Wrong. That was wrong.

With all the sand and wind out here, even the shabbiest establishment would at least have some latch to keep the screen door from flapping. Something was out of whack. I chewed my lower lip. I might be being watched. I should go inside, not hesitate. Turning back to Aric would signal a problem to a watcher.

But if I went inside, the "people" behind all of this could be waiting for me.

I turned back to Aric. "Honey, I'm going to look around back. I need the bathroom. It might be out here."

"Sure," was all he said.

I walked around the building. No cars. No tracks. A

small brown lizard scooted out of my way. A window facing east had a cracked pane. I stood on tiptoe, shielded my eyes and peered in.

I couldn't see much. Dark. Wood floor. Shelves. This wasn't working.

The wind stilled, and as I walked around the building, the sand crunched beneath my feet and the hot sun warmed my cheek. All desert here and a ring of mountains to the west. So beautiful, so austere.

The back door was locked.

I continued walking, and soon I again faced the front door. I didn't feel much safer, but I'd done what I could not to play the fool. I wondered why the hell Aric wasn't coming inside with me.

I checked my cell phone. I had a signal. Not a great one, but it was there.

I pulled open the screen door, held my breath as I stepped into the cool darkness.

No one had switched on the lights for the day. No fans, either, which I found unusual. At least no one had jumped out at me and gone "boo!" I exhaled and . . .

Hell.

The unmistakable smell of dead flesh and feces and other odors of death mingled like a noxious perfume. There was a something "other," too. Something unfamiliar.

Happy I was wearing sneakers—so aptly named—I sidestepped behind a shelf of canned green beans, peas, and corn. I opened my cell phone, switched it to camera, and peered around the grocery. Nothing out of the way appeared on the small screen, but I snapped off some shots.

For the millionth time, my foster mother's words about getting a gun rang in my brain.

I sucked in a breath, almost choked on the stench, and stepped from behind the shelf. I crept forward. Where the hell was Aric?

Another step, where packages of pasta and tacos and

Oreo cookies towered over me. No one in the aisles. Not so far.

Dammit, Aric.

Lights blazed, and I stumbled, grabbed what turned out to be canned jalapeños, and furiously blinked.

"Tally," Aric said.

"Yes?"

"It's okay. Come out."

I peeked around a corner, then walked down the wooden-floored center aisle until I neared the front counter.

Except it wasn't okay. Not one bit. Aric was bent over a supine body encased in jeans, a plaid shirt, and cowboy boots that lay behind the counter. Beside the body, a gray furry mutt that looked half coyote oozed blood from his shoulder.

The mutt was breathing. The human wasn't.

Above them loomed the scarred wood counter with its ancient cash register. The drawer was closed. Other than the corpse and the dog, nothing else was out of place.

I ran over. The body belonged to an old man. Oh, dear. The dog whimpered.

I found a clean dishrag and kneeled by the dog.

"Don't," Aric said. "You'll lose your hand."

"I might." I talked to the pup, tried to soothe him, but each time my hands moved near his wound, he growled. Understandable. I'd growl too.

"Can you hold him, Aric? Just until I get this bandage on."

"You're loco. Swear to God."

"Yeah," I said. "Most likely, but he's stood by his master until he's too weak to move. If we stop the bleeding, we can take him to a vet and . . ."

Aric snorted, jumped up, and returned with a pack of Handiwipes, several of which he tied around the dog's snout. He then took Coyote into his arms, and I sprayed the wound with some Bactine from the shelves, then bound the wound. Oh, Coyote did not like that one bit.

I retrieved a clean bowl from a shelf in aisle three, snared a bottle of spring water, and used the latter to fill the bowl. I opened some food and put it in another bowl.

"Ready?" Aric said.

"Yeah, I think so."

Aric released Coyote and jumped back.

"What?" I said. "Are you expecting an attack? He's half dead."

Coyote's wiry muzzle twitched. He managed to get his two back legs under him, but he was too weak to stand, and he collapsed. I moved the water bowl closer, and his tongue slithered out. He began to lap.

"Good pup," I said.

"Can we get to the problem at hand, Tally?" Aric said.

"Yes, yes, sure. Of course."

I took my first serious look at the old man. Poor soul. Two bullet holes marked his chest. His face was gray, his cheeks sunken, and stubble covered his chin and upper lip. Flied buzzed around his head.

He'd deserved better. *I'm so sorry, old man.* I crouched down. Hard to tell if he was Anglo or Indian or both. He looked like, well, like an overcooked . . . Geesh. "Awful."

I reached to touch Old Man's face. Such a sad, lonely way to die. Coyote growled, and I smiled. At least Old Man hadn't died alone. No.

Inside my purse, I found my phone. I felt naked without my camera, long lost in the accident, but the phone would do. I snapped off half a dozen shots of Old Man and Coyote, and then I walked around the trading post taking photos of shelves and goods and pawn and pottery and anything else I could think of.

The dust made me sneeze, and I purloined a box of tissues.

"You done?" Aric said.

"Almost." I walked behind the counter, and took photos there, too. I hoped the camera would capture what I wasn't seeing. The fluorescent light sputtered above my head. Time to change the bulbs. I guess it didn't matter much now, at least not to Old Man.

Aric was pacing in front of the corpse. I sat on the dusty floor and crossed my legs.

"See anything?" I asked.

He shook his head. "You?"

I shrugged. "Nothing that strikes me. Is he the Bone Man?"

"I don't believe so. Natalie was a cautious kid. I doubt the Bone Man would be the operator of a trading post. Too obvious. Too—"

"Public? So who *is* the Bone Man? Or *what*, maybe? I wish I could see how this old man's death connects to a twenty-first-century woman's skull found in an ancient pot."

I began to dial 911. I punched out the nine, and Aric put his hand over mine.

I stood. "What?"

"Are you nuts?" His lips had thinned in anger. "Do you forget what's happened? The accident? The man who tried to kidnap you?"

"Yes, but . . . we have to call this in. He shouldn't be left here."

"We have to leave him, Tally."

"But . . ."

"We must."

I bent again to Old Man and apologized, and for the first time noticed the burn marks surrounding one of the bullet holes. And Old Man's face . . . I sat back, tried to see with my gut. Huh. His expression was one of . . . surprise. Yes, surprise.

"I think he knew his killer," I said. "Nothing's out of place. Burn marks on his shirt. The killer got awfully close to him to leave those marks. And he's got a look of surprise on his face, too."

"I think so, too." Aric slapped his thighs. "C'mon." He pulled at my arm.

I tugged it away. "Not a chance without Coyote."

He slapped his hands on his hips. "I thought you had dead friends. That you wanted to find out who did them in."

I shook my head. "He's alive, Aric. Coyote's alive. He's wearing a collar. I'll get a leash and . . ."

"He'll bite your sorry ass."

"Screw off. He'll die if we don't take him with us." I found the tiny pet section and took a leash. I also saw one of those bright blue cloth muzzles. I pulled off the tags and took that, too. Found a box of dog treats and ripped open the plastic top with my teeth.

I realized I was hungry. Funny.

A phone rang, and I jumped. I scanned the low-ceilinged room. There, a pay phone. Ringing.

"Answer it, why don't you?" I said to Aric.

He cocked his head. "Finally, a good idea out of you."

I crouched before Coyote. He growled, but didn't make a move for me. I talked to him softly in what I hoped sounded soothing to his ears, about how we had to leave his master, that it would be okay, that we would take care of him. His growls subsided.

I glanced up as Aric lifted the pay phone receiver off its cradle. "Yeah," was all he said.

He listened, nodded. "I'll check. Hold on."

He was handling the call, and I turned back to Coyote. He let me scratch beneath his chin and between his ears, a favorite spot of Penny's. "All right, boy, I'm going to snap this leash on, okay?"

His golden eyes regarded me with a mixture of distrust and pain and hope. I fed him a soft treat and snapped on the leash. Okay. That went well.

"This is not going to be fun, but I've got to do it, Coyote." I sighed, began slipping the muzzle over his snout. He moved—lightning—and bit down on my hand.

"*Shit!*"

"Shut up!" Aric hissed, his hand over the receiver.

Coyote whined, looked guilty, and licked my hand. Remorse. Didn't help the pain. Crap. Crapcrapcrap. I shouldn't have done anything until Aric was with me. Whatever. My own fault.

I sat there, talking softly to Coyote, watching blood ooze from my hand, and waiting for Aric to hang up. I cursed my own stupidity. I imagined tetanus and rabies and other nasty stuff.

"Oh, Coyote, we're screwed."

CHAPTER SIXTEEN

Aric gently replaced the receiver on the wall pay phone.

"Aric, I, um . . ."

He didn't see me as he approached. He sure didn't hear me, either. Aric was all inside now, thinking about whatever he'd learned from the person on the other end of the phone.

My hand throbbed, but he needed time to process the call. I sighed. Aric would shoot me once he saw what had happened to my hand. I could take it. The dog wasn't at fault.

I waited. Long minutes passed. Aric walked right by me and rounded the counter. He reached into his pocket and pulled out what looked like latex gloves. How *handy*. And how interesting. I sure wasn't seeing the whole picture here.

"Be right back," I said as I headed for the sign that pointed with a metal arrow and said BATHROOM.

Aric mumbled something, and I made my escape.

The large bathroom-cum-storage room was piled with boxes to the ceiling. It appeared semi-clean, and its one stall seemed usable. I checked, used the facilities, then found soap and turned on the water. A few drops piddled out. That was it. Damn. I retrieved another bottle of spring water, lathered up, and rinsed. The whole process hurt like hell. Using the soap, I managed to tug off the ring Veda had given me from my pinkie finger and slip it onto my left hand. I wasn't thrilled about the swelling.

"Shitshitshit." My hand hurt like the dickens. I rinsed again, toweled dry with a new Handi Wipe, sprayed on a ton of Bactine, and Band-Aided the site of the tooth marks. Who knew where Coyote's mouth had been. I sure didn't need an infection right then. Rabies? Tetanus? Absurd. I knew I was up on my tetanus shots. And how many people got rabies nowadays?

What had Aric found out? And why would a Zuni be carrying a pair of latex gloves in his pocket? Oh, there were lots of mysteries here.

I punched out Hank's number on my phone. It went directly to voicemail. I left him my new cell number, told him where I was and who I was with, and then I dialed Carmen at the restaurant.

The phone bleeped once, twice . . .

BLAM! Right here. A gunshot. Like thunder.

I found my pepper spray, started to run.

Hank's voice in my ear stopped me.

Are you nuts, woman? Bullets trump pepper spray. Hide, then help.

Another shot. Different gun? Shit.

Hide, then help.

Did Aric have a gun? I couldn't remember.

I flicked off the bathroom light, ran to the stall, closed the door that damnably creaked. I wanted to lock it. I shouldn't. If someone came in, saw the door shut tight, they'd know.

I hung my purse over the back hook. It weighted the door enough to mostly close it.

I pocketed my pepper spray, and cradling my bad hand, I hiked myself onto the toilet seat. I saw stars. My hand looked worse. It definitely felt worse.

Quiet. I had to get quiet. And calm. Yes, calm. Crouched atop the toilet seat, I listened.

No sounds from outside the bathroom. But that meant nothing. A pause in the action.

Was this right? Should I blaze out of there? What? I chuckled. Pepper spray at the ready? Oh, yeah, that would . . .

The bathroom door creaked open.

I swallowed. My legs were going numb, my hand throbbing, my face covered in sweat that was starting to drip down my forehead. The sweat of fear.

Just breathe, Tal. Calm. Ohm.

Lights on!

A weakening bulb sputtered above my head.

I wished my legs hadn't gone numb. I wished . . . Screw it.

I held the pepper spray in front of me, facing outward. I pictured some killer flinging open the door—bam!—me spraying him in the face.

I closed my eyes, asked for strength.

Footsteps snapping on the wood floor. The guy didn't call out. Didn't say a word.

But he was getting closer.

No, he was headed toward the sink, away from the stall.

If I stood, maybe I could see him. Had to do it.

I pushed my thighs, and somehow grew tall. I could almost see . . .

The toilet seat wobbled.

Shit, I mouthed. I got quiet. Very quiet.

There, a guy, tall, stocky, black Stetson with a frickin' feather in it. He turned, and I saw blood dripping down his arm. From Aric?. Where the hell *was* Aric?

The seat wobbled again. Crap!

I grabbed for the side of the stall, missed, started to keel forward. The guy swiveled around, gun at the ready, aimed at my head.

I caught myself, sprayed the pepper.

The guy was wearing glasses. He laughed as he pulled back the trigger of a huge revolver.

"Don't!"

Bam!

A patch of red blossomed on the guy's left temple, and brains and bone spewed from his right. His gun slid from his hand, and he crumpled to the floor.

The pepper spray fell to the floor as I reached for the stall door. I gripped it tight, but my legs shook. I was afraid to see who'd fired the gun.

I turned my head. "Aric!"

"I wondered where the hell you went." Arms crossed, hip jutting casually against the wall, he was the picture of the laconic Westerner.

"Oh, God." I held the stall door while I climbed down on wobbly legs. "I didn't know you had a gun."

"Lucky for us I did."

Lucky? I doubted luck had anything to do with it. I stuttered in a breath.

Aric put his arm around me. I leaned into him. It felt good. Solid. I needed solid at that moment.

"You okay?" he asked.

"Just *peachy*, Aric. Sure. We find a dead guy, and we get shot at. Who wouldn't be?"

He snorted. "Sarcasm is the refuge of the weak mind."

"Who said that one?"

He shrugged. "Hell, I don't know."

I chuckled. Hank always made me laugh, too. I missed him so much. "Are you okay? No bullet holes?"

"Not a one."

I leaned against the sink, poured some of the bottled water on a wipe, and brushed it across my face.

"Nice firearm." He pointed to my pepper spray.

"Speaking of sarcasm." I walked around the dead man, whose blood was pooling onto the wood floor. I made sure to keep my swollen hand hidden. The dead man looked like a pretend cowboy. He wore a soul patch, a day's growth of beard, and a tattoo of Lara Croft on his neck.

"Go sit down," Aric said.

"In a sec. This guy . . . there's something definitely off about him."

"That's an understatement," Aric said.

The guy's jeans were stonewashed and floppy-loose. I got a pen from Aric and used it to raise the bottom of the dead man's jeans. His cowboy boots were tall, with lightning bolts carved on them. The soles were barely worn.

"Pricey boots," I said. "You've got the gloves. See who made the shirt?"

"Who the fuck cares?"

"It matters. And stop playing clueless with me. I know you're just waiting until I leave the room to check him out. So don't bother."

Aric said nothing, but crouched down beside the dead man. "The shirt. Huh. Patagonia."

"I thought I recognized it. I gave one like it to my boyfriend for Christmas. Anything in the guy's pockets?"

He searched. "Odd. Nothing."

"Well, then we'd better get going. Someone dropped him off here, and they'll surely be back to retrieve him."

Dust billowed as we pulled away from the trading post. I kept looking over my shoulder, half expecting to be chased by a ghost. We'd left behind two dead men—a sad old one and one freshly shot. Coyote slept in the backseat. I wanted us to be safely away before I mentioned my hand, now throbbing like the dickens. Infection was never pretty. Maybe it was just a bone bruise. Coyote had gotten me but good.

Something about the dead man back there . . . I'd seen him before. But not out here. I shook my head. Maybe I was imagining it. I didn't remember anyone with a Lara Croft tattoo. Except . . .

I caught a flicker out of the corner of my eye. Far across the flat desert landscape, another vehicle billowed sand.

"See that?" I said. "Over to your right."

"Yeah. Five minutes ago."

"The driver's going to be in for one nasty surprise."

He hooked a right at a four-way. We were pointed toward distant mountains, the names of which I didn't know.

"Or," he said, "he's a pal of the dead guy, and he'll be hightailing it after us."

I couldn't keep my eyes open, even though the truck smelled of unwashed dog and sweaty human, yet when I closed my eyes, all I kept seeing was Mr. Soul Patch level his gun at my face.

That poor old man. A long life with an unhappy ending. I reached back and scratched Coyote with my good hand. He snorfled. Away from his master's remains, he was more benign.

The sun blazed my right cheek as I pressed it against the glass. Had to tell Aric about my hand. But I was beat.

A little snoozle. That would do it. "I'm gonna nap."

"Go ahead."

A symphony. In my head. No, wait . . . I blinked my eyes open. Still playing. Of course.

I reached into my pocket and pulled out the cell phone. An unknown number. I'd bet it was . . . "Hello?"

"Where the hell are you?"

Yup, Hank. God, I was glad. "New Mexico. On the way to Gallup. I've got—"

"Don't!" Aric grabbed the phone and threw it out the window.

"What the hell!"

"You can't," he said. "You can't tell anyone. No talking. No nothing."

"You knew I bought the phone in Gallup. What's your problem? My people back home are going to wonder. They're going to come looking for me. That was my boyfriend."

"When we get to Gallup, you can call from a pay phone. I don't trust anything."

"Do pay phones even exist anymore?"

"When you got poor Indians, they do."

"Nasty," I said. "If you weren't an Indian yourself, I'd think you were prejudiced."

"I am."

I sank back in the seat. Hank was having a fit right about then. At least he knew I was in New Mexico. "How long until Gallup?"

"Maybe forty minutes."

"Good. We need to take Coyote to the vet. Me, too."

"Is that some joke?" He flipped open a can of Red Bull and glugged.

"No. I'm not feeling so hot." My hand was swollen and black and blue and, unless I was mistaken, oozing puss. I held it up to show Aric, which made it throb even worse.

"Holy shit."

I stretched, and everything ached. I blinked a couple of times to get myself in gear. I was still in the Land Rover, but we'd stopped at a gas station. A more modern one than the trading post, with not anywhere near its charm. When Aric slid back into the driver's seat, he handed me a mug that said *Allsup's*.

"OJ," he said. "Drink up."

I swallowed, and my throat burned. "I'm not very thirsty. I think I might have a fever."

"Drink anyway."

I took a sip, and acid would have been smoother. I reached for the door. "I'm going to get some water and call Hank."

He jammed the truck into gear and took off.

"Dammit!" Even yelling hurt. My head spun, and I heaved twice, then puked on the floor. I could barely keep my eyes open.

"We're gonna take Coyote to a guy I know. You, too. No calls until then."

"Whatever you say." My hand—a giant sausage. "We'd better get there pretty soon."

I awoke in a dark place. That was becoming a habit. Not a good one. My mouth tasted like furry yuck, and my hand still throbbed. I groped with my good hand for a light, found nothing. I sat up, and the black world twirled.

"Damn." I took a couple breaths. "Aric?"

My good fingers crawled to my sausage hand, felt cotton or gauze. *Ouch.* Hmmm. Odd, but it felt different, maybe better?

What the hell was I thinking?

I had to get up, get out. I was way too dependent on Aric. I'd assumed he was a good guy. What if he wasn't? What if I'd been fooled all along?

Was I even thinking straight? Hell if I knew.

My feet found my shoes, and I slipped into them. I used the bed and managed to wobble to a standing position. I took a few breaths and somehow remained vertical. A good thing.

Maybe the killers had gotten to Aric. I'd be next.

I groped beside the bed and finally found the nightstand. Something rattled. Pills? Two bottles? Sure, maybe. I took them, slipped them into my skirt pocket. My wallet. Yes. Into the other pocket. That was all I needed.

I found the wall and began to fumble about for an exit. God, I felt lousy—stomach bouncy, head throbbing, hand achy. But I could do this. Had to. I wanted out of there.

When I reached what felt like a door, I pawed for the knob, turned it slowly, softly, cracked the door.

Dim, smoky light filtered in. Tiles on the floor. Maybe I was at the doctor's or the vet's. That's who'd bandaged my hand. I slipped outside the room, hugged the wall. I just wanted to get away. I needed to talk to Hank.

Voices, low and melodic, filtered in from somewhere. I peered around a corner. There was Aric, leaning against a counter, drink in hand, smiling at a sexy brown-haired woman. Across what I could see of the room—a kitchen, most likely—was a sofa. Coyote lay on it, his shoulder bound with what looked like a fresh bandage. Okay. Good. But the setting didn't feel right, and I sure didn't either.

The pills. I held the two bottles to the light. Percocet. No wonder I felt loopy. And amoxicillin. My hand—encased in a baseball mitt of gauze, definitely felt different.

Then why wasn't I trusting here? Just because.

I sidestepped to the right, opened another door. A laundry room, complete with stacked washer/dryer and steam press. I flipped the twist lock, walked across the laundry and out the door.

Great. Not.

The courtyard was lavish, with a pool and cabana and cacti and waterfall and a lovely iron gate that probably was locked. Now what?

I slid down the wall. Had to think. I'd been in worse places. Sure.

A car drove past the gate. Then another and another.

Except it was the *same* car, wasn't it? Driving back and forth. How bizarre.

I wanted to wave, jump up and down. Yeah, that wasn't going to happen.

Hell. What if I was trapped? Fear closed my throat and I shook, couldn't stop. I rested my head on my knees.

"Hey, girlfriend!"

Out, across the courtyard and through the gate . . . a hand, waving like mad, fingernails painted a frantic pink. What the . . .

"Hey! Get over here, you wicked woman!"

Someone calling to me. I must be hearing things.

"Hey you, girlie!"

I pushed against the wall, managed to stand and staggered over to the gate. The car that kept passing. Huh. Out poked a head. It was sheathed in a red scarf, from which a riot of red curls escaped.

I should know the person, shouldn't I? The face . . . ? Oh, I was really drugged but good. I pulled at the gate, which was locked tight.

"Help." My voice, a whisper. "Can you get me out of here?"

"Hang on," the redhead said.

A bang. I whirled around. Aric in a crouch, his 9mm aimed at the car.

CHAPTER SEVENTEEN

"No! Noooo!" I stumbled toward Aric, who shifted and again squeezed the trigger.

"Get in the house," he barked.

"Stop shooting!"

"Get inside," he said through clenched teeth.

"Not until you stop shooting."

His hand clamped around my upper arm, and he dragged me through the door. He released me, leaned back and closed his eyes.

"You, woman, are the biggest pain in the ass I ever met."

"Well, tough." I reached for the towel bar and hung on for dear life. I took a breath, then another. "What's going on here? Why am I being held prisoner?"

He swiped a hand across the back of his mouth. "Prisoner? C'mon, we've got to get going."

Stall. "We can't. I've got to go to a doctor."

"You have been. Your hand will be fine once the infection's gone."

"I'm not going anywhere."

He waved the gun like a cigar. "Yes, you are." He

gripped my arm again and pulled me through the laundry and down the hall toward the back door.

I struggled to get free, but I had no strength. "Dammit."

He tugged harder.

We neared the backdoor sliders when a crash stopped us. Aric turned, whipping me around. Down the hall the redhead was on one knee, gun drawn, aimed at Aric.

"Shit," Aric said. "I'll be back." He pushed me forward.

I tried to catch myself, staggered, and fell.

I looked behind me. Aric was gone, and I was in the hands of some crazed redhead with a gun.

On my hands and knees, I stared at the floor. I hadn't the energy to get up. I expected to be shot any second. Aric had just . . . left. How could he do that? I couldn't quite believe it.

A shadow above me. I didn't budge. Then hands reached beneath my arms and lifted me to my feet. Arms wrapped around me and pressed me close, where I fit perfectly beneath her chin. *Her* chin?

I knew that fit, had felt it a million times. "Hank? In drag? Why the hell are you dressed as a redhead? Oh, God, I'm so glad to see you. You shaved your mustache!"

The arms tightened, and I wrapped mine around him and squeezed tight.

He leaned down, kissed my head, my cheek. Oh, that felt great. Nothing had ever felt better.

"Tal," he said, his voice soft and caressing. "Hon. I'm glad you survived, because I'm going to kill you."

Not for the first time, I willed Hank to drive faster. I sat strapped into the seat of the rental car as we drove down a busy two-lane street near a golf course. Men and women were out swinging their irons on this chilly, blazing-blue day. My stomach flip-flopped, and it took all my energy not to ask him to speed up. I closed my eyes. Back home the skies would be lead gray, and the leaves would have turned party colors, and people would be bustling in their light coats, chilled by gusts off the Charles, yet refusing to give in to down parkas just yet, not this early in October.

The car stopped. We were in the parking lot of the Red Rock Animal Hospital.

"Be right back," Hank said. He slammed the door and marched into the vet's sans wig and fake boobs and makeup. He hadn't said a word on the way over. You'd think he'd be curious, but apparently he was just pissed.

I was glad to see him go, since he'd been taciturn and angry and altogether miserable to me. I trolled in my purse, but, no, my phone was gone. That's right. Aric had trashed it. A whimper from the backseat. I turned, and was surprised to see Coyote's nose peeking out of the blanket that covered him. How the heck had Hank gotten the dog? I couldn't imagine. Didn't want to, actually.

Coyote was dreaming his doggie dreams. He whimpered and thrashed his legs, perhaps in pursuit of some illusive rabbit. I always wondered what dogs dreamed. Were people featured? Or were they all-animal dreams? Were there pictures? Sounds? Smells?

Coyote whimpered again, and I thought he might be back with his master, Old Man. I knew Hank would never hurt a dog.

My brain wasn't working right. Why had Aric left me? He'd shot at Hank, but I believed he thought Hank was one of the bad guys. Why couldn't I think straight? I'd momentarily seen Aric as the enemy. He wasn't. I believed that. At least, I thought I did. Cripes. I wished nobody had given me the Percocet. Obviously that ship had sailed.

I flipped down the visor to look in the mirror.

Ohmigod! Medusa hair out of control, milk-white face, zombie-like lips. Scratches and bruises and ugly stitches on Izod man's cut.

I looked like an escapee from a Tim Burton movie.

Movement at the entrance to the vet's. A white-coated

man—tall and stick thin—walked beside my bear of a lover. I sighed. He was like a bear, that Hank, but funny, too. I realized I was thirsty and groped for water. No luck.

Odd. Hank and the stick man were talking, and the stick man cradled something in his hand. I wished I could see better. I pushed myself up. Crap. Everything ached.

Oh, good, they were coming to the car. Except they walked right past me, and opened the back door. Hank reached for Coyote, and the dog growled, and then Stick Man jabbed him with a needle before I could even react.

"What are you doing?" I said.

Coyote wuffled a sigh, and his head lolled on Hank's forearm.

"Did you kill him?" I said. "What did you do?"

"Stop barking, Tal," Hank said. "He's just asleep. He's fine. Fine."

"Oh. Okay."

The men talked in murmurs, voices low and deep. Then Hank lifted a limp Coyote out of the car and carried him into the vet's. I tried to follow, tugging at the door, finally getting it unlatched, pushing it open, which was really hard.

Had I ever ached so much? I staggered toward the entrance, and somehow I made it inside. Coyote was *my* responsibility, not Hank's.

"What are you doing?" I said.

A man with a Chihuahua on his lap stared at me, but no one said a word, not even the girl at the counter. Then her lips thinned, and her eyes grew wide. She looked frightened, which was really weird.

I took a seat and leaned to pet the Chihuahua. The man hugged his dog and inched away from me.

Boy, nobody was being very nice.

I was too pooped to say anything, and so I let my lids drop and I slid into sleep.

I see Aric, his head and back sheathed in a white buffalo robe with horns and a bonnet of feathers. His chest is naked but for jacklas of turquoise and orange spiny oyster shells that bounce as he dances. A weaving is wrapped from his waist to below his knees, met there by a circle of bells and soft moccasin boots. Brightly colored beaded bands surround his biceps, and turquoise and coral and silver adorn his wrists. He carries a lightning arrow, with points at each end, and a gourd that he rattles. He's dancing and singing to a rhythm that's more familiar than life. And I sway to the rhythm.

He smiles at me. He holds out his hand. I take it.

I join the dance, moving with that Zuni rhythm of the drums. It pours through me, and Aric smiles. And there's his auntie, smiling, too, and his grandma, teeth missing, but grinning.

Aric moves faster. I can't keep up. His legs pump up and down, pistons, and when he twirls, the white fur fans out, like liquid platinum. And now we're joined by Ben Bowannie and Natalie and Ben's aide, and we're all dancing, swirling, leaping to the rhythm that pulses faster, faster, faster.

A cold shadow creeps across my shoulder. Fingers of ice. I shudder with fear. Aric shakes his head, waves to me, but . . . oh, I want to move, but I can't.

"Come," Aric whispers.

The chill crawls across my back and down my arms and up the back of my head and down my spine. An undulating wave of fear.

"Come," Aric says. And he's twirling now, sweat beading, flying from his face, his chest.

And I hear him even though his lips aren't moving.

His face, close to mine, but lips unmoving. A halo of white fur. I reach out to touch it, the tips of my fingers almost feeling the softness, the warmth.

But the cold, like an evil lover's arms, wraps around me. I can barely move.

You must, Aric says. Chaco. Come. Come to Chaco.

I touch his face, warm as the sun from the dance.

Chaco.

And the cold envelops me.

I shuddered in a breath. Let my head fall to my chest. Blinked myself awake. I knew something important. I did. Aric was neither evil nor the enemy. I had betrayed him by not believing in him, when all he'd done was help me. How could I have been so foolish? Where was that sense I so relied on? Now he was gone. I had no way to get in touch with him or apologize or anything. His father and cousin were dead.

What had I been thinking?

"C'mon, Tally." Hank crouched in front of me. "We've got to go." He helped me stand. "You're in crummy shape."

"Am I?" *I have to get to Chaco.*

"I'm taking you to the hospital."

"I don't need to go to the hospital."

Hank's eyes, those wonderful caring eyes, wouldn't meet mine.

"What?" I said. "What is it?"

"Nothing, hon. Let's just go."

I pulled my arm from his hand. "Wait. What are you doing to Coyote?"

His lips thinned. "We've got to test the dog."

I leaned against the wall so I wouldn't fall on my ass. "Look, I may feel pretty woozy here, but I want to know what's going on. Now."

"You're about to pass out. C'mon." He moved forward.

I sat down, hard. "No. I'm not going anywhere. You are *not* my keeper."

His lips thinned. "You need one."

"Bite me." I stood, wobbled, sat again. "Miss?" I called to the receptionist. "I need to talk to the vet about my dog."

I squinted. She was looking at Hank, not me. I crossed my arms. "Fine. I feel so crappy, another hour or so won't make a difference. I'm not leaving til—"

"The vet," Hank said. "He's sending the dog to Albuquerque to be tested for some stuff."

"Oh, okay. Some blood tests?"

Hank's chest billowed out and in. He sat beside me.

I slid my hand through the crook of his arm. "Thanks, hon. I need to know. He's a good and faithful dog. What does the vet think is wrong with him? When will they know?"

"C'mon, Tal, you're not feeling well. We should go."

"*When* will they know what's wrong with him?" I repeated.

The receptionist whimpered, and I turned to her. Her eyes were saucers, her face pale, her lips wobbly.

"What?" I said to her. "What is it?"

"They cut—"

"Don't!" Hank shouted at her.

"Oh, yes, sorry," she said.

The man with the Chihuahua mumbled some Spanish words and ran out of the lobby clutching his dog.

"Goddammit, you tell me the truth, Hank Cunningham." I sounded drunk. But I folded my arms. I wasn't budging until he fessed up.

Hank sat back, threaded his hands together. He still wouldn't look at me. "The truth. Here it comes. That dog might have rabies. They have to cut off his head to learn whether he's rabid or not."

Hank lifted me by my upper arm and steered me toward the door. "Hospital."

I gathered what little strength I had left and dug in. "No."

"Yes." He tugged.

I sat.

"Tally, dammit."

"No one. *No one* is chopping off Coyote's head."

He peered down at me. "That's the only way. Period."

"You mean to tell me, there are no blood tests, no saliva tests, nothing else that can be done?"

He shook his head.

I whooshed out a breath, wrapped my arms around my bent knees. What could I do? Thinkthinkthink.

"Here's the deal," I said. "I believe Coyote is a good animal. I also think that he's probably been vaccinated for rabies. But I don't know and we can't find out." My head spun and my stomach flip-flopped. Hank was right. I needed a hospital. I rubbed my eyes, tried to focus.

"So here's my solution." I smiled up at him. "We'll have him boarded, keep him muzzled. And I'll get the rabies shots."

Hank rolled his eyes, walked away. He was ticked, for sure. He pulled me to my feet.

"We'll talk about it on the way to the hospital," he said.

I leaned against him. "Okay. But I'll never forgive you if you kill him."

"Whatever you say, Tal."

I let him haul me out of the vet's. I was too weak to fight.

After a flurry of the usual emergency room hooha, I found myself in a bed in some hospital in Gallup. All I wanted to do was sleep, except they kept fussing with my hand. "They" meaning the people behind the masks and wearing the latex gloves. It felt surreal.

They unwrapped my hand. I peeked, and saw it was swollen and angry and ugly. But someone else had done something to it that almost looked like packed dirt. They gently lifted the dirt off, and I couldn't help watching. You know, sort of like watching a train wreck or something equally horrible.

I flexed my fingers. Didn't hurt so much. Oddly, the hand wasn't nearly as swollen as I'd expected. Someone—Aric?—had given me some care.

They rinsed it off and washed it with Betadine and I grew sleepy, and then, bada-bing, a bunch of shots.

"I am not a pincushion!" I tried to shout. It came out a mumble.

"You sure look like one, honey."

And I fell asleep.

CHAPTER EIGHTEEN

I peered around the room. At least this awakening, the lights were on and noises penetrated my membrane of wooziness. Right—a hospital. I had a window bed, a little plastic canister of water beside me, and someone snoring in the next bed who was unavailable for viewing due to the starched curtain hanging between us.

"Hank?"

Nowhere to be found, I guessed.

I lifted my right hand, the bandaged one. Not bad. Oh, it throbbed, but not bad at all.

I wheeled the IV cart with me and peed. Then I pulled it to the closet, where I found not a single stitch of my clothing.

Hank knew me too well. I'd bet he took my clothes. Then again, given the last few days, maybe he'd burned them.

I sat back down on the bed. I wanted out of there. Veda's death had only worsened my loathing of hospitals.

My head throbbed a little, but I felt a thousand times better than when I'd entered the hospital. I buzzed the nurse, sat back, and waited.

A whirlwind varoomed in. "Yes? You buzzed?"

She wore her black hair in braids, bound to her head, and her face was gorgeous and exotic.

I smiled, tried to look pleasant. "Hi. I feel pretty good. I'd like you to help me shower, get dressed, and get out of here."

She smiled. "The detective said you'd say that. Since you're under arrest, I'm afraid that's not possible."

I again saw the man, dead, in the trading post, the one who'd tried to kill me. How had the authorities found out I'd been there? And did they think we'd killed the old man, too?

Except . . .

"This detective, um, what's his name?"

She blushed. "Lieutenant Cunningham."

That bastard was flirting with the nurse to keep me here. "Of course."

She turned, smiled. "Here's the doctor. He'll explain the shots and all."

"Shots?"

She disappeared and was replaced by a round, balding man of indeterminate age. "Hello, hello, hello."

A jolly one. Hell. "Hello, doctor."

"Call me Popie."

This was like a bad dream. "Of course, Dr. Popie."

"No." He chuckled. "Just Popie."

I forced my lips upward, into a smile. "Of course . . . Popie." I was going to kill Hank.

He read my chart. His jolly face became rigid with what sure looked like fear. He pulled a chair up beside me. But not too near. Oh, boy—this guy was terrified of me.

"I'd like to explain the shots, if I may."

"The rabies shots," I said. "Go right ahead, Popie." I reached out to touch him, and he jerked backward.

He cleared his throat. "As you may know, rabies is incurable once symptoms appear."

"Deadly. Yes, I know that." I leaned toward him and, in concert, he leaned backward. "Do go on."

"We've given you three vaccines. Immune globulin, a tetanus shot, and the first dose of rabies vaccine."

I nodded and pressed my left hand to my stomach. "It doesn't hurt."

"No. We don't do rabies shots in the stomach anymore. Your right arm will hurt, though."

I ran my fingers across my right upper arm. "You got that right, as Mainers would say. It aches." Rabies. Horrifying. Now I remembered. Coyote. Oh, geesh—I hoped they hadn't killed him. "What's next?"

"Tomorrow, and then in five days, then two weeks, then three, you'll get additional vaccinations using the rabies vaccine. Not so bad anymore."

Oh, no. I'd kissed Hank. Aric had touched me. "What about my friends? Those I've kissed or touched?"

His face folded into a grin, all except his eyes, which spelled fear. "They're fine. Fine. Rabies is almost never passed from human to human."

"What do you mean, 'almost'?"

He clutched the chart to his chest. "Known cases include corneal transplants and other organ transplants."

"You're kidding? You mean people have gotten transplanted organs from people who have rabies?"

He nodded. "I'm afraid so."

"That's horrible. Well, I haven't given anyone any of my body parts lately, so I guess all is well. I'm safe. They're safe." I smiled. "So what's with you? What are you so scared of, Popie?"

"Scared? Of course I'm not scared."

"I'm a shrink. I know these things."

He began to backpedal out of the room.

"Hold it!" I said, starting to feel a familiar exhaustion. "What are you so scared of?"

"Isn't it obvious? You've been cursed."

* * *

Later that afternoon, Hank paced back and forth, back and . . . the term "caged bear" came to mind. He scratched his upper lip, where his mustache had grown for so long. I could tell he missed it. I missed it, too. He looked odd.

Every few seconds, he'd shoot me an annoyed stare while I continued to put on the clothes he'd bought for me.

"I feel like a kept woman in these clothes. First Aric, now you."

He seemed ready to explode out of the denim shirt he wore. He wanted to holler at me, I could tell. Except he wouldn't do that, especially not in a hospital. I kissed his cheek.

"I don't like anything about this, Tally," he said.

I kissed his cheek again.

"There are things you've conveniently left out of your tale."

I shrugged as I zipped up the boot-cut jeans. It would have been easier to spray them on. "I don't want to talk here."

"I've booked us a flight from Albuquerque."

I slipped into the white shirt with pearl snaps. "You can't run my life."

"You made that clear a year ago. Yup, ya did."

As I reached for the socks, I turned away. I needed some privacy. I'd hurt him badly with my feelings for Kranak. I'd like to relent, go back home, be with Penny, cozy up with Hank by the fire. Snuggle. Make love. Talk.

Except when I closed my eyes I saw Delphine's face and dear Didi floating in a pool of her own blood.

"Your pal Kranak is the CSS on Didi Cravitz's murder," he said. "I can't stand that guy."

"So what if he's my pal. He's just a friend. I thought we got that straight. And, yeah, Kranak's good." I sat on the bed and tugged on a sock and a left cowboy boot. "Really good. But it's all about out here, not back there."

"Delphine's disappearance is being looked into, too," he said.

"She's dead." I tugged on the other boot, stood, looked over my shoulder at his sweet face. "They feel good, Hank. Thanks. I always liked cowboy boots."

He grinned. "I know. I got you a pair of Merrells, too."

"Cool. And a room in town?"

"Just for tonight."

"I get another shot tomorrow."

"And then we leave for Boston." He pulled me close, kissed me hard and long. I rested my head beneath his chin.

The good-byes would be harder than most.

I couldn't say I was feeling a hundred percent, and maybe I was hallucinating, but as Hank drove us down Route 66 in the heart of Gallup, I was sure I'd stepped into an old movie, one made just for a girl who'd grown up loving anything Western.

"What a trip," I said.

He nodded. "Not Maine. Nope suh."

"Route Sixty-six! If this wasn't all so awful, I'd love being here. It's so cool."

"Ayuh, that it is. I should have rented us a Corvette."

I laughed, and then I remembered. "Uh, oh. Where's Coyote?"

"In quarantine with the vet for six months. You really impressed those people with your love for that mangy dog."

I snuggled next to him. "You're full of it. He's not mangy. You liked him too. He's a good dog. He only reacted when I tried to put the muzzle on him. Where are we headed?"

"Surprise."

I took in the sights of auto sales and gas stations and a million neoned hotels—Best Western and Travelodge and Days Inn and Comfort Inn and Red Roof Inn—all shouting *Stay Here!*

Hank slowed, and before us stood a huge neon sign proclaiming EL RANCHO HOTEL & MOTEL. HOME OF THE MOVIE STARS. ARMAND ORTEGA'S WORLD FAMOUS INDIAN STORE.

"Wow," I said.

He pulled into the parking lot out front. For all its proclamations, the place looked like a two-story motel. "Home of the movie stars?"

He nodded. "I had a lot of time to read while you were busy being sick."

"I'm sure." I tried to keep the sarcasm out of my voice and failed.

"Look, you were in the hospital for twenty-four hours. It's getting to be a thing with you. Aside from getting you some clothes, what was I supposed to do?"

"I don't know," I said. "Go out on the town?"

He tweaked my breast, which felt awfully good. I swatted his hand away. "Behave."

We left the car, and he wrapped his arm around my waist. "About El Rancho. It was built by the brother of D.W. Griffith."

"The famous movie director? Huh. I didn't even know Griffith had a brother. So there ya go."

Inside, I stood in the immense lobby and was amazed. "Well, it certainly is an improvement over the outside."

The two-story open lobby was what I'd call Old West rustic. Or maybe Old Movie rustic. A huge double staircase on either side curled up to the second floor, and dark wood and light fixtures that I'd swear were old-time stamped aluminum. The twin staircases surrounded an immense stone fireplace that blazed away. The place was full of Navajo rugs, which I loved, and deer, elk, and antelope trophy heads, which I definitely didn't. The floor was brick and just about every wall was plastered with photos of movie stars from a bygone era.

While Hank checked us in, I walked over to a Spencer

Tracy photo signed by the man himself. They were all signed, and pretty amazing. Katharine Hepburn and Jackie Cooper and Ronald Reagan and Alan Ladd. Joel McCrea and Errol Flynn and Troy Donahue and Suzanne Pleshette and more.

"This sure is something," I said as Hank led us up the curving staircase. Our room was far less interesting and certainly the most conventional place I'd stayed at since arriving in New Mexico. There was something to be said for that. We even had a balcony that overlooked the courtyard pool. "I say it again—wow."

"Let's eat."

I was starved, but hesitant. I looked at him. He was un-packing, making everything neat. He seemed normal, but he wasn't. He knew something, and he was also furious. His explosions were too calm and quiet. I hated them.

I wanted to bolt. Instead, I ate a huge lunch, just like a girl who was having her last meal on the planet.

Hank stood facing the balcony. "Are you ready to tell me what you aren't telling me yet?"

I pressed my hands to the back of my neck. I wanted Hank to know *everything*. Not only was he my lover, but he was also a damned fine homicide detective.

I bowed my head. If I told him, he'd force me to return to Boston.

The hunt was more than about Delphine, or even Didi now, or Governor Bowannie. It was about a gun-shot old man, a murdered Zuni girl, and an attack by an anony-mous killer who'd ended up dead. Whatever these people wanted, they didn't care how they got it.

Hank cracked the slider, and a soft breeze played through the door. I walked up behind him and wrapped my arms around his chest. I pressed myself to his back and hugged him.

"Love me," I whispered. Just saying the words made me

wet. "Now. Please." Up on tiptoe, I kissed the back of his neck. My hand moved from his chest to his groin, and I massaged his hardness. It felt fine.

He tipped his head back and groaned. I pressed him tighter, moved my hand faster.

He flipped around, held me at arm's length. "Jeeze, Tal."

"Hank."

"You're doing this on purpose."

"Of course I am. But it's real. You know that."

He chuckled. "Ayuh, I do."

I sighed when his fingers found my crotch, and he moved them back and forth.

"You're a devil," I said.

He lifted me, and I wrapped my legs around him. "God, you feel good."

We fell onto the bed, and I couldn't stand the clothes between us. I tugged at his chinos while he ripped open the snaps on my shirt. We were naked in an instant, and I guided him inside me, held him tight for a moment.

"Don't move," I said. "Wait." I was breathless, panting, and I licked his chest, relishing the salty taste of him.

He suckled my breast, and I inhaled slowly, felt the pops of sensation across my nipples where he sucked and pinched and massaged.

"Can't wait anymore, babe." He moved, slowly, deeply, and I did too. Our dance lasted until his fingers touched me once and the pleasure arched my back, and I thrust against him one . . . more . . . time.

"Me too," he gasped.

And we both spun higher than kites in the wind.

Six A.M. I checked Hank's watch, which I now wore on my wrist. Yes. I was used to the time change—two hours earlier than Boston. Hank, normally an early riser, was not.

I'd showered last night, packed, so he thought I was preparing for the trip back East.

I slid out of bed, watched as that dear man's chest rose and fell.

I looked down at him. I couldn't even brush his lips good-bye. His police officer instincts would awaken, and I'd be sunk. It was so hard not to touch him.

I love you, I mouthed.

I turned. So hard.

A hand shot out and captured my wrist.

"You didn't really think . . ." Hank said.

I was still turned away. I couldn't look at him. "I've got to go, Hank."

"My *ass!*"

Several things happened at once. I broke free of Hank's grasp, stumbled backward, Hank flung off the covers, and the glass in the sliders shattered.

Hank flew out of bed and on top of me.

"You're smothering me, dammit!"

He rolled off me and crawled, flat-bellied, toward the nightstand.

Another shot.

On hands and knees, I backpedaled to the bathroom, making sure I still had Hank in view. "What the hell is going on?" I said.

"You're the one who should know." He inched open the drawer and pulled out his Sig. "Get the fuck down."

"I am down."

"I can see you."

"And I can see you. All of you."

He snorted. He crept back to the bed, raised his gun, and aimed for the window. The shot boomed. "That should keep him busy for a sec. Ayuh."

"Sure should," I said.

He fired again. "Tally Whyte, what the hell have you gotten into down here?"

I inched to the door, reached for the knob. I felt like a traitor.

"Throw me the boxers that are in the bathroom."

Oh, dear. It was now or never. Still on my hands and knees, I flung the door open and crawled outside hauling my backpack. "I love you, Hank."

"Goddammit, get back here!"

"Don't worry, hon. I'll call the cops."

I fled.

I stopped at the desk and told them someone was shooting at us, then hightailed it out of there. I took a cab to the hospital, and although they hassled me that I was early, I got my rabies shot almost immediately. The nurse also changed the bandage on my hand, which was looking much better.

I kept watching the door, hoping I wouldn't see Hank barreling through it. I didn't, and I made it out of the hospital before Hank arrived.

I raced out to my waiting cab, hopped in, and we were off.

I had four days before my next rabies shot. It didn't seem like much, but it would be enough time for me to find Aric.

CHAPTER NINETEEN

Cars whizzed by as I slid back into the cab. I could rent a car at the airport, but first I needed a phone. Off we went to Gallup's Radio Shack, and I bought one of those prepaid phones, a best bet to keep Hank away just long enough for me to find Aric. I bought a map, too. I was sure I knew where Aric was headed—Chaco Canyon, sacred site and homeland of the Old Ones, the Ancient Ones, the Anasazi. My dream of Aric in the white buffalo robe had been more than that. I believed it.

The Peabody's broken pot was from Chaco.

The skull—Chaco. Or so it would seem.

Chaco Canyon had to be my destination. Aric was going to go alone, and I couldn't have that. It was my fight as much as his.

The taxi dumped me at the small Gallup airport. I knew what I had to do, but before I rented a car, I sat on a bench, where the wind whipped my hair and face, and I unfolded the map.

It looked like I had about fifty miles to travel. I had to take I-40 to Thoreau, which was sure an interesting name for a town in New Mexico. I walked to the counter and explained I was headed to Albuquerque, but I wanted four-wheel drive. I paid for the Ford rental with a credit card—Aric said I shouldn't, but I had no choice—and pressed the pedal to the metal.

I-40 was a pretty highway that wound through New Mexico's high desert. I was headed east, just as if I were going to Albuquerque. The land was scrubby and dry, with blue skies overhead and air that was crystal. I traveled through the Fort Wingate Military Reservation, whatever that was, and saw signs for small towns and the continental divide. It was so different from Zuni and yet the same. I felt more at home here in the wilderness than I did in any city.

I sighed. I was alone. I was scared. Something deep in my belly told me I was still in grave danger. I could have had Hank with me. He might have come. Except he had fought me each step of the way. I didn't want that.

Somebody had once said that fear put all our senses on alert. I hoped that was true in my case.

I saw piñon pine and juniper trees, sagebrush, tumbleweeds, and some short, sparse grasses whose names I didn't know. The day was warm, nearly sixty. But the night would be cool, even cooler than back home. I needed to find a place to stay. I hoped that would be in Thoreau or Crownpoint, or another town I'd pass through on the Navajo reservation before reaching the vast expanse that was Chaco.

I approached Thoreau in less than a half hour. I was zoomin'. Beautiful red mesas lined the way and up ahead, a silver water tower.

Why had I thought Aric was the enemy? Made no sense. He wasn't abandoning me or hurting me. He was trying to protect me, just like his father had. He believed in the evil that was out there, disturbing the atmosphere, the evil that had killed Delphine and stolen the Old Ones pots and left Didi swimming in blood.

I should let him handle it. He was more suited.

Except he'd said I was a part of it.

I shook my head.

Up ahead, Thoreau.

Oh.

An abandoned motel, some buildings, several schools. Not much of a town. I slowed. I didn't even see a gas station. There was a Navajo Nation Chapter House that looked beautifully built and well maintained. Churches. And a rather lovely mission called St. Bonaventure. But not a welcoming tourist mecca, for sure. I didn't see zip in the way of accommodations.

Over on the side of the road, a sign read GO HAWKS! in green and gold letters. I smiled. Some things are a constant.

I checked Hank's watch. Not late. Only around eleven. What to do? Hell, there had to be someplace to stay in Crownpoint.

I took the left off I-40 onto NM-371 and away to Crownpoint I went.

More dust, more scrub brush, and a severe beauty I found inspiring. I checked my gas gauge. Plenty. The road grew hilly, and some small trees dotted the landscape.

Another half hour—not bad—and I arrived in Crownpoint. I looked around at the small, flat town, which was certainly larger than Thoreau. But poor, at least in dollar terms. I was aware that the Navajo in this part of New Mexico were poor, but I hadn't realized how poor. Again, in dollars, which was very much a white man's perspective.

A man in a checked shirt and blue bandana walked down the main drag. I pulled over. "Hello. Is there a supermarket or gas station in town?"

He nodded. "Yup. We got real modern stuff, lady." He smiled as if it were some inside joke.

I smiled back and said, "Super." I thanked him and drove to Bashas' Supermarket. Sand and dust gusted around the truck as I parked next to a Chevy pickup at

Bashas', which sat at the crossroads of 9 and 57. A good spot, looked to me.

The market was well stocked and clean and had a good feel. I ordered a sandwich at the deli, used the women's room, and bought an ice chest, some water, juice, and Diet Coke, as well as crackers, almonds, yogurt, and V-8. I picked up a flashlight, some white socks, a *New Mexico Magazine*, the Gallup paper and four Hershey bars with almonds. I retrieved my turkey sandwich, filled the cooler with bagged ice, and asked the checkout girl where I could stay in Crownpoint.

She shook her head. "Sorry. No place."

"None?"

"Nope," she said. She rang up my purchases.

"Any thoughts on where I *can* stay?" I asked.

She shrugged. "Grants?"

"How far is that?"

She wagged her hand, smiled. "Maybe an hour. Maybe a little more. Depends."

"On how I drive. Right. I'm headed to Chaco. Anything else?"

"Farmington. Up north. Should I put this stuff in the cooler?"

"Sure. Let's." No one lined up behind me, so she and I arranged all the groceries I'd bought in the cooler. "How far is Farmington?"

"Pretty far. Like, almost three hours. Yeah." She nodded.

My watch now read noon. "How far is Chaco Canyon?"

She shrugged. "I've never been there."

Before Bashas' I'd passed a gas station. I'd try there and see how I did.

I filled up the Ford with regular. The guy at the station suggested Grants, too. Grants it was, which I found incredibly frustrating. I was going in the opposite direction from Chaco.

On the way back to Thoreau, I checked out my spiffy new cell phone. I had service. Cool.

While I drove back the way I'd just come, I downed my turkey sandwich. I also got an itch, as if . . . I looked in my rear-view mirror. Nothing. The road was empty.

No one knew I was here or where I was going. Maybe Hank could find me. I doubted anyone else could. I'd covered my tracks well enough.

When I got to the four-way in Thoreau, I decided to check one more thing. I drove to the St. Bonaventure Indian Mission and School. Inside, I found a nun. I realized it had been years since I'd seen a real nun.

"Sister." I almost curtsied, even though I'd never been Catholic. "I'm looking for a place to spend the night. Someone suggested Grants, but it's pretty far out of my way."

She folded her hands. "What's a pretty girl like you driving around New Mexico alone for?"

I grinned. "Sightseeing."

Her eyes narrowed. They were gray and soft, with gray brows above them. I felt instantly guilty. I'd just lied to a nun!

She smiled. "Well, I guess it depends on the lodging you're looking for. We have a film crew tenting just a few miles east of here."

I held up my hands. "No tents, Sister!"

She chuckled. "Not for me, either. Most folks do go to Grants, but you look like a Navajo Pine Lodge girl to me."

"I bet I am," I said.

"It's lovely. Off the beaten track. Very pleasant."

"Perfect."

She led me to the front door and pointed. "Right about thirteen miles from here down Route 612. Very close, really."

"Thank you." I turned to leave.

"You're not in trouble, are you, miss?"

I turned back to the sister. "I might be. Believe me, Sister, I have done nothing wrong."

She tapped her finger to her lips. "Do be careful."

"Yes. Um, I do have a question." I asked her about Delphine—if she knew her as an art dealer. If she'd seen her.

"No. I'd remember a beautiful Frenchwoman." She moved closer and placed her hand on my arm. She was so short, she had to look up at me. "There would be more people in Grants who might know your friend. We're a poor area with not much to offer."

"I wouldn't say that." I kissed her cheek. "Thank you."

I called ahead, and the Lodge's owner, Tom McGuire, said that he had a room for me, but no one might be around, and so I should make myself at home. He even gave me a room—Number Three. He'd leave it unlocked.

It sounded like heaven. It was after two P.M. when I pulled into the Navajo Pine Lodge. Driving just those few short miles, the topography had become mountainous. Much like Taos, in fact, with lovely vistas and trees and even the sight of a lake.

The lodge was simple, yet comfy, as if you were stopping at an old friend's home. I loved it on sight. I dumped what little stuff I had in my room and went exploring. The front room—I called it the living room—had a fireplace and three cozy chairs and a card table all set to go for a hot game of Spite and Malice. The TV was on, but no was seemed to be around.

"Hello?" I said. Nothing.

I was tempted to watch some tube, but I kept on down the narrow hall. Midway on my right was a powder room, with all the necessary plumbing. On my left I found a small tidy room with another fireplace, sofa, furry rug, and shelves of books. Perfect.

There was no one in that room, either, but within a few

minutes of looking, I discovered the book I was searching for. I found two, actually.

In the middle of the oak shelf sat two books on Chaco Canyon. I pulled them out and sat on couch. Bliss. The first book was for kids, which was fine by me, by authors Vivian and Anderson. It looked wonderful, but I put it aside. The second, *Chaco, a Cultural Legacy*, with its magnificent door on the cover, insisted I read it first. I got a chill when I looked closer at the cover. There, in a photo, was a frog fetish carved in some black stone, maybe jet, and inlaid with turquoise squares across its back. I had its replica at home on my mantel. Frogs were important fetishes in Zuni because of the need for rain. Made perfect sense. I hadn't realized my frog was a replica of one found in Chaco Canyon.

I opened the book by Strutin and Huey. The first spectacular spread was of a place called Chetro Ketl. Hard not to be awed by the structures built in such a harsh climate so very long ago. I began to read and learned about great houses and kivas—rooms used by Pueblo Indians for religious rituals—and roads thirty feet wide. The pottery, so abundant, with its geometric and iconic designs, rippled down through time to the Hopi and Acoma and Santa Clara and other modern American Indian tribes.

Here was a six-toed foot and there sandstone cliffs and timbers as wide as a man. The contemporary photos were spectacular, but it was the old ones from the early discoveries that made my pulse quicken. For just an instant, I felt I was a time traveler and discoverer of magic.

And then I saw it—my first glimpse of Pueblo Bonito. The giant D-shaped building contained rooms upon rooms upon rooms, some circles, others squares, in some strange order yet to be deciphered. Snugged up against the north wall of Chaco Canyon, Bonito looked like something aliens had built for a king. I tried to picture it in its heyday and for a minute I forgot why I was out there and all the lives that had been lost in the process.

The book was a fast read, and I raced through words and images knowing I hadn't much time. And as I read, I felt the pull of Chaco and an odd familiarity, as if I'd walked the roads and bent beneath the T-doors years earlier. Grasses grew throughout Chaco, and in spring I assumed wildflowers blossomed among the rocks, for most of Chaco was rock and masonry and light.

The Chaco petroglyphs fascinated me, as did all petroglyphs. They were classic spirals and stars, hands and people, animals and symbols of harvest and corn and, most especially, Kokopelli, the wizard and trickster and flute player extraordinaire. At least that's how we Anglos saw him. I should ask Aric.

I bit my lip. Where was he? Was he all right?

My Coyote-bitten hand throbbed with memory. And the future. The oddest thing about Chaco was how I knew it was pulling us all forward to some destination I could feel but not see.

I read on until my eyes grew heavy. Then I slipped upstairs to Room Three and crashed on the bed.

I awakened disoriented and woozy. Out the window, the sky had faded to a softer shade of blue. I checked my watch. I'd been asleep for two hours. It didn't feel like it.

I showered, lathering my bumps and bruises, while trying to keep my bitten hand dry with the shower cap, a fairly annoying process. I toweled off, rubbed a second towel through my hair. I felt almost human again. Boy, I'd needed that.

I tugged on my jeans and a baggy white shirt from my limited wardrobe. Didn't matter. I was clean and not running from someone or something. I flipped open the cell phone. Huh. I sure didn't have much reception here, but it might be just enough. . . . I called Aric's cell phone, the number he'd given me days earlier. It went straight to a mechanical voicemail. Now what?

I looked around the room for a phone book. No luck. I needed to get some numbers in Zuni. I slipped on the Merrells Hank had bought me and trotted downstairs.

A blond teenaged girl in an apron appeared in the hall. I introduced myself.

She rolled her eyes and blew a pink bubble, reminding me of Gert. A wince of pain. The girl's cute face pruned up. "Par for the course. Pops is out somewhere."

"Tom, the owner, you mean?"

"Nope. My pop's Niall, the manager. I'm making dinner. Gotta get back to it." She pivoted and fled.

"But . . ."

She didn't even look back. Ha! Teenagers, gotta love 'em. So where was the lodge's phone book? I walked into the living room. My steps slowed. I couldn't quite believe what I was seeing.

Slowly, carefully, I walked closer. A pot sat on a large shelf beside the fireplace. The pot was a duplicate of the one broken at the Peabody Museum in Salem. It looked just like Didi's sketch and was sized the same.

My breath caught in my throat. Was it possible? It couldn't be a coincidence.

I was mesmerized as I walked toward the pot. I needed a close-up view. I needed to see *inside* the pot.

Halfway across the room, a chorus of voices froze me to the purple shag carpet. I swung around. A clutch of middle-aged-to-older folks looking amazingly fit entered the lodge, all chattering away. So much for privacy. They streamed past me, cheeks flushed, doffing coats and gloves, and beelining it for the tea and scones provided by the lodge. Enthusiasm grew as one tall balding fellow opened a cabinet and began pulling out bottles of red and white wine, Seagram's, Old Granddad, and a host of other liquors.

The noise level escalated. A petite woman turned to me and opened her mouth.

I smiled and walked backward out of there but fast.

CHAPTER TWENTY

Out back, I caught my breath. I wasn't comfortable being around all those people. They made me nervous. I didn't know why. Maybe I just needed some peace and quiet to think, not a bunch of folks out jiving it up in the New Mexico wilderness.

The late afternoon breeze felt good on my face. I walked down a path soft with pine needles and paused to look over the hill at the lake below. What a view! The lake's crystalline beauty enthralled me—so still and quiet and deep. No ripples. Smooth and soft.

Sadly, it provided no answers about who had killed my friends or Aric's location or any of the things foremost in my mind.

Reality called. I headed back up the path.

Really, things were in a pickle.

I had no clue where Aric was. Didn't know what Hank was doing. Or who'd shot those bullets into our hotel room. I might have gotten rabies from Coyote. Natalie was dead. If I continued my litany, I might as well just shoot myself. Things were grim, and, worse, I saw no end on the horizon.

So what the hell was going on?

I rubbed my hands up and down my arms to stop the chill that crept into my bones.

Why was that skull so important? At least three lives had already been lost. I couldn't make sense of it. I walked onward. Minutes later, something just off the path caught my eye.

I walked over to the path's edge. Before me lay acres of pine. I hesitated, then left the path. There, beneath a fallen pine bow, something shined white. I crouched down, and with a stick I pushed some of the earth and needles away.

A shed antler. A small one, from a young deer. Lovely. Nature was incomparable. Beside it sat a rock shaped like a faceted heart in the colors of red and ochre and green. It glittered in the blue-sky day. The rock just fit my hand, and its sharp edges dug into my palm. It was worth taking. Its beauty reminded me of the Southwest. I slid the rock into my jacket pocket and the small antler into the opposite one. Treasures. My favorite kind. I stood, turned, and slammed into a burly oldster smelling of booze and sweat.

"Pardon me." I went to sidestep around him.

He smiled and matched my step.

I wasn't amused. "Don't," I said. "It's annoying."

He laughed, and his hands slid onto my upper arms. He squeezed, and pulled me toward him.

I pushed. And instantly knew he was no oldster, but some guy made up to look geriatric. I looked toward the lodge. I'd walked farther than I'd realized. "What's your problem?"

"Now?" he said. "None. You're coming with me."

He had that flat, Minnesota-Scandinavian accent, and a vision of *Fargo* and the wood chipper bounced into my head. "My ass I'm coming with you."

"The baby in my pocket says you are."

"Screw the baby."

He jerked his head back. "Do I look stupid?"

What a great opening. He still held my upper arms tight enough so that I had little mobility. I could knee him, but I wasn't close enough. "Sad to say, yes."

He threatened to backhand me across the face. "Bitch."

I bent my head, tried to reach his hand and bite it. No luck. *Dammit.*

He laughed.

"Screw you," I said.

"You'll get your chance."

"In your dreams." I squirmed to get away, and he laughed harder. He stood there like a chunk of petrified wood until I exhausted myself. That was when I recognized him. He was the fake cop who'd come to pick me up in Zuni. Then he'd been wearing a hat and a uniform and a mustache.

He began to drag me down the path, away from the lodge. I squirmed some more, but I had trouble finding purchase. I tried to swing my leg around to kick him in the balls. All I did was fall flat on my back. He hauled me back up again and dragged me forward.

"Don't fuckin' do that again," he said.

"Or what, you're going to kill me? Looks like you have that in mind anyway."

"You don't know shit, lady."

"I know you're an asshole."

He backhanded me. My neck snapped, and for a moment I was stunned as blood filled my mouth. Bastard. I spit at him. Bull's-eye, right on his shirt.

He raised the back of his hand again.

Painful as it was, I smiled. "Go for it, asshole."

His hand squeezed into a fist he raised high in the air.

I felt myself cringe, forced my body to relax. "Like I said . . ."

He punched me in the face.

My ears rang, and dizziness nauseated me. I twirled, stumbled, and became a bouncing boomerang from his hold on my wrist. I spit blood, then more, then began to heave.

The world slowly stopped spinning and my panting sounded loud in my ears. The guy would kill me or turn me over to people who would. "Why?" I mumbled. Already my face had started to swell.

He pulled me to my feet, and we walked forward, and that's when I realized he'd released his death grip on my upper arms. My head pounded with each step, and my vision blurred.

Yeah, he'd kill me. I slid my free hand into my jacket pocket as we bumbled along the trail. I grabbed the heart-shaped rock. My right hand. Not my best or strongest.

If I went for it and messed up, I'd be in for a beating. I'd never been punched in the face before. I shook. That fist pounding into my face had been shocking. It was fast and furious and painful.

I tightened my hand on the rock. *Okay. Here goes.*

I faked a stumble, fell to my knees. Pissed him off, as I knew it would, and he began yelling at me. I slid the rock out of my pocket.

"You stupid bitch." He leaned down, his splayed fingers with their black, broken nails, reached to pull me up. "We're gonna fuckin' use you up."

I whammed him in the face with the rock. That feeling sickened me, but I made sure I followed through on the swing.

"Fuck!" His hand went to his face, and blood gushed between his fingers as he stumbled backward.

Just as he righted himself, I leapt up, pivoted, and slammed the rock into his temple, which was softer and even more horrible. He staggered. Blood streamed down the right side of his face into his stubbled jaw. He blinked over and over. He growled, a mixture of pain and fury.

I ran, clutching the rock, not letting go, out of the

woods to the path and up the hillside. I slipped on pine needles, stumbled onto my knees. I stretched out my arms to catch myself, but I couldn't. I landed on soft earth and hard rock.

Pain shot into my knees and elbows, and my eyes watered. Fuzzy vision, woozy. *Shit.*

I pushed myself up just as I heard him, close, behind me, there, breathing, panting. Closer.

I lurched to my feet, and something brushed my long curly hair. I bolted, stumbled, caught a branch to steady myself, and ran on.

"Fuck!" came from behind. "Arrhhhh." A crash, rolling.

I looked back, and he'd fallen, was rolling, and I almost went to help him. I shook my head. No way.

I ran uphill toward the lodge. "Help! Help!"

"What!" came the voice up ahead.

"I'm being attacked!"

"Coming!"

On the crest. There. A middle-aged man and several oldsters, branches in raised hands. I laughed, and just then . . .

My feet flew out from under me, the rock bounced away, and my head snapped back from the tug on my hair.

A hairy fist shot toward me, but stopped midair with the boom of a gunshot.

I tumbled backward—still attached to my pursuer, who rolled over and over down the hill.

I reached for roots, branches, anything to hold on to that would stop us. Nothing worked.

"Let go!" I shrieked.

Faster and faster, and dirt and needles billowed around me. I had to stop us. I flailed my arms, dug in my feet, except nothing worked. In my ears, screams and hollers and shrieks.

I forced my legs apart, and on my belly, pretended I could run uphill. I pedaled my legs, digging my feet into the slippery, pine-needled soil as I swam the breast stroke, all trying to stop our roll, but it wasn't helping, not at all, but . . .

Yes! I grabbed the hard thing, tucked my arms around a huge surface root. Cuddled. Again my neck snapped. Couldn't let go, couldn't, couldn't. The pressure on my scalp. I was being pulled and pulled and . . . Holdon-holdonholdon.

A sob burst from my mouth. I was so scared. "Damn you!" I screamed over and over and over.

Pebbles streaming around me, then feet, then a sudden glorious easing of the pressure. I flattened to the earth, let it cradle my cheek. Struggled for a breath without tears.

"Am I free?" I finally said.

"Yes," someone said. An arm wrapped around my waist and lifted me to my feet.

I leaned against the middle-aged man, just one of my clutch of rescuers.

"Welcome to Navajo Pine Lodge," he said. "I'm Niall, the manager."

I chuckled. "Thanks. So much." Atop the hill, Niall's daughter gave me the thumbs-up, and I gave it back. As I relaxed, I sensed a recession of adrenaline, replaced by the sting of scrapes that went from the top of my head down to my ankles.

Soft murmurings that I couldn't hear as Niall helped me up the hill toward the lodge. I looked behind me, and my legs grew rubbery when I saw the precipice that would have launched me into space just a few yards away.

"Ohmigod."

"You can say that again," said an oldster.

"I definitely need a good shot of bourbon," I said.

"Coming right up."

We stumbled onward, Niall half-dragging me up the hill. "Will you be able to get him back to the lodge?" I asked.

"We'll wait for the sheriff's deputies. They'll be coming from Grants."

"But . . ."

"He's dead, Ms. Whyte," Niall said. "He won't care one way or the other."

CHAPTER TWENTY-ONE

I took a long, steamy bath, complete with soothing aro-
matherapy oils and three fingers of bourbon on the rocks,
courtesy of Niall. It helped all of me, even the throb in my
jaw where the guy had punched me. It took almost two
hours, but I finally felt clean. My shaky legs managed to
get me out of the claw-foot tub, whereupon I melted to
the plush bath rug laid on the floor.

The tub drained with slurps and sloshes, and I rested my
cheek on the roll-tub edge and closed my eyes. I was alive.
I. Was. Alive.

I yipped at a knock on the door.

"You okay in there, Ms. Whyte?"

"Oh, uh. Yes. I guess I fell asleep." I was freezing, too,
sprawled on the bathroom floor, half on, half off the matt.
My God, I was a mess.

"Good bourbon'll do that."

"You're so right. I'll be out in a sec." I hoisted myself up.
At the sink, after I got over the sight of my black-and-blue
and swollen face, I began smearing on the antibacterial

cream Niall had left for me. At least now I could get a good look at that pot on the mantel.

"Someone's here to see you," he called through the door.

My heart stuttered. Maybe Hank. That would be wonderful. I was an idiot to leave him. "Who's that?"

"The deputy sheriff."

I peered down the stairs at the leathery woman who stood waiting in the front hall, thumbs hooked to her Sam Browne belt, one cowboy-booted foot tapping.

"Hello," I said as I walked down the stairs.

She didn't smile, but gestured me into the small library at the back of the lodge.

She wore a brown pant suit over her boots, which were polished, but well-used. She'd traveled a lot of miles, I suspected. She'd bitten her nails to the quick. She'd tied her straight brown hair in a ponytail, but her bangs softened her face. She didn't look like someone who smiled easily.

The minute I sat across from her, she pulled a small silver recorder from her pocket, pressed it on, and sat it on the table. The officer noted the date and the time. Niall sat across from us in a chair, but she shooed him away.

"I'm done with you, friend," she said.

"C'mon, Louise," Niall said.

She shook her head. "No. I want to talk to this lady alone. Now go."

"Be careful," he said to me as he left. "She looks all warm and fuzzy. She's not."

I didn't think Louise looked warm and fuzzy in the least.

"You're a problem," Louise said. "One I wish I hadn't encountered."

"Okay," I said. I had no idea what to make of her words.

"There's a BOLO out for you."

"Why should the cops be on the lookout for me?" I shrugged. "I haven't done anything wrong."

"We got a guy in the backyard here dead."

Now was exactly the time I wished I still smoked. "He tried to kill me."

"So you say."

I sat up straighter and winced. "Yes, I do say. Just ask Niall and the others who came to help me."

She flicked a speck off her pants. It felt like a dismissal.

"Since arriving in your fair state," I said, "I have *not* had a pleasant time. Now you're implying that Mr. Creepola wasn't attacking me. Lemme tell you, lady, I almost died amidst the piñon pine out there."

"Yeah, I guess." She flipped open a slim notebook. "Says here you came to New Mexico for a job interview in Albuquerque. I also got that the car you rented at the airport was found bashed in and burned. That true?"

I hadn't thought of it that way. "Well, yes, actually, but—"

"That in Gallup, you were involved in a gunfight between an unknown assailant and a Mass. State Police detective. And that you abandoned the detective during the gunfight. That true, too?"

Put that way, it sounded pretty grim. "Um, in one sense—" Thank heavens she didn't know my real reason for being there.

She flipped a page. "I got one other thing before the, ah, 'incident' here. Says you believe that your friend's skull was found in some old Anasazi pot and that another friend of yours got her throat cut over the same pot. That true, too?"

I really didn't know how to answer without sounding like a crazy person. So I said nothing. I folded my hands on my lap.

She leaned forward, one hand pressed to her knee. "You know what I think? I think you're trouble. I think you're crazy, and that we'll be glad to see your back. So you know what I'm going to do? I'm going to drive you to Albuquerque, and I'm going to watch while you get on a plane that's nonstop to Boston. And I'm going to let them handle it. You see?"

I saw, all right, but I refused to be railroaded out of New Mexico.

Her phone bleeped, and she turned away from me to take the call. Not native, not Anglo, but seemingly both. She might be Hispanic. I wondered if she had trouble fitting in at all. I told myself to focus.

Why try to make me leave? Not that anyone really could, but . . . Someone from back home? Massachusetts's medical examiner had a long reach. Maybe Addy wanted me out of here. I could see Veda doing that, but Addy?

The situation was weird and confusing, made stranger by the deputy having so much information about me and my doings.

The deputy turned back to me. "Why don't you go up and pack. Get ready to go."

"I'm not going anywhere," I said.

"Sure you are." She smiled. "Niall?"

The lodge manager appeared at the door. "You rang, babe?"

"You're full up, right?"

His brows beetled. "Full up? Now? You crazy?"

She notched her chin. "Sure you are."

He looked from her to me and back again. "I, uh, I guess I am."

"What?" I said.

The deputy smirked. "Like I said, I'll give you a lift."

"Just like a little sheep," I said. "That's swell, but I have to make a plane reservation. I also need to crash. How about first thing in the morning?"

She looked from me to her notebook to me again. "I guess I can do that." She slapped her knees and stood.

I'd leave before she came back in the A.M.

The deputy walked over to Niall and gave him a soft punch in the belly. "I don't feel like drivin' all the way back to Grants. You can put me up, right?"

"Sure, Louise!" He wouldn't look me in the eye. "Sure I can."

"I'll just get my kit." She saluted me and walked outside to her cruiser.

Upstairs, I tossed the few things I had into a bag, then sat on the bed. I was screwed. Of course, I had no intention of flying out, and I sure didn't like the prospect of traveling to Albuquerque with a woman who obviously despised me.

What if the bad guys, whoever they were, had sent her? She could easily do me in on the way. Plenty of barren stretches, from what I imagined.

But that made no sense. Niall knew her.

How did she learn so much about me?

Sounds in the driveway drew me to the window. A black, dust-covered panel truck pulled up, and out piled four guys in jeans and cowboy hats. They carried ropes and a stretcher, and I assumed they were here to take my attacker to the ME's office in Albuquerque. One of them carried a CSS kit and another a camera. I suspected two were just for the heavy lifting, as the guy had died in a fairly inaccessible place.

Who was he? Maybe I was wrong about him trying to kill me. Maybe rape and assault were his agenda. But he was just a flunky. I was sure of it.

But for who, dammit? For *who*?

I made a list of possibles, or rather, I tried to. All I did was stare at a white sheet of lodge notepaper. I showered, lathering my hair with Prell, the shampoo I'd used as a kid. Funny, the passage of time and how I could be right back there when my dad was alive, when Carmen and I had played with our buddies on the beach at Echo Lake.

I lay down on the bed.

The thump of a woodpecker awakened me. But when I opened my eyes, I realized the tapping was at the door. "Yes?" I said.

"Dinner, Ms. Whyte," came the call.

My "okay," came out like I had a bag of marbles in my mouth. "Coming!" I danced my fingers across my cheek. Yikes. I skittered by the mirror, only glimpsing my balloon cheek, as I left the room. I'd seen enough, though.

My right cheek was swollen and black and blue, and I looked like a chipmunk. When I pressed it, it ached. On my left cheek, I wore a pink, scabby line where the man on the Vineyard had knifed me. Two different men, but from the same source. I'd certainly pissed off someone. Seemed like they wanted me bad.

I walked downstairs, my hand tight around the banister. I was a fricking wreck. But each day I'd get better, and I had no intention of spending a single night at the lodge.

Three A.M. by Hank's watch on my wrist. I slipped out the lodge's side entrance. The moon was full. I hadn't realized how much light could be in the sky. Cripes. It was practically daylight. I sure wasn't being particularly clever. I didn't know how to *be* clever when I was out in the middle of nowhere with a deputy on my ass. I had to take the rental car, since I sure as hell couldn't walk out.

I zipped up the fuzzy jacket loaned to me by Niall. The temperature had plummeted, and I saw my breath mist the night air. Had to be below freezing. I wished I had a fuzzy hat instead of my ball cap. My wet hair was becoming crunchy in the cold.

The earth crunched, too, as I stepped on pine needles and dirt. Oh, golly gee—what other noise could I make?

I unzipped the jacket's pocket, felt the car keys. Whooeee, it was cold. I kept my back planted to the wall of the lodge. I was almost to the corner. I peeked around. There was my rental.

As I ran up to the car, I slipped the keys from my pocket. I unlocked the car with the key, not the beeper, and slid into the driver's seat. Almost there. I whooshed out a breath, watched it fog the night air.

I slid the key into the ignition and turned it.

Nothing happened.

I tried again. Hell. The engine didn't even *try* to turn over. What was the deal?

I felt around with my hand, then snapped on the light to make sure I hadn't imagined what I'd just felt.

Oh crap. A bunch of multicolored wires hung in a tangle below the steering column. They'd been cut or pulled or whatever. All I knew was the car wouldn't start.

Louise had checked me.

Well, dammit, I'd been through too much. It wasn't checkmate. Not by a long shot.

One night in the woods wouldn't kill me. After that, I could hike out, get a lift, and no one would be the wiser.

I ran a ways up the dirt road, then searched for a low-hanging pine branch. I found one just a few yards into the woods. I tugged like mad, but couldn't get it off the tree. I turned a circle and finally found a weenie-looking little thing that might work. Again, I tugged, fell on my butt with the thing, and ran back to the road. I dropped one of my precious socks. Oh, well. Then I did like I'd seen in the movies and brushed back and forth with the pine-needled branch as I backed off the road.

I carried the branch into the woods and left it. In the moonlight, I could see fairly well. The wood was a place of silver-gray shadows that flowed into night. Cripes, it was cold. I did a little dance. The luminous dial on my watch read three-thirty. I walked farther from the road and downhill, closer to the lodge and farther from the sock.

A dog like Penny could find me. But I wasn't a fugitive or a lost child. Given the expense, I doubted they'd bring in the scent dogs. I guessed I had three hours, before they'd awaken and that crazed deputy would come hunting for me. If she bought the note I'd left about hitching back to Gallup, things would be a lot easier.

Once the deputy's hunt was headed for Gallup, I'd hike to the main road, hitch a ride, and be off to Chaco. I'd return the jacket by mail. Niall had my credit card number, so I wasn't leaving him holding the bag. It felt like I had every contingency worked out.

In fact, this was a better plan, given that someone had followed me to the lodge. This way, I'd leave no trail.

I found a large clump of pine, lay the blanket I'd taken on the ground and sat. Brrr. Oh, yeah, cold. But I could stand it for a few hours. Sure I could.

I wished I knew where Hank was and that he was okay. I believed he was, but I wouldn't call him until I got to Chaco. If I called earlier, he'd insist I go back to Boston. And then I'd be right where I started.

In three days, I was due for another rabies shot. Lucky me. But I could get to Chaco in the morning, look around, see if I could find something before I called in the troops.

Okay, if I was honest, I had no clue about what I was doing. All I knew was I had to get to Chaco Canyon and fast.

Fingers of cold morning light awakened me. I checked my appendages. They all seemed to move, but with pain. The bod had definitely taken a beating yesterday.

I took a minute to listen to the busy birds and the forest sounds. Nice. Comforting. The breeze was chill on my cheek, and it felt good. I could stay here for a while, wrapped in my blanket, cocooned in the safety of the woods.

It was *definitely* time to go.

On the way back to the lodge, I checked Hank's watch. Seven-thirty. *Damn.* I'd slept later than planned. As I walked in the woods—hating every time my foot made a crunching sound—I paralleled the road. I also listened for anything out of the ordinary. The place was silent. Oddly so.

I finally stopped across from the parking lot, still in the comfort of the woods. Disturbing. Where the hell were all the cars, Niall's truck? Where was my rental? The cop car?

Everybody would not have left the lodge en masse.

I started to run, skidded to a halt. A trap. Sure. The deputy had hidden all the vehicles, so I'd think they were gone. Of course.

Except as I peered out from the edge of the woods, I could see everywhere. And I saw nothing. I walked onto the driveway and looked up the road. Since the lodge was on the side of a mountain, I could see pretty far down. Trees clacking in the wind, pines swaying, birds chirping. I even heard the skitter of small animals, and the plane that buzzed overhead.

What I didn't hear were humans.

I sat on the bench beside the lodge, wary of going inside, where, I was sure, the trap would be sprung. I had no car. No way out of there. At least, none occurred to me.

Screw it. I was always one to bring the inevitable closer.

As quietly as possible, I pulled open the screen door. I reached for the knob to the entrance to the lodge that would lead me into the back of the place, by the kitchen and laundry.

That was when I noticed a smear that looked way too much like dried blood.

I stilled my hand. Damn and double damn.

For all I knew, the red smear was raspberry jam.

Except I'd bet it wasn't.

It could have been from me, yesterday, or from my attacker or any number of things.

Like I believed that. Sure.

This cat-and-mouse had gotten awfully serious awfully quickly. I'd been playing a stupid game, but maybe not. Maybe not at all.

I piled my hair up in a bundle and slipped on my ball cap. I leaned over to put my gear and the blanket beside the house.

Someone was watching me.

I pivoted around. All I saw was the parking area and scrub brush and empty space. Talk about the jitters.

I looked in the kitchen window. The room was empty. I moved across the back of the house, looked in another window.

The spare room. Niall said he sometimes used the room for overflow. The door to the back hall was closed, so if I . . .

I stood on tiptoe and pushed against the window. It flew up, and I tumbled backward. The body-beating thing was getting tiresome. I struggled up, braced my hands on the sill, and climbed in. I left the window open.

The whole procedure felt bizarrely familiar. I vowed that this was the last time I'd climb in a window. Period.

The lodge remained quiet. No voices, no sounds of any kind. I walked to the spare room door, cracked it, and peeked into the hall. Empty.

It wasn't that this was so easy, but rather that it felt pointless. Maybe they'd all caravanned back to town for the local movie or something.

I padded out of the room and down the hall. I stood still, and that's when I heard an odd snuffling. I tilted my head. Where was it coming from? The library? Maybe. I peeked in. *Cripes.*

CHAPTER TWENTY-TWO

A wicker end table lay on its side, a mug of coffee spilled across the carpet. Not what I wanted to see. Nothing else looked out of place as I skimmed the bookshelves and phone table and pine desk.

And there. That snuffling sound again. I licked my lips. Nerves. Something bad was going on. I slid my pepper spray from my pocket. An old friend, for sure.

I walked down the long, pine-boarded hall. The lights were out, and as I moved forward, the windowless space grew darker. I came to carpet. Just ahead was the front door. On my left, the front parlor the lodge used as a dining room. On my right, the other parlor, the living room. I was afraid I'd make a mistake, go the wrong way.

I looked up the stairs. A book lay half open in the middle of one stair. Not reassuring.

I moved to my right, the living room. I pressed against the wall that framed the archway and inched toward the opening. The snuffling sounded like someone . . . *drowning*. I couldn't see much, not really, but a dark stain that hadn't been there yesterday marked the carpet. My hand tightened around the pepper spray, and I crouched as I entered the room.

The smell was terrible. My stomach lurched. Oh, boy. Feces, urine, and blood. Death's cocktail. I slipped down onto my hands and knees, crawled around the blotch that I now saw was congealed blood. Lots of it.

Something bad had gone down there. Really bad.

I inched around a chair. The snuffling grew louder, and I saw the source.

She lay facedown on the carpet surrounded by blood. I skittered over, lifted her torso onto my lap, turned her and brushed the matted hair out of her face.

"Deputy?" I said. "Louise?"

Blood had dried on her face, like a deep red birthmark, and a thin trickle ran from her mouth.

"Deputy?"

She appeared unconscious. I lay her down on the floor, but with a throw pillow beneath her torso, which I hoped would help her breathing. I scrambled for the phone that sat beside one of the room's wing chairs. I lifted the old-style receiver and was met with silence. I pushed the button—*click, click, click.* Nothing.

I slid the cell phone I'd bought from my jacket pocket and flipped it open. The same iffy service. I tried, but got nothing. Nothing.

Back beside the deputy, I searched for her wounds. Her jacket was matted with blood, and so was her shirt. I opened her shirt, saw a gaping wound that oozed blood. I was no nurse, no doctor. I knew so little.

I got some towels and a glass of water and a cloth. I packed the wound with the towels, hoping they'd stop the bleeding. Then I lifted her onto my lap again, and held the glass of water to her lips. "C'mon, try to sip."

She didn't move. Her mouth was partially open, so I moistened the cloth and dabbed her lips. Then I squeezed out some water onto her tongue.

That sound of her labored breathing. Terrible.

I put my lips close to her ear. "I'm not going to leave you, but I have to go outside and try to make a cell call. We haven't any reception in here. Okay?"

Silence.

Outside, I again flipped open the phone. I had no bars, nothing, no service. Damn.

She was dying, and I was doing nothing.

I ran back inside and raced into the library. The closet door was closed. I flung it open, and there was Niall's computer all ready to be fired up, which is exactly what I did.

Took forever, and I thought I would scream until the thing was finally ready to roll. Once I had a screen, I clicked on the e-mail program. Of course, I didn't know anyone's e-mail out here. Swell. What was I thinking?

I went on the Web, signed on to my e-mail, and wrote to Gert and Kranak and Hank. I typed like blazes, explaining everything, told them exactly where I was, and all about the deputy. I told them to call both Grants, the deputy's home base, and Thoreau, which was closer to the lodge. I told them to hurry. I hit Send.

I prayed Hank had brought his BlackBerry with him. Then he'd get my e-mail.

Next I tried for Grants's and Gallup's police departments, and I came up empty. Now what?

State police. Of course. I found the New Mexico State Police online, e-mailed them in their online form, and prayed something, anything would work and help the deputy.

I sat back in the chair. This was bad, really bad. I closed my eyes, rubbed them. I'd better get back to Louise. I didn't want her to feel alone. But as I stood, I saw a shadow, just a flicker, cross the library door in the hall.

Damn. I didn't need that. Not now. I had the pepper spray, which had one hell of a reach. I wanted more. I padded out of the library and down the hall to the kitchen. Right where I remembered them were Niall's kitchen knives. His chef's knives clung to a magnetized board screwed to the wall. As I grabbed one of the large ones, I said a silent prayer of thanks. I swallowed. To stab someone took nerve I wasn't sure I had.

Of course I did. Absolutely. Oh, boy.

Back in the hall, I pressed my back to the wall and slid toward the living room and the deputy. It was me and nobody else. Even if my message got through to Gert or Kranak or the state police, the drive here was a good twenty to thirty minutes.

I was on my own.

One, two, three. I pivoted into the arch that framed the living area. I saw nothing. Heard only the deputy's shallow liquid breathing. I swallowed, almost coughed. My throat was dry with fear.

Again I tried to peer into every shadowy corner of the room. I then went over to the deputy. I was so glad she was still alive. I made sure to put my back against the wall.

We could wait. I couldn't help her any further. I didn't know what to do. And if some guy was playing hide-and-seek with me, he'd have my pepper spray and knife to deal with.

Keeping my eyes on the room, I sat beside her and leaned forward. "Help is coming. They're on their way. Please hang on."

Her right hand twitched, and then slowly squeezed into a fist with the index finger pointing to the closet door.

"Thank you," I whispered in her ear. "No worries. I'll take care of you."

All I had to do was keep my eye on the door and the pepper spray ready. Hell, the thing could spray more than thirty feet.

I moved to my knees, feet planted beneath me, toes bent so I could spring up at the ready.

A chuckle came from the hall, then a crunch. I pivoted in time to see a sawed-off shotgun pointed at my face.

A pinup-handsome man cocked the trigger. "Put that crap down, babe."

"Don't call me babe, asshole," I said as I stood. "And if I put them down, you're going to blast me with that thing."

He whistled. "Oh, you are *so* wrong. We don't want to kill you or mess up that pretty face. Boss wants you. You saw the note."

I raised the pepper spray. "What note?"

He dropped the barrel of the gun, so it pointed at the deputy's face. "C'mon now. Play nice. She's not dead yet, but she will be if you don't behave. Drop them."

I glanced at the deputy. I'd swear she twitched her head "no."

"Do it nice now," he said.

I bent over and placed the pepper spray and knife on the floor. "Fine," I said. "Let's go."

The blast jerked me around. But I wasn't hit. *Dear God!* No, the deputy's face was now a mass of fleshy pulp. No sound. No nothing. She was dead, of course.

I drew in a sob. *I'm so sorry!*

The monster reached for my arm. "We go."

I dropped to my knees, pretended to retch, scrabbled for the pepper spray. "You bastard!" I twirled on him, pressing the nozzle hard. Of course I missed him, and he leaned in to grab my arm, his face masked in fury.

I drew my knee up and got him in the balls.

He doubled over, but he clung to the gun. I reached for it, and he slammed the barrel against the side of my head.

Pain knifed from my ear into my brain. I fell to my knees, gasping.

"You little bitch!"

Kaboom!

I looked for another shooting pain, knowing the shot

was for me, that my face or arm or leg would be pulp, too, just like the deputy's.

I bent over, crouching on the floor, left arm holding me up, barely. I squeezed my eyes tight.

A thunderous noise and clattering.

"Open 'em," said the voice.

Did I know that voice? But . . .

I pried my eyes open and gasped. The handsome monster was missing the left side of his face. His mouth was open in a silent scream as blood dripped down his forehead and into his open mouth.

That time, I really did puke.

Minutes later, someone yanked me to my feet. I fisted my left hand and swung. A quick hand stopped my punch.

"Cut it out, Tally!"

I shook my head, cleared my eyes, peered up into the face of . . . "Aric?"

"Come on." He pulled me to my feet. "We've got to get going."

"What about the deputy?"

"She rests now. She's gone. We can't help her."

"No." I sighed. "One sec." I ran back to her and kneeled. *I'm so sorry. I won't forget your gift of my life. I wish . . .*

"Hurry up, Tally."

I scooped up my spray and the knife. "Stop rushing me. I've got to check something."

I ran to the shelf where the pot sat. It looked the same as it had the previous day, a replica of Didi's sketch of the Anasazi pot—maybe a foot at the base, it bowed out to around eighteen inches with a narrow, six-inch neck. I got this eerie feeling looking at it, and I wondered if anything was inside.

"It's fake," Aric said. He was rifling through the dead man's pockets.

"How can you tell?"

"I just can."

Cute. I sucked in a breath and plunged my hand inside the pot. Empty. I lifted the Old Ones' pot and turned it. The red-and-white pot looked authentic to my untrained eyes. I lifted it higher and checked the bottom. Huh. "Hey, Aric. It says made in 2001. Replica of an ancient pot found at Chaco Canyon. You were right."

"I'm consistent that way."

In the kitchen, I washed off the deputy's blood, then followed Aric out the door.

I looked around. "Where's your truck? Car? Whatever?"

"A couple miles down the road."

I sat on the bench. "I don't know. I'm pretty much a wreck. Yesterday—"

"So what? Let's go." He shouldered his shotgun and began to walk.

"Wait a minute. I don't think there are more of them. At least not here. Why don't we wait for the cops?"

"What? You lost your nerve?"

"You could say that. These pot thieves are sure doing a job on me. I pretty much hate being a target."

"It's complicated," he said. "C'mon, let's vamoose."

But I didn't go. The sun felt good as I sat there. The breeze was warm and comforting, and the scent of the piñon pines soothed me. If we waited for the police, we could hand everything over to them. No more running around. I tilted my head back against the side of the lodge. The sun warmed my face and soothed my soul.

Enough. Delphine and Didi were both gone. They'd understand if I gave everything I knew to the cops and went home. Hank was right. I ached. My face throbbed and my shoulders and thigh and my cheek where I'd been cut.

I lifted my hand. I'd lost the bandage on it somewhere along the line. I traced the scabbed scar on my face. Hank hadn't said anything about it. Maybe I repulsed him now.

Natalie. The Zuni girl had tried to help me, and look where I'd gotten her. And the deputy. Maybe it was her job and all, but I didn't really think so. I'd been suddenly on her agenda, and now she was dead. The old man, too.

These pot thieves were determined to get me. The pursuit, the obsession. I didn't understand the death in all of it. A skull. A pot. Perhaps an old fetish carving. The blood fetish. I still couldn't see it.

"Tally."

I opened my eyes. Aric stood there, angry and tired and . . . different.

"Aric, I don't think I can go to Chaco. Um, I'll stay here, wait for the cops. Fill them in and all. Thank you for today, but there's been too much death. Too much."

His face boiled with anger. "There's going to be more if you don't get your ass in gear."

I stood so we were face to face. I refused to match his anger. I'd walk away, except I didn't have the energy for it. "I'm sorry you're disappointed. Or angry. Or whatever it is you are. I can't help thinking of Natalie. And now the deputy. I ran away from Hank, and some guy yesterday tried to kill me, and the rabies shots because of Coyote—"

"Don't."

I searched his liquid brown eyes. Something. "What am I missing here?"

He backed off, reached into his back pocket, then held up a folded baggie with a paper inside. "This."

We've got Niall and his kid. Come to Chaco, Chetro Ketl grand kiva by sunset or we kill them.

My hands shook as I held it. I stared at the thing, then at Aric. "They wrote it in the deputy's blood, didn't they?"

"Yes."

CHAPTER TWENTY-THREE

Aric wasn't even breathing hard by the time we got to his truck. I, on the other hand, clung to the side by the bed and wheezed.

"It's the altitude," he said.

"Maybe. I run at home. I can't stop thinking about Niall and his daughter. I did this to them."

He cupped my chin. "You didn't, Tally. You didn't do it to the deputy, either. I've learned how you think."

"Is that so?" I kissed his cheek. "Thank you. You're right. I know that, intellectually. But my gut. Ah, that's another story. Let's go."

I walked around the Land Rover and slid into the passenger side. I didn't want to talk or to think, not for a few minutes at least. He gunned it, and I was glad I wore my seat belt. We bounced and jounced until we made it to the main road, which was paved.

"I bought you a present." He pointed to the pickup's dash. A pink thing the size of a TV remote sat next to Aric's can of tobacco.

"What is it? Do I look like a pink person to you?"

He laughed. "You don't know what it is?"

I picked it up with care. *Taser* was written on the side. A *pink* Taser. "Oh, I don't think so, Aric."

"Hey, it's not a gun. I know you won't carry one of those." He was grinning.

"You're awfully pleased with yourself."

"I got it cheap. They're trying to dump the pink ones. Guys won't carry 'em."

"This girl doesn't like pink, either. Well, not much. I don't think so, Aric. Not now, anyway."

"Whatever. Your choice."

I nodded. "Good." I sensed we weren't done with the subject. "Look, I've got to say it."

"What?"

"The elephant in the room."

He stuffed some chaw into his cheek. "You've lost me."

"I apologize for leaving the way I did in Gallup. It was all very . . . weird."

He nodded. "My friend thought so."

"The woman?"

He powered down the window, spit. "Yeah. Me? You don't surprise me anymore, Tally Whyte. I take it you knew the, um, strange person who was after you."

"Um, well . . ." I explained. He snorted, laughed, and shook his head at my recitation.

"So should I expect this Hank to come and kill me?"

"No. He's not like that."

"Oh, wow," he said. "Gee, this Indian's relieved."

"Funny. Not. Let's move on, huh, Aric? See, I don't get it. Why all the murder and mayhem for a pot and a skull."

"I can't say I get it, either." He spit again out the window.

"You shouldn't do that. It's bad for you."

"I'll keep that in mind, *Ma*."

"Cute. How long until we get to Chaco?"

He shrugged. "Depends."

I leaned back, closed my eyes. "C'mon, Aric."

"Go to sleep. It'll be a while."

The rabies shots. I didn't tell him. I'd have time. I'd make the next one.

I sensed this would be over sooner, rather than later.

A droning in my ear awakened me. What now? A flat tire? A sandstorm? Pirates? I waited, listened. Hank would have been proud of me.

The truck was noisy, but the open window felt good. So did the scents of sage and desert and clean. Hard to get the deputy out of my mind. The radio wasn't on, so what was the humming?

I forced my eyes to stay closed. Aric. Talking in what I assumed was Zuni. He sounded angry. But whoever he spoke with was in charge. He flipped the phone shut, and I was about to "wake up" when he gave it another voice command.

"*Kesh'shi,*" he said, soft and low.

Without moving, I slitted my eyes open. He was smiling, nodding. *Heavens*, Aric laughed. This call was very different from the last. Again he talked in Zuni, and he finally said what sounded like *dohoechma*, and shut the phone.

I made a noise, groaned with supposed waking.

Aric turned on the radio.

"Hey," I said. "Got anything to drink?"

He reached into the backseat and handed me a Coke. Warm. Who liked their soda warm? I didn't get it at all. I popped the tab and drank deep.

"You were on the phone," I said.

"Naw. Talk radio. This satellite business is pretty cool."

Golly, it sure was. Grrr. Now Aric was lying to me. I longed for Hank's straightforward honesty. "You have a girlfriend?"

His lips thinned. "Why all this . . . intimacy now?"

"You know me," I said. "Or at least you said you did. It matters that I understand my friends. To know them."

He slapped the wheel. "Don't bother, Tally Whyte. It could get us both killed."

"That's a conversation stopper."

"Intentional."

"There's someone in your life, Aric." I rested my hand on his shoulder. "Someone you love. You seem worried. You certainly can tell me—"

"I don't choose to."

His face was all shadows and mystery. He wore a ball cap atop his short hair. His handsomeness, so reminiscent of an Edward Curtis photograph, hid what lay inside the man.

He rolled up the sleeves of his snap shirt. He was the son of a former Zuni governor, a man who was also a clan chief. A powerful man. Aric was powerful, too. I sensed a depth in him I barely understood.

The Aric I knew wasn't the man beside me who was hurting. I wished I could help. "Are you sure that I—"

"Positive."

I let go for the moment. "Where are we?"

"Almost to Crownpoint. Then we head east to Chaco."

I pulled out my cell phone. I still had coverage, and I doubted I would in Chaco. I dialed Gert.

"Who are you calling?" Aric said.

"Just a friend back home. To get the news on Penny, my dog, and work."

He gave me a stolid and long look. "I thought you said you weren't working."

The air grew hot and tense. Why the hell should I be feeling that way with Aric? Cripes. "I'm not working. Not officially. But I started the program at OCME, and I'll always have an interest in MGAP. It's my baby."

"Huh," was all he said. "You better not be long."

"Why? I mean, am I under guard or something? Because that's what it sounds like."

His hands tightened around the steering wheel. "Just be quick."

I dialed Gert. It bounced right to voicemail, and I left a message. I hoped she reached me before we were out of range. I punched out Kranak's numbers, got the guy on duty, a CSS I'd known for years.

"Hey, Wes, how goes it?" I said. It was great to hear a friendly and familiar voice. "It's Tally. I'm looking for Rob."

"He's out on a case."

"I'm not surprised. I'll try his cell. Have a good one, huh."

"Wait," Wes said.

"What's up?" I tried to play it casual, but I heard the catch in his voice.

"I just wanted to say I was sorry."

"About . . . ?"

"You don't know. Shit."

"Whatever 'it' is, I don't know it, Wes." Panic. "Is Doc Morgridge okay?"

"She's fine, Tal. Let me put you through to Gert."

I rubbed my forehead. "Look, Wes. I have not a clue what you're talking about. Gert's on the line. I already tried her. What's the deal?"

"Fine. Um . . ." A sigh. "I don't feel good about this. Just remember that, okay?"

"Go ahead."

"Did you catch that? I do *not* feel good about this."

"I caught it. I caught it. *What?*"

"Your boyfriend. That Cunningham guy."

My heart stopped. "Yes?"

"He's been shot up bad."

"Bad?" I whispered. "He's not dead, right? You'd tell me, wouldn't you?"

"Yeah, I'd tell."

Aric shook my arm. I pulled it away and mouthed, *Stop it!* "Go on."

"Some gunfight or other," Wes said. "I guess he's out there in some hospital."

My throat squeezed tight. "Where is he?"

"Place called Crownpoint."

"Not Gallup?" I said. "How bad is he?"

"Not good, Tally," Wes said. "Not good at all."

"Okay." I signed off. The world spun. Hank. *Hank.* Nothing could happen to Hank. But something had. I couldn't bear it.

"We're on our way to Crownpoint, right?" I said.

Aric's sideways glance was anything but comforting. "Yeah."

"I've got to get to the hospital there. Now. Period." I folded my hands in my lap and searched for calm.

Aric slapped the steering wheel. "No time."

No time? Of course, our deadline to make it to Chaco Canyon. For Niall and his daughter. Except . . .

I shook my head. "I can't help it. I have to stop." I explained about Hank and what had happened.

Aric got quiet. Too quiet. It was obvious he had more to say, whereas I had nothing else to say. I was going to the Crownpoint hospital. That was it.

Mile after mile of scrub and desert passed as we climbed one hill and drove down another. I slung my hand onto the swaying door strap. The rhythmic motion felt good. Time, time, time.

It was taking forever, and all I could see was Hank as a little kid with a crush on me. Hank, the sheriff of Hancock County. Hank, in bed and walking Peanut and playing hockey and . . .

What had happened? How had the shooter gotten to Hank? It made no sense. Of course, I'd been the one to screw up. I'd left him there in that motel room. I was sure he'd be fine.

I was wrong. So wrong.

I spotted a dozen cows grazing on the scrub, then three coyotes slinking toward them.

A sign for Crownpoint. A jackrabbit leapt across the road. Aric swerved so he wouldn't hit it.

"How far are we from the hospital?" I said.

"Not far." He tapped a tune on the dash that I guessed played in his head.

My head was silent, lonely. I tried to see Hank in my mind's eye, but I was alone, and he was gone, and I couldn't see him at all.

The land flattened. Up ahead, simple homes, maybe a school, and I thought I could see the hospital. My heart beat faster, my mouth dried.

"I guess, well, turn wherever."

Aric nodded, tapped the dash, faster, harder. I bit my lip. *Please let him be okay.*

On the right. There. The hospital. "There it is, Aric."

He flew past the street, letting the truck pick up speed.

"But, Aric."

We raced across the desert, through the town.

"You've got to stop," I said. "I'll walk if I have to."

"I can't, Tally. We've got two people who might die."

I cracked the door. I could leap out, roll. I *would* see Hank.

"You'll kill yourself."

Faster and faster the truck moved.

And suddenly a sound. A siren.

Aric looked in the rearview mirror. "Cop. Shit."

"I see." I slid my hand to the door handle.

As we coasted to a stop, I leaned my shoulder against the door and raised the handle.

"Don't," Aric said.

I turned the handle. Beneath the red bandana that sat in Aric's lap was a semi-automatic handgun. The barrel pointed straight at me.

A chill skated down my spin. Aric wouldn't shoot. Of

course not. But I was intimate with how the bullet from a nine mil could rip through your gut.

I waited. In the side mirror I watched as the cop approached. The men talked low and slow, so I couldn't hear. The cop was Navajo. Zuni and Navajo were never the best of friends.

Then the cop walked away. I looked at Aric, his eyes dead and angry. The gun never wavered.

Screw it.

"I have to." I flipped up the handle and leapt. I hit the ground hard, and my crappy left knee gave. But my right one held, and I sprang forward, stumbled, ran.

"Tally!" Aric hollered.

I heard the whine of the truck door opening, but I ran on, past the cop and headed to town. It wasn't far, and someone beeped. And then this ancient green pickup was keeping pace with me.

"Hey, lady!" someone hollered.

"Yeah." I didn't stop running.

"Why's that crazy Zuni chasing you?"

I glanced up to see a straw-hatted Navajo smiling down from his truck. "That crazy Zuni wants to marry me." I was panting hard now.

"You wanna marry him?" the Navajo asked.

"Hell, no!" I said.

"So get in," he said.

The green truck stopped, and I ran around to the passenger side and hopped in.

"Tally, dammit!" Aric hollered.

The Navajo laughed and put the pedal to the metal.

CHAPTER TWENTY-FOUR

People stared as I walked through the doors of the Crown-point hospital. Because I might scare Hank, I went to the ladies' room and splashed some water on my face. I didn't bother to look. I knew my face was a train wreck. Hank had seen worse.

Aric might have arrived by now, but I didn't much care. He couldn't drag me out of the hospital by force. I couldn't believe the Navajo cop had let him go.

The small hospital's waiting room overflowed with people—men, women, old, young. I found the reception desk. The young gal at the desk had her nose buried in a textbook.

"Excuse me," I said. "I'm looking for a friend, Hank Cunningham."

She slid a place mark into the book and smiled up at me. "I'm sorta new. Does this Cunningham work here?"

"No," I said. "He's a patient."

She bobbed her head. "I don't think so. I never heard of him."

"I've been told he was shot and brought here."

Her forehead wrinkled. "I don't think so, lady. We got only one guy here who's been gun-shot, and that's my cousin's brother-in-law. He shot himself in the foot. Can you imagine that?"

I had to think. "I'll be right back."

"You know, I'm just the temp while Sally goes to lunch. I bet she knows."

"Where can I find her?"

"Out back, having a smoke." She smiled. "I hope you find your friend."

"Me, too. Thanks."

I found my way out back. It wasn't far. Except way too many men and women were smoking, maybe a dozen, with more than half of them women. Some leaned against the building, while others paced and talked on their cell phones.

I walked up to a Navajo woman who wore jeans and a fluffy top.

"Hi," I said. "I'm looking for a gal named Sally. She's the receptionist."

She wagged the cigarette. "Over there. She in trouble?"

"Not at all."

"Well, *that's* different." She flicked her ash, shrugged, and turned away.

The wind picked up, and I tightened Niall's fuzzy. As I walked toward Sally, I shielded my eyes from the midday sun. She was short and stocky and wore a red windbreaker and jeans. Her long hair was bound in a single braid. She looked around fifty. "Sally?"

"Yeah, that's me." Her sing-song voice was almost musical. "Boy, you look like you been through the wringer."

"You could say that. Um, I'm looking for a friend. The girl at the desk said you might be able to help me."

She ran her cigarette across the wall, where a million other marks existed, and dropped it into to another large can labeled *Butts*.

"I probably can't," she said. "But run it by me. C'mon, walk with me. I'm supposed to walk. Helps the diabetes."

"I'd be happy to." I fell in beside her as we walked the perimeter of the hospital. I hesitated. Fear tightened my throat. What if Hank were mortally wounded? Or brain damaged? Or paralyzed? I had to know, of course.

"My friend," I said. "His name is Hank Cunningham. He's law enforcement from Boston."

"Anglo, right?" she said.

"Yes. I just found out he was injured. I came right away. I'm scared, Sally."

She led me inside. "I gotta call up first. Okay?"

"Sure. Is he . . ."

"Can't say. Not allowed." She shooed the other gal from the receptionist's desk. She reapplied her lipstick, popped a Tic Tac, then lifted the phone to call. Her eyes were sad when she looked at me.

Oh, no. "What?" I said. I couldn't believe this. I just couldn't. My stomach cramped with fear.

She shook her head. "I'm sorry. I am."

The same thing Wes had said on the phone.

The waiting room chair was soft, too much so. I fastened my eyes on the bowels of the hospital and didn't move. People entered and left. Occasionally I'd glance at the entrance, half expecting to see Aric stride through. But he didn't come.

I dozed, which seemed impossible, but I did. And my fear grew. I checked Hank's watch for the hundredth time. I rubbed the dial, the band. He'd worn the watch forever. I *had* to be at Chaco by sunset. I didn't know how long that would take, but I suspected an hour or so.

I couldn't leave, yet I would have to leave sooner, rather than later. What was taking so long? Why couldn't I just go up and see Hank?

I held my hands up to Sally, a silent *how come*. She gave me a shrug and went back to the phones. I slumped back in the chair. Hank was dead. I was sure of it. Someone was coming to tell me, and that's why there was the wait. I wanted to stand up and scream.

Shouts at the entrance made me turn. Aric zoomed through the front doors at a run.

He held out his hand. His eyes worried, fearful. "We gotta go, Tally. We gotta go now."

He was right. Of course we did. Niall and his daughter would die otherwise.

"Yeah," I said. "Let's go. I'm . . . I'm waiting for nothing." I turned to leave.

"Wait." Sally shook her hand at me.

"Can't, Sally. I . . . I'll come back later."

She raced around the reception desk. "You can't go!"

"*Now*, Tally!" Aric said.

I walked forward, and we were almost to the front doors when . . .

"Tally!"

The voice whipped me around. I blinked. Rubbed my hands across my eyes. Hank stood right there, wearing his chinos, a green crew shirt, and boat shoes. "*Hank!*"

I ran up to him, threw my arms around him, and hugged and hugged and hugged. I began to sob, and then I kissed him long and hard and, finally, when I felt semi-sated, I sighed and tucked my head beneath his chin.

God he smelled good and felt good and . . .

His arms were tight around me, and he was rocking me back and forth. Except something was very wrong.

I peeked up at him. "I don't understand."

He kissed the top of my head. "Nothing *to* understand, Tal."

I sighed again, content in his embrace. Except . . . sure there was something wrong. I moved to back away, but he held me tight. Too tight.

I pushed, and his arms remained locked around me.

"Let go, Hank."

"Tally . . ."

I jammed my foot on his instep and pushed hard.

"Damn!" he said.

I was free, and I backed away, watching him try to stare me down with that Cunningham doggedness I knew so well.

I looked behind me, and there was Aric, chaw in cheek, arms folded, legs crossed, hip against the wall. The relaxed Zuni, except he was anything but. I moved toward him, and he straightened.

"What the hell's going on?" I said, trying to grasp a wisp of sanity.

Aric snorted. "Simple. This thing with lover boy has all been a scheme to get you to do what he wants. Isn't that right, Detective?"

I looked from Aric to Hank. But no. Hank wouldn't give me that kind of unnecessary grief. "Hank? Wes said you were hurt. Badly hurt. Is Aric right?"

Hank walked forward, eyes on me, but he spoke to Aric. "I don't know, Special Agent Bowannie. Is it right or not?"

"*Special Agent?*" I said. "Like in FBI Special Agent?" My world was spinning. Hank unhurt, Aric an FBI agent.

I looked around. A dozen faces were turned to us, as if we were stars in some soap opera. I guessed we were. I read pity on some faces, humor on others, fascination on others.

Sally the receptionist's face wore regret and guilt. She'd been a part of the scam. I guess most of OCME had been, too.

Let's trick Tally into coming home. For her own safety.

Yeah, right.

"Sorry, guys." I saluted and ran out the door.

I ran beside hedges and around cars, zigzagging around anything that might hide me from view. I made it to a parallel street, heard shouts, and stuck out my thumb. Almost immediately, an old woman in a battered van gave me a lift. I ducked down, peeked out the window, and saw Aric and Hank racing after the van. I was away. I sighed with relief.

I embellished a tale of two rival men, which the old woman found quite amusing. She was a neat old gal—a sheep farmer and weaver. She dropped me at the high school, per my request. I needed time to think, and I doubted Frick and Frack would figure out where I'd gone.

I thanked her and entered the school.

I checked Hank's watch, the one I'd lovingly massaged minutes earlier. Pa-thetic. It was two. I still had time to make the sunset appearance in Chaco. Inside the school, I signed in at the front office, saying a friend who was moving to town wanted me to look at the library. That got me by, and I found the large room with no trouble. The school was small and low-ceilinged, but a sense of pride was everywhere, from the banners that read: Go Eagles! To a trophy case with athletic and academic trophies.

In the library, computers marched in a row, with a few students pounding the keys. The library stacks looked just like any other, and I felt a sense of home that made me long for Boston.

I certainly was a stranger in a strange land. Hank and Aric—both men I trusted had lied to me. I'd survive. I took a seat at one of the desks.

Why couldn't I figure this thing out? What was *really* going on? The pots weren't that valuable. Oh, an undamaged one would bring thousands of dollars. True. But so many deaths? That meant higher stakes, so why couldn't I see what was really behind all the killing. Didi had started to write *bloodfet* in her own blood, no less. That mattered. I guessed the Bone Man did, too, but I had no clue about him, either.

The Bone Man might be the killer, the guy who was after me. I felt a central will in all the attacks, yet the actual person remained illusive.

There was no way I wasn't going to Chaco that night. I kicked the leg of the desk.

"Ma'am, are you angry at our desk?"

I looked into the face of the pretty Navajo girl peering down at me with questions in her eyes.

She made it easy to smile back at her. "No, I'm not. I just have a lot on my mind. Do you have a map of Chaco Canyon?"

She returned my smile, and out popped two dimples. "Of course we do."

I followed her through the stacks to shelves beneath high windows. Inside what appeared to be a bound notebook, she pulled out a large, folded map. She spread it on the top of the shelves.

"Where do you want to go in Chaco, or do you just want to tour around?"

I studied the map. "Here." I pointed to Chetro Ketl, whatever that was.

She nodded, her eyes again smiling. "Oh, yes, that's very beautiful."

"What's this road?" I asked. "The one off Fifty-seven."

She held up a finger and walked off. The map looked good, but not good enough. I needed details so I wouldn't end up eaten by the death squad, or whoever they were.

A soft grunt made me turn, and I stared into the serious face of a Navajo teen. He wore cowboy boots and jeans and a plaid shirt, with a red bandana tied around his page-boy haircut. The outfit struck me as traditional, intentionally so, right down to his Navajo turquoise bracelet.

"You bothering my sister?" he said.

"Hi. My name's Tally. And I don't think I'm bothering her. She offered to help me, and so she is."

He grunted again, folded his arms, and set his face into a rigid stare. The fact that I topped him by a good five inches didn't seem to bother him one bit.

"What's your name?" I said.

"Joe. And don't try to get friendly."

"I wouldn't think of it, Joe. I just like to know names, is all. I'm from Boston."

He snorted. "So? You think you're better than us?"

Oh my, this was one angry boy. "No. Why would I think that?"

"'Cause of money."

"Really? So you believe money defines a person?"

His chin jutted. "No. But *you* do."

"I'm afraid I don't, Joe. People are people. I try not to judge and to take them for who they are." I shrugged. "That's about the best I can do."

"So who am I?" he spat.

I was *really* too tired for this. "I don't know—"

"Gorman!" barked a stern woman in a pressed pair of jeans.

I looked from her to the boy, who hadn't moved an inch.

"He was helping me with this map," I said.

She sniggered, smooshed her hands into her too-tight pockets. "Sure he was."

"Isn't that okay?" I said.

She walked toward me. Swaggered would be a better word.

"You look like you been through a blender, lady," she said.

I shrugged. "I sort of have."

"Gorman, two demerits." She flicked her red nail–polished index finger. "And go sit over there."

The kid gave me a black look and moved out.

"That's sort of harsh," I said.

"Yeah?" She smiled. "He knows he's not supposed to talk to Anglos."

"Pardon?"

"You deaf, too?" She sauntered toward the boy, again wagging that finger, and talking in what I presumed was Navajo.

I stood there for a moment, frozen to the linoleum floor. I felt foolish, like I'd just been chastised for breathing. But I was also annoyed with her narrow mind, which was obviously tainting the boy's. I went back to looking at the map and had trouble focusing on it. Boy, that exchange bugged me.

"Hey," came the chipper voice.

The pretty girl was back, and her eyes were welcoming.

"What's your name?" I asked.

"Kai. It means willow tree, which I find sort of funny, since, well . . ." She gestured to her full breasts.

"It's a lovely name. Mine's Tally. That boy over there, Joe, said he was your brother. He was told not to talk to me because I'm an Anglo."

She didn't bother to look. "I know just who you mean. It's a clan thing. He's not my biological brother. And, yeah, he's really into the Diné point of view." She flushed. "He's a pretty angry kid. So's—"

"—the woman?" She looked over her shoulder, and her long ponytail swished across her shoulders. "That woman *is* my biological half-sister. She hates everybody. Don't let them bother you."

"No. Thank you." Kai was lovely and petite, and her smile welcomed the world. Life was complicated, for sure. "So what did you bring to show me?"

"Oh! Yes. Here." She laid a pad and pen and another map of Chaco on the counter. "You can take these with you. And I'll give you directions into the canyon."

She talked, and I began to write while two pairs of hostile eyes burned into my back.

CHAPTER TWENTY-FIVE

"That's it!" Kai said, dotting the final *i*.

"Great." My smile was at half mast. Time to go meet the beast. The question was, did I use Navajo or park law enforcement? "One more question, Kai. Do you have any books or articles here on fetishes? I know they're mostly the province of the Zuni, but you're so near Chaco that I thought you might."

She smiled. "I think we do. Are you looking for something specific?"

"A carving called the blood fetish."

She flushed and bit her lip. "That sounds bad. I don't like it."

"You've heard of it?"

A student waved, and Kai said, "Excuse me," and walked off.

I followed and waited as she showed the student a program on one of the computers.

"Kai?" I said.

She turned back to me. "Why do you ask about the blood fetish?"

"I saw it written once. And a man I met spoke of it."

"It's probably nothing but a rumor," she said. "But it's an old one. And not necessarily a good one."

"You're the first person I've met who's even heard of the thing. Or at least admits to it. It's as if I've been imagining the words, the object."

She undid her long ponytail and refastened it. Her sparkling brown eyes grew serious. "I'm sure I'm not the first person who knew of the blood fetish," she said. "Not if you've been asking Indians. But most folks won't talk about stuff like that."

"What *do* you know about it?"

She shrugged.

I hooked my arm through hers and walked her to where others couldn't see us. I leaned close, and I told her all that had happened. The only thing I didn't say was about the deputy's murder. Grants was way too close to home. The last thing I wanted was this gentle girl involved.

"Like I said, I know a few things," Kai said. "That Zuni guy. That Aric. He knows. I'd bet on it. Zunis carved it in the first place. Long, long time ago. I'll show you something."

She led me across the library to a stack near a corner of the library. "How do you know Aric?"

She shrugged. "The blood fetish is not one of those for-sale fetish carvings," she said. "Not like the ones they do for tourists and collectors. No way. It's got some hoodoo in it."

"'Hoodoo?'"

"Yeah, magic. I don't want to talk about it. It's bad stuff. Talking makes it worse."

"What did you want to show me?"

She didn't look happy. "I shouldn't."

"Hey, Kai!" Joe hollered.

He'd appeared out of nowhere, along with Kai's sister. Both wore angry frowns.

Joe snorted. "Why're you talkin' to this Anglo? She's trouble."

Kai rolled her eyes. "Oh, yeah, right. All Anglos are . . . to *you* and sis. You're idiots! Now get out of this library, unless you're gonna study, which it's obvious you're not."

"Screw you," Joe said.

"I'll screw you, all right," Kai said, cheeks flushed, hands on hips. "Now get out, or I'll tell Ma what you've been up to with that one." She flicked a finger at her sister.

They melted into the darkness of the stacks.

"He sure is angry," I said.

Kai nodded. "It didn't used to be like that. Pretty sad, if you ask me."

She turned toward the farthest stack. "This whole row is weaving and pots and carving and stuff. You'll find some things here." She pointed to a lower row. "But this is really where the important articles are kept. See how old these books are? At least a century or two, some of them. They've got magic."

Her words cloaked us in mystery. The air became charged with portent, and I sensed that Kai was far more than a sweet young librarian. There was something here, and if I were lucky, I would find it. Kai knew exactly what it was, this magic. But maybe all books held magic for Kai.

"You're right, all books do," she said, as if answering my thoughts. "Look carefully, okay? Be respectful. And you may find what you're looking for. It's not up to me. We don't just show anybody these."

I laid my hand on her shoulder. "Thank you. Now forget what I'm looking for, do you hear me?"

Kai seemed to grow taller, older, *wiser.* "I cannot. It's done."

I took her hands in mine. "Then stay safe, Kai. Please."

She nodded, solemn and silent. Finally, she said, "You, too. Remember, respectful. I can give you twenty minutes with these. That's it. Or someone will sense . . . Just be fast, okay?"

"Yes, I will."

"Good." Then a student called, and she was Kai again, the young girl with few cares and fewer years on her shoulders. She gave me a wave and a "good luck," and off she went.

Aloneness wrapped around me again. I might have been the only person in the world. The corner I stood in was dark and quiet, as if time itself were muffled. I bit my cheek. I believed I was about to open books no Anglo had seen for many years.

I took a deep, life-affirming breath.

The higher shelf held such familiar books as Oscar Branson's *Fetishes and Carvings of the Southwest*, Kent Mc-Manis's series on Zuni Fetishes, Hal Zina Bennett's *Zuni Fetishes*, a Facsimile edition of Frank Hamilton Cushing's *Zuni Fetishes*, Rodee and Ostler's *The Fetish Carvers of Zuni*, *Zuni Fetishism* by Ruth Kirk, and others, many of which I had in my personal library.

I skimmed through the Cushing book, the original of which was written in the late 1800s. He'd spent years in Zuni and was the first Anglo to document their fetishes, many examples of which were in the Smithsonian. I'd read the Cushing book several times, so I did a quick look-through for a blood fetish, or anything resembling that. No mention, which was what I'd expected.

I slipped the book back on its shelf. The other books on Zuni fetishes were modern, and I knew them well enough that I didn't need to review them.

The books that mattered, according to Kai, were on the bottom shelf, and so I sat on the floor. I pulled the first book from the shelf. It was old, published in 1896, and it talked about American Indian rites and magic. I looked through it, checked my watch, replaced it and pulled out book two.

I went down the stack that way, and so I made it to the middle of the shelf when my twenty minutes was up. I'd thought I'd find something. I really had.

I scrambled through the final three books, handling them with as much care as possible. Nothing. *Nothing* about a blood fetish.

Think, think, think. I replayed Kai's words.

I was getting nowhere, and my watch said it was time to go.

Kai hadn't misled me, so what wasn't I seeing?

A mumble of angry voices distracted me. Navajo, yes, but voices I recognized. At least one of them. Who, though?

Breathe, look, breathe, look.

I ran my finger down the row of books and found *Respect and Indian Magik.* Why hadn't I seen it before? Kai had told me to be respectful.

I eased the book out of its slot in the row. It didn't resemble any book I'd ever opened. It was maybe ten by twelve, larger than most. The cover was soft and pliable, with pen-and-ink letters across the front. The cover and binding were some kind of unusual skin. Maybe buffalo. The book was about half an inch thick and sewn together with sinew. I opened to the cover, and the smell of "old" reached my nose. I ran my fingers down the page, feeling the wonderful texture of the ink and handmade paper. I closed the cover to look for the author's name.

I almost laughed out loud—The Bone Man. He'd written the book. Oh, boy.

I couldn't read the right-hand pages. The language was alien to me. But on the left-hand pages, someone had attached on English translation, slipping the paper into black photo corners. *This* was the book. The Bone Man's book.

I scanned the first page. It talked of secret Zuni ceremonies and a land far away where water was plentiful and the people had originated. But the writing described the mountain, too, Corn Mountain, sacred to the Zuni, and its Zuni name Dowa Yalanne.

I felt hope, as if the book could give me some answers. I turned a page, skimmed, then another. Then . . .

The voices again. Arguing. A woman's—gruff and angry, then another woman . . . It sounded like Kai's sister.

I couldn't tell what they were saying, but I sure didn't like the tone. I pressed the book to me and walked around a stack. The last thing I wanted was to be in the midst of some confrontation.

I kept reading. Page after page.

And then . . .

The blood fetish, now lost, was once our most sacred and powerful. The fetish is the red of our enemies' blood, and it glitters in the morning sun. Maybe Old Man Natewa carved it. Or The Bone Man. Or maybe the gods who bring the red rain. It comes from far away, from the sacred place of our ancestors. Hold it, and it makes you young. Wield it, and you will flatten your enemies as if with a scythe. Covet it, and . . .

"So, hi there, ma'am."

I jumped. Down the stack stood an elderly woman. My heart's thumping gradually slowed. "Hello. You were at the lodge, yes?"

"We sure were." She was waving, and her smile was welcoming.

I waved back. "What a coincidence!" I never much liked coincidences.

She kept smiling as she walked toward me. "Coincidence? Not really. We Elderhostelers love libraries, and the one here at the high school . . . well, it's pretty good. It really is. The whole crew's here, except . . ." She frowned. "Sorry."

She'd been referring to the man who'd tried to kill me. The killer had disguised himself as elderly. For all I knew, this woman was his partner, out to finish the job. No, I didn't like coincidences much. Nor did I enjoy the sense of enveloping paranoia. "Not a problem, ma'am. They've got some wonderful books here. So where'd you go this morning? I didn't see any of your group."

"We checked out real early," she said. "We all thought you left last night."

"No, I didn't. Good seeing you." I backed away and turned.

"Hey now, what's that you're reading?" Over my shoulder she reached for the manuscript.

"Um, just an old book that—" She tugged it from my hands.

"Well, look at this." She began paging through the manuscript.

"I haven't finished reading it yet," I said.

"No, well, that's too darn bad." She turned and began to walk away.

I reached for her arm. "Hold it! I was reading that."

"Were you, now?" Her smile didn't reach her eyes. "Well, I want to read it myself. You'll excuse me."

I grabbed for her, and she shoved me away, into the stacks. I stumbled, but didn't fall. I couldn't let her take that book.

I ran after her. She began to run, too. She was headed for the exit by the special books. Just as she reached the door, Joe appeared, blocking her path.

"Where you going, lady?"

"Get out of my way, kid," the woman said.

"White women don't get to read that book."

"Yeah, they do." She punched the boy in the face.

Joe fell backward and hit his head on a table. He went down and stayed there.

"You monster!" I screamed.

She slammed open the door. "I am, aren't I? You'd better hurry, or those folks are gonna be dead."

I raised the Taser and pressed the button.

Nothing happened! I pressed again. Same thing.

And then I was looking at empty space where the woman had once been.

I ran to Joe, who was shaking his head. "Joe, I'm sorry. Are you okay?"

"Fuck off," he said.

"Joe—"

"Just leave me alone."

I ran and got Kai and told her what had happened.

"I'll be right back," she said, and returned in a few minutes with bandages and antiseptic.

She worked on Joe's head until he slapped her hand away and walked off in a huff.

"It looks like he'll be okay," I said.

"Oh, yeah," she said. "That Joe's a tough one. His pride's bruised, that's all. A woman getting the better of him. Ieeee."

"I'm sorry, Kai. I'm so sorry about the manuscript."

Her beautiful eyes didn't hold a speck of anger or recrimination, but rather, empathy. "You know," she said, "it is just a book."

"But an important one."

She rested her hand on mine. "Yes. But people are more important. Those people who took the book, they're not meant to have it. It won't help them. Not at all. They won't understand the blood fetish, even if they find it."

I searched her face. She believed what she was saying. I wished I could do the same.

She led me to a different exit.

"Here," she said. "You can leave this way. No one will see. The alarm doesn't work. Let me come with you."

"Not a chance," I said. "You've got to be really careful. These people are killers. I don't want them to know that you even exist."

Her eyes clouded. "I guess so."

I gripped her arms. "Promise me you'll leave this alone. I'll get the book back."

"Yes. Okay."

"Say it!"

"I promise."

I released her. Exhaustion crept through my body. "Good."

With a pink-polished finger, she traced my pink scar. "I wish I could fix you all up."

"That's the last thing I'm worried about right now." I pressed my hand to her cheek. "Thank you for all your help. Be safe."

"Not only will we be safe," she said, "I will make sure little brother is on watch duty. We'll be fine. He will let no one hurt me."

I clutched the pad and map tightly in my hand. "I'll find a car or truck. Four-wheel drive, I guess. I'll make it to the park, then I'll alert the rangers and go from there. I've got to get to those people. Niall and his daughter."

She looked at me, so worried. I had to leave right away, before I fell apart. I hugged her and left.

I trotted down the street well aware that I had to get a ride or hook up with Aric and Hank. The latter was the smart thing to do. So how come I was so reluctant?

I spotted the town's one gas station. If anyone had a car to rent in Crownpoint, it would be there. Afternoon. The town was a-bustle. I really wanted to be on my own. Common sense said I should find Aric and Hank. Except nothing about this whole thing made sense.

I leaned against a telephone pole stapled with fliers proclaiming Indian rodeos, powwows, and job counseling. I was stuck, afraid to move. I caught a whiff of frybread on the air. My mouth watered. Few things tasted better than frybread with honey or sugar on top.

Maybe food would get my brain going again. I needed time to think, to put stuff together, to understand what was really going on. I looked at Hank's watch. I was running out of time.

I was missing something. Whatever. I had to do the best I could do. I walked toward the gas station. A couple of cars sat on the lot. One, an old pickup, looked like a prime rental. I broke into a trot.

The blast of a horn made me stumble. My heart raced. I turned, ready for who-knew-what. Aric's Land Rover zoomed toward me. I cringed, but held my stance. Hands waved at me from the open passenger's and driver's side windows.

Oh, dear.

Aric was at the wheel and Hank sat in the passenger's seat.

CHAPTER TWENTY-SIX

More bumpy roads with numerous potholes in the packed dirt. I sat between the two men and ate the sandwich handed to me by Hank. Turkey, mayo, lettuce, no tomato. He knew me well. Maybe too well.

The sandwich had appeared out of a Bashas' Supermarket bag. I wondered if he'd gotten me a pickle or chips. I didn't dare ask, lest I unleash the floodgates of his fury.

No one was talking. Neither man had yelled at me. Neither, in fact, had said a word.

I pretended to be upset. Actually, I was pretty pleased with the silence. I took a sip from the huge water bottle provided by Hank. The water slid down cool and refreshing.

A sea of desert sprawled beyond the bug-spattered windshield. Strips of clouds banded the bright blue sky. A few miles back, we'd turned left at the long-abandoned Seven Lakes Trading Post. Our route took us on or near The Bisti Badlands. I'd always wanted to visit and see the Hoodoos. Some were strange outcroppings of pedestal rock with tilted flat pancake hats atop them. Others looked like giant mushroom-shaped fields of stone. I'd seen photos and had been amazed.

Over a small rise, cattle stood in clumps. What a wild place for cattle to graze. How could they possibly get enough water? But they must.

The land undulated, and for miles and miles we saw no sign of humankind. Hawks danced on the air currents overhead. The clouds gradually coalesced, and a soft rain began to fall.

"That won't help," Aric said.

"Ayuh," Hank said.

"I wish we could go faster," I said.

The two looked at me as if I'd grown a second head. The gray, fading light slowed us even more.

I worried about the time.

I thought of all that had happened and wondered what Governor Bowannie would have made of all the blood and violence over pot shards and a skull and the blood fetish. I wished he were here to guide us. I believed he was the only one who understood what was going on. Or maybe that was simply my wishful thinking. Maybe there were no answers.

The rain hardened, and the road became less and less visible.

I checked my watch—maybe for the fiftieth time.

"We've got less than an hour to make the meeting," I said.

"We'll make it," Aric said.

I waited. Neither man spoke.

And then my anger bubbled up. I wanted to tell them about the old woman at the library. About Kai and the blood fetish and the useless Taser. Except neither man was saying a thing.

I leaned forward, retrieved my purse and plucked out my cell phone and lipstick. Few things seemed to annoy men more than donning lipstick when the world was falling apart.

I moved the rearview mirror, which I knew would annoy

them further, and slashed peach something across my lips. Aric grunted, which I found oddly satisfying. Hank's chuckle was simply irritating.

I felt like a mackerel sandwich between those two.

I flipped open the phone, saw I had coverage, and called Gert.

"Hey, G, it's me," I said.

"It's about time," she said.

"Let me tell you a few of my adventures, since we last spoke." I launched into a litany, which was punctuated by *oohs* and *ahs* and *yikes* from the other end.

I checked my watch. We had fifty minutes, which felt like not nearly enough time.

In the background, Aric seemed to be grunting, while Hank began to softly curse. At least they'd stopped the silent treatment.

"Anything on the carbon dating?" I asked.

"Yeah, finally." Exasperation filled Gert's words. "Took me forever to get Kranak moving, and then *he* had to do this whole trip on this really dumb judge. I mean, the guy was one nasty piece of—"

"Gert! Please, hon, I'd love to hear later, but now, what were the results?"

"Cool your jets, Tal. You sound really stressed."

"Didn't I just explain what's been going on? Stressed is sort of an understatement. The pot? Please!"

"Yeah," she said. "It's one of those old things. Like from A.D. 1100 or something. Wait a minute, let me get the paper, huh?"

"Um, yeah. Sure. Get it."

I glanced at Hank while I waited. He must have sensed me watching, because he turned, slowly drew off his sunglasses, and stared. His cool blue eyes blazed hot. Then he leaned down and kissed me, and I became lost in his passion.

I surfaced gradually. The radio was on. Aric was saying

"Get a room, guys," and Hank had crossed his arms and was facing forward again, as if we'd never kissed.

Maybe I'd imagined the whole thing. Except my belly was jelly, and my thighs burned and . . .

"Gert?" My voice sounded weak and strange.

"Where ya been?"

"Outer space. Sorry. You have the paper?"

"It's just what I said. One thousand years old, consistent with Anasazi. The composition of the mud marks it as Southwestern, too. If they had more time, they could tell us exactly where the pot was from because of the makeup of the mud or something. Really weird stuff. I looked 'em up online and everything makes sense, ya know?"

"Yeah, I know. I do. I can't believe it, but I do. Thanks, hon, so much." I flipped the phone closed.

"Well?" Aric said.

"The pot was authentic. So now I don't get what's going on at all. How did Delphine's skull get in a pot from A.D. 1100? A pot that *had* to be built around the skull?"

The rain turned to mist, and again I checked my watch. We had forty minutes to make the meet. None of us had been to Chaco before, and I wondered in the gloom and wet if we'd be able to find the Chetro Ketl grand kiva easily enough. I hoped they'd gotten a map of the park and the canyon. If not, we'd have to stop at the ranger station.

"I read about it, you know." I said the words hoping either Aric or Hank would respond.

Aric grunted. Wow—a victory.

"Do you guys have any idea where Chetro Ketl is? Or even what a grand kiva is?"

We landed in a huge pothole, and I bumped my head on the roof of the truck, even wearing my seat belt. On landing, the Land Rover fishtailed badly. I fisted my hands in my lap. No way would I hold on to Hank. Their silence was really pissing me off.

"I've had it, guys. And, Aric, your damned Taser didn't work when I needed it. I almost got killed."

"Which time," drawled Hank.

"Not that funny," I said.

"We didn't think so, either," Aric said. "You acting like a prima donna."

Hank chuckled, and I elbowed him in the gut.

"Cut it out," he said.

"My ass, I will," I said. "The situation is deadly. We may not reach Niall and his daughter in time. And I'm stuck here with Misters Silent One and Two. Do you not see how lethal this all is?"

"We see," Aric said. "But we journey to where my ancestors lived or at least worshipped. Don't you feel it? The power?"

I breathed deeply, tried to relax. Of course he was right. Chaco had power. I'd always known that. And when I looked out on the austere landscape, I realized it mattered more than I'd thought. I felt dizzy with the pull of Chaco. "You're saying your ancestors will help us?"

Aric shook his head, spit out the window, and pushed a fresh chew into his cheek. "I'm saying there's more here than us and our hunt. I'm saying we should try to feel the power and use it to help us. It was a travesty, the skull in the pot. One we must fix."

I stared at Aric, and in the closeness of the truck cab, where the air was thick and musty and tight, I saw a different man. Not the FBI agent or the Indian, but the man who was comfortable being close to the spirits.

I leaned toward Hank, tilted my head. "Do you feel it?"

"I feel the truth, Tal." Hank brushed a lock of hair from my forehead. "No more than that. But truth is a powerful thing. Maybe different from Aric's power, but a strength and its own kind of power. More than that, I can't say."

I leaned back, closed my eyes. I couldn't believe it. I was in a truck with the Obi Wan twins. I slipped my arms through theirs. For the first time in days, I felt safe.

All well and good, until someone shot out our tire.

"Someone shot it, Aric." I paced by the side of the road in a vain attempt to keep warm. Aric and Hank were making swift work of changing the thing. But time was getting tighter and tighter, like some damned hangman's noose.

"How soon?" I said.

Aric's jaw tightened, but he didn't answer.

"Sorry," I said. "I know you're both rushing. I'm terribly worried about them."

"And we're not?" Hank said.

"No, of course you are."

Hank stood, arched his back. He walked around the Land Rover. I continued to pace. "Damn, it's cold out here." I hoped Niall and his daughter had warm coats to wear.

"Here," Hank said.

I looked up, and he handed me a lidded styrofoam cup with "Basha's Supermarket" on the side.

"Coffee?" I stood on tiptoe and kissed his cheek.

He flushed. "Cocoa."

I couldn't remember the last time I'd seen him blush. Made me smile. "Thanks, hon."

"Get in, you two lovebirds." Aric hopped behind the wheel, and I ran around the side. Hank slid in beside me, and we were off.

"Crank up that heat, please," I said. I took a long pull on the cocoa. "Boy is this good."

"Tal," Hank said. "It makes no sense that someone shot out our tire."

I had to think. "Maybe they didn't want us to make the meet. Maybe this is all about the *time* we get there."

"No," Aric said. "It was a rock."

"Ideas, then, about what we do when we get there?" I said.

"You'll see." He floored it, and we flew over the road as if we wore skates.

Minutes later, the rain stopped, blue sky appeared, and so did Chaco.

"Do you feel it?" I said.

Hank slipped off his glasses. "Pretty striking."

The world was painted gold and white. We neared the canyon.

"No," I said. "I mean do you feel the pull, the . . . otherness?"

No one said a word. We were almost there. And yet . . .

"Hank?" My voice . . . slurred . . . odd. Tired. I was so . . . I gasped. "The cocoa."

Hank took the mug from my hands just as I slipped into sleep.

I swam up from some sludgy depth that didn't want to release me. I pried open my eyes. Blankets swaddled me, and outside . . . emptiness. Where was I? The sun was setting on the far horizon. Where . . . ?

Pueblo Bonito! I recognized it from the books I'd read. Impossible not to. My eyes felt heavy, and I let them droop. I could nap for just a little while longer. Sure I could.

I pushed myself up straight.

Dammit! Where was Hank? Aric?

I fought my arm out of the blankets to look at my watch. 6:30! I'd been out for what, two hours? Long after we were to meet the kidnappers who'd taken Niall and his daughter.

Then where were they? What had happened? Why was I alone?

"Shit!"

Hank had doped me. That cocoa. He'd put something in it to make me sleep. They'd been planning this all along, even before they'd picked me up. Geesh.

I flung off the blankets, found some gum in my purse and jammed it into my mouth. Anything to stay awake. I trolled in my purse, found the Taser. I needed that, needed it to work. Rotated it around and around in my hand. Pressed the button. No button. No nothing.

What was I missing? I . . . Ahhhh.

I slid back a plastic hood on the top, and there, within the red circle, was the real button I was to push. Finally!

I laughed. A safety. *Of course.* Now that I'd solved that dilemma . . . I searched under the front seat, found nothing, slipped into the back, explored and, yes. I held one of those mini-flashlights. Perfect. With that, my cell phone, and the Taser, I'd be all set.

I pulled up the door handle and pushed.

The door didn't open. What the hell?

I peered out the window. They'd strung some kind of wire tight to the front and back door handles, so I couldn't open them. Couldn't get out, couldn't interfere with their big-boy plans. Talk about lame!

Those two paternal idiots.

I checked the driver's side and that was the same deal. It wouldn't budge, either. I scrambled in back, twisted the back tailgate, and that wouldn't lift or push out. Stuck. I was stuck.

Okay, now what?

There was no way I was sitting in this truck for who-knew-how-long. *Think, Tally, think.*

The truck was old, with vinyl duct-taped seats, a cracked windshield, and plastic steering wheel. The windshield could be broken. I was sure of that. But I'd hate to do it. I scoured the truck again, which made me dizzy. I found no rock, no ice scraper, nothing I could use to pound out the passenger-side window. All I really wanted to do was sleep. Maybe I should just let them be, crawl under the blanket and doze.

That was when a sense of dread crawled up my spine. I

was trapped. Someone could set fire to the Land Rover, and I'd be burnt to a crisp. I couldn't breathe and was suddenly gasping for air.

I clutched the armrest, shook the door, screamed to be let out.

Stopstopstop.

I took a deep breath, said a couple oms.

If the Land Rover were burning, I would . . .

I lay on my back, legs flexed, and slammed my feet against the passenger-side window. On the second kick, out it went. At least, part of it. I wrapped my hand in the blanket, lifted some of the spiked glass shards out, then reached outside and tried the door. I hadn't expected it to open, and it didn't.

I pulled out the remaining glass shards and crawled out. I "oomphed" when I landed, then crouched and peered around. I saw no one. But I heard, in the near distance, what sounded like laughter.

I left my purse and the blankets I'd carried through the window beneath the truck. I took the Taser and the flashlight and my cell, pulled on my gloves, and off I went.

Night was closing in. Fingers of the sun glowed on the horizon. The moon, fat and promising, bobbed in the sky like a giant Necco wafer. My rubber-soled shoes made no sound on the desert floor.

Around a curve, while climbing one of the brick walls, I skidded on a slick rock and went down.

I panted. Nothing broken. Not even too badly scraped. But I'd twisted my bum left knee, and it hurt like mad. I had to be more careful.

As I pushed myself up, I felt a rock, a nice one, a pointy one. Sure, I had the Taser, but I really trusted rocks. I slipped the baseball-sized stone into my jacket pocket and ran again. At least the pain would keep me awake. I still couldn't believe they'd drugged me.

The air was cool and getting cooler. Yet sweat drooled

down my back and between my breasts. More laughter. I felt a punch of adrenaline.

I crouched lower, ran faster. *Don'tslip . . . don'tslip . . . don'tslip.*

I shaded my eyes and looked up at the dying sun. I was running east from Bonito toward what I guessed was Chetro Ketl. So Aric and Hank had gone past the meeting spot, locked me in and doubled back. Except I was sure something had happened to derail them. Something bad.

Night was closing in, and I panicked. I *had* to find them. I ran around clumps of sage dotted with raindrops and over chunks of rock. I hustled through an arch, then down a well-trodden path, my footfalls like a beating tom-tom.

But I wasn't going fast enough.

A shriek knifed the night.

Someone was in pain. Or fear. Or both.

I ran faster, slipped, fell to my knees. I hurt, but not as much as . . .

Another shriek blasted the night.

Wait, I told myself. I had to play it smart if I was going to help anyone. I rubbed my knees, got up, flexed them. I was okay.

Taser, phone, rock, flashlight—check. I ran on.

Chaco was bigger than I'd imagined. That shriek. Maybe an animal? No, it had been human.

Someone hissed, "Fuck you!"

I ran even faster. Hank. That sounded like Hank.

Another shriek.

The world blurred as I moved in some dream, faster, rhythmically, shooting through time and space.

And then I was there. Fear grabbed my gut, and I pressed my hand to my mouth so I wouldn't sob out loud.

CHAPTER TWENTY-SEVEN

I could see nothing. I crouched behind a boulder just out-side of what I thought was the great kiva at Chetro Ketl. I took enough breaths to make sure I was somewhat calm, not that I really ever could be with Hank and Aric in ter-rible straits. Cold seeped into my bones as I listened. Be-fore I entered, I had to know just where they were.

The wind grew in volume, and an owl hooted, and some creature scurried with scratching sounds.

And then . . .

"What the fuck are we gonna do now?" came the voice.

"Shuddup," came another.

Two men. I recognized neither voice. But I now knew where they were. I waited another heartbeat, and . . .

"Do what he says." A third voice, low, slow, command-ing. A *woman's* voice. The woman at the library? It didn't sound anything like her.

Sweat bathed me, and I shook. I gripped the rock tighter, rested my cheek on its cold face. I wanted to run, leave, *escape*.

I slapped my hand over my mouth as I laughed. What sane person wouldn't?

I flexed my hands, loosened my shoulders, then crept forward.

I came face to face with a wall. The dark was a bitch, all right.

Now what?

I tried to picture again the photos I'd seen of Chetro Ketl. The Anasazi had built the great house in a semi-circle, more like a D, really, with large squared-off stones, like huge bricks, and squared windows. It once had a roof, but no more, and part of its walls had collapsed.

Originally it rose several stories, or so I remembered. But now? The pictures showed only one story remaining, and that a jagged one where walls had collapsed. Even so, the walls around me still felt immense.

I thought Chetro Ketl was the great house with the raised plaza and large kiva, but I wasn't sure. I did remember it had a huge, straight back wall hundreds of feet long.

I peered up, but could see nothing. The windows would be too high up for me, anyway. There was something I was forgetting.

I closed my eyes, tried to see with my mind. I pictured the great kiva and its stonework and the small square windows and . . .

Staircases. Short ones. They led to the main floor of the great kiva.

I rested my hand on the wall and walked. I heard no noises from inside. They'd gone silent. Had they heard me? I wet my lips. I was toast if they'd heard me.

But that couldn't be it. I'd been quiet, and they'd been busy.

I stopped walking for a minute and listened. It seemed like voices, low, mumbling. Angry, maybe?

I began walking again, almost trotting, feeling the wall

with my hands, the ground with my feet. My knee throbbed. I walked faster.

The stone was rough beneath my fingers. Would I ever find that damned door?

And then I touched space. I stumbled forward, almost fell on my face so a shower of pebbles tumbled downward.

"Did you hear something?" said the one voice.

"Yup," said the second. "You're a real jerk. Some animal makes a noise, and you get spookier than Casper the Friendly Ghost. Get over it, bubba."

"Nope," came the first voice. "I'm gonna check."

I flattened my back against the kiva. If I zapped him, would everyone hear the noise? No time to figure that one out.

Footsteps. It sounded like they were on the kiva steps.

And then he was in front of me, blocking the moon. I couldn't see a gun. I was sure he had one, but still . . .

I gasped, he turned, and I pressed the Taser button.

It failed to go off, or I missed or something.

He lunged at me, and I sidestepped. I saw something bright and shiny in the moonlight. A gun. I tried to twist out of his reach.

He grabbed me with one hand, squeezed hard, so I yipped in pain. I tried to kick him, failed, and got slammed in the face. I tumbled backward, but he held on and laughed.

"Fun, eh?" I said. "C'mere, fella. You don't know what you're missing." I used my sexiest voice, and he chuckled.

"You wanna see it?"

"Of course," I said. "You've got me good."

He made a slurping sound and pulled me close. "I do, don't I?"

"Oh, boy, do you ever, sweetie." I hauled off and whammed him in the face with the rock.

He crumpled right into me, and I tumbled, too. We

rolled over and over down the kiva steps and poured out onto the kiva floor.

I rolled away into deep velvet shadows. The dark was my friend now.

"Dick?" called a second voice. "You playing one a yer lame-ass jokes?"

Dick sure as hell wasn't joking. I got on all fours, clutched the rock, except I had to put it down to check on the Taser.

A beam of light sliced the night. Over to my right, across the great kiva, another doorway, with fire flickering in its center, led to another room in the great house. That's where they were.

Now all I had to do was get to that light across the kiva while the other guy kept calling for Dick.

I crawled. I was fast, but it was still crawling. And now they were alerted. Some alien was among them—me. Why hadn't that damned Taser worked? The thing was stupid and useless.

Pebbles bit into my already bruised knees. I paused, caught my breath. All I heard was silence and some wet, heavy breathing.

I glanced at the stars once for courage. Oh, my, they were magic.

I got my feet beneath me and duck-waddled on. When would they hear me? Know I was there? Cripes, where the hell were Hank and Aric?

My breath sounded loud in my ears. I tried to calm down. I was getting closer to the light. I had to get there without them noticing me. My thighs burned as I waddled my way forward around the edge of the kiva.

"You look pretty funny, lady. Hey, what'd you do to ol' Dick?"

I was afraid to look, but, yes, the silhouette of a man stood maybe six feet from where I was crouched. Moonlight splashed on the barrel of the gun he pointed at my face. My breathing became shallow. I grew dizzy and put my hand out to steady myself.

"Don't move, lady!"

"Sorry," I said.

I was blinded by the sudden flashlight sprayed on my face.

"Don't," I said.

He spit. "The dead live here, missy," he said. "Have some respect."

Where had I heard that? Wait a minute. Something . . . I used my hand for balance and stood. "Who the hell are you, and what do you want?"

"You're a pisser, all right," he said. "I knew you would be. I've got a good memory. Do you?"

Did I? *The dead live here.* . . . Ahhh. The National Geographic people a lifetime ago at The Grief Shop. *I'd* been the one to say those words. Now, how to play it. "No, my memory's not so hot."

"We've been looking for you, lady."

"Well, here I am, big boy." Did I really say that?

He ran the flashlight beam up and down my body. "Just like I remembered. Nice."

"Well, thanks, mister."

"Ohhhh, she's frisky."

I stepped forward.

"Hold it!"

I stopped. "You know it's freezing out here. Isn't there somewhere warm where we can go and talk?"

A rustling in the dark. Maybe the guy I'd conked on the head. I didn't have a lot of time.

"Go and talk," said my captor. "Three of my pals are dead 'cause of you. You've hurt our business. Bad." The snick of a gun. "Come with me." He waved his gun, and I was forced to lead the way.

He beamed the flash so I could find my footing. Nice

guy. The wind rose, and a howling in the distance gave me shivers. I walked beneath a squared arch into a dark passage. Someone breathing, labored, forced.

"Who's in here with us?" I said.

"Your boyfriends."

I looked around, frantic. But I could see nothing on either side. "Where are they?"

"Not your business."

He moved closer, and I smelled his glee. He took hold of my arm and dragged me forward, through the arch and across a smaller kiva. I stumbled once on a rock, almost went down. He kept me vertical.

Across the kiva and inside another arched tunnel. Here, there was a whirring sound and I smelled gas. He flung the beam around, as if to show me his hidey hole. Two inflated air mattresses lay on the floor, with a crumple of blankets atop them. To my left were two large, flat boxes. I walked toward them. One box contained hundreds of potsherds, all jumbled together. Another box was sealed and addressed to . . .

He twisted me around, pulled my hips to his and ground his pelvis into mine. His erection nauseated me. I turned away.

"Look at me, bitch."

I did. His gun hovered near my face.

I gasped for breath and finally glimpsed his face. I was right. The curly-haired Geographic guy filled with arrogance and pride.

"Oh, yeah," he said. "That feels great. Too long, baby, out here. One sec, and we'll be good to go. Yes, we will."

With the gun still pointing at my face, he reached into his pocket and produced a plastic pull tie, the kind I'd seen used by cops in place of handcuffs. They were almost impossible to remove. If he got that thing on me . . .

My mouth dried. He'd rape me and kill me without a

moment's regret. I stepped back, tried to focus on a plan, came up empty.

"You don't go anywhere." Both hands reached for me.

I stepped backward, stumbled on the rocks, landed on my back in the dirt. I lifted my hand. Blood seeped where one of the ancient potsherds had cut me right across my palm. "Shit on you!" I hollered.

"Oh, honey bitch, that's not what I'm gonna do."

He propped up the flashlight so it splayed across the floor onto me. I wasn't sure I could even move. I sensed his grin, although I couldn't see it. Everything outside the sea of flashlight was coal black.

Okay. On my back. Focus. I moaned. It sounded fake to me, but what the hell.

"That's it, honey bitch. Get ready and wet for ol' Paulie."

Ready and wet? Cripes. I moaned again, since it obviously entertained him. At the same time, I slid my hand slowly downward.

He pulled out his penis, shined the light on it. I felt his grin broaden. "Look what I've got for you."

Oh, *Christmas.* He was certainly primed for action. "Wow," I said, hoping I sounded positive. "That's really something." Maybe I could bite it off. Yeah, but I doubted he'd let me get that close. My stomach heaved at the prospect of rape.

"Sure is, honey bitch."

Get over it, Tal. Do something. Anything. I tried to think of something, but all I could do was pant in fear.

He rubbed himself, grinned. "You are a pretty pussy. Even all beat up."

Oh, God. I slipped my hand into my jacket pocket, danced my fingers around in search of the Taser. Cripes, it was in the other pocket.

"You're awful quiet, honey bitch."

"I don't mean to be," I said in a faux sexy voice.

He kneeled in front of me, but not near enough so I

could grab him. The gun in his left hand never wavered. It was like a snake, one I couldn't take my gaze from.

I'd arrived in this nightmare place and time, and no one could come to my aid. No one was near. No one to hear my cries. My rape. My end.

I scooted a couple steps backward.

"You got nowhere to run, honey bitch."

"Why are you doing this?" I said.

He tittered. "Stupid. Money. You're dumber than you look. But I've got to admit this part's fun."

"Money. All these people dead for money."

"Lots of it, honey bitch."

"My name is Tally."

"Yeah. I know." He turned and cranked up the heater.

I couldn't believe this jerk was the man who'd killed Delphine and Didi and the governor and Natalie and . . .

I readied my foot. I'd push it into his crotch the minute he came near. Who was panting? Oh, it was me. Loud and shallow in my ear, like some fearful stranger.

He slipped his penis back into his pants and moved forward. "Time to tie your little pretty self up."

His right hand shot out, and he yanked me hard, so I fell forward onto my left side. Something cracked, and tears came as I was blinded by the pain. I growled, refusing to give him any satisfaction.

"Oh, did I hurt the little girl? I liked it." He laughed harder.

I swooped my hand into my right pocket. This was my last chance. Third time and all. I pulled out the Taser, pointed it at him and zapped!

Nothing happened. *Nothing.*

"Bitch!"

I scooted across the dirt floor, flopped onto an air mattress.

He grabbed my feet, unsnapped my jeans button, and tried to pull down my pants. "You'll be sorry."

The jeans were tight. He was having trouble. He pulled,

and I squirmed, anything to get away from him. My jeans went down over my bum.

He hit my ass, hard.

I gasped.

I felt him above me, moving, about to . . .

I raised the Taser one more time, didn't know what else to do, twisted around and . . . *Hell.* I hadn't pulled back the safety. I pumped my legs, kicking and twisting as I slid back the plastic on the top of the Taser, a beam of light and a glow around a red-marked button.

"What the fuck!" he shouted.

Clawed hands reaching for me! And I pressed the button, hard, harder. *Pressitpressitpressit.*

I panted, harsh, guttural sounds of fear. *Pressingpressing.*

The Taser's wires flew out and zapped him.

I sucked in breaths.

Ohgodohgodohgod.

Calm, I told myself. *Calm. Ohm. Ohm. Calm.*

I shook my head twice. *Focus, dammit.* I looked, saw him writhing and barking like a dog in pain in the light from the Taser's beam.

Clutching the Taser, I scrambled to my knees. He still writhed on the floor of the tunnel, and I was afraid to touch him, but I had to. I wiped one hand, then the other, on my shirt to get rid of the greasy feel. I wanted to pull up my pants, but I didn't have time. How long would he be in pain? I had no idea.

I reached for his gun, wrapped my hand around the stock, and pulled it toward me. Took the flashlight. Oh, God, I wished he'd stop moaning. Searched, found the black pull ties. Wrapped one around his hands, faster. He kicked out, and I lurched back, but I'd gotten his hands tied, had the gun.

Panting, couldn't stop.

Could I Taser him again? I didn't know. And if I did, would it kill him?

He was still rolling around, moaning.

I felt this incredible sense of satisfaction and instantly felt guilty. I *had* to calm down. I was dizzy, hyperventilating.

Okay. Calm. No matter what. Calm.

I looked at my hand. I held several ties, the flashlight. His gun. I looked sharply to my right. There it was. Okay.

I tugged my pants up and fastened them.

Maybe I should hit him on the head, knock him out.

Om. Calm. His hands were bound. He couldn't get to me. Maybe I could tie his ankles. But the ties weren't long enough.

I was sweating and shaking. A fricking mess.

A sound, just outside the entrance to the tunnel. I pressed my back against the wall, flicked off the light. Still a light! Shit! Shit! I slid the Taser door closed, so the other guy wouldn't see the light from the Taser.

Pitch black. Safe.

"Paulie?" It was the voice of my first attacker.

Dread crept over me. I was in some monster nightmare that would never end. I knew what I had to do, hated it, but I made myself pick up a rock, and I brought it down on Paulie's head. It make a sickening thud. I didn't think he'd awaken anytime soon.

"Hey, Paulie, you there?"

Stumbling and shuffling sounds. Then a flashlight blazed on just outside the end of the arched tunnel.

What to do? I could Taser him. Maybe. But I wasn't sure it would work a second time. No, I had to draw the guy away from Hank and Aric. Yes, that made sense. How?

One, two, buckle my shoe.

"Here I am!" I shouted.

The light went off, and everything got quiet. Again, I heard labored breathing, a moan. Okay, if I stayed there, I might be able to take him out. That was probably the better thing to do.

A bullet ricocheted off the side of the tunnel.

I ran. Over my shoulder, I hollered, "Catch me if you can, sucka!"

Between my pants for breath, I heard him following.

"Gonna get you, bitch!"

Yup, he was after me.

Then I tumbled over a rock and fell into emptiness.

Chapter Twenty-eight

Whoomp. I blinked, adjusted to the moonlight, wiped the dust from my face. Just a small fall, into what looked like another circular room, this one lower than the others.

Laughter, coming from behind me.

I pushed myself to my feet, reached into my pocked.

The Taser was gone!

I scrambled on all fours, feeling the crusty earth, rocks, dried grasses, droplets of rain. Nothing. *Nothing. NOTH-ING!*

Now what? Oh, cripes.

I would not let this son of a bitch do me in. No way.

I crouched low, listened. Okay, he didn't know exactly where I was.

Bullets. A hail of them. I ducked.

But, no, he didn't have my location. He was heading off in another direction. I could go back, try to free Hank and Aric.

I should wait, listen. Just for a minute.

I sat, huddled, arms around my knees. I hugged myself,

tried to find that quiet place I knew existed that was safe and serene. Just for a minute. My head felt light, woozy.

I rubbed my temples. Was I going crazy?

Think practical. Right. I tried to picture the kiva, the maps. Cripes. All I could see was the stupid sign saying DON'T CLIMB PREHISTORIC STAIRWAYS—VERY DANGEROUS.

They hadn't looked that dangerous in the picture I'd seen. I'd bet the sign was for their protection, not the climber's.

I tilted my head back. Oh, my—the blanket of stars. They were there as always. Beautiful. Wonderful. A freshening breeze caressed my cheek, oddly warmer than the night.

The stairs. A whisper.

The . . . stairs.

I was hearing that, as if in a dream.

I grew calm, quiet, tried to listen to words that felt inside me, yet . . . whispers on the wind. Maybe I was living my end, where, they say, clarity drowned one in truth. I strained to hear. The desert sounds, the rustling and scratching and small yips and chirps all receded.

The air grew even clearer. Softer, warmer, yet charged with electricity. Chaco glowed.

My head swirled, and there, in front of me—Chaco as it once had been.

She was magnificent, with her people busy building, cooking, dancing, worshiping. The great houses wore roofs, and some of her people wore much finery. And over there, macaws—three of them—had leashes of leather on their feet. They sat on perches and watched, their heads swiveling back and forth.

I was dreaming . . . I was crazy . . . what . . .

To my right, the canyon walls glittered red and yellow and ochre in the blinding sun. A stream, clear and melodic, wove beside the canyon wall. Where some small trees grew, a man, a warrior, walked to a woman, young and fair who had a twisted foot and hair down to her thighs.

He kneeled before her. She nodded, then rested her hands on his shoulders. She kneeled, too, and they kissed and made love by the stream.

What was going on? I rubbed the cut made by the potsherd that had sliced my palm. Except my palm felt smooth. No cut. I held up my left hand. Nothing. My other palm was uninjured, too.

I held up both hands, and the sun felt warm on the backs, my fingers, all warm. This couldn't be real, yet . . .

I stepped toward the couple, wishing to be closer, to understand what they understood.

When they were sated, he leaned over her and plucked a string of brilliant yellow desert roses that vined across a rock. He wove it through her hair, and they laughed, and then they made love again.

Where was I in all this? A voyeur, yet somehow I was a part of it, too. I didn't really understand, except the same warmth beamed down on me, healing my body, my heart, my soul.

Time to go! the warrior said. He looked above Chetro Ketl, to a tall, winding stair cut from the cliff rock itself. *Time to go!*

The girl shook her head. *Not yet!*

Now. He reached down for her and helped her up. He handed her the carved crutch she carried always.

You will die, she said.

I will be safe, he said.

She shook her head, fought the tears that dripped from her eyes.

Yes, he repeated. He reached for the amulet pouch that hung from his neck. He widened the leather thong and reached inside. He pulled out something and hid it in his hand.

What? she said.

See? He unfolded his hand.

On his palm rested a fetish. Crudely shaped, but smooth and cared for. It was blood red and glittered in the noon sun, like a ruby. A line humped its back—a tail bent upwards. The body was long, lean, with a rounded head.

I carved it. For safety. Mountain lion will keep me safe.

What is mountain lion?

You will see when we go to the new place in the South. Dowa Yalanne. I have heard of it. We will make our home there. You will see. But for now, he said, *I must go.*

They kissed again, passion incredible, and when they parted, her face was wet with tears.

But her eyes, brown and liquid, glittered with hope.

She raised . . .

Gunfire!

I shook my head. What had I been doing? Where was I? Where was the sun? But it wasn't day, it was night. Not then, but now.

The canyon, now. The breeze, sharp and biting.

But the stairs. I'd seen them in my vision. I knew they were there. I turned. If I went straight . . . The moon shined on a glitter path. Yes, if I went straight, I would find them.

A bullet whooshed by my cheek.

I ran.

Laughter followed. "I know this place, little lady," he said. "You ain't gonna get out. No, you ain't. So I'm just gonna wait."

I stopped, bent over and caught my breath. My side ached. Now what? Ummm. I turned, so the wind slapped my face. I climbed up onto a hump of sandstone and hoped he could see me, *and* that I was out of range. "Oh, you're so wrong, Dumb Dick. I know of a place. One that will lead me to freedom."

"Why the hell are you callin' me that, goddammit? I'm not dumb."

"Sure you are, Dumb Dick." I laughed, hard, leapt off the rock, landed in my usual awkward manner.

"Where ya goin', little lady?"

This time I crouched. "Oh, Dumb Dick, I'm going up, up, and away!"

A beam of light cut the night. It wove back and forth. I had to be crazy, but . . . I believed my vision. This was Chaco, after all.

I stepped forward, let the light catch me, then turned and ran. Then I stopped, flattened myself on the ground, and Dumb Dick peppered the night with bullets, just as I had imagined he would.

It actually felt good, lying on the sandy earth, some nasty clumps of something pricking my belly. Then again, maybe he'd just walk right up and shoot me.

I pushed myself up and ran forward, hollering "Catch me if you can, sucka!"

I ran through halls and tunnels and across kivas round and square. Like some party maze, it seemed to go on forever and ever.

I ran straight into a cliff projection and was flattened.

I saw stars, and not the celestial kind. I lay there on my back, took a couple breaths, rolled on my side and staggered to my feet. I felt giddy with frustration.

If he didn't get me, I'd get myself.

Now if I could only find the stairs. I saw them so clearly in my mind.

I flattened my hands on the sandstone, searching for the stairs in the dark where an overhang might hide me.

I inched along sideways, hands pressed against the cliff wall, feet trying to find purchase on the uneven, rock-strewn ground, all the time listening, listening for Dumb Dick.

He was there, shining his beam of light to my right, while I moved left. I sure as hell hoped I was going the correct way. My left knee, the bum one, ached. But it held.

My hands stung from the scrapes and bruises. Yet I didn't care. I couldn't quite believe I was still standing.

Seconds later, I wasn't, as I tumbled to my left, into another hole.

"Gotcha!" Dumb Dick yelled.

He was right.

No Taser. I searched for some rocks.

Instead I found the stairs. I felt one, then the second, then another.

I slipped some stones into my jacket pockets. God, my fingers ached. Had to do it. I began to climb. I was amazed the stairs were so well cut and defined. The Chaco masons had been brilliant. How could these stairs possibly have lasted so long? Yet they felt marvelously intact. Thank heavens.

From the photo I'd seen of one stairway, it was a long, long way up to the top of the mesa. I sucked it up again, and climbed. "Come and get me, Dumb Dick."

"You call me that again, and I'll . . ." A shot rang out, then another.

"Up here, baby!" I hollered.

I paused, listened. He was coming.

I climbed. And climbed. And climbed. The stair was narrow, but not so that I could put out my two hands and touch both walls. I could almost feel the warrior guiding me. What a reassuring hallucination.

I loosened some stones. They cascaded down, and Dumb Dick hollered curses at me. My heart sped up, and I climbed faster.

The moon gave me enough light to see the twists and turns of the stair. Dumb Dick's beam of light couldn't follow me.

I paused, caught my breath. I was in the high desert, which meant altitude. And I was high up on the stairway. Really high. Yet from what little I could see, I sensed I was still far from the top. Down below, the stair vanished around a curve. But I saw Dumb Dick's light, heard more curses.

I climbed higher, panting, searching for breath.

I turned, looked down. Below, far below, Chaco spread out like a magic carpet in the moonlight. Stars, big as the kind kids stick on their ceilings, winked back at me. There was Chetro Ketl, the visitor center, and there, Pueblo Bonito. From up here, it looked . . . alien. As if visitors from long ago and far away had gifted man with this amazing creation of circles inside squares inside the shape of a D. Words always had been inadequate for this place.

A cloud drifted across the moon. I remembered my mission.

"Up here!" I shouted.

He didn't answer, but I could see enough of the beam and its bobbing to know where he was. He was far below me. I couldn't imagine what was taking him so long.

Again I heard cursing. He was coming on, getting nearer.

I had my rocks. I slipped my hand into my left pocket and pulled out a bunch of stones. As soon as I saw the light nearby, I'd crouch in a corner of the stair and pelt him with the things.

One more time. I could do this.

I leaned against one wall of the stairway. I was exhausted. I slid down the wall and sat, held my head in my hands.

A scream!

I jumped up, blinked over and over. What had happened? Gunfire, more screams, a piercing yelp, then . . . silence.

I waited for a bit. "Dumb Dick?"

Only the wail of the wind answered me.

It could be a trick. Sure. But if I stayed where I was, unmoving, I'd freeze to death. At least, that's how it felt. And I had to know. I couldn't just sit there. Could not do it.

This was going to be hard. Really hard. Harder than going up.

The wind howled and clouds scudded across the sky.

Maybe I'd just sit here for a while. Yeah.

I sat down again. My teeth chattered. My knees did, too, and I thought of Hank and Aric, freezing in that small hallway.

I stood, gripped the rock in my left hand, moved to the other side of the stair and guided myself with my right.

Down I went.

Down and down and down, until I had to stop. I was dizzy and wobbly. I checked my jeans pocket and came up with two Jolly Ranchers. I unwrapped both and stuck them in my mouth.

Good God. Was I really eating Jolly Ranches on a Chaco Canyon staircase with a murderer waiting for me down below? I swallowed again and again. Felt good. Energized.

Down I went. Nine, eight, seven, six, five, four. "Dumb Dick?"

The sky cleared, hushed. Light from the east, just a hint of it, but it washed out many of the eastern stars. Dawn was on its way. I had to hurry. No dark, no way to hide.

I almost ran down the stairs. Even with the twists and turns, I sensed when the floor of the canyon was near.

I stopped once more. "Dumb Dick?"

Nothing.

He wasn't that clever, was he? Or patient?

The screams had sounded real.

I never prayed. Except right then it felt like I needed to. So I prayed for safety and goodness, and I talked to Buddha and Jesus and all the gods of Chaco.

I raced down the final stairs. If he were there, waiting, I'd surprise him with my speed.

I hit the floor of the canyon like a rocket, and then I tripped.

Flat on my face. My cheek stung, my shoulder ached, my knee. Geesh. My bad knee.

I rested just for a sec, then gathered myself into a ball

and turned to see what I'd tripped on in the watery morning light.

Dumb Dick lay there, crumpled, bloody, with a bone sticking out of his shin and a rock stabbing into his neck.

I inched forward. "Hey?"

He was dead, all right. Just beyond where the stair emptied into the canyon. He'd fallen amidst a jumble of rocks. That was the scream I'd heard. I didn't see how, but I didn't much care, either.

Just to be sure, I pressed two fingers against his carotid artery.

Silence. His skin was cold, clammy. I shrank back.

The flashlight was still on. It was one of those heavy-duty ones. I reached for it, and flashed the beam on his face.

Christmas. I wished I hadn't. His look of horror, stubbled gray beard, milky eyes, tooth poking through his upper lip.

I shook my head. Horrible. He would have killed me. But I still felt sorry for him. I'd been lucky to make it. That was all. Lucky.

I thought it was only right to thank the gods, and then I ran back toward Chetro Ketl and Hank.

Dawn was near. Streaks of red fingered the sky now lit with a pale light. I stumbled my way through the warren of rooms large and small, back to the tunnel in Chetro Ketl. I flicked off the flashlight. I didn't really need it, and I didn't want to be any more a target than necessary. As I crossed one of the larger kivas, the wind picked up, slapping my clothes and tangling my hair.

Where was I? Lost? God, the noise was intense. Every time I thought it was dying down, another bluster pushed me in some crazy direction. I rubbed my forehead. After all the crap with those men, I sure as hell didn't need this.

The howling was driving me nuts.

I pushed forward, trudged up a small set of stairs, and

there was the tunnel. I leaned against the stone wall. I was beat. I couldn't make it to the tunnel.

Of course I could. Had to.

I put one leg in front of the other. The wind had steadied, and now a frothy mist drifted onto my face, like a soft caress.

I trotted the last few yards across the round kiva, up and over a small projection, then around a rectangular hole of stones maybe a foot deep. I looked up. Black clouds boiled on the horizon. I didn't know when the rain was coming. I just feared it.

I ducked inside the tunnel. At the very edge, the howling was even louder. I tightened my fists, took some calming breaths. It was darker here in the tunnel.

Paulie could be lurking. I pointed the flashlight at the ground and pushed it back on. Where had I left him? Not far from the exit.

I hugged the wall. That's right, they'd had some kind of light in here. So where was it. My mouth dried. He was alive. He'd gotten free. He was going to shoot me.

I flicked off the flashlight, walked forward, so quiet, except of the wind bringing her howls into the tunnel.

Where were Hank and Aric?

A presence. Someone. In front of me. Paulie!

I dropped to the floor. Pulled a rock from my pocket.

Then someone grabbed me in both arms, pressed me tight. I tried to raise my wrist. If I could just nail him with the rock.

He tore it from my hand. Gone. Done.

I was done.

I caught a sob in my throat. Now wasn't the time to whine.

And then I was lifted by my shoulders, my hands released, and I flipped around and . . .

"It's me, Tal. Hank. Calm down."

And I leaned against him, saying nothing, nothing, and all I could hear was the cry of the wind.

CHAPTER TWENTY-NINE

The Ring Ding tasted great. God, it was luscious and creamy and just perfect. Perfect! I licked the center and . . . Geesh, what was I doing? Every so often, I'd close my eyes and cry. And Hank would say, "Please, don't," but I couldn't help it. I leaned against the wall of the tunnel. It was surprisingly small and cozy, especially with the neat fire Aric had built. He was gone to get the rangers and call his base and find some way to remove Paulie and Dumb Dick's dead body.

"Except he wasn't dumb," I said to Hank. "I don't think so, at least. I just called him that to piss him off."

"Sweetie," Hank said. "You've explained that twelve times."

My chewing slowed. "I guess. Yeah, I guess."

"How's your hand?" He poked a stick at the fire, which danced.

"My hand." I held up my palms. No cut across either one. Nothing. Something had happened to me in Chaco. Something that I felt more than understood.

"Tal?" Hank said. "Coyote's bite. Remember?"

"Oh!" I laughed, slapped my thigh. "Coyote's bite. Yeah. Sure I do."

He shook his head. "Less than two days. We gotta get back for your shot."

"Oh, right." That all seemed like another reality completely. What did anything matter after last night? I rested my head in my hands.

He threw an arm over my shoulder and pulled me tight. He rocked me, and I wept. And then slept.

I dreamed of Chaco and the limping girl with the hope in her eyes.

Noise! I jumped, moved into a crouch.

"It's okay, okay, Tal." Hank massaged my hand, kissed my palm.

"No! It could be—"

"It's Aric. The rangers. We're all set."

"Oh. I meant to tell you," I said. "I recognized Paulie. He was part of a phony National Geographic team I met back in Boston. My gut says he and his buddies were the ones to kill Didi. We'll see." I told him the story, and he took notes.

"Once we ID the guy," he said, "this thing will start to break."

"I hope so."

Several rangers filed into the tunnel. Aric was at the head. He led them over to Paulie and pointed.

Two rangers conferred, then hoisted Paulie onto a curved red stretcher, much like they used in ski rescues.

"Aric!" I held open my arms, and he hugged me. "I'm so glad you're safe."

"Us. Yeah. Right." He hugged me tighter.

"How's Paulie?"

Aric frowned and shook his head. "He didn't make it, Tally."

I sprang up and ran to the body that rested in the

stretcher. I tugged back the part of the blanket that covered his face.

I turned away and leaned against the wall. I rested my forehead on the cool stone. What had gone on? I didn't understand.

"What is it, Tally?" Hank said. "You've seen plenty of dead people."

I nodded. "Yes. But his face. It didn't look like that when I left last night. Now, it looks . . . well, it looks just like Dumb Dick's face. Horrible."

Two of the men looked at each other, and it was obvious they thought I needed a lot more rest. I sucked in a breath, turned to a ranger.

"Come with me," I said. "I'll show you where Dumb Dick is. He's by the stairs."

"Why don't you wait here," Aric said.

I looked from Aric to Hank, both so concerned, so paternal, so wanting to believe none of the things I'd done the previous night. They'd see.

"Do come along," I said. "Gentlemen, ladies, I'll show you the way."

The sun was a fat yellow lollipop, the sky the color of turquoise. The day had warmed, the rain had vanished, and the air was crisp and light.

I wore Hank's jacket. It was huge on me, and I felt like the abominable snowman as I followed the woman ranger across Chatro Ketl. I wasn't sure if I could find the staircase again.

Hank held my hand in his huge one, and the comfort warmed me far more than the jacket. Everyone chattered, as if two men hadn't died in Chaco the previous night.

"Here we are," said one of the rangers.

And there lay Dumb Dick's hideously crumpled body. The park rangers loaded him onto a stretcher, and I sure didn't need to see *his* face. I remembered it all too well.

"You say you climbed the stairs?" the female ranger said.

"Yes." I nodded, arms tucked at my sides in an attempt to look strong. I think I swayed anyway. "If not for them, I'd have been dead meat."

"Um, ma'am," she said. "I'm not really clear about this."

Aric snorted, shook his head. "What does she have to say? Huh?" He rounded a bend. Silence.

"Aric?" Hank said.

"Hold on!" Aric called.

"Problem?" Hank said.

"Come," Aric replied.

I felt like I was watching some play, as each person disappeared around the bend. Hank vanished, too, and I was so beat, I slumped against a rock. The two remaining rangers—two others had already left with Dumb Dick's body—milled around, giving each other and me long looks.

I just wanted to go home. Or, at least, to a warm bed where I could sleep for a week.

Hank reappeared. He slid his arm around my waist, peered down at me, all serious business.

"What?" I didn't know what else to say.

"Hon, tell us again about last night and the stairway and Dumb Dick."

"Oh, why not!" I repeated the whole thing, blow by blow. Yawn. I caught Aric listening, too.

When I finished, Hank turned to the rangers. "Another canyon staircase around here?"

They shook their heads, looked down and left, a perfect "tell" that something was off. Maybe they thought I'd murdered Dumb Dick in cold blood. That I hadn't been pursued.

"Hank," I said. "He was after me. I know the sign says not to climb the stairs, but I *had* to get away. He was shooting at me. You'll find the bullets and . . ."

My voice trailed off. Now *everyone* was looking weird.

"People!" I shouted. "I am, after all, a psychologist. What the hell is wrong?"

The wind that had been howling so furiously, quieted. I heard canyon noises. Scurrying and bird chatter and pebbles tumbling to the canyon floor.

Aric held out his hand. "Come. I'll show you."

I took it. "Hank?"

"Let Aric take you. I'll be waiting for you."

Aric held my left hand, and we walked around the large boulder that hid the entrance to the staircase.

Impossible.

I stared at a jumble of rock, and the vague memory of a stairway cut into the rock. Steps had crumbled. Many no longer existed. Others were impossibly narrow and smooth, and still others gaped or were worn to near nothingness. At the bottom of the stairway, near where we stood, a chaos of rocks and boulders, so that the base of the stairway was pretty much impossible to reach.

The stairway before me *could not* be climbed.

I turned to Aric. "This isn't it."

He nodded. "It is, Tally."

I waved my hand. "I couldn't climb this in a million years. No one could. There's nothing to climb!"

He looked at the ground. "I know."

I threw back my shoulders. "Obviously there's another stairway around here, one that's well defined and easy to climb."

"There isn't, Tally." He raised his hand to the stair. "This is the only one nearby. This is where we found Dumb Dick."

I stormed back around the boulder. The two rangers and Hank stood there wearing expressions of expectation. Hank's eyebrows inched up. "Well, hon?"

"Don't 'hon' me. Where's the frickin' stairway I climbed?" I first looked at Hank, who shook his head, shuffled his feet. I walked over to the rangers. "Well?"

"Um, ma'am," the man said. "You've obviously had a long and terrible night. We understand. We do." He tried to smile.

"Understand what? I climbed the stairway to get away from Dumb Dick. I got halfway up. I know because of the view."

"I'm sorry," said the woman ranger.

"Don't be," I said. "Look. Let me explain again. He was chasing me, and I felt along the wall, and then I came to the bottom of the stair. I began to climb. The steps were wide. Wider than four feet, I'd say, and well defined. Well cut, you know. They were deep enough, too, that I didn't feel tippy. I have lousy balance. So just to make everyone happy, please show me the other stairway, okay? I assume it's farther away from here, but in the dark, distances can be strange."

"That's true about distances." The woman ranger dug her hands into her back pockets. She looked from me to Hank to Aric to the other ranger, then back to me. "Sure. I'd be happy to do it, okay?"

"Thank you." I began to walk beside her. "They just think I couldn't have made it so far or something. Sure, I was beat and terrified, but the adrenaline was pumping like mad."

"I understand," she said. "Except we found the dead man at the bottom of the stairway we were just—"

"Humor me," I said.

"Sure."

We headed across the canyon floor.

"Wait, please," I said. "I didn't cross the canyon."

She turned to me, her face sad. "Look, ma'am, you've had an *ordeal*." Her voice had a Southern lilt that fell softly on the ear.

"Yes," I said.

"It was dark."

"Yes, but the moon was out. It was brighter than you think."

She tilted her broad-brimmed hat back. "Ma'am, I don't know how else to say it kindly. It's either where we're going, across the canyon, way over there. Or way down the canyon, there." She pointed, and I knew I hadn't traveled anywhere near the distances she was showing me.

"But—"

"Or it's the stairway we just showed you. You couldn't've reached anything else. I *am* sorry, but those are the facts. Even the stairway across the canyon isn't . . ." Her voice trailed off.

The ranger's unlined, sunkissed face looked genuinely sad. Squint lines fanned from her green eyes, and freckles dusted her nose and cheeks. Most of all, she wore truth on her face. She didn't look down or away or anywhere but right at me.

"So, that's the staircase," I said, pointing back to where we'd just come from.

She nodded. "That's it. Right where we found the man you call Dumb Dick." She held out her hand. "C'mon. Let's walk back and join the guys. We're freakin' 'em out."

I took her warm, leathery hand in mine. "You're a good person. Your name?"

"They call me Gimp because, well, I limp. I have a lousy foot."

"I hadn't noticed."

She smiled.

On the walk back to the tunnel, I tried not to think about the stairway or how I'd climbed it or the looks I was getting from the other ranger and Hank and Aric.

Gimp held my hand, and, yes, she did walk with a limp.

Her strength seemed to move from our clasped hands up my arm and into my heart. I felt better. I looked at her—

with her confident, limping stride, straight shoulders and flushed cheeks—and saw a face I'd seen before . . . in my dreams or that waking dream or whatever last night's vision had been.

She must have felt me staring, because she looked straight at me and smiled. The sun was in that smile.

"I'm, um, uncomfortable calling you Gimp. What's your given name?"

"Doesn't matter. 'Gimp' reminds me of someone I'm fond of. Use it, please."

"Of course."

"How 'bout you stay at my apartment today?" she said. "Get some rest. We need to talk."

I had the strangest feeling that she knew things. Things I needed to understand. "Yes. Okay. I'd love a place to lie down."

Back at the tunnel, we examined the box of potsherds, which was about the size of a fresh fruit box used at farm stands.

"I've seen no stolen pots," Aric said. "None that are whole."

Hank paced the breadth of the tunnel. "No."

With gloved hands, Aric and Hank lifted the sealed wooden box.

Gimp walked over, her hands also gloved. "I figure you don't want to open it, right?"

"Not a good idea," Aric said. "We might be able to get some prints, some trace of something off the outside of the box."

Gimp nodded. "Shake it a little."

Hank and Aric gently shook the box as the two rangers and I watched. It made a soft, rattling sound.

"I wonder," I said. "Could it be more potsherds? Unwrapped? I don't get it at all."

They carefully replaced the box on the floor of the tunnel. Aric pushed a chaw into his cheek. "Maybe. Boxes aren't shaped right for a whole pot. Too small."

"So why would they want a bunch of shards?" I said, more to myself than anyone. "I've seen a few on eBay. What does it give them? They're not that valuable."

Hank picked up the flashlight and shined it on the box. "You see where it's headed, Tal?"

I leaned forward and read the address. "Wow. Huh. Salem, Massachusetts. What goes around . . ."

"Yup," Hank said.

I pulled Hank aside, into a darker recess of the tunnel. "I wanted to ask . . . any word or sign of Niall and his daughter?"

He brushed my lips with his. "Leave it to you to ask."

"Isn't everyone asking?"

He pressed me closer. "Some rangers found 'em just a little while ago, hon. While we were out walking to the stair."

I closed my eyes, took a deep breath.

"They're dead, aren't they?" I said. "Just like Didi and Delphine and . . ." I didn't need to open my eyes to feel the sorrow and kindness in Hank Cunningham. He hugged me tight.

"We did our best, babe. They were dead long before the five o'clock deadline."

I melted into him, and we held each other, knowing that we both were feeling the horror of the world and glad we had each other.

"It's probably time to go home," he said.

"It is."

I refused to leave at that instant, and so we were right back to reality. We had a fight. Not a big one, but I sure didn't need it, and I bet Hank didn't either.

I insisted on spending that day at Chaco. He wanted

out of there right away. Gimp offered to drive me to Albuquerque, but Hank would hear none of it, so he and Aric hung out somewhere, while Gimp took me to her apartment in the housing area where most of the rangers lived.

The one-story apartment had a wooden porch and was made of stucco. Inside, it felt like any other apartment just about anywhere on the planet. It was clean and plain, with photos of Gimp's family as decoration. I slid beneath the clean, white sheets. Heaven. I didn't dream. Or, if I did, I had no memory of it when I awakened.

I sat up in the bed, rubbed my eyes. Every damned part of my body ached, from my skin right down to my core. I had cuts and bruises everywhere. My knee throbbed, and so did my head. My face . . . oh, boy—I didn't even want to go there. All I wanted to do was sleep some more.

Instead, I fluffed the pillow and sat up in bed. I smiled when I saw the bottle of ibuprofen on the small wicker table beside the bed. I was sure it was courtesy of Hank. It would help, for sure.

I shook three tablets into my hand, then poured some water from the white ceramic pitcher that also sat on the end table. They went down easy. Funny, it felt good to do small things, like pouring water and plumping a pillow. It felt good to *live*. I should pay attention more often.

I'd been damaged, outside and in.

But maybe not my heart. Maybe not that. Yes, it felt bruised, but not broken.

I hunkered under the soft down comforter that was just light enough on my aches and pains to keep me warm. My eyes slowly shut, and I pictured a small red boat I'd owned as a kid back in Maine. The paint was flaking and there was a hole—a big one—in the bottom. I'd found the boat near our home on the Surry Road and asked my dad if he'd fix it for me. He said I was nuts, that it wasn't worth fixing, but he did it anyway, and he and I used to row in the boat out to the big rock where he'd pretend to fish and I'd read my book.

"Ready for our walk?"

I jumped. "Gimp?"

"Yupadoodle." She leaned in the doorway, one foot inside, and one out.

"I think I need to sleep more."

"I go on duty in an hour. We don't have much time. Let's go."

"How about a rain check, huh?"

She burst out laughing. "I'll meet you outside in five minutes."

CHAPTER THIRTY

She handed me a chilled water bottle, and we strode across the housing area, then hopped into the Jeep she'd left running.

The sun from the sunroof felt good, but Gimp stuck a ball cap on my head.

"No sunstroke here," she said.

I snugged it on. "Gotcha."

With one hand, she fished in the cooler on the floor behind the seat.

"I can do that," I said.

"All set." She handed me a Diet Coke. "Figured you needed that to wake up."

"You got that right." I popped the top and took a long swig. "Thank you, Gimp!"

"Pleasure."

She shifted gears, and the Jeep took off, thumping and bumping over the chip-seal road.

"I'm surprised the road's not dirt," I said.

"Everyone is." She laughed.

The golden sun fingered the canyon with jeweled beauty. The red and yellow rock took on even deeper hues.

"This is the quick tour," she said.

I looked at everything, drank it in as the best nourishment in the world.

She pointed with her right hand. "That's Una Vida."

I nodded.

Minutes later, as we drove down the canyon she pointed out Hungo Pavi and then . . .

"Chetro Ketl," I said. "Yes?"

"Yes. And there," she said. "Pueblo Bonito. Chaco's crown jewel. Can't you see it filled with people?"

And suddenly it was dark, and I again saw a hive of activity, and the man with the carving and the woman with the crutch and . . .

"Do you?" she asked.

"Yes."

She parked the Jeep. "C'mon."

We walked inside Pueblo Bonito, down a small stair, and onto the floor of the great house.

"I'd love to see the six-toed petroglyph," I said. "It's in Bonito, right?"

She shoved her hands into her back pockets. "Is . . . was. We had to backfill it. Someone vandalized it. You can't see it anymore."

"How sad."

"Yeah," she said. "Happens. Let's sit."

We sat on a floor of stone surrounded by four circular kivas excavated to about four or five feet down. Grasses, now brown with winter, grew on the bottom.

The stone was chilly on my bum, but it reminded me that I was alive.

"How long have you been at Chaco?" I asked.

"Forever."

"It's a good place, isn't it?"

She nodded. "As long as we can keep the evil at bay. That's why you're here."

"Pardon?"

She handed me a granola bar and unwrapped one for herself. "You were meant to come here, to protect Chaco."

I looked around at the brown clumps of grasses, the fine stonework, the round kivas, and raised walls of Pueblo Bonito.

"Chaco doesn't need me to protect it," I said. "Not that I believe I could."

She finished the bar, rolled the paper, and tucked it into her pocket. She took a deep swig of virulent pink Gatorade. "I don't say I understand it. I just know it to be true."

I thought of the many deaths—good people and bad. Odd how I felt no further along in learning who'd killed Didi and Delphine. "Sounds like a lot of woo woo to me."

She grinned. "It does, doesn't it?"

And then Gimp sat very still. The wind, which had been our companion all day, quieted. She moved to sit cross-legged, closed her eyes, and rested her hands, palms up, on her knees.

The sky darkened, not night, but softer, as if the world were wearing a chiffon party dress.

And she transformed into the Chaco girl I'd seen the previous evening, the one with the crutch and the warrior lover. Gimp's hair darkened from blond to black. Her eyes tilted upward and her figure slimmed to fragile and young. Her hands shrank to delicate, and a dull henna polish coated her nails.

Her left ring finger was bound with a bright gold ring, braided and inlaid with turquoise and jet. And resting on her right palm sat the carving done by the young man, the one of the mountain lion. Or was it? The carving was the same, yet different, more . . . detailed.

My breath came shallow and fast. Obviously I was hallucinating. Maybe she'd spiked my water or soda. Sure. Or maybe it was a real vision, like the stairway.

But I didn't believe in visions.

We were sitting so close. I leaned closer to see better, and she said with her mind, *Take it.*

I lifted the fetish from her hand.

The carving was heavy and rough and hard. It glittered, and its turquoise eyes seemed to move, to watch me. On its back bound with sinew was a black arrowhead, which looked hand flint-knapped, and random shell heishi. A nugget of turquoise, small and crude and a deep blue, had a hole in the middle, through which passed the sinew.

The lion's mouth yawned, but it was all interpretive, really. The fetish had just a hint of a form, with the tail bent over its back. And someone—the young man?—had rubbed a rust-colored substance, like clay, on the body. Part of a ritual, maybe.

The fetish warmed my hand. It felt secure. *I* felt secure. And strong. Powerful. I wrapped my fingers around it. The arrowhead stung as it pierced my flesh, but I didn't mind. I rubbed my fist against my cheek.

Was this the blood fetish? The one Didi had meant by the words written with her own blood? The one demanded by the man on the Vineyard? Was I really seeing It?

"Hey there, Tally," said the voice.

I was leaning on my arms, which were folded across my knees. I looked to the left. "Gimp?"

"Where you been?" She was smiling, and she was blond and sturdy and wore her tan ranger hat.

"I'm not sure," I answered slowly. "Things seem clearer here, don't they?"

"Mostly." She offered me a hand up, and I took it.

"I'm weaker than I thought." I chuckled.

"Oh, but you're not."

I clutched the fetish tight in my hand as we walked back to the Jeep. I knew I couldn't take it with me, but I wanted to hold it for a little while.

"This is very weird," I said. "I don't ordinarily talk to people. I'm pretty closed. But I'm talking to you."

She brushed her hat against her thigh. "People say that I'm a good, well, I'd guess you'd say sounding board. Or somthin'." She smiled. "Haven't we known each other for always?"

We climbed into the Jeep.

I smiled back. "Maybe we have. I've learned things."

"Yeah?" Off we went.

"I've been drifting."

She glanced at me. "I thought you were hunting a killer."

"Yes. But that's not what I mean. I'm talking personally. Ever since my foster mother died, I've felt adrift, not knowing how to get on or what my place is in the world."

She slowed the Jeep, pulled to a stop beside the tall canyon wall. "Maybe you don't want to let her go, huh?"

I chuckled. "Oh, I definitely don't want that. I miss her madly."

Gimp removed her hat and wiped her forehead. "My pops died fifteen years ago now. Long time. But it's not. It's yesterday. He's here." She pressed her palm to her heart. "But I've let him go. I've found my place. I suspect you've found yours. You just don't know it yet."

Her eyes were clear. What I saw was depth and purpose. Chaco was her life. Perhaps MGAP was mine.

"Yes," I said. "Maybe."

"We'd better hustle," she said. "I go on duty soon."

"This drifting . . ." I powered down the window, let the wind scour my face. "Now I understand the place to go."

"New Mexico?" She put the Jeep in gear and gunned it.

I liked her takeoff. "I thought maybe. But no. I think my place, at least for now, is back in Boston. Back where I used to be. It's home. Back at MGAP."

"What the hell's that?"

I looked out at the beauty of Chaco and talked, telling her about my work with the families of homicide victims, how my dad had been murdered, how I'd met and fallen in love with Hank. And about Veda. Beloved Veda.

She nodded. "Whew. Lotta stuff."

"Yeah."

"You gotta be half crazy to do what you do."

I grinned. My heart lightened for the first time in months. "Yeah, you noticed. But first, I've got to find out how two friends were murdered and why. I'm closer, but not there yet. I'll get there."

The Jeep lurched down a pothole and up. "Ugh!" she said. "Sorry. Paulie and Dumb Dick were a part of that."

"Yeah," I said. "Unfortunately that's true. But so are you. I wouldn't have missed that."

"There's Casa Rinconada." We approached the top of the canyon, near the museum and visitor center. But before she rounded the curve, she stopped the Jeep.

She pointed. "Just one more thing."

An incredible table-top mesa sprouted like a jagged, giant pillar from the ground.

"Fahaja butte," she said.

"It looks like the place in *Close Encounters of the Third Kind!*"

"It's not, but it sure could be. Didn't a guy build a mashed potato mountain or something in that movie?"

We laughed and took off, and a fullness filled me right up.

Hank and Aric stood by the Land Rover in front of the visitor center.

"You ready?" Aric hollered.

"In a sec." It was hard, but I unwound my hand to return the fetish. "This belongs here."

Gimp looked at my hand. "You mean that rock?"

I looked down. A rock, smooth and egg shaped and

blushed with red, rested on the palm of my hand. "Um, did you give this to me?"

She shrugged. "I don't think so, but . . ."

"It's illegal for me to bring it from here, isn't it?"

She hugged me. "For you and your journey? I think you *must* bring it. You need a bit of Chaco with you. Return it when the time is right."

"Thank you, Gimp," I said. "For everything."

When I climbed into the Aric's Land Rover, Hank asked what I was holding.

"Oh, just a mountain lion." I laughed. "I really need a bath."

He wiggled his auburn eyebrows. "How 'bout a shower, honey bunch. With me!"

"You betcha. And then we go to Salem."

Albuquerque. I got my next rabies shot. Two more to go, day fourteen and twenty-eight. Then I'd be done. I had my cuts and bruises looked after. Gave the FBI a deposition about Paulie and Dumb Dick. I took a shower with Hank—great fun—and a bath alone. I apologized to New Mexico's Chief Medical Investigator, declined the alluring position he'd offered, and said a temporary farewell to the state.

Aric would meet us in Boston in a few days. Hank and I planned to steal a little R&R before diving back into the case. I intended to see how the land lay at MGAP regarding my return. But not until we'd found Didi and Delphine's killer, the Pot Thief.

I suspected we'd also find The Bone Man's book.

The flight was long, and I dozed. I was still exhausted from being chased around Chaco by two killers. Each time I awoke, I found Hank holding my hand. We still hadn't discussed his moving from Winsworth to Boston.

I awakened slowly from the mud of dreamless sleep. "Hey."

Hank smiled down at me, sleepy eyed himself. "Hey, yourself."

A paperback lay open in his lap. "What are you reading?"

He held up the book. *The Lost Constitution* by William Martin, a popular writer from New England. "Thought I'd get some background on my new state. Plus the book's got some baseball. Can't go wrong with that."

I simmered, tried to keep my lips zipped. I looked out the window at clouds, down the aisle to the flight attendant marching forward with his cart, to the woman across the aisle, mouth open, snoring away.

Up front, some new film with Hugh Grant played on the screen. I smiled at Hank, slipped on the earphones. Smiled again.

Tally? he mouthed.

Smiled broader, turned my eyes to the screen.

He slipped the earphones off my head.

"Hey!" I said.

"What's bugging you?"

"Nothing." I reached for the earphones.

"Tal?"

"Okay," I said. "You, Hank Cunningham. You're bugging me. You should have told me you'd applied for a position with the state PD, that you wanted to move down here. I don't understand why you'd keep such a life-changing move secret. I don't. It sure looks like you don't trust me or our relationship."

He nodded, lower lip out. "You could say that."

Now I was pissed. "I just did, smartass."

"See how you get?"

"What?"

"All defensive," he said. "Panicked."

I turned in the seat. "I'm not—"

"Yeah, you are." He cupped my face in his hands. "I love you, babe. But I didn't want to tell you because you'd have thought up a million objections why I shouldn't do it. I didn't want to hear 'em. I've loved you forever, and I couldn't stand being away from you, especially when you were near that guy."

Kranak. That was justified. I'd hurt Hank. I'd hurt Kranak, too. "You know, that night in the canyon, when I heard your screams and that woman's laughter, her orders to hurt you, I . . . well, I almost died. I swear."

"What are you talking about, Tal?"

I sighed. Sometimes men could be so hard to deal with. Hank's macho was emerging. Geesh. "Hank, I heard your whimpers, your screams. That woman's voice. Then men's laughter. I heard it all."

He tilted his head, his eyebrows scrunched. "Um, we were never tortured. Those two idiots were too busy looking for you. And there was no woman. None at all."

I was losing my mind. "I heard it, Hank. Her. You. Aric."

He shook his head, kissed my lips long and deep. "It wasn't. There *was* no woman. And how, my dear, *did* you climb those stairs?"

I turned away from him to the window, pulled the thin airline blanket to my shoulders, and closed my eyes.

Like Scarlett, I'd think about it tomorrow.

CHAPTER THIRTY-ONE

Home. It felt great. I unlocked the door to the front hall of my apartment. Penny leaped upon my chest, and I hugged her madly. I buried my face in her soft fur and relished her yips of joy.

"Hey, girl!"

I couldn't seem to stop hugging her, and when I finally let her down, I realized I was crying. I wiped the tears away as I knelt in front of her. She instantly flopped on her back for her favorite—a belly scratch.

"Pens. Oh, Pens. I am so happy to see you."

She woofed a reply, and I laughed.

"Hey, stranger."

I looked up the stairs. It was Jake, my long-ago lover, my friend. We had history, and it felt good. "How's my favorite landlord?" I said.

"Worried about you." He trotted down the stairs wearing a grin. We shared a big hug, Penny nosing her way in, of course. When we broke apart, his handsome mug was marred by a frown.

"You've had a tough time," he said.

I had trouble holding his eyes, so I hugged him again. "Yes. It's not over yet, Jake."

He snorted. "Penny missed you a lot."

"Me, too. Oh, boy, me too."

He stretched, so I was at arms length. "I know. It's good to see you, Tal, especially since you're in one piece. But I confess I'm glad we're not together anymore."

My turn to snort. "Thanks a lot, buddy."

Beaming smile. "My pleasure."

I reached for the door to my apartment, the one that led to my bedroom. "Boy, do I need a bath. See ya for dinner, huh?"

"Love it. Takeout sushi?"

"For you, only the finest. Later." I leaned into the old door that perpetually stuck.

"Tal? Wait a sec, huh? I, uh, found some girl trying to buzz into your apartment."

"Really? Most people knew I was away. What'd she look like." I reached down and petted Penny's head.

"Pretty. Young. Milky-white complexion. Incredibly long blond braids. Tons of them. Right to her nicely packed ass."

That made me think of only one person—Zoe. "Good thing you're a sculptor. I'll chalk up your revolting words to that."

He grinned. "You know sculpting has nothing to do with it."

"So what did you tell her?"

"Nada." He walked toward me. "That's why I didn't like it. She scurried out of here pretty fast. Then, a couple days later, Penny started barking like crazy. The girl was back."

I sure wasn't liking the sound of this.

"This time, I watched from upstairs. She stood in the hall." He tilted his head. "She'd broken into the building, Tal, and was working on the lock of your door. I stepped forward, and she saw me and took off. You know her?"

I nodded. "Zoe. The dead woman, Delphine's, assistant. Thank God she didn't break in. She disappeared weeks ago. I'm thinking she's involved in this ring of pot thieves."

He moved past me toward my half-opened door. "That's the problem. She did." He pushed the door wide.

I stared at my bedroom. Chaos. I raced into the living room, which was neat and tidy, except . . .

I walked to the fireplace, where, on its mantel, I'd placed my favorite Zuni fetishes from my collection. Just dust remained, and the outline of the carvings. I turned, found the Inuit sculpture, the tiny Pangnark that looked like nothing more than a little square piece of gray rock, and next to it, the red rock given to me by the governor. At least they were safe.

I went back to the bedroom and stared at the damage. The bedroom mess was all about anger, and since I understood it, I should have accepted it. But all I could see was the broken glass vase Veda had given me years earlier. "*Damn* her."

I gathered the shards, and Jake gently took them from my hands. "I can fix it."

I saw Delphine's head and Didi's blood and the dead old trader and . . .

Jake couldn't fix it, but I intended to.

I breezed into The Grief Shop. How bizarre for a morgue to feel like home. I waved at Sarge behind the desk and beelined it to MGAP. I'd been gone a couple weeks. It felt like forever.

I reminded myself I didn't work there anymore.

As I walked into MGAP's central office, I glanced at the white board. One new case that day. Not bad.

"Hey, Donna!"

The pretty young woman looked up from her paperwork and smiled.

"How do you still look like twenty after all these years?" I said.

She blushed and grinned. "Great genes."

"Is Gert in her office?"

She peered at her paperwork. "Um, I don't think so. Not today."

I walked over to her desk. "Really? How come?"

Donna wouldn't look at me straight on. "She's been in a really bad mood lately, Tally. I don't know what's going on. I'm worried. Maybe she's decided to hate me."

I hugged her. "Now that's just plain impossible. Nobody could hate you. Gert's crazy about you. So you think she's home?"

She looked up, her eyes brimming with tears. "I . . . I guess. I really don't know. She's changed. Just this week, she's gotten all weird. I wish you'd come back."

"Hey, hey, hey. Gert's the best. Maybe she's just having a rough patch. You know how that can be."

"Maybe." She blew her nose. "And maybe she's just decided to hate me."

Oh, dear.

Gert's office door was locked, so I returned to MGAP's main office, headed for the giant fern that hung from the ceiling in the corner.

"Forgot something," I said to Donna. "Gotta water her. For luck!"

I lifted the yellow plastic watering can, filled it with water in the bathroom, and returned to the fern. The thing was huge, half brown, and hideous, but someone's superstition insisted we keep it alive and in place. It was a legacy from when Crime Scene Services occupied our suite of offices. Some police sergeant before Kranak had macraméd the fern's equally awful hanger.

As I lifted the watering can, I looked over my shoulder. Donna was deep in her paperwork. I pushed the jute rope with the yellow bead aside and removed the key to my former—and Gert's current—office. I finished watering the fern and left, shutting the main office door behind me.

I swiftly unlocked Gert's office door and slipped inside. I locked the door and turned, prepared to hunt for the two remaining Anasazi potsherds I knew were in the office.

"What the hell are you doin' here!" Gert shouted as she swung the chair around to face me.

I jumped. "You scared the hell out of me."

"What're ya doin' here?" she repeated. "Get out!"

Whoa. Gert clung to the arm of her leather desk chair, as if it were a life raft. Her legs were spread, her face flushed and dripping with sweat. Spiderwebs of red crisscrossed her eyes, and snot ran down her nose.

I walked over to her and kneeled. "What's wrong, Gertie?"

"Get out. I hate that name."

I took her left hand in mine. It felt clammy and limp. At least she didn't remove it. "You never used to hate the nickname. C'mon, sweetie, what's up? Let me help."

"Get outta my office. That'll help."

It wasn't the time to have a heart to heart. That was obvious. "Whatever you want, Gert. Where are the potsherds you borrowed for the carbon dating? The Anasazi ones."

"Right there. What's left of 'em." She pointed to a plastic bag. "That's all you wanted, isn't it? So get out."

"I wanted them. Yes." I picked up the bag with the two shards. "But I care more about you than some pots. Can we talk?"

Her bloodshot eyes blazed. "Get the fuck out, Tally, and don't bother coming back."

That night, I sat on my living room couch. On the redwood coffee table, Hank had spread plastic, then clean moving paper. He'd brought over five or six potsherds he'd taken from the open box in the Chetro Ketl tunnel. Aric was to have opened and forensically examined the sealed box bound for Salem. He then would have the box resealed and sent on its way to Salem, Massachusetts.

The Chaco potsherds sat on the paper on the table. The ones from Didi's office that once held the skull sat in their plastic evidence bag beside them.

I hadn't mentioned my disastrous meeting with Gert. I didn't know what to say, who to tell. Something was deeply wrong with my good friend, but I couldn't imagine what.

I'd called the Chief Medical Examiner, but Addy was away for the week at a conference.

Gert's reaction had scared me, but at that moment, I didn't know what to do. "Hell."

Hank returned from the kitchen bearing our bourbons on the rocks and a bottle of Rebel Yell.

"What's up?" he said. He placed the drinks on the table and sat beside me on the couch. He wove his fingers through my hair. "Hon?"

"Nothing." I leaned forward, poked a pencil at the sherds in the baggie. "These are real, Hank. Real. Around A.D. 1100. Anasazi. From the pot that was broken at the Peabody Essex Museum in Salem. The one with the skull."

I poked at the loose shards that we'd brought back from Chaco. "These are real, too. We know that, since you had them tested yesterday, just to confirm. But they're just that—shards. Dime a dozen. I exaggerate, but it's the whole pots that are rare and valuable, although not too many have skulls of twenty-first-century women inside them."

"Tally, the reconstruction could simply have looked like your friend," he said. "Which makes a lot more sense, don't you think?"

"No, I don't." I reached for my drink, leaned back on the couch and sipped. "She hasn't been seen for weeks and weeks. Hasn't communicated or returned my calls. She's abandoned her shop. She's gone. She's dead, Hank. Dead. With her skill found in . . ."

"Fine," he said. "I'll go with it."

"Gee, thanks."

He raised an eyebrow.

"I know, I know," I said. "You love my sarcasm."

"Only sometimes."

"You've got to take the good with the bad, hon."

He put his arm around my shoulder, and I leaned into him. It was swell to have someone to lean against. Not just someone, but Hank. He was a good man. And he made me burn with lust. I chuckled.

"Huh?" he said.

"Nothing, sweetie." I kissed his cheek. "I'm just horny. You need a shave, by the way. Look, even the whole pots aren't insanely valuable. Not enough for so many lost lives."

He picked up a shard, twirled it in his hand. "So what are we missing?"

"That's the trouble. I don't know."

I looked at the mantel, where I'd put the old Chaco stone given to me by the governor, then felt the one in my pocket that offered a warm comfort. "The blood fetish, whatever that is. Not just some red rock, but something of material worth. I don't really get what these pot thieves think it is."

"They're gonna keep after you, babe." He poured another finger of bourbon into his glass.

"Me, too." I held out my glass. "I know they are. Thing is, just like with the pots, I don't seem to have any answers."

"We'd better get some. Fast."

"Ayuh," I said.

Right then, the lights flickered and died.

I began to shake. I was transported to Chaco, being chased by Dumb Dick. Sweat dotted my upper lip, and I slid off the couch in search of my Taser. In the light from the streetlamp, I saw the glint of Hank's gun.

"Stay put," he said.

"I want the Taser."

"Tally, don't."

"I need it, Hank. I don't give a shit that it's not legal in Massachusetts. I will not be intimidated by these people."

He hissed. "They're not out to intimidate you. They aim to kill you."

"My point exactly." I scrambled across the carpeted floor and into my bedroom. I reached into the drawer in my bedside table and wrapped my hand around the Taser. The shaking eased, not totally, but it was better. A cold nose nudged my cheek. For just a moment, I buried my face in Penny's fur.

"They won't get us, girl," I said to her. "*Pozor!* Guard, Penny. *Pozor!*"

A knock from the hall on the bedroom door. I pressed my back against the side of the bed and pointed the Taser straight at the door.

The door creaked open. "Tal?"

"*Jake?* What?"

"Sorry about the lights," my landlord said. "I messed up. You know how I suck at home repairs."

I let out a relieved breath. I realized I was totally paranoid. Dear heavens. "Oh, I sure do, Jake. I sure do."

The following morning, Aric called to say the package would arrive at the Salem post office the following day. I was glad. I couldn't live the way I'd been going on for the past few weeks.

I saw monsters everywhere, jumped at the least thing, feared constantly for my life. And I had no idea why *I* was the prime target of the pot thieves.

I wished I understood the meaning behind the blood fetish and the words written by The Bone Man. At least then I could figure things out. Now . . . ? I was flailing around like a beached whale.

"A beached whale?" Hank said as he breezed through the front door.

"Where have you been?"

"Work. I've got the eight to three."

"That stinks."

"I've had worse," he said.

"So what's up?" I went into the kitchen and returned with a mug of black coffee. "Here you go."

"Thanks." He took a long pull. "What a cliché. The coffee at the station is so damned lousy. C'mon. We need to go on a road trip. I'll explain on the way. I got Penny's leash." He held it up.

I peered out the window. A light rain had turned the world gray and gloomy. So typical for early October in New England. While Hank leashed up Penny, I slid into my Keene boots and down jacket, wrapped my favorite scarf around my neck, and pulled on my fishing hat, the one with the broad brim that made me look like an Australian cowboy.

Just as I was locking the door, the phone rang.

"Leave it," Hank said.

"I should, but . . ." I ran back inside and checked the caller ID. MGAP. "Tally Whyte, here."

"You told, didn't you?"

It was Gert. "What do you mean?"

"You told everybody." A sob.

"Gert, I don't know what you're talking about, hon. I said nothing. Please."

She clicked off.

I looked at Hank, who stood in the doorway wearing his usual mask of patience. The man could be a saint.

"We've got to stop at MGAP on the way," I said.

He shook his head. "Can't, Tal. This package won't wait."

"What package? Hank, I've got to." I walked past him leading Penny, headed for my 4Runner.

He grabbed the collar of my coat, swiveled me around. "This isn't a request, Tally. You're there. Know what I mean?" His serious eyes stormed with anger.

"Hank?"

His frown squinched up the dimple in his chin. "I know just how pissed you're gonna be, and I never like that. But you're coming with me."

"Gert needs me," I said.

"I don't much care if the queen needs you. Sorry."

"But, Hank, dammit."

"*Now!*"

CHAPTER THIRTY-TWO

We took Storrow Drive to the Northeast Expressway.

"Where are we going?" I asked.

"Revere."

"*Revere?* What, for a day at the beach in the rain? How romantic."

"Not quite so nice."

We ended up on Route 1A, to Ocean Ave., to finally Revere Beach Blvd. I could almost hear the yips of the greyhounds at Wonderland Park, except I wasn't sure if they ran this late in the fall. To my right, the steel-colored Atlantic blended with the leaden sky, which continued to spit chilling rain. Oddly, I longed for snow.

I cracked a window and listened to the wild sound of a rainstorm at the beach. The rhythm of the whooshing tires added to the surreal feel of the day. A quintessential New England October day, for sure.

We pulled into the state barracks across the boulevard from Revere Beach. The tall buildings of Boston rose behind us, but the station was old and moody, built in the late 1800s. Its tall tower always reminded me of a watch-tower, with its weathervane twirling in the wind. Today, it was twirling like mad. We parked inside the chain-link fence, and Hank led me in.

We threaded our way through the bullpen. Hank waved to a woman I presumed was an old friend. Or maybe a new friend. Huh. She was awfully cute, with a bob of brown hair and a perky smile. Too perky.

"Tal?" Hank said.

"Oh, right. Coming."

We walked through an arch and then turned left into a room where a tech sat at a small console and another plain-clothesman slept in a chair, black bandana across his eyes.

Hank kicked the sleeper's foot, and the guy nearly lifted off the chair. *Aric!*

I gave him a huge hug. "Wow. I'm so glad to see you."

"Yeah. Me too." His eyes smiled at mine with genuine joy. Made me feel swell. He looked at Hank. "Time to get started?"

Hank sighed. "I guess so." He lifted a manila folder from the wall holder and breezed through a bunch of pages. "You sure about this?"

Aric made a face. "More than sure. She's a rainmaker."

Hank's eyebrows shot high. "If you say so. Back in a sec."

Aric dragged up a seat for me and helped me with my coat.

"What's going on?" I slipped off my hat and scarf and laid them on the table in front of me.

"He didn't tell you?" Aric said.

I shook my head.

"We got the girl who broke into your house. And I brought in a specialist to chat with her."

I didn't like the sound of that one bit.

I sat between Aric and Hank and stared at the blank wall in front of us. Aric had donned an earpiece, and he began to motion to the tech at the console.

He held up fingers. Three, two, one.

Lights came up in the room just behind the blank wall. It looked like an interrogation room. It was small and rectangular, with cinder-block walls. We could see inside, but I guessed we were hidden from those in the room behind a mirrored wall.

Our room was darkened, but the interrogation room's lights gave off a yellow cast, and the walls were greenish gray and shiny. The room was empty, but for a pitcher that sat on the table along with two glasses. Minutes passed. I sipped the Diet Coke Hank had brought me.

We waited. It felt like just before the curtain rose on a Broadway show. Tension was heightened. Anticipation was huge. Everything was staged. Aric leaned close to me. "It's about sixty degrees in there."

"Why so cold?" I asked.

"To make this girl uncomfortable."

"What are we waiting for?" I said.

His smile was grim. "The show to start."

A door on the right opened. In came Zoe, the girl I'd spoken with on the phone and met nearly four weeks earlier on the Vineyard. The one who had worked for Delphine. She wore her hair in long, thin braids, except stray wisps flew everywhere. I wondered when she'd last had a comb in her hand. Instead of clothes, she wore a sheet wrapped around herself, like a toga. A hand pointed her to the one wooden chair, and she sat.

"The back of the chair tilts slightly forward," Aric said. "It's incredibly uncomfortable."

It all looked and sounded grim to me.

"She's been grilled by a mean-ass guy," he said.

I turned to Hank. "I can't say I'm liking this."

"She hasn't been harmed or deprived of sleep or tortured in any way."

"She better not have been," I said. "You know I'd mouth off."

Aric pointed at the room. "Watch."

A woman entered on the left and shut the door behind her. She wore a calf-length denim dress that didn't disguise the broadness of her shoulders or fitness of her body. The cardigan she wore over the dress looked handmade. It was gorgeous and oddly out of sync with her persona. The sweater was lime green, with a knit fuchsia ruffle up the front of each buttoned side.

This girl didn't appear like any frou-frou I'd ever known.

Her honey-blond hair was clipped short, in a bob to her ears, and parted off center, so two semi-bangs danced on her forehead. She carried a carpetbag with twin handles of bamboo. I wished I could see her eyes. They were large and round, but I couldn't catch their color. She was lean and lithe and sturdy, with squared hands like mine. But at five-foot-ten, I would top her by a good five or six inches, I guessed. She was bigger boned, too, and her lips were lush and strong. She was quite a package. I had a feeling she was a woman to be reckoned with.

"How old is she?" I said to Aric.

He slipped a hunk of chaw into his cheek. "Around twenty-eight. Something like that."

"Who is she? What's her name?"

Aric slung an arm around me and leaned close. "Who she is, well, that's for her to say. Her name is Styx."

"Sticks? Like, sticks and stones?"

He shook his head. "Like the river that separates the living from the dead."

That shut me up fast.

The two women faced each other. By now, Zoe was shivering.

"You want my sweater?" Styx smiled, and her whole being changed from stark to gentle. Anyone would want to see that smile again.

"Thank you," Zoe said and reached for the sweater.

As I watched Zoe slip on the garment, I'd swear she was just a sweet, young girl who'd lost her way. Now I knew she was anything but. She might even have been Delphine's killer.

"Thank you," Zoe said. "It's freezing in here!"

Styx nodded. She leaned down to her bag, opened it, and pulled out two knitting needles and a long hank of knitting that she began working on. "Let's talk."

Zoe swallowed. "I'd love to."

Styx began to knit. Her hands made the needles fly. They looked like black steel and flashed in the light. We could hear the sound in the observation room, and the rhythmic *clack-clack-clack* became unnerving. Styx's eyes never left Zoe, and yet soon the sweater, or whatever it was she was crafting, began to grow. So did Zoe's unease.

The knitter finally looked down at her work. She smiled what I'd call a secretive smile. "Want to talk?" she asked Zoe.

"About what?"

Styx looked up. "Oh, you know."

"I . . . I do?"

"Of course you do." Her smile was so warm, so welcoming. Who could resist it?

"I have no idea what everyone wants me to say," Zoe said.

Styx knit faster. "No?"

Zoe's eyes darted around the room. Her nose ran. But then she looked back at Styx. "I swear, I didn't kill Delphine. I don't know where the bitch is."

Faster and faster Styx knit. The black garment swayed and jigged, and Zoe's eyes couldn't seem to leave it alone.

"Huh," Hank said.

"I know," I said. "I've really never seen anything like it."

"Or her," he said.

Aric laughed softly. "She's part Abenaki. The People of the Dawn. Is it any wonder?"

Abruptly, the knitter halted. She leaned forward, clasped Zoe's hand in one of hers. I moved closer to the mirror, so I could see what she was doing. Back and forth, she rubbed her thumb across Zoe's hand. A comfort move. Also, a hypnotic one.

Tears waterfalled from Zoe's eyes. "My friend, Jerry Devlin. He called me."

Styx leaned closer. "Is he a friend or your boyfriend?"

Zoe nodded. "Boyfriend. I . . . I guess. He said he and another guy were going to come to the shop. They were gonna get this woman from Boston."

I looked over at Hank, and he nodded.

"Jerry told me what to do and how to act." Her voice sank. "I was only following orders. And then this jerk of a guy came. I mean, he was such an *idiot*." She wound one of her braids round and round her fingers. "He's dead. Bloody dead."

Styx lifted her chair and brought it around beside Zoe. She set her knitting on her lap and wrapped her right arm around Zoe's shoulders in such a way that we could still see both women.

"But Jerry's not dead, right?"

"No. No, he's not," Zoe said.

"You're crazy about him still, aren't you?" Styx said.

Zoe nodded. "And I like working for Delphine. I really do."

"I know. But something bad happened, right?"

"*Yeah*," Zoe said. "Delphine's daughter showed up, and, well, they had to take her."

I couldn't believe what I'd just heard. Delphine's daughter, Amélie. Where was she? I'd seen her months ago, but since then . . . I turned to Hank. He shook his head that he didn't know, but his whole body tensed.

Styx's spine had stiffened, too, just the slightest bit. It was a tell, but one I doubted Zoe noticed.

"And where is she?" Styx asked with a warm, honeyed voice.

Zoe shrugged. "I dunno. Why do you care about her?"

"Because she could affect your safety. But let's talk some more about you. You're right. Where's Jerry?"

The younger girl pouted. "He hasn't done *anything*. He knows I'm here and—"

"Where is he, sweetie?" Styx said.

"Where he always is," Zoe answered. "At that damned museum. I hate it."

Styx moved away from the girl and resumed knitting.

"Why are you doing that again?" Zoe folded her arms in a huff.

"Because I'm the knitter. I stitch things together, Zoe. Like why you broke into Tally Whyte's apartment."

"Oh, come on. I didn't break into anyone's apartment."

Styx smiled, and again the room glowed. "Yes, you did."

Zoe inhaled a stuttering breath. "Will you still like me?"

"Oh, Zoe," she said in an incredibly warm and friendly tone. "Nothing you say could change my feelings for you."

The younger girl beamed. "She's got the key."

The key? I held my palms up to Hank and Aric. I had no idea what she was talking about.

Aric whispered in the microphone. Styx nodded, then said. "I don't understand. What key?"

"The key, the key. That old fetish everyone's been after. I was supposed to find it or something. Maybe it was never there. I don't know. Just a bunch of new junk that I took with me."

"I don't know either." Styx carefully folded her knitting and slipped it back into her bag. Her eyes went to us, behind the mirror. Aric leaned forward, into the microphone. "Thanks, Styx."

The woman nodded and rose to leave the room.

"Wait!" wailed Zoe. "Aren't you going to stay with me?"

Styx slipped out the door and closed it behind her.

We found Jerry Devlin in the system. When a bland, nice-looking guy stared back at us from the computer screen, I knew I'd seen him before.

"I know this guy," I said.

Hank leaned over my shoulder for a look. "And . . . ?"

I tapped a key. "And, nothing. I know him. He was the anchorman for the National Geographic team. Allegedly, they were going to film the reconstruction and the skull. Two of them are dead." I explained who they had been. "Things are coming together, Hank."

"I'll be back in a sec," he said.

I printed out the image of Jerry Devlin. I wondered if he'd look the same. The other two men, Paulie and the killer at the lodge, hadn't.

"I need to get out of here for a while, okay, Aric?" I said.

"Sure."

We headed toward the front of the barracks.

"I'd like to meet her," I said to Aric.

"Styx?"

I nodded. "She interests me. A very unusual girl."

"She doesn't like people much," Aric said.

"She's talented," I said.

"She is," Aric said. "She works for the FBI part time."

"She could help with the case."

He shook his head. "She always gets what we need. But at a price to her. It's painful to watch. C'mon. Let's walk."

"Should we wait for Hank?" I asked.

"He had to do something with the prisoner. That kid's a pistol."

Our footfalls sounded hollow on the polished linoleum.

"You mean Zoe?" I said. "She's been in this from the beginning, I'm thinking. She's a nasty little piece of work. Only out for herself."

"Seems so," Aric said.

We blew through the front doors, and the minute I inhaled the sea, I calmed. "Zoe's dangerous. I'm terribly worried about Amélie. If Zoe's even half right . . ."

I couldn't help imagining the fear she must be feeling. How they might abuse her. How they'd kill her, just like they'd killed her mother. And we still didn't know who *they* were.

I didn't for a minute believe that Zoe's boyfriend Devlin was in charge of the operation.

We walked to the beach. That day, it was pristine, with few footprints and no people. The rain had stopped and the sun emerged, but the ocean still roiled with the storm's energy. I cherished its vastness, that feeling of smallness, much the same as I felt in the desert.

I sat on the wet sand, legs crossed. The cold seeped into my bottom, and I didn't care. The cool spray refreshed me, and I felt cleansed, if only for a moment.

"The ocean always amazes me," Aric said. "She's probably dead."

"Amélie? I can't think that way. Not one more corpse. Please. All for some stupid pots."

"You *should* think that way," he said. "It's sensible."

"Oh, and sensible sure describes me, Aric."

He walked to the sea and let it lap the tips of his boots. "Your point of view affects everything."

I jumped to my feet. "Well, dammit, Aric. I refuse to believe that girl is dead. So let's get Hank and haul our asses to Salem and figure things out once and for all."

His lips thinned, and he scraped a hand through his clipped black hair. "Yes. It's time."

CHAPTER THIRTY-THREE

The drive to Salem didn't take long. We were already on the North Shore, and so we just shot up Route 1A to 107 to 114. Penny and I sat in back, and Penny's ears stayed at attention the whole time. She knew something was up.

The men tossed around different ideas about the case, and at some point, Hank made sure we'd have backup at the museum.

We arrived in front of the mall that housed the museum in less than forty-five minutes.

The electric feeling in the car gave me goose bumps. Inside the museum was Jerry Devlin, going about his daily work as one of the museum's Native American curators.

How could he so betray his profession? His passion? I guessed that Paulie had said it all: money.

"So what's our plan?" I said.

Hank turned to me wearing his Serious Sheriff face.

"What?" I said.

"Our plan is, you stay here."

"No way."

"You must, Tally," Aric said. "Our worry for you could

jeopardize the whole operation. Devlin knows this place in and out. To get him, we must use surprise. You, Penny, do not constitute surprise."

"But Aric, Hank . . ."

"We won't go in," Hank said. "Unless you give us your word."

I hated this. Hated it. But I looked from Aric's face to Hank's and back again. They meant what they said.

"Fine. I'll stay here."

Hank stabbed a finger at the dashboard. "Right here. In this car. You will not leave it. Deal?"

How could I make a deal like that? Not to go after Devlin, to sit passively by? That wasn't me, not at all.

I sighed. They weren't kidding.

We could either drive away and let others handle Devlin. Or I could stay put.

"Deal."

I scooched into the backseat of Hank's Chrysler and tried to sleep. The rain had started again, playing a melodic tattoo on the metal. I found it soothing. It would lull me to sleep.

I couldn't believe this was happening in Salem, of all places. Talk about creepy. Here women had been hanged as witches and a man pressed to death beneath stones. The air was different in Salem. The town thrived on that difference, and its gabled homes and Gothic churches only enhanced that feeling.

I watched Hank and Aric walk across the street toward the museum, one of the most wonderful in the state. I didn't like their leaving. Penny didn't like it, either.

"Right, Pens?"

She woofed a sigh.

I closed my eyes . . . and saw the governor. He wore the sweetest expression of caring and love. I began to cry.

I sat up, sniffled. I was being stupid.

I reached into my bag for some tissues. Nothing like getting all maudlin to bring on the waterworks.

As my hand searched for the tissues, my fingers found cool silk. I pulled whatever it was out. "Look, Pens, Delphine's gloves." Good thing I hadn't brought them with me to New Mexico. They'd have been destroyed. I didn't remember tucking them into my purse. I was glad I had.

I laid them in my lap. They were beautifully knit, and the colors of the rainbow. I wondered if we'd ever find her remains. I sure hoped when Aric and Hank caught up with Devlin, he told some good tales.

Penny whined.

"Huh? What's up, Pens?"

She scratched at the window, but I wasn't getting it.

"What?"

She scratched again, an obvious bid to get out of the car. An urgent one.

I assumed she needed the bathroom. I leashed her up and opened the door.

She took off, yanking the leash from my hand.

"Penny!" I shouted.

The rain was falling faster and thicker, and if she wasn't black and tan, I wouldn't have been able to see her. "Penny, dammit!"

She sat perfectly still at the end of the parking lot, head tilted, waiting. As if she had something to show me. I'd seen it plenty of times, but . . .

I'd promised Hank I'd stay in the car. But Penny definitely had something to show me.

Oh, hell, Hank should know me better than that.

I slipped out of the car with a confidence I was far from feeling. I wore my hat and jacket, and wished I'd brought the Taser. I tucked the gloves in my pocket.

I crouched in front of Penny. "What is it, girl? Something, eh?"

She whined and sat in front of me, as if she hadn't just disobeyed me.

I picked up her soggy leash. If I were right, she'd take off like a bat. Then I pulled the gloves from my pocket. "Is it this?" I held them out to her.

She whiffed them once, twice, and off we went.

Boy, was Penny in a hurry. We flew.

Across the street, Penny paused by the stately Episcopal church, with its majestic stonework and green window trim, past its pocket-corner graveyards and soaring Gothic dignity. Then we ran again, down the brick sidewalk, past the church hall, and more buildings. Past a parking lot, where we had a gorgeous view of town and beyond.

"Pens?"

She trotted on, down the hill to a seedy parking lot and an ancient barn and an abandoned building out of witchy nightmares. She paused on the gravel surface, nose twitching. I tried to catch my breath.

The old stone building was massive. It took up a city-block corner. It sprawled across acres, and there, on the side of the building, over to the right—geesh—was an old graveyard, the kind out of a Washington Irving horror story. Hard to imagine anything spookier.

The empty building stopped me short. Penny tugged on the leash. "Stand still. *Ruce vzhuru.*" Even for Salem, the place was disturbing, with upsetting vibes that seemed to make everything worse. The building was constructed of large, rectangular blocks that appeared to be granite. It must have been flush at one point, since it was trimmed in copper. Two strange cupolas—one pointed, the other with a round adornment—sprouted from the roof, as did numerous brick chimneys. I shielded my eyes trying to read the engraving on the side of the building. I stood on tip-toe. 1884.

The two-story building was surrounded by heavy wire fencing, atop which were several rows of barbed wire. Dying vines threaded in that inhospitable place, up the fence and around the barbed wire. How unlovely.

Why had Penny brought me to this empty relic, with its disturbing vibe and blown-out windows?

The rain was coming faster, the wind whipping the drops into a frenzy. This was the last place on earth I wanted to be.

"Penny, can we go now?"

She whined. I let her smell the gloves, and . . .

"Take that dog home!" came an angry voice.

I turned. A woman bundled like a polar bear was shaking her fist at me.

"Pardon?"

"Look at this rain," she said. "She'll freeze."

This was incredibly annoying. "Her coat is thicker than mine. Excuse me."

As I went to walk around the woman, she slammed something hard on my wrist. I reflexively loosened my grip on Penny's leash, and she trotted away.

"Dammit!" I raced after my dog, while the woman's cackling laughter sent a chill down my spine.

Something was wrong. "Penny!"

The wind stole my voice, and Penny ran on, alongside the raggedy barn with the collapsing roof and through a hole in the chain-link fence.

"Penny! *Zustan!* Don't do that! *Fuj!*"

She wasn't listening. She was on the scent.

I looked behind me. The woman wasn't there. It didn't matter. I had to get Penny.

I followed Penny through the hole in the fence, scraping my jacket on the broken steel link.

It was a lot creepier inside the fence than out.

Penny loped down the hill, and I ran after her. The wind gusted, and the sudden blast of rain blinded me. I couldn't see Penny. I called again and again, but I didn't see her anywhere. I tried to find her paw prints, but of course I couldn't spot them in that terrible rain.

I ran down the slope, stumbled, caught myself. I ran up to the building. I shivered. There were bars on all the windows. Maybe the place had been an insane asylum.

Think, think. Why would Penny run there? The gloves, of course. Had to be. Pens was a good cadaver dog. Delphine's remains?

I ran from window to window, plowing through increasingly nasty gusts of rain. The storm was a real Nor'easter, the worst kind.

Bars, bars everywhere. I rounded a corner and . . . there . . . a door, cracked open enough for Penny to slip inside. Could I?

I reached the door, tried to squeeze inside. No way. I pushed and pushed, and nothing happened. I began to call, then clamped my teeth tight. If the pot thieves were inside, they'd hear me.

I pressed all my weight against the door, imagined it opening, pushing inward. I pushed and pushed and . . . The door flew open, and I tumbled inside, landing flat on my face on the cold, filthy marble floor.

A boom.

The place went dark. Someone clamped my hands together behind my back. Brutal hands yanked me to my feet, and rough arms dragged me up a set of jagged stairs. I couldn't see a thing—no light whatsoever—and when I struggled, a man's voice growled in my ear, "Cut it, or we kill the dog."

At the top of the stairs, I was hauled down a corridor. Metal clinked, a door opened, and the guy gave me a shove. I flipped around and slammed inside a small room, right into a cinder-block wall. Pain shot through my elbow. The door went *snick-snick* behind me.

Hell.

But it wasn't all bad. At least, that's what I told myself. I'd seen his foot. He wore cowboy boots. Dark ones with lightning bolts up the sides. I'd seen boots like that before, on the man who'd tried to kill me at the trading post. Yet another of the National Geographic guys. I should say fake Geographic guys. I doubted homicide was part of their job description.

What was with the lightning on the boots? What was I missing here?

Didn't matter. I looked around and shivered. The room was freezing. I felt all that granite surrounding me and the weight of old, old souls pressing against mine. There was a terrible wrongness to the place. It was suffocating, like a stone squeezing my chest, like that poor old man pressed to death beneath those stones.

I walked to the window. Pale watery light filtered in from outside the barred, glassed, and wire-meshed window filthy with grime and age. The room—crypt?—couldn't have been more than six-by-six, and I told myself that now wasn't the time for claustrophobia. Right. A ceiling light dangled above my head but shed no light because the bulb was broken. Given the stairs I'd been dragged up, I was obviously not on the first floor. I wet my fingers, tried to clear a bit of glass, but failed. The mesh was too tight. My stomach cramped with fear.

I hunkered down, close to the chipped beige floor tiles. They, too, were grimy with age and coated with dust. So no one had been in this room for a long time. That all meant something. Why couldn't I put it together?

I sat in the corner, my back against the chilly wall.

If Penny were okay, she'd find me. My captor said they had her, but I didn't believe him. Couldn't. Yes, Penny would find me. If not . . . I refused to think about it.

I pictured Aric and Hank. First, they'd be annoyed that I'd waltzed off. Then angry. Then worried. But by then it would be too late. I didn't see how in hell they'd know where I was. Too bad I hadn't left any bread crumbs.

I peered around the cell for spiders, webs, anything that spoke of life. I found nothing. The place was empty and cold, with a horrible absence of life. The tips of my fingers had lost feeling.

Think, dammit, I yelled at myself. I doubted they intended to kill me, at least not at first. So why lock me up? What did I have, what did I know, what could I do that they wanted?

I pushed myself up and began to pace. Movement, action, that was the ticket. I breathed in and out, listened for sounds. Other than my breath, all I heard was silence. I paced. Rhythm.

The boots were the same. I'd recognized four of my assailants, yet I had trouble placing them in my world. Back and forth. Pace. Rhythm.

A clanking made me stumble. *Ignore it.* Now was the time I must understand, or I would die. I believed that.

The clanking grew louder. *Think. Think, Tally, dammit!*

Lightning. On the men's boots. And where else? A breeze from a crack in the window brushed my face. A collar. A shirt collar.

The anchor-style guy I now knew to be Devlin had a lightning bolt embroidered on his shirt collar. Two pairs of boots and a collar. Not a coincidence. And there was one more. What? I paced, paced. The clanging grew louder still, yet . . .

A man formed in my mind, a shadowy one with a predatory disposition. I'd sure met enough of them lately. Anchor man? No, I recalled the lightning bolt on his shirt. It wasn't he. Then who? *Who was I seeing?*

The cell door flew open, and I jumped.

"Who's there?" I said.

"You killed Paulie," came the whispery voice full of hate.

I backed up a step, right into the wall. I braced myself. "Why would you think I killed anyone?"

"You killed him."

I caught the glint of something. Gun? Knife? It didn't matter. I had nowhere to go.

"You're wrong."

"You're dead."

I dropped to the floor just as something clattered against the wall. Footsteps entered the room, and I rolled. A large, round person was bent over retrieving the big knife that lay on the floor. He was vague, like a shadow, with eyes that burned.

I leaped on top of him, and he laughed.

I bit, kicked, tasted blood. A swat across my face snapped back my head. Hands, heavy and tight, squeezed my neck.

I gasped for air and groped for some place to grab on to. I found a smooshy area and clamped down hard with my fingers and nails, scraping along a surface.

The floor hit me in the head, and I saw stars while I kicked myself out of his way. I could hardly make out his face, but I saw streaks of red, and I pushed to my knees. His teeth glinted, and he watched me as he reached for the knife.

With both hands I grabbed for his balls and squeezed down hard.

Howling!

I squeezed harder and tighter, and he pushed me away, but I pushed back, using his energy, his force. Then I suddenly released him.

Wham! His head smacked into the cinder-block wall. He slid down it, aware but stunned, and I grabbed his knife, wrapping both palms around the hilt, and I thrust it into him, my back arched, seeking an energy I didn't feel.

He screamed, and I fell back. And he collapsed. His head tilted to one side, his eyes were closed, and blood ran from the wound in his side. I gasped for breath. Couldn't believe I'd gotten the better of him. I sucked in air until the voice in my head shrieked, *Run!*

I lurched to my feet. God, it was hard. I couldn't leave him like this. When he came to, he'd come after me again.

I'd only wounded him. I rifled his pockets, pulled out a Zorro poker token. Stupid. Finally, in his shirt pocket, I felt something metal, something like . . . a key. Yes. He had a flashlight, too. I took both of them and crept out of that vile room.

I locked it behind me, and the satisfying *snick* told me that for the moment, I was safe.

CHAPTER THIRTY-FOUR

In the hall, the howl of the wind sounded like madness. It reminded me of Chaco. Different, but the same.

I should leave, get Hank and Aric. But I couldn't leave. Not without Penny.

Fear seeped into my brain like a poisonous oil. I ached for a courage I wasn't feeling.

The corridor was pitch black, but for one greasy window that allowed in a pale light. That was to my advantage. I slipped into a nook in the hall that might have once held a water fountain. I pressed on the flashlight. A halogen with a direct beam. Perfect. I listened for Penny, but heard only silence. I had two choices—I could turn left, down that hall, or go right, deeper into the labyrinth.

Left . . . it made little sense that anyone would be there. Passing cars might see someone walking in the building. Right it was, and so I went deeper into the bowels of the place that felt like a snake pit.

I walked quickly, again thankful that Hank had bought me the Merrells. The farther I traveled, the colder it seemed, until, another right and . . . I saw a light down the end of the corridor.

I realized I was shaking and tried to catch my breath. What a place! High ceilings, cold, damp walls, bars on the windows, stone everywhere. A medieval prison or a madhouse or the catacombs of Moria.

Get it together. My teeth began to chatter. Those people wanted to kill me or worse, torture me. I'd been lucky to make it this far. How long would my luck hold? Maybe I should run. My soul said: *flee.*

I slipped my hand into my pocket in search of some gum, Altoids, anything to feel a little normal. Instead, my fingers touched something hard and egg shaped. It felt warm. I laughed out loud, slapped my hand across my mouth. But I couldn't help smiling. The rock I'd brought from Chaco. I'd slipped it in my jeans for a pocket fetish. I rubbed my thumb across its surface. It comforted my heart.

And a lightning bolt of recognition hit me. Almost literally. I found another alcove down the hall and backed into it.

My brain had finally put the insignia in its proper place. The lightning on the boots and the one on the National Geographic guy's shirt. Lightning bolts. And just now, the monster who'd tried to kill me, he had what I'd taken as a Zorro poker chip. I nearly laughed again. Of course it wasn't that, but it was a chip with a bolt of lightning on it. And, yes! I'd seen another one. Izod-man's gold tooth. I'd taken the mark on it for a Z, but, again, it was a bolt of lightning.

I knew just what those lightning bolts meant.

According to Zuni belief, humans lived in an underworld before they emerged to the surface of the earth. The earth was swampy and humans couldn't live there. So Sun Father created twins. These brothers were to take care of the humans. The twins created lightning, which could ignite fires that would dry the earth. And so the surface became livable and humans emerged.

Except many were eaten by ferocious beasts.

So the twins turned the creatures to stone, all except for their hearts, which continued to beat. The twins then told the stone animals to serve as guardians for humans. They have done this ever since. And so fetishes were born to protect and aid the Zuni.

Could the pot thieves believe that a fetish would protect their work? I had trouble getting my head around a desire for a particular fetish over and above all else.

The lightning was some fetish cult formed by these non-Zunis.

I could sort that out later. I shook myself. Right now, what I believed didn't matter. What *they* believed was what counted. I had to get moving.

I eased out of the cranny and continued on down the hall. The farther I went, the more disturbing the vibe. The place was a hellhole. I wished Hank knew where I was. From its abandoned look, no one ever ventured into the building. No one except people doing very bad things.

The hall tilted downward and widened a bit. I wondered if that was real or my perception. From a bend down at the end of the corridor, what looked like the shadow of fire flickered on the wall. It stopped me.

I'd seen that in some dream. Nightmare. I'd swear it. Go beyond that turn, and I would die.

I sagged against the wall, clammy with sweat and fear. I had dreamed this very scenario. Foolish, foolish. But in my bones, I knew it to be true.

At that turn, right there, right beyond where I could see, monsters awaited me with arms wide. Their embrace would be slow, but final. I would go insane. I would lose myself. Forever.

I leaned back. What was wrong with me, seeing these things, believing them?

I closed my eyes, willing myself out of there. I stroked the stone in my pocket. It calmed me. Penny. She would never, ever leave me in a place like this. Never.

So how could I leave her?

I straightened. Whatever that right turn held, I refused to go gently. Knife in my left hand, flashlight in my right, I walked forward, toward the flickering, shadowy light up ahead.

I took a breath, was about to make that hideous right turn, when I heard a familiar *clack-clack.*

I flipped around, and saw a low shadow in the dark hall. I ran uphill toward it, and the clacking grew louder, and in an instant, two paws slammed into my chest.

I buried my face in Penny's fur and cried. "Safe. You're safe."

"I found her," said a woman's voice.

I jerked up. *"Pozor!"* I commanded Penny.

"She doesn't need to guard you, you know."

I beamed the light up, toward the sound of the soft voice. Five feet up the corridor stood a pretty, young woman. I walked toward her, kept my knife at the ready. Penny hugged my side.

"Here," I said to Penny. "Come."

As I closed on the young woman, I saw that she was filthy. One side of her face was bruised, and her hair hung in greasy hanks. She looked unwell, feverish or starved or sick at heart.

"You are?" I said.

"Um . . ." She rubbed her lips with her finger, back and forth. "I'm . . . I'm not sure. They've been drugging me. I'm confused."

She began to collapse. I grabbed her waist, but I couldn't keep her upright. We both ended sitting. She tilted her head back against the wall.

"Let's get you out of here," I said. "All right?"

"I don't think I can."

"Take a few breaths," I said.

"Okay. Yes."

Hard to tell, but I'd swear the girl was Amélie, Delphine's daughter. I felt her forehead. She was burning up.

Her frail hand reached out and buried itself in Penny's fur. "She saved me."

"Her name is Penny."

"She . . . she found me."

The gloves. Maybe they weren't Delphine's but Amélie's. I pulled them out. "Do you recognize these?"

She held the gloves as if they were fragile glass. She smiled. "Yes, yes, I do. Mama knit them for me. Long ago."

"Come on." I got to my feet. "We're leaving."

"Can't."

"Yes, you can." I snugged my arm around her waist. "Help me, now."

"Yes," she said with a whisper.

I pulled and she pushed, and we somehow got her to her feet. We wobbled, but managed to stay upright.

I looked up the hall, which now seemed a monumental hill to climb. Yet I could see no other way out of here but back the way I'd come.

"Okay, Amélie. Here we go, huh?"

One foot, then the other, then again. We inched slowly up the hall. For such a petite girl, she had to weigh four hundred pounds. One foot, then the other. I prayed our snail-like progress would be enough to get us out of there.

I looked ahead, flashed the beam once, and saw that we'd almost made it to the upper hall. Once there, no more hills, but flat until the downward stairs took us out of the hellish place.

"You okay, Amélie?"

"Okay."

A surge of joy.

Then a flash of light doused hope.

A burst of pain in my head, then . . .

I awakened slowly, as if a hangover made breathing hard. I was sitting, but my head was bowed, my feet on the floor. Maybe the Fun House of Horrors had all been a bad dream. Yes. I smiled. I was home. With Hank. Sitting on the . . .

No, I wasn't.

I opened my eyes, but didn't look up. My hair hung like a curtain, shielding my face.

I sensed a vast room, well lit, warm. I wiggled my fingers. They were bound in front of me at the wrists. My ankles were bound, too.

Murmurs, chatter. I couldn't tell what was being said. Strange.

"We know you're awake," came a voice.

Rat-a-tat of footsteps moving closer.

"*Bonjour,* Tally."

I looked up. Blinked a dozen times. The ghost remained.

She wore a black turtleneck and tight black pants. Her signature black hair was pulled back into a long ponytail and she wore bangs, as always. Silver yei figures dangled from her ears. A wide red belt wrapped her tiny waist, and a slash of red covered her thin lips.

"Flies will get in your mouth," Delphine said, "if you don't shut it."

"Delphine," I said.

"*Oui.* In the flesh." Laughter poured from her lips.

"Penny!" I blurted out.

"She's alive." She pulled over another straight-backed chair and straddled it.

Relief made me lightheaded. "Where?"

"There." She pointed, and I saw Amélie asleep on a couch with Penny sprawled across it, her head resting on Amélie's lap.

"You are dead," I said. "You were dead. What's going on?"

"I assure you, I am not dead."

That was obvious. I took in the room. Comfy. A small kitchen, three couches, two beds with curtains like in a hospital. Several work tables with potsherds resting on them. Tubs of water, giant mortar and pestles. Another table with heat lamps. Naked pots beside some paints. One was half painted with Old Ones' motifs. A man sat at that table, and he dipped a stick into the paint, then applied some to the pot. Shelves on the wall with whole Anasazi pots and bowls and other pottery items lining them. And on yet another table, a smaller one, the Zuni manuscript from the library alongside a pair of leopard-print eyeglasses and a grouping of modern fetishes. My fetishes.

"I get it," I said. "Of course." I couldn't stop looking at Delphine.

"What do you get, Tally?"

"What you're doing. It's so simple. You're crushing the old Anasazi potsherds, then reconstituting them into clay and making new pots that you're selling as antique. That's why the carbon dating is inaccurate. You reconstruct the Old Ones' pots using spring water, right? Have a potter make new ones. And you're all set."

She nodded.

"And that's how you got the skull in the pot. You put it in there before you made the thing."

Her aristocratic face flushed. "I did not do that stupidity. Gerard did." She gestured to the pot painter, who looked up and winked at us. I recognized the handsome guy from National Geographic: Zoe's boyfriend, Jerry Devlin. "Stupid, Gerard."

"It was a joke," he said. "I know it was stupid."

Her Gaelic shrug of "whatever" boggled my mind.

"Whose skull?" I said. "Whose skull was in the pot?"

She waved a hand. "The woman who Gerard replaced at the museum. We had to make an opening, you see?"

"She must look just like you," I said.

"*Moi?*" Delphine said. "*Non.* Not at all."

"You have killed so many people," I said. "Didi, the governor, his aide, many, many others. I . . . What the hell, Delphine? Weren't you making enough money at your shop? To kill all those people. How could you? For what?"

"Shut up, you stupid woman. You really think I made money at my shop in genuine antiquities? What a fool. They don't matter." She frowned. "Except for you! Not that we didn't try, eh?"

I'd found Death, and she made no sense to me. None.

She held out her stained and roughened hand. "Give it here, and I won't kill your dog. See? Easy."

"Not so easy," I said.

She shot me a dark look and reached down for the knife, the one I'd taken from her henchman.

Her cell phone rang the Harry Potter theme. She checked it, leaped from the chair, and flipped open the phone. Barking into the phone, she walked over to the man painting the pot. She sat on the bench beside him and finished her conversation. When she flipped the phone closed, she rested a hand on the painter's shoulder, kissed him, and he left.

All that time, I'd tried to chew my way out of the nylon straps holding my hands. I'd made zero progress when she turned back to me.

"Let's focus, Tally, shall we?" She again sat on the chair facing me, legs widespread, hands on the chair back. A smirk marred the lovely face of the woman I thought I'd known.

"Trust me," I said. "I'm focused."

"Ah, the woman with quips."

"I've got to do something, since I have no idea what's going on. A woman I thought I knew is a pot thief and murderer. From what I saw at your home, you love your daughter, yet she's been starved and beaten and abused."

Delphine rubbed her neck, and for the first time I saw a vulnerability. Something was off, and it had to do with Amélie.

"Why did you do that, Delphine?" I said. "Why hurt your sweet daughter?"

She slapped my face so hard my neck snapped backward. Black night and stars blinded me for a moment. When my vision cleared, Delphine was shaking her hand.

"That hurt," I said. She'd split my lip, and warm blood trickled down my chin. I tried to wipe it using my shoulder.

"Here." She leaned close and dabbed at me with an embroidered handkerchief. "Sorry. I don't like being out of control. Amélie knows nothing about me. This. Nothing. I had two of the men take care of her, as she was jabbering on way too much, just like always. They got a bit carried away. They've paid. Oh, yes." The anger in her black eyes looked feral. She was mad. Delphine could hide an army of corpses here, and they might never be found.

"Why, Tally?" she said. "Why could you not let things alone?"

"Me?" I'd heard that one before. Many times. "You killed my friend Didi and the governor and others. But I also believed you were dead, killed by the same person who'd murdered Didi."

Delphine's sculpted eyebrows shot up. "What would ever make you think that?"

"Didi's reconstruction. It was your twin. I was sure you were dead."

"That?" She pointed to her left, and there, lying on its side on one of the tables, was Didi's re-creation from the skull.

"Yes," I said. "That."

She retrieved the clay head and sat it on her thigh. "I don't understand."

I didn't, either. I stared at the re-creation. The face looked *nothing* like Delphine. A stranger in clay stared back at me.

I shook my head, wished I could rub my eyes. I blinked again and again to clear my vision. But it remained the same. Not Delphine. "I . . . I don't know how to explain it."

"Let's get on with it," she said. "I want Amélie out of here before she awakens."

So she intended to keep her daughter forever in the dark. I doubted that was possible. "Fine," I said. "I still don't know what we're getting on with."

"Simple," she said. "I really never took you for being stupid. The blood fetish, of course."

"Ah. I know something about it, ever since you've been looking hot and heavy for it. It has been you, yes?"

"Of course. It's all I want."

Swell. I was supposed to give her some mythical fetish. "Here's what I know. Well, not even know, but what I read."

Delphine leaned forward, an eager child. "Yes. You must see, my dear, how you're a part of all this?"

"All what? My hands are numb."

"A shame. Let me say one more time, where is the blood fetish?"

"In my pocket, of course."

Time stopped.

I am back in the Navajo school library. Kai smiles at me. I read the description of the fetish and how it runs red with the enemies' blood. The Bone Man had written the book. The Bone Man has carved the fetish.

Could he possibly be the young man in my vision, who'd loved the crippled girl?

I am in Chaco. The young warrior and the young woman are saying their farewells. I see the mountain lion fetish, and then later, the fetish again, when I am with Gimp. Only with Gimp, the fetish has changed. It now wears a bundle of obsidian and turquoise and heishi.

I breathed out, my mouth forming an O.

"Don't do that!" Delphine barked.

I refocused. "Do what?"

"Whatever. We searched your pockets. There was no fetish."

"Of course there is," I said. "Why do you want it so very much?"

Her eyes lost focus. "Ah, yes. The blood fetish. I learned about it when I began collecting American Indian art. An old man told me, the old trader."

"The one you had killed?"

"Yes," she snapped. "He wasn't so smart. It's incredibly powerful. It can rule others, bring great wealth and power."

I almost blurted that she was being absurd. Given the look of madness in her eyes, it was a good thing I hadn't. "So you want the power."

"Yes," she said. "Of course. And the beauty. After all, it's carved from a huge ruby."

A ruby. Swell. I thought I could pull something off with my rock. A ruby, eh? "Ah, of course. If you cut my bindings, I'll show it to you."

Amélie moaned, and Delphine ran over to her. She kneeled in front of her daughter and felt the girl's forehead with her palm. The gesture challenged my ideas of her as a stone-cold murderer. But that's just what she was.

A sudden memory of Niall's daughter at the inn. A pretty blond girl even younger than Amélie. Delphine had tossed Niall and his daughter aside like refuse. I knew what I had to do.

"Hey, Delphine," I said. "Let's get going here, huh?"

She looked over her shoulder. "What's your rush to die?"

"I like bringing the inevitable closer."

She stood, brushed the dust off her black pants, and strode over. "A stupid attitude." She had a gun in her hand, a small one that she waved at me. She crouched down, lifted the big knife, and cut the plastic binding my wrists.

They snapped apart, and the blood cascaded into my hands with painful force.

"Hurts, doesn't it? Get the fetish, and let's get done with this."

I figured I could get the stone, show it to her, and convince her it was the real blood fetish. After all, she'd never seen it. Either that, or I could bash her on the head with it. Two brilliantly stupid plans, but I was fresh out of ideas.

I slid my hand into my pocket and . . . *Cripes*. Not there. I moved my fingers around. Nothing. Nope, not there at all. I tried the other pocket. Same deal.

I glanced at Delphine, whose thunderous expression reminded me of a death mask I'd once seen in a museum.

I looked around on the various tables, chairs and . . . There it was, on the table next to us, along with a pack of my gum and fifty cents. I leaned over, but couldn't reach it.

With what little feeling had returned to my fingers, I waggled them at the stone. "There it is. That's it."

"Don't move." The gun she had pointed at my face never wavered.

She walked over to the table, looked back at me, and pointed. "This?"

I nodded. "That's it."

"Do you take me for a fool?"

I wanted to say yes. "Of course not."

"Does this look like a ruby to you? Or a carving? Or both?"

"It's the blood fetish," I said with as much certainty as I could muster. And for a moment, I believed it as truth, knew it to be so. It *was* the blood fetish.

"Now, you die." She aimed the gun and reached for the stone at the same time.

I held my breath, and the world ended. But not as I'd imagined.

Delphine dropped the gun, shrieking, "It burns!"

All I could do was watch as she tried to release the

stone, shrieking and screaming and fighting the pain that began to consume her. Fire arched her back as it flew up her arm to engulf her. I leaped to help her, tripped and fell, with the chair on my back. I was still bound by the ankles.

I began to crawl to her as she writhed on the floor, her body a mass of flame, screaming and screaming for help and forgiveness, hollering, "Oh, God" over and over and over, slapping her hands at herself, as if trying to put out the flames consuming her.

And in one hand, I saw it. The blood fetish. Nothing like the rock I'd brought home, but instead, Mountain Lion—Guardian of the North, Chief of All the Directions, the Greatest of All Hunters.

An angry roar came from mountain lion's mouth, its fiery tail flicking back and forth, its arrowhead and turquoise bundle strung around its neck, like an adornment, the arrowhead stabbing Delphine's heart.

I had almost reached her when a roar, more suffocating than all the others, filled the room with sound and blinding light. Delphine was being ripped apart.

I snapped my eyes closed, covered my ears.

And then silence. Absolute.

I opened my eyes. My egg-shaped stone rocked back and forth on the floor. No fire. No heat. No anything. Just Delphine. On the floor, as if asleep.

I didn't believe she was asleep.

Still on my belly, I swiveled around. There were Amélie and Penny, both snoring on the couch. I gingerly touched my lip. Split, now swollen. There was Didi's reconstruction that looked nothing like Delphine.

I hadn't imagined it. Not any of it.

I reached for the stone, touching it first with only the tips of my fingers. It welcomed them, and I wrapped my hand around the stone, Delphine's obsession—the blood fetish.

* * *

I retrieved the knife and cut the bonds around my ankles. I ran over to Penny and Amélie. Both were fine and sleeping soundly. I ran over to Delphine.

She was gray as death, eyes open, milky white. For a moment I couldn't look at her. Then I turned back and pressed two fingers to her neck. No pulse. Icy cold, not a sign of blood anywhere.

I didn't understand any of it. But that didn't matter. I went in search of Delphine's phone, called, and waited for the troops to arrive.

CHAPTER THIRTY-FIVE

Days later, I still failed to comprehend what had happened in Delphine's workshop. But I had learned a few things that settled at least part of my mind.

Aric, Hank, and I sat around the fireplace one evening, doing a wrap-up for Aric's FBI files and Hank's state police records. It was incredibly tedious, but it had to be done. So both men wrote while I yapped, and we all sipped some Vino Verde from Portugal.

"Delphine's workshop." I shivered. "One of the all-time creepy places."

Hank chuckled. "What do you expect, it used to be the Salem Jail, babe. Lots of ghost stories about that place."

I made a gagging sound. "I know. You told me. Too ironic. Still creeps me out."

"I guess it creeped Gerard out, too," Hank said. "He spilled his guts fast as I've seen anyone in trade for his life. He confirmed what you said about the skull belonging to one of the former curators at the museum."

"Massachusetts doesn't have a death penalty," I said.

"No," Hank said. "But there's a federal one, and that's how we threatened to prosecute. He's done forever."

Aric looked up from his paperwork. "You were dead on, Tal, about how they were reconstituting pots. They were making nice money at it. They should have stuck with that."

I leaned back on the sofa and watched Aric and Hank write. Hank was hunched over on the new red leather club chair he'd given me that he'd somehow appropriated for his own.

I shook my head. Hank and I seemed to be one cozy couple. Oh, dear.

The phone rang, and I grabbed it. I sighed. "It's for you." I handed it to Hank. He nodded several times, smiled, said, "Thank you," and, "Great news," and hung up.

He looked at me, all serious, yet smiling. "I thought you'd want to know, so I placed a call."

I tilted my head. "What?"

"Coyote's doing well. They doubt he's rabid, even though, yes, you must complete your shots. And he's got months more of quarantine. But the vet's become attached to him, and so Coyote's found a home."

I laughed, maybe for the first time in what felt like forever. "That's great. And I know I have to finish the shots, just in case."

He went back to writing. I'd told the two men exactly what I'd seen happen to Delphine. Much grunting went on during my recitation, but I doubted they believed me.

Addy had supervised the autopsy, and unless the blood tests changed things, Delphine had apparently died from a heart attack.

I knew better.

Amélie was doing well in the care of an aunt who lived on the Vineyard. She'd inherited the shop, and no one saw any reason to tell her about her mother's horrible doings.

Penny, curled up next to me on the sofa, hadn't suffered, either. We were all lucky.

Too soon, it was time for Aric to leave. Hank went into the kitchen to get him a snack for the plane.

A light shined in Aric's eyes, one that I hadn't seen there before. A joy.

"You're returning to her, aren't you, Aric?" I said.

He nodded. "Yes. I never talk of her while I'm on a case."

"I understand." I hugged him. "I'm happy for you, but sad that you're leaving. I have a question."

"Yes."

I leaned toward him. "Why me, Aric? Why did I see Delphine's face on Didi's reconstruction? The ancient man and woman in Chaco? The stairway? The blood fetish? Why me?"

He looked at me for a long time. Then he shrugged. "Why not?"

"Aric!" I stood. "That is not an answer."

Aric chuckled. "You're always so easy to get going, Tally. My father entrusted you with more than a piece of red rock."

Hank walked back in the room. He looked from Aric to me. "You two having a powwow?"

I looked from one man to the other. I laughed. "I guess we are."

I walked to the mantel where all my precious fetish carvings sat once again. I reached for the oval rock, the blood fetish, I'd brought home from Chaco. I hated parting with it, but I felt I should return it to its people.

I lifted the simple oval rock from the mantel. As always, it warmed my hand. "Here, Aric. The blood fetish."

He stared at the rock, shook his head. "You're really willing to give it up?"

"Of course."

"But, you see, Tally, that's not the blood fetish. This is." He pointed to the red rock given to me by Governor Bowannie.

"*That* is the blood fetish." I held my Chaco rock in one hand and, in my other hand, lifted the red rock. "I feel . . . nothing but two lovely rocks."

He nodded, smiled. "As it should be."

"Here." I handed him the blood fetish, the real one. "Delphine thought it was a ruby."

Aric shook his head. "Foolish." He closed his hand around the blood fetish, and I was suddenly in Chaco with the young couple as the young man promised to return. And he had, of course, and married the young girl and had many children and grandchildren. He'd become a shaman, like his descendent, Governor Bowannie, and he had written the manuscript.

He was The Bone Man, and his face was Aric's and Aric's was his.

I shook my head and all was normal again. Thank heavens.

We said our good-byes, and I knew I'd see Aric again, and that felt good. After he left, I cuddled with Hank on the sofa.

"So what are you going to do about MGAP," Hank said.

"Oh, not tonight, Hank. I don't even want to think about that place. I don't want to think about anything."

He'd switched to beer, and took a long pull on his Bud. "Well and good, but you better decide soon, especially with Gert pregnant."

I sat up fast. "What?"

"You didn't know?"

"No, I didn't know, dammit."

"It gets worse," he said. "She told me it's Fogarty's kid."

"Oh, hell."